happy
family

happy family

a novel

TRACY BARONE

A LEE BOUDREAUX BOOK

LITTLE, BROWN AND COMPANY

NEW YORK BOSTON LONDON

Copyright © 2016 by Tracy Barone

Lee Boudreaux Books / Little, Brown and Company
Hachette Book Group
1290 Avenue of the Americas, New York NY 10104
leeboudreauxbooks.com

First Edition: May 2016

Lee Boudreaux Books is an imprint of Little, Brown and Company, a division of Hachette Book Group, Inc. The Lee Boudreaux Books name and logo are trademarks of Hachette Book Group, Inc.

The publisher is not responsible for websites (or their content) that are not owned by the publisher.

The Hachette Speakers Bureau provides a wide range of authors for speaking events. To find out more, go to hachettespeakersbureau.com or call (866) 376-6591.

ISBN 978-0-316-34260-5
LCCN 2015952379

10 9 8 7 6 5 4 3 2 1

RRD–C

Printed in the United States of America

For Zoë Anne

Happy families are all alike; every unhappy family is unhappy in its own way.

—Leo Tolstoy, *Anna Karenina*

happy
family

AUGUST 5, 1962

Marilyn Monroe found dead, drug overdose

Jamaica celebrates independence

Nelson Mandela arrested for illegally leaving
South Africa

Trenton, New Jersey: Generator blowout at
St. Mercy's

Twelve-car pileup on the New Jersey Turnpike, worst in state's history

PART I

the baby

MIRIAM

The pregnant girl enters the Trenton Family Clinic, looking like she parted the Red Sea to get there. The lower half of her dress is wet with amniotic fluid, and the upper half is streaked with sweat. She stands, shifting her weight from foot to foot, in the waiting room near the check-in window. She breathes in quick, sharp breaths; no identification, no insurance card. The entire contents of her plastic purse: one dollar and thirty-nine cents, half a roll of Necco wafers, a chewed pencil, and a hand-shaped pendant with an eye in its center. She's sixteen or seventeen, with white-white skin and black hair. She smells like tobacco and spices that don't come in tins at the Stop and Shop. A jolt of pain makes her feel like her flesh is being stripped from her bones. "Hey." She pants, gripping the ledge of the window. "Hey, somebody."

The somebodies around don't have white coats, caps, or name tags. They sit or stand, pressing towels to wounds, looking dazed or scared. An elderly man wearing a janitor's uniform strains first to pull, then to push a fat man off a chair and onto a gurney. The man has lost a shoe, has blood spatter on his pants. During one

7

attempt, the janitor tips into the gurney, sending it caroming into a wall.

"Nurse?" the girl asks.

On a regular day, the nurses wouldn't have been in a rush to help this girl. They see poor kids like her all the time—although they're not white, not in this neighborhood. But this is not a regular day. It's a short-straw Sunday, and the majority of the clinic staff are off; they're in movie theaters or dipping their feet in water, anywhere to get out of the record-breaking August heat. The nurses and lone doctor on duty are in the back, overwhelmed with trauma patients—victims of a highway collision—who, due to a generator failure at St. Mercy General, have been routed to the clinic because it's the only medical facility within miles.

The girl feels faint. The only fan stopped working long ago, and the air is close and thick with the rust smell of blood, bleach, and something nasty somebody's just thrown up all over the floor. A teenage orderly slops over with a bucket and mop and swipes at the vomit, which streaks close to the girl's bare feet. She squeezes closer to the window just in time for another pain, this one sharper, longer, harder to endure. The orderly's eyes dart from the floor to the girl. He can see the dark rings of her areolas through the thin fabric of her dress. The girl moans and the boy quickly looks down.

"Orderly!" A nurse with a name tag that reads *Syl* sticks her head into the waiting room, points at the kid, and then disappears. He looks up—*What, me?*—and his left hand involuntarily starts curling as if around an imaginary ball. The girl closes her eyes and sees floating specks of orange and gold.

When the girl's contraction has subsided, the orderly and the janitor are gone. She waits. She walks, she sits on her heels, she breathes and forgets to breathe; she waits for the next pain to come, then waits for it to go away. She waits—it could be minutes or hours—until she feels a nurse's fleshy arms around her, pulling her to a standing position. "Come on, you can walk. Just around the corner."

Just around the corner is one big room sectioned into cubicles by curtains. All of the cubicles are full of what the nurse calls "real emergencies."

"Wait here," Syl says, trotting off.

The girl is left standing. Movement had blunted the pain for a few seconds, but her next contraction is so intense she bites the inside of her cheek until she tastes blood. Between ragged breaths—she's already determined that calling for help will do no good—she focuses on the little tables next to each patient's cubicle. On the tables are pink, kidney-shaped trays filled with bottles of medications, pills in paper cups. No one is paying attention to her. The nurses' station is untended. The girl moves toward a table parked beside the bed of an unconscious person with a surgical mask over his or her face. In one quick movement, she swipes a syringe and two bottles identified with a typed strip that says *Morphine*. Her hand shakes from the aftershock of labor pains, but she'd shoot up right there if it weren't for Syl's returning.

Syl is nothing if not efficient; she's converted a corner next to the bathroom into a birthing station and an IV awaits. Within minutes, she's got the girl hooked up and lying on a cot, covered with a paper sheet. Syl feels around inside the girl to see how dilated she is. The girl clenches the vials in her hand so hard her fingernails bite into her palm.

"No time to put you out," Syl says into the chasm of the girl's open vagina. And the nurse is off to retrieve something, a doctor perhaps.

I'm going out, all right, the girl thinks as she plunges the syringe into the first bottle of morphine. She's on a first-name basis with Dilaudid, Nembutal, chloral hydrate, opium smoked from a hookah in Chinatown. She taps the side to make sure there are no air bubbles and sticks it in the feed to her IV line. As the girl feels the first gold filigree spread its fingers through her body, she thinks she is lucky. Lucky to be in the last bed in this, her Last Resort.

Syl's back, lifting something wet from underneath the girl. She barks at the orderly, who has suddenly materialized. The girl doesn't care. She's warm and open, lying in the sun. She squints a little from the heat, then closes her eyes again. "Doctor's coming," Syl says. To the girl, everything sounds like it's underwater. Maybe she's floating on her back in the ocean and her ears have dipped below the surface. She is aware of friction in her womb and the need to bear down and push. And yet the pain is hovering above her, outside her body.

"Don't bear down. Hold on for the doctor," Syl says.

The girl is laughing because the baby is popping out. She hoists herself up on her elbows and sees a white-crusted head, the neck still inside of her.

"Don't bear down!" Syl insists. As if the girl had any control. As if she could stop the head from opening its eyes, locking onto her. The doctor appears in bloodied scrubs, but with one push, the baby flops out like a bass. "Girl," Syl says. She already knows that because the baby's speaking to her in thoughts no one else can hear. *I am here to love you, Miriam,* the newborn says. At the sound of her name, Miriam starts to cry.

Before, Miriam couldn't feel connected to another person, even when their bodies were fused and melting into each other. Having a man inside of her, lying stomach to stomach, thigh to thigh, forehead to forehead, she felt only the nothingness of herself. She yearned to be filled, yet when somebody was inside her, she wanted only to escape. Now, as she and her baby are separate yet still one, united by the cord that still joins them, Miriam understands the ecstasy of connectedness. Her thoughts and the baby's thoughts flow through the cord effortlessly. Miriam pictures herself, eyes ringed with kohl, standing in front of the sea in the blue dress her mother made her. She holds the baby up to the sky like an offering. Miriam is breathing in her child's sweet, sweet breath and listening to her words. *We'll fly to bliss,* she says, and her baby carries them up and into the clouds.

But her baby is being taken away. The doctor has cut the cord with his scissors and has given the crying infant to Syl to take someplace to weigh and measure and clean.

Miriam is shivering so badly she thinks she'll fall off the gurney. She's alone and her body aches and is so cold. She wishes she had a blanket. She tries to go back to the blue dress, the sea—but they are only thoughts. She still has the other little bottle; she'd meant to save it, but she can't wait, she's shaking with cold and can't feel her lips. She'll have to worry about later later; she needs it now.

Whhhhhhssshhhhh—the liquid is hot in her veins and she hears the *blip* of someone else's machine. She can wriggle her toes and feel the sun, just like the one on the postcard from the Jersey Shore—the one she'd sent to that nice man after she'd found out he'd made her pregnant. She didn't know why she felt the need to go south; maybe she was a confused bird, or because after they'd make love he'd cry in her hair and call her his treasure. What was his name again? Something with a *J,* like Jesse or James or Jerry. He'd let her stay with him and didn't ask her where she was going and when she'd be back. He'd stroke her hair and make her something with potato chips and soup from a can. And he made this baby. How could she tell him that opium is beyond sex? All she wanted was to suck the white dove of smoke out from under a glass and then eat a chocolate bar. What is she supposed to do with a baby? She's never had a pet, though she likes turtles. She keeps losing herself, how can she hold on to someone else? She feels no pain now, but she knows it is coming, that she has only so long before she's in worse pain than when she was in labor and there will be no more little bottles or nice Jerrys.

Miriam knows her baby is safe. She's being wrapped up in a soft blanket and the nurse is washing her and kissing her head like in a baby-shampoo commercial.

Miriam thinks of the child in *The Red Balloon*. It's the only movie she's ever seen, wearing kneesocks, eating sticky toffee, and drinking soda pop that made her burp out of her nose. No matter that the man she was with pushed his hand between her legs during the best part. She doesn't care about any of that because it's so nice lying here—just one more moment with heavy lids, drifting—one, two, three, four, let's walk out the door. Five, six, seven, eight, get up now before it's too late.

Miriam sits up and takes the saline bag off its hook. Nobody has come, nobody is watching. She keeps the IV in her arm and puts the tubing and the bag under her dress. She was supposed to remember to do something. What was it? She wanted to write something down. She looks around and finds her purse, fishes for her pencil. She smooths down a semiclean part of her crushed paper sheet and writes what she thinks is the father's full name and where he lives. Then she picks up her purse and, as an afterthought, pulls out the hand pendant—it should protect her baby now. She places it on the sheet next to Jerry's name and walks out of the clinic. Nobody notices. Nobody except the teenage boy who leans on his mop, watching her disappear into the hot blast of day.

BILLY BEAL

Billy Beal runs. He runs because his pops insists he train year-round despite the fact that high school baseball season doesn't start until the spring. He runs in the predawn darkness, accelerating his pace when he feels the headlights of Pops's station wagon lick the back of his legs. It's all uphill from here—he'll have to beat his time from yesterday or do another ten miles. "You're falling behind," Pops yells, "get a move on, Billy Beal. Motivate." It doesn't matter that Billy Beal was the only East Trenton High School junior to play in the Great Northern League Baseball Tournament, or that, with his team trailing five to three in the third inning, he came in and struck out the side for six innings in a row, paving the way for his team's championship victory. He can always do better.

This morning, like almost every morning for the past two weeks since the girl left her baby in the clinic, Billy Beal's brain is stuck in a groove. Each day it gets worse because it's one day closer to the start of school and one less chance he's got of seeing her again. When school begins, he will have done his community-service hours and will have no excuse to go back to the clinic. What if she comes to pick up her baby the day after he leaves? Then he'll never see her again. If he never sees her again, he can't give her back the charm she'd left among the dirty towels. He'll say something like: "I think you forgot this." Of course the charm won't be what she's coming back for, he knows that. Just like he knows she didn't abandon her baby, at least not forever. "You're a romantic, Billy Beal," Moms had said when he told her the girl would be back.

"Focus, son," Pops shouts out of the station wagon's open window. They've reached the bottom of the hill, and Billy Beal's American Legion T-shirt has a dark V of sweat at the neck. He would have pitched in the American Legion World Series in California last month if he hadn't gotten involved playing lookout for Manny Cannerni's liquor-store robbery. Eight weeks of community service at the worst clinic in Trenton was getting off light, the judge had said. Billy Beal never thought about anything other than the baseball he was missing as he pushed dirt around on the floor of the clinic. Until the girl came in.

She didn't look like anybody he'd seen before. Certainly nothing like the girls who went to his high school. If she had gone to his school, he would have wanted to ask her to homecoming— if he'd ever go to a dance or dare to ask a girl her name. True, he wasn't seeing the girl in the best of circumstances—there was a lot of puffing and heaving going on—but she had clean nails and a nice dress. It didn't matter that she didn't have shoes; she had pretty feet. She didn't scream when nobody paid attention to her, or freak out about the vomit on the floor. He thought she looked at him when he was mopping around her; she noticed him. Which was unusual because Billy Beal felt invisible except on the pitcher's mound.

As far back as Billy Beal can remember, his world has been

dominated by men: Pops, his two older brothers, and everything baseball. If high school girls were prey to the letter-jacket-aphrodisiac effect, Billy Beal was unaware of it. The girls he knew—cousins who smelled like corned beef from working part-time in the deli—were like old socks. His brothers didn't bring girls to the house; they went to Asbury Park with beers they'd pilfered from the deli and came home with hickeys on their necks. But Billy Beal wasn't blind. He noticed how girls changed in high school: their circle-pinned shirts got tighter, their pleated skirts shorter, and everywhere he looked there were legs. Legs in the bleachers, legs crossing and uncrossing under the desks. Girl legs that were frighteningly downy and soft; coltish thighs and calves speckled with blond hair, ankles covered with bobby socks that would sometimes slip down to expose a curve of bone.

None of this came close to preparing Billy Beal for the pregnant girl. The few times he'd seen women come into the clinic to have babies, they were taken behind a curtain, and he'd drown out their cries by running baseball stats in his head. The inner workings of femaleness made him squeamish. The last thing he wanted to see was a baby coming out of a girl—especially a girl his age. He stared at a scraped-up patch of linoleum on the floor and inhaled the ammonia vapors from his bucket. Then Sylvia was snapping her fingers at him, saying, "Are you deaf? I asked for towels!" The girl was losing a lot of blood. He'd gotten down on his hands and knees and scraped up all kinds of clots and body fluids but he'd never associated those remnants with a face before. Billy Beal not only looked at this girl's face, he memorized its contours. She didn't frighten or shock him. Her face was soft as she turned toward him, and he could swear her eyes flashed out a message to him in code. *I know you, Billy Beal,* they said.

Billy Beal thinks about the girl's eyes, which were practically transparent, like drained Coca-Cola bottles, like he could see through them right into her. Was she doing the same to him? Billy Beal runs past their mailbox, might have kept going but for Pops yelling and holding up his stopwatch: "Made it by three-tenths of a second. Sometimes I think you're somewhere else, I swear to Christ." They're walking in the front door, which has a perennial Christmas wreath nailed on it, and Billy Beal's mouth is a desert. "Peg? Peg? Did that goddamned Ralphie take the extra keys, because I couldn't find them. Peg, goddamn it!" Pops looks up and there's Moms with that crooked smile of hers, holding out the extra keys to the deli. Her long silver hair is still restrained in its nighttime net, and her face is rumpled like an unmade bed. "Well, why didn't you say something?" Pops says, barreling past her toward the kitchen, where breakfast is ready and waiting.

Billy Beal is at the icebox, guzzling milk from the bottle, leaning into the cool electric air, when it occurs to him: they should take the girl's baby. "We should take the girl's baby," he says.

"What?" Moms says.

"We should take her baby," he repeats, because it makes perfect sense.

"What the hell are you talking about?" Pops says, looking up from his plate of bacon and eggs.

"He's not talking about anything, close the door, Billy, you're using the electricity up."

Billy Beal wipes milk off his mouth with the back of his hand, "Just for a little while, until she comes back. It's the right thing to do. That's what you'd say, Moms—"

Pops jumps out of his chair like a jack-in-the-box. "Jesus Christ, you know about this, Peg? I can't believe it! I can't believe you snuck behind my back and knocked someone up . . . who is it? Who's the little slut? How the fark did this happen, you son of a bitch? " "Hey, now," Moms says, moving her body between Pops and her son. "Get the hell out of the way, woman. You can't protect him on this." Pops puffs his chest out like an ape. "I'm going to kill you, Billy Beal. You're going to wish you'd gone to jail by the time I'm through with you!" "Al, Al, Al, you've got it wrong." Moms waves her hands. Pops pushes her out of the way and thumps on his son's chest, pushing him backward into a chair. "What's the matter with you, huh?" Thump. "Are you a moron?" Thump. "You got a baseball scholarship to think about, you farking idiot, you farking fool. You got shite between your ears—" Pops jumps on the floor and wrestles with Billy, trying to get him in a headlock.

"Al, Al, Al," Moms screams, pulling on his shirt, "it's not his baby!"

"I'm going to farking strangle you . . ." Pops uses weight to his advantage—he's about to sit on his son when Moms screams in his ear: "Al, stop! I said it's not his baby!" Pops looks up at Moms, and Billy gets out from under.

"Jesus, Pops," Billy says, holding up his hands in disgust.

"Are you trying to kill me?" Pops says to Billy. "You scared the shite out of me. I should pop you one just for that." Billy Beal looks down at the floor, pictures all two hundred and thirty pounds of his father running while he drives the station wagon up his ass. *Die,* he thinks, *die.*

"Farking baby, what's he got to do with a baby?"

"It's a good idea," Billy says, staring into the mid-distance.

"If I were you, I'd leave well enough alone . . ."

"Okay." Pops slams down his cup, sending rivulets of coffee out into the universe. "Since when does he have ideas that I don't know about? What the fark's going on?"

"Get upstairs, Billy."

"But you said I have to eat—"

"The two of you are stepping on my last goddamned nerve . . ."

Moms swoops up Billy's plate of food and hands it to him. "Go," she says, waving him off. "Shoo, shoo . . ." Moms's eyes mean if he has any hope of getting her on his side he better scram right now.

"Lucy, you've got some 'splaining to do," Pops says without a trace of irony.

Billy Beal paces across his bedroom floor, making the boards squeak because he can. He hates being treated like a little kid, being told to go to his room. He hates it when Moms babies him and Pops jumps on his neck, blaming him for everything.

His idea is genius. It's so simple he doesn't know why he didn't think of it sooner. Moms taking the baby would solve everything. The girl would come to him, and Moms would tell her how it was he, Billy Beal, who saved her baby from being what Moms called a ward of the state. The girl would be so grateful she'd agree to go get a root beer with Billy and he could make a cord for her pendant and put it around her neck as a surprise. And Moms is so good with kids she'd help the girl take care of her baby and maybe the girl would stick around awhile. Moms did it for total strangers and the girl, well, it's not exactly like he knows her, but after what they went through, it feels like he does. Moms has to be on his side on this one, she just has to.

It takes Moms a while to tell Pops the story about the girl and her baby, mainly because Pops's frequent eruptions and subsequent spills slow her down. He's finally stopped flailing enough that she can start in on the juice and coffee that have found their way onto his pants. "I don't know why he cares, but he cares. It's the first time I've seen him care about anything other than baseball. He's showing a bit of compassion, which is more than I can say for you." Moms dabs his pants with a moistened towel.

"Compassion? For a nigger slut who leaves her own baby in a clinic? That girl's never coming back and you know it. It's the goddamned state's problem, not ours. You're rubbing it in, not taking it out!"

"I've got to blot. And she's white, not that that should make a difference."

"You're not saying you think this is a good idea, are you? Because if you did, I'd say you're out of your farking skull. Or I'd think this isn't about the boy, it's about you. How many times do I tell you, my wife doesn't work! I provide for this family, and, what, the deli's not doing well enough for you? You want to go back to running crumb-crunchers nobody wants through here like it's a farking summer camp? I let you do that *once* and you're forever throwing it in my face. Fostering, you'll be fostering a bruise on your head, woman, if I hear one more word out of you." He spits when he talks, white gunk starting to form at the corners of his mouth.

"You're way out of line, Albert Beal," Moms says, dropping the towel. She turns her back on him and starts to do the dishes. The only thing that breaks the silence between them is the rush of water from the faucet and the timpani of rubber gloves on porcelain.

Billy Beal heard Pops calling the girl a slut. Forget that the walls are thin; Pops communicates in only two forms: loud and louder. He could take his father; he's known that for a while. He's strong and quick—he doesn't have to let himself be pushed around. Billy Beal hasn't heard a peep from downstairs in a while. He hates his parents' silence more than their fighting.

Pops and Moms sit in the kitchen listening to the tick of the

Budweiser wall clock that Pops got for free at Wally's Liquor Shop. After what feels like forever, Moms says, "Okay, then. I accept your apology. And I was thinking, with Terry taking off for the South Pacific—"

"It's not in the South Pacific," Pops says.

"Wherever it is, we'll have an extra room."

"It's off China, what's it called? Where's Ralphie? He knows. Ralphie! Ralphie!" There's no response. "Don't tell me he didn't come home again!"

Elvis's "Good Luck Charm" starts playing so loud Moms has to raise her voice:

"Can we stick to Billy? If we did it, I'm saying *if,* it would only be temporary, until they could find a home for the child." Pops goes to the closet and grabs a broom. He punches the handle against the ceiling. "Turn that shite down, goddamn it! And you, don't you go thinking I'm considering it because I'm not." Moms hands Pops a sack lunch she made for Billy last night.

"Viet Nam," she says. "They're sending Terry to a place called Viet Nam."

CICI

Carlotta Matzner gets goose bumps when her husband blows on the back of her neck. Tonight he's doing it to cool her off; the late-summer nights are hot, even in the country, otherwise known as Montclair, New Jersey. *"Scopa me,"* she whispers. He loves it when she speaks Italian, especially when she talks dirty. She could be reciting the phone book right now and it would sound sexy. *"Scopa me con tuo cazzo duro,* Solomon." Even though they have no family left to share their happiness with, this was worth it.

She's burning him up, and at this rate, Sol won't be able to last. "Aiiieeeeeee!" she cries.

"What? What did I do?" he says, pulling out.

"Aiiiieeeeeeee!"

"Are you okay, did I hurt you? Where? What, *chérie,* tell me?"

"Solomon, the baby, he arrive. You stir him with you generals!" Her eyes are earnest; he wants to be concerned but her malapropisms slay him. "Oh, *chérie,* no," he says, trying not to laugh. "You're just having a cramp, remember, like the one the other night, and the day before? Nothing to worry about."

"This is no like the last time. We make him arrive, we should no be doing this. *Porca Madonna, la minchia,* it hurts."

"Breathe," he says. She breathes and he breathes; they breathe.

"For a second there, you scared me," he says. "But trust me, the baby's totally protected in there, from things much bigger than the mister here."

"*Pronto,* Solomon," she says, "call *dottore, per favore.*"

Panic happens often, though never while they are making love. Rationality doesn't work when Cici is like this, so there is no point in saying you can't bother a doctor in the middle of the night for nothing, especially when he just saw you the other day and everything was A-OK. No point in saying you've got another month to go and at this rate the obstetrician will be so fed up that by the time the real thing comes he'll play an extra set of tennis before meandering into the hospital. No; Sol listens and comforts, he looks at his watch and says, "Just to be sure, we'll see how long it takes between pains." He manages to keep his eyes open for half an hour, and when all is quiet on the baby front and Cici's thinking she'd like some runny cheese and a cigarette, he says, "I'm okay if we don't make love. I want you to know I would never want you to do it just for me." He's out of bed, in his bathrobe, ready to get her snack. "I mean it; I abstained before and I can abstain again." She looks up at him and whispers something impossibly sexy. "Look what you do to me," he says, "you're incorrigible."

As Sol is looking for the runny cheese Cici likes, he trips against a leather bag that's parked next to the kitchen door. God-damned handyman, leaving his stuff all over the place. Sol hired Gusmanov to check on the house and see if Cici needs anything because he (a) had pimples the size of boils on his neck and was no threat, and (b) spoke a little Italian he learned from his neighbors in Brooklyn. Sol worked such long hours, he didn't like leaving Cici alone all day in a new house in a new neighborhood. Cici was still nervous about driving so he'd also recently hired a housekeeper to clean and run errands.

When Sol goes back upstairs, Cici is sleeping. The moon shines through the still-curtainless windows, bathing Cici in a faint glow. He has made a hobby of looking at his wife. Her naked body is ravishing, but something about seeing her fully dressed, reaching a hand up to screw in an earring or fasten the clasp on her necklace, is magical. As she lifts her hair to pin it up or adjust her jewelry, he can see the mole behind her left ear and it startles him, as if he's discovering it for the first time. There's an equal thrill when she unpins her hair and it swans down her back. Hair that Sol loves to feel the weight of when wet. Her honey licks of hair spill over her pillow and onto the sheet. Her face is dewy from the moonlight or pregnancy or, Sol would like to believe, because of him. How did a thirty-two-year-old redheaded radiologist whose best features are his calves and his mind, not necessarily in that order, get a twenty-one-year-old shiksa goddess? Looking at Cici ripe with his child, well, could life possibly get any better?

The next morning, Sol gets up early and decides to surprise his wife with coffee in bed. *My wife.* He loves to say that—*I'll just go call my wife; sorry I can't cover your shift, the missus is waiting for me.* While the espresso percolates, Sol peruses the newspaper, folding each section in half lengthwise and then again crosswise. His long, tapered hands are spotted with freckles even though he's barely been in the sun all summer. Between the move, Cici, and his radiology caseload at the hospital, he hasn't been able to play much tennis. He hastily butters a roll, eats it in a few bites. This gives the pot enough time to bubble over, making a gritty mess Sol decides is best left to the new housekeeper, whose name he thinks is Coffee. Who names a child Coffee?

When he returns to their bedroom, Cici is bent over next to her open closet. She's making a series of exasperated *Oooooffs*, followed by a bout of cursing. Sol pulls the espresso cup from behind his back. "For the missus."

"Do you know my bag, is big like this?"

"The one by the kitchen door that I almost killed myself tripping over last night?"

"Ah, I forget! I put it there so it is ready to go."

"Where exactly is it going?"

"*Buuuu,* to the hospital, you silly."

"They say first babies are usually late so don't get your hopes too high."

"No say that, Solomon." The corners of her mouth start to droop and he remembers he's got another surprise. At the last minute he'd gone into the yard to forage for flowers; he proffers a few lilac sprigs that he's been hiding behind his back.

"You find one that is still alive? In the heat? Oh, *caro mio.*" Cici clasps the flower to her chest and her face brightens. He hopes it will always be this easy to make her happy.

By the time Cici's plopped down on the sofa, she's on her third espresso, second croissant, and fifth cigarette, which she stamps out in a saucer. She traces the back of her fingernail over a silk pillow, feeling its cool surface—a habit she's had since she was a baby—and goes to lick the jam off her last half a croissant. She lets the clumps dissolve on her tongue, enjoying how it sweetens the tobacco aftertaste. The living room is empty except for the sofa she's on, but she doesn't mind. She was brought up to believe that quality is far more important than quantity, be it in a woman's essentials—handbags and shoes—or home furnishings.

The house is still so new and it takes time to find antiques, the right colors for fabric, paint.

In a minute her legs hurt and she's perspiring underneath her breasts. Maybe she should have a bath or ask the housekeeper to drive her into town. What would she do in town? Go to the market, where she'll have to deal with American money—it's so ugly and only one color—and feel bad when she forgets the words *toilet paper*? If the housekeeper goes with her, then she'll have to talk to her and it's tiring to translate in her head. Cici can't get a command of English; its irregular verbs and genderless nouns have their way with her. American names are strange. Like the housekeeper: "Ah, *come biscotti,*" Cici said when Solomon introduced them. "No, ma'am. Not like *biscuit,* that's with a *B.* It's *C.* It's *Cook,* like stirring the pot, making you food. *Cook,* add the *e,*" Cookie said loudly and slowly. Cici hated when people spoke to her like she was a deaf child. And Cook and the *e* had a dialect she couldn't understand, like the *stronzo sicilianos.*

Cici has yet to dream in English, which Solomon says is the sign that you really know another language. These days she just wants to read the Italian magazines they get in Little Italy, keep up with the gossip about this prince and that princess. She hasn't been in America long enough to understand their royalty, except of course that Marilyn Monroe had taken too many sleeping pills and died. Sol won't let her walk around in the city by herself now she's so far along so she'll have to ask him to bring some home. "Speak to Gusmanov, he knows Italian," Solomon said. Her husband was so sweet. He thought that because Gusmanov grew up with Italians he knew how to speak the language. Although he tried, he butchered it with his Russian accent and it made Cici's ears hurt. She doesn't even think Gusmanov is coming today. It's too hot and she's too fat and *buuuuuuu, no lo so.*

Cook and the *e* must be cleaning the toilet because Cici hears the water going on and off, on and off. It's too quiet. She'd wanted this house because the grounds were big and filled with fragrant lilac trees. She'd pictured their children playing and running in and out of the house all day. She likes a noisy house. It's how she remembers life with her real papa; something always bubbling on the stove, fighting but also music—Papa's piano, Mama's opera on the Victrola, the ocean in the background. The complete opposite of her stepfather's house with its dark, shuttered windows, everyone speaking in lowered voices because Mama was sick again and couldn't be disturbed.

Cici shuffles through a stack of papers on the counter; all bills go to Sol. Sol is good with money. Her mother taught her that it is déclassé to discuss how much money one does or does not have. She claimed to be a descendant of the Borgheses but neglected to tell her children why they moved like ants up and down the Liguria coast to stay one step ahead of the debt collector or why Papa spent his weekends betting on horses instead of riding them. Why she had to marry a devout, humorless man after Papa died, a man they all knew she couldn't have loved.

Beneath the bills, Cici finds pamphlets from St. Clare's about the sacrament of baptism and the naming ceremony. There were only two Roman Catholic churches in Montclair, and Sol had left the decision up to her. Cici thought St. Clare's was fine for their immediate purpose; while not marble, the baptismal font was clean and simple. Father Padua seemed kind and—best of all—young.

Cici had had her fill of decrepit priests in Varese's Chiesa Brunella. Just thinking about it evokes the smell of Father Dante's onion breath seeping through the confessional grate. How she'd walk to church chaperoned by humpbacked old signoras who would stop at the bar for a shot of espresso chased by grappa and appear an inch taller going into Mass. The only thing Cici liked about Catholic school was the lives of the saints, because it included women and featured stigmata. Her favorite saint was Teresa of Ávila. People loved Teresa of Ávila so much that when she died, they stole her body parts. Sister Agatha said she knew someone who knew someone whose great-great-grandmother had touched Saint Teresa's finger. Cici loved Saint Teresa because of the ecstasy of her visions and imagined that's what sexual intercourse felt like. If it was a sin to have sex with a boy for pleasure, then why wasn't it a sin to give yourself to Christ? Teresa of Ávila's rapture certainly seemed to give her pleasure. Cici had these kinds of thoughts often and was certain something was wrong with her because of it. But she couldn't help herself. When she was alone at night she'd remember the words of Teresa of Ávila and imagine Maurizio the altar boy's lips pressed against hers.

Besides Maurizio the altar boy, the other good thing about church was how it smelled: a distilled concoction of old wood, bitter oranges, Christmas pine, death-sweet lilies, rotting beams, and bergamot smoke children thought was the Holy Spirit fogging out from the priest's censers. St. Clare's had no odor. Maybe it wasn't old enough to have acquired its own fragrance, but Cici made sure that Father Padua would use scented oil for the baby's baptism, and she hoped to convince him to bring out the censers.

Cici was in no rush to go to Mass at St. Clare's. She was finally free from the irons of family obligation. An obligation that came as part of the bargain her mother made by marrying Marco D'Ameri and promising him that she'd raise her daughters as good Roman Catholics. What would they think of her now? It's what Sol thinks that's important. He adores her and will adore his son. Ever since Cici looked down and couldn't see her feet over her stomach, she knew she was having a boy. Her older sister Genny had three children, all girls, much to Marco D'Ameri's disappointment.

Cici hasn't felt the baby kick or move since the cramp last night, and she is as listless now as she was excited when Sol helped her off the plane and onto the tarmac at Idlewild airport ten months ago. She'd spent much of her life in the provincial town of Varese, and although she'd worked at her stepfather's retail store in Milano, no city she'd seen in Italy compared to Manhattan. New York City was the big sister she'd always wanted: it moved fast, burned bright, took her by the hand and threw her into the action. She was used to the cold uniformity of Milano, the gray faces of businessmen, the small weariness of the housewives who spent all day shopping to feed the businessmen, putt-putting through the narrow streets in their itsy-bitsy cars. Everything in New York was big: big taxis, big hot dogs in big buns, big buildings, and big music. She was like a Russian doll, and Cici loved to explore the smaller and smaller cities nestled within. Sol took Cici to Little Italy, Chinatown, Greenwich Village, the Lower East Side. Cici vowed to become a New Yorker right away. *Go, New York!* became her bible, and she devoured any and all guidebooks she could find in Italian. She learned how to take public transit and read the grid system, discovered that museum headsets were more fun than Berlitz tapes and that Harlem wasn't a place for the many wives of Turkish men. Most important, she figured out where to shop.

With the one pan Sol had in his Gramercy Park apartment, Cici made *risotto con funghi* and *costoletta alla Milanese* and brought it to Sol at St. Vincent's. They'd eat lunch and nuzzle in the spare room at the back of the radiology department where the nurses stored people's old X-rays. They went to the New York Philharmonic on Sunday afternoons to hear Bernstein conduct Mahler or to the Met to see the latest exhibits, even when there was standing room only. Afterward, they'd peel off their clothes and squeeze into the tub, she leaning back into him, hugging her knees to her chest so they'd both fit. There, they'd take turns reading from an Italian/English version of *The Inferno,* coconspiring in their lexicon of mixed languages and touch, laughing long after the soap-scummy water had grown cold.

In those New York City months, Cici thrived in the womb of their twosome. They went out with a few couples—acquaintances of Sol's from the hospital—but mostly kept to themselves. Cici's main obstacle to broadening her social life and knowledge of the city was her English. She'd thought she would pick it up quickly, and when that didn't happen, she felt self-conscious and frustrated. As long as she could communicate with Sol and get around, what else did she need? She could become a New Yorker without grammar. But as soon as Cici started to show, Sol decided a one-bedroom apartment in Manhattan was no place to raise a family. All roads led to what their real estate agent called the "Florence of New Jersey." Sol stretched farther than he should have and bought a turn-of-the-century Colonial house in suburban Montclair with a view of New York City. By Cici's twenty-first birthday that June, they were official New Jerseyites.

Cici's world waned as her belly waxed during the hot summer months. Montclair was quaint, with oak and poplar-lined streets, manicured gardens, and a respectable art museum. Cici could walk places, and the public library had a decent listening room and some rare opera recordings. She could go to the park and watch women tending to their children and think, *Soon, soon, I'll have a whole brood and my life will be so full I'll wish I had a quiet moment to myself.* Some of Sol's colleagues had also moved to the suburbs, and a few of the wives had gotten together to give her a baby shower. Still, Cici was isolated. She swore what happened to her mother would never happen to her—her luster wouldn't be worn down by choosing a safe, bourgeois life. She was in America, after all.

"Remember who you are, Carlottina," her mother always said. Her girls had classical educations and perfect teeth, no matter the cost. They ate only the best cuts of veal, no white, no trace of gray, only pale pink; they knew that the best rubies were pigeon-blood red and the reasons why Verdi was superior to Wagner. Her mother made sure her girls had everything that was important to her, even when she had to stay up all night making stuffed animals out of fur to sell to department stores and spend her days giving piano lessons to children who left their seaside homes at summer's end while their family stayed on as caretakers in the winter, often without heat.

Sol is Cici's family now; she doesn't need her mother or her sisters, why is she giving in to such sentimentality? She'd written to her sister Genny on a whim, not expecting a response to the news that she was pregnant. Well, maybe she harbored the fantasy of a kind word, but she was surprised when the postman delivered a box covered in Italian stamps. She ripped through tape and wrappings like a child at Christmas and found lots of goodies—Italian *Vogue,* unfiltered Nationales, Pasta del Capitano toothpaste, risotto, *gianduiotti, stracchino* cheese that looked like a green eyeball, a blue baby blanket—but no note.

Cici sighs. "You belong in another century," Sol liked to tease her, "one where women always wear pearls and lingerie and go around audibly sighing." She goes to Sol's den, where there are boxes of records, picks out a bel canto recording, then heads upstairs. Cookie, a young black whippet of a thing, is descending the staircase, arms loaded with cleaning supplies. "I need some Brillo, Mz. M. After I do the kitchen, I'm going to run down the screet if that's all right with you." Cici freezes. What's a *brillo*? A *screet*? Cici doesn't understand, doesn't want to try to understand any more of what Cook and the *e* is saying—it makes her want to cry. Cookie doesn't know what to do when, without answering, Cici walks into the baby's room and slams the door.

With shaking hands, Cici puts the record on the portable player. She grabs her white fur elephant out of the crib and sits on the rocker, hugging it to her chest and waiting for the emotion to subside. The walls of the room are painted a warm yellow and everything else is blue. She closes her eyes and listens to Maria Callas. Callas was her first. First opera she ever saw at Teatro alla Scala, first voice that could bring her to tears of joy and sorrow at the same time. Callas in *Il Pirata*—commanding, fragile, passionate. As she listens, Cici feels like Callas's voice is entering her body, reverberating in the hollow of her throat as if she could open her mouth and such beautiful music would pour out. Cici's throat doesn't feel so good. Is it Callas or heartburn? She feels clammy, and saliva starts to pool beneath her tongue.

Cookie is cleaning the kitchen, a blur in her black-and-white maid's uniform. It's two sizes too big, as she used it most of the way through her three pregnancies and didn't want the added expense of buying a new one now that her littlest one was ten months old. She's happy to have full-time work, because her husband, That No-Good Nigger, went and got himself thrown in the big house and she's got her kids and her mama to feed. That

Mz. M. is a strange one. Cookie thinks she can't be much older than her, but Mz. M. seems like a child. She's got no family to look out for her and she's crying up there, listening to all that loud Italian singing. Cookie feels bad, but it's none of her business. Cookie keeps to herself because you never can tell with white folks.

Cici's about to stretch out on her bed when she notices something perched on top of the overnight bag Sol moved back upstairs. Dingy, once-white slippers that are frayed around the edges. Just as she's picking them up to inspect them further, she sinks to her knees with pain.

Cookie turns off the kitchen faucet. Is that screaming or Mz. M.'s music? When Cookie finally decides to go upstairs to investigate, Mz. M. emerges from her room looking an even paler shade of white. She's clutching her stomach. Mz. M. doesn't have to make a steering-wheel motion with her hands; Cookie knows what her boss is asking, and she nods her head. True, she doesn't have a license. But she made good and sure That Nigger taught her how to drive his rusty canoe of a car before they came and hauled his skinny ass away. "C'mon, let me help you. Cookie knows what to do."

⸻

When Sol Matzner hangs up the phone with his new housekeeper, he's not convinced that Cici is going into labor. However, he's not at all sure that she isn't. Cookie's voice had a surprising authority. He's concerned enough to call Dr. Dubin and head out to Grand Central Station to catch the next train back to Montclair.

It starts with a spot. Cici notices a red stain in her underwear when she pees in the bathroom on the ground floor of the hospital. She had to pee so badly in the car, she didn't know which was worse, her full bladder or the contractions. By the time she gets to Dubin's office on the third floor Cici has had another couple of contractions. Cookie thinks about making eye contact with the nurse but instead she does that make-yourself-small thing she's learned to do in all-white places like this.

"My husband, he call *dottore,*" Cici says between exhales like she's blowing out a candle. The nurse isn't responding to her in that singsongy voice she uses when Solomon and Dr. Dubin were there. Cici is scared; she needs her doctor-husband, her man. Another nurse takes her into the back after the first nurse whispers something to her and hands her a chart.

Cici's out of her "below the waist" clothes, covered with a sheet in an examination room. Where is *il dottore,* they keep saying a minute but it has been many, many minutes. Solomon will be here soon, holding her hand and talking the way he talks. She just has to wait. Cici feels another cramp and then a gush of warmth between her legs. She's scared. She can't see over her belly. She scrunches up her eyes and when she opens them and sits up, she doesn't need to pull back the sheet to see what's going on. Cici is bleeding.

LUCKY CHARM

Ralphie is listening to his Bob Dylan LP in Terry's old room, smoking wacky tobacky, and it's making Billy Beal's eyes sting. That and the fact that he's so tired because the baby was crying all night and Moms kept coming in and out of his room to get her. Billy Beal can usually sleep on a rock in a construction site, but the baby's cry manages to get through where jackhammers can't. He hates to hear her cry and not just because it's annoying. Ralphie's moved into Terry's room now that Terry's shipped out to Asia, so Billy Beal has to bunk with the baby.

"You wanted her, you sleep with her," Pops grumbled. Billy Beal doesn't really mind having the baby in his room, but he's hanging out with Ralphie because she's finally taking a nap and Moms and Pops are fighting downstairs. "Gotta fly, little man," Ralphie says mid-toke, clapping Billy Beal on the back and crawling out the window. Ralphie used to climb down the tree in front of Terry's window so he could go to Asbury Park after curfew. Billy Beal hasn't a clue why he's doing it now, in the middle of a Saturday afternoon.

"For Christ's sake, if I'd wanted another kid I'd go knock up Mab—"

"It's not like she asked for twelve kids, it's men who can't keep it in their pants!"

"My ass, woman, my woolly ass. That baby's on borrowed time so don't you dare name her because we can't keep it like the goddamned stray cats."

Billy Beal puts a pillow over his head. When the baby wakes up maybe he can take her for a walk. He doesn't know why Moms worries; he's good with her, and she's an easy baby. She shuts up when Moms shoves a bottle in her mouth. He likes to look at her while she's sucking on her bottle because she's in a whole other world. He knows Moms must have done some quick talking with the bat from the Children's Home Society— he watched them through the glass door and at one point Moms slammed her hands down on the table and the bat looked like she'd shoot up to the ceiling. He can tell Moms likes having a baby in the house. "Nothing like the smell of new life," she'll say, sniffing the baby fresh from a bath or when she's changing her diaper. Good and bad even out inside Moms.

"With all we're blessed to have, you cheap, stingy bastard."

"Who do you think you're talking to? Who gave you all these things? If he loses the chance of a baseball scholarship because of this, he's nothing."

It's no use. Their words are missiles and the fallout gets him. He touches the charm he's got hidden under his T-shirt. He's never seen anything like that, with the watching eye, it's got to ward off evil spirits. He put the girl's charm on a string and kept it in his underwear drawer but recently decided to wear it for good luck. He could use some luck right about now. He touches the charm on the back and the front six times because six is his lucky number.

Pops yells at Moms, even if he never hits her. He's smashed his hand through walls and broken his share of furniture and lights, punted a cat once, but never touched Moms. Billy would like to go down there and protect her, but she'd just tell him to mind his own goddamned business. She's got a point about money; Pops is tight with a dollar, and when business is bad at the deli (which is a lot of the time), he blames Moms for having to go and have three farking kids who were eating them into the ground. One time, Pops drove away and said he was leaving for good. Billy Beal cried because he thought he'd never see his father again and he and his brothers would be like his aunt Mab's kids. When Moms couldn't shut him up, she walked him a ways down their street and pointed to a neighbor's driveway. There was the Country Squire, lights off, parked. Pops was inside, his head tilted back, mouth open. He walked in the kitchen the next morning and nobody said anything.

Billy Beal's gone from waiting for the girl to show up at the clinic to waiting for her to knock on their door. Moms told him that people from the family welfare office were still trying to track her down but hadn't been able to find any record of her or her next of kin. The information she'd written down about the father didn't check out. Moms warned him that they could only keep the baby so long, that soon she'd have to go to another foster home. "It's complicated business. There's a whole lot more to this than you can understand, Billy," she said. Billy Beal understands more than they think. He may not change diapers, but he's doing all his chores. He even helps out with the laundry if he has to. He doesn't want the girl's baby to go to another family; the other family won't have someone like Moms.

The baby sleeps like a snow angel. Billy watches as she makes little sucking motions. She's gotten bigger, but she looks tiny in the crib Aunt Mab loaned them. Moms had put in a couple of rolled-up blankets to make it cozy, but she's got lots of room to grow. Billy Beal thinks the baby looks like Gramps did at his wake. Which makes him think maybe she's stopped breathing. He holds his hand above her mouth until he feels her breath. He'd never looked at a baby up close before. Or from afar, for that matter. It's funny because the baby likes what he likes. She gets fidgety sometimes but calms right down when he turns on the Yankees game and gives her the play-by-play along with Mel Allen. Maybe later, if the coast is clear downstairs, Moms will let them watch the Yanks/A's game on TV and he can give her the lowdown on Ralph Terry and Bill Fischer. He thinks he might be ready to try to hold the baby on his own.

There's a slam and a crash and he imagines one of Moms's porcelain dwarfs got the worst of it. And then he hears the front door bang and the sound of Pops flooding the engine of the wagon. When Billy Beal bounds down the stairs three at a time in his bare feet so as to avoid making noise, he finds Moms in the living room sweeping up what's left of Dopey or maybe Bashful. "I can do that," he says.

"All done," she says. She smiles but doesn't look her son in the eye. She turns her back and throws the dwarf bits into the trash can. There's something in the way she takes her time brushing out every last shard that makes Billy Beal feel ashamed.

SMALL, HEAVY THINGS

Cici is in the dream room.

There was blood. So much blood on her thighs and on the floor as the nurses lifted her onto the gurney. They were packing things inside of her to get it to stop and all she could say was "Solomon, *dov'è* Solomon?" She felt cold and light-headed and then sleep.

Cici dreams of Rapallo; huddled under the tent of Papa's arms on the hill. Looking down at the town, the *processione* wending through the city ways, heading toward the sea. Watching the huge gold cross rise up in the arm of one strong man, pass through hands and dip down into the harness of another strong man. There are the bright colors of people's clothes and the *festoni,* the winking of lit candles the women and children carry and will put out to sea. The last man bearing the cross walks slowly into the ocean. Papa's fingers, dyed with the stain he used to retouch a countess's piano, comb the hair away from her face. He hums a moony song, does his crooked dance, and carries her home. The warmth of Papa's body next to hers, reading until she is too sleepy to understand words, just the licorice tone of his voice.

She dreams of reindeer.

"What do you see, *cara?*" The empty clothesline, stones with moss growing in the cracks. "You see him there? With grass between his teeth?" "A reindeer?" Papa laughs. "It's your pony!" "Is he coming, Papa? Is he coming for my birthday?"

Running to the window, looking. *Torta di noce* with five candles on the table, handmade gifts. Opening the crinkly paper to find a white fur elephant with a red velvet collar. Mama saying, "*Buon compleanno,* Carlottina." Running to the window, looking. No Papa to play monster-chase when the dinner dishes are washed. Running to the window, looking. No *compleanno* call, Papa's not home; day turning to night turning into day. Mama scrubbing the bathtub Papa uses to make his special drink in, then he takes the bottles with him on trips. Genny not letting her stop for an orange soda after school. Her wanting that soda so much, her tears, pounding Genny with her fists when she carries her up the path to their house. Running to the window, looking. Past Mama and a man in a black suit with a white collar who holds a Bible. Screaming, "I hate Papa. I hate Papa!" Sitting in the dark of her closet, holding the elephant, waiting to be punished. The knock. Mama's mouth pulled down at the corners like it does when she's angry, only she's not angry. Mama going down on her knees, "Do you understand what I am saying, Carlottina? It means we won't see Papa again, not ever." Mama's mouth keeps moving, but Carlottina is thinking about her pony. If Papa is in heaven, how will she get him? What if the pony is hungry and all alone, trying to find her?

When Sol arrives at the hospital, he's told that his wife needed emergency surgery and is now in intensive care. By the time he learns exactly what the emergency was, and the remedy, he is standing over an incubator the size of a large breadbox, staring at the tiny, intubated form they say is his son. He puts his hand on the clear plastic; the fan of his fingers obscures the infant's body. The shape of the incubator reminds him of a dog carrier, or an iron lung. There must be noise in the room but Sol hears none of it. He expects to feel something great, and yet all he feels is a small heat on his hand. He wants to see Cici, to touch her. He wants to charge into the recovery room like a husband who is overcome by the notion that he could have lost his wife. He wants to behave like a man who knows he's about to lose his son.

Sol cannot bear to look at the baby, and he cannot bear to look away. He is a doctor, trained in life and death, and yet he's never experienced the crossing over—having to hold a patient's hand at the moment of death. Telling a man's wife, his child, that he did all he could do and his all was not enough. Leave that to the surgeons with their God complexes. Yet here he is, holding this child the only way he can, a thin shield the only thing and everything between them. Without seeming to move Sol, a nurse opens the incubator and takes the tube out of the baby's mouth. Disencumbered, he looks so peaceful, he could be perfect. Sol thinks he hears the nurse say, "I'm sorry." There's a terrible moment where neither of them knows what to do. Shut the incubator? Wrap him up in a receiving blanket and transport him somewhere, wherever they take dead babies? They do an awkward shuffle. Now he hears the definitive cries of newborns; someone running water. Sol leans over the open container; brushing his hand across the infant's curled-up fingers that make a fist the size of a penny. They're already cool against the gush of warm air. "She's starting to come to," he hears Dr. Dubin say.

Before Cici realizes where she is and that her throat is so sore from being intubated it's hard to speak, she's trying to say, *"Dov'è il mio cavallino?"*

Cici swats the oxygen mask that's on her face. Someone's hands put an ice chip in her mouth. When she focuses enough to feel the crashing pain in her head, to understand that it's not limited to her upper portions and seems to be everywhere at the same time, she's waving her arms and using whatever voice she has to call out for her baby.

If Sol had arrived at the hospital just five minutes later, he would have raced directly to Cici's bedside to console and support her. But he catches Dubin before the doctor's had a chance to tell Cici. As much as Sol hates being the bearer of horrible news, as much as he's frightened about what this will do to his wife, he couldn't live with his cowardice if he let another doctor say what he is going to have to say now. He strokes her hand over the IV catheter. She struggles to sit up when he says, in response to the question she's been asking the ICU nurse over and over, "We lost him. We lost the baby." She blinks and shakes her head. "My baby, I must see my baby." It is clear that Cici will not rest until he honors her request, and, despite this not being protocol, Sol talks Dubin into allowing the nurse to get their son ready to bring to his mother like any other newborn. He stops her; it is his burden to bear, this small, heavy thing. Sol cannot look at Cici's face as she pulls back the blanket and clasps the baby to her chest in anguish. But he hears the deep guttural moan she makes, like a wounded animal, and then the great *O* of a wail that is the sound of all hope and joy being extinguished. It is a sound he will never forget. When the nurse gives her more medication,

Sol stays with her. He talks softly and strokes her head as she slips in and out of consciousness. He exists within this vacuum for as long as they'll let him: five minutes per hour, per hospital regulations.

Sol gets to know every inch of the waiting room. It looks the same as the one at St. Vincent's except he's never had to wait there, looking at the happy faces of a family who have just learned whether it's a girl or a boy. When he's called into intensive care for the last time that evening, Cici is sleeping. He looks at the space between her parted lips; he can't begin to describe why that gap fills him with both dread and longing.

When Sol gets home, he realizes he hasn't had anything to eat since his morning roll. That feels like years ago. Now that Sol's away from the hospital, his brain goes into overdrive. He feels like he did the night before a final exam: too hyper to sleep, brain whirring through notes, charts, definitions. As in *placenta previa:* implantation of the placenta over or near the internal opening in the cervix, through which the baby must pass to be born.

Sol's drawn to the simplicity of bread. If it were Wonder Bread, it would be better, as that was verboten in his mother's house and thus a great goyish delicacy. But Cici buys bread only at the local bakery. He cuts two slices off the loaf and closes it back up in its bag with its red twisty. He puts the bread in the toaster and depresses the button, takes the butter out of the fridge, opens a drawer and grabs a butter knife. Dubin didn't need to be condescending, giving a lengthy explanation of the differences between total and partial placenta previa. He talked to Sol like he was a technician, not a physician of equal stature. Goddamned surgeons.

Nobody needed to hand-hold him. Once Dubin said they couldn't stanch Cici's bleeding, there were only two possible outcomes. When Sol heard she was alive, he didn't dwell on what had had to be done in order to keep her alive. He didn't need justifications, he needed to see her, right then, right there. Now, while he's listening for the pop of the toaster, he replays it all. The logic of the C-section, the medical necessity of a hysterectomy—anything to stop the bleeding, to save the mother; it's always the mother first and that's the way he'd want it, he'd insist. The mother. They'd told him every part of "the mother" they'd cut out, listed a scrum of side effects and postoperative risks— hair loss stood out, for some reason. Cici's beautiful blond hair, he can't imagine.

The toast pops up, still pale. He presses the lever down again. Sol hates surgeons the way he hates lawyers. There was something smug beneath Dubin's concern. The way he tossed out *cesarean hysterectomy* like a towel he'd used to wipe himself off with between tennis sets. How dare Dubin declare that discussions with Sol's wife regarding the ramifications of her surgery were best left to the attending physician. As if Dubin knew Cici, as if he were better equipped to soften the blow than Sol. Too emotionally involved—that's what Dubin had said. Of course Sol's emotionally involved. It's his wife. He wasn't going to let them say, *Sorry, Mrs. Matzner, your baby died and oh, by the way, we had to remove your uterus.* Cici had barely had a moment to absorb today's loss; to immediately follow that with the news that she could never have any more children would be too devastating in her fragile state. So Sol played the "professional courtesy" card and prevailed on Dubin to allow Cici some time to recover before she was told about the hysterectomy. He double-checked to make sure this instruction was noted on Cici's chart—Sol had been around hospitals long enough to know you can't be too careful, can't follow up enough. He'd spoken to the head nurse and found out which nurses were on the next day and talked to them personally about how to handle Cici: *She will wake up and have questions about the pain, the stitches—they had to make ugly vertical and horizontal cuts—and the bandages. She'll be frightened and forget her English.* He'll be there first thing in the morning to help her through it, answer her questions.

Sol is pulled from his thoughts by a waft of acrid smoke. Nothing works anymore, nothing's made of quality, this piece-of-shit toaster. Now he's sounding like his father and that makes him so angry that, without knowing it, he's squeezed the now-burned toast in his fist. It rains black crumbs when he opens his hand.

Sol will be vigilant this time. He watches the minute hand on his Bulova—a present from his parents when he graduated from Yale. When the golden toast rises, the Bulova says it's been three minutes and two seconds. Their son lived for two minutes and forty-nine seconds—less time than it takes to hard-boil an egg; less time than it took Sol to make and eat his two pieces of toast.

On his way to the bedroom, Sol stops outside the baby's room. The door's ajar; the phonograph makes a whirring noise and is hot when Sol switches it off. He has the impulse to clean out the nursery so there's nothing left when Cici gets home. He'd enjoy the busywork, but is that what she would want? What's worse, to have all vestiges of baby gone without a trace or to come back to things exactly as they were before? Sol can't afford to make a mistake at this point—better to do nothing than do the wrong thing.

The bag. Cookie must have taken Cici's overnight bag with them to the hospital because it wasn't in the kitchen. Why didn't he listen to her? Would it have made any difference? Sol reminds himself to call Cookie first thing and tell her not to come in. There's so much to take care of: he'll have to call work, make arrangements with his partner; he needs to reschedule the man about the septic tank, find a neighborhood kid to mow the lawn. Lists usually bolster Sol, but he's beyond easy comfort. His legs are suddenly so heavy they threaten to buckle from exhaustion and he barely makes it to the bed. There's a lump underneath his back—he's lying on Cici's fur elephant. He pulls it out and it smells achingly of her. He pictures Cici's yearning eyes looking up at him, asking for their baby. He had promised her he would give her everything; it is too cruel, too painful that he's now helpless to give her the one thing she most desires. He folds his arms over the elephant's trunk and collapses into dreamless sleep.

A FEW CRISES

Solomon, when do they say we can start again, when we can make another baby?" Cici's pulled off her oxygen mask and is looking up at Sol. It's her second day in intensive care and her voice is weak. *"Quando?"* she asks. Her innocence cuts Sol and suddenly he can't respond with rehearsed words. He takes a deep breath, like a swimmer who knows he's going to be underwater for a long time, and tells her the truth. "Sweetheart," he says, stroking her hair, fighting to keep his own voice strong, "I am so sorry."

Cici refuses the shot to dry up her milk and the medications Sol and Dr. Dubin try to get her to take for her confused hormones. She's moved down to the maternity ward, and whenever a baby cries, she starts to lactate. She falls into fits of weeping that threaten her stitches. She barely eats. She clutches at Sol's neck one moment and then talks about how they'll have a baby girl next, he'll see. "Give her time. Time and the Lord's love can heal all wounds, physical, emotional, spiritual," the hospital chaplain tells Sol. Days pass in the hospital and all Sol can hang on to is things will be better once Cici is home, in her own surroundings. She will adjust. Time, it appears, is all he can give her.

When Sol makes it back to their house, the front lawn is spattered with newspapers and the air inside is hot and smells of garbage. Mail litters the hallway. Sol gathers and organizes, settling into the den to pay bills. How did it get to be the week before Labor Day? It's that last-gasp-of-summer, when families pack up coolers and kids and go to the Jersey Shore or Fire Island. The house seems to groan with neglect, and it's not the only thing groaning. Sol can hear the muzzled Jew inside of him saying, *Bury your child, for Christ's sake, it's time already.* He'd spoken to the hospital chaplain about a funeral but didn't want to go ahead with arrangements until Cici was well enough to attend. *It's disrespectful;* the voice turns into his father growling at him when he asks if they can wait a day for Grandma Minnie's funeral. Sol doesn't want to miss capture the flag at summer camp. "I don't care if you have to miss the president's bar mitzvah, you don't question the word of God. When He says bury, you bury. You think I'm tough? I'm nothing compared to God. I'll die, but Him? You have to answer to Him forever."

But now it's become clear that Cici won't be up for a funeral even if he waited another week, when she'll be released from the hospital. So he makes arrangements for the plot and a service. The procedural part is easy, but no one wants the task of calling family to invite them to a funeral. Moot point here. In his fantasy, Sol has a family like the Cleavers—people who resolve disagreements with handshakes and promises they keep. Family members who swoop in bearing starchy foods and know better than to ask you every two seconds how you're doing. The family you want to get rid of until you're alone and realize how much better you felt when they were around. Sol can't allow himself to indulge in this kind of illusion, because then he'll get in touch with the rage he feels. In reality, Sol's parents disowned him when he married

Cici. As if they had ever owned him. No question, he's better off without them and their narrow-minded bullshit in his life.

The story of how and why Sol was cut off from his parents is fodder for a joke: "Did you hear the one about the Jew who converts to Catholicism in order to marry the Italian bombshell?" But Sol prefers to think about the how-we-met part. Mainly because it makes him seem more adventurous, more heroic, than he actually is.

Sol met Carlotta D'Ameri because he was lost. He was in Milan attending a radiology conference, got confused, and stumbled into the Sierra Milano—a yearly textile convention housed in the same building. To escape the crowds of well-heeled Italians, Sol dipped into a booth with rolls of leather on display. It smelled of tobacco and tannin and then, suddenly, a deep, plummy scent, like fig or pomegranate. Sol saw a young woman, dressed in white, laughing and waving her hand at something a man in a suit had just said. She laughed like she smelled. Sol wanted to make her laugh like that. All he could think to do was offer her his hand. "My name is Solomon. Dr. Sol Matzner." He points to the *Dr.* before his name on the identification card around his neck. "Apparently, I'm lost."

"Carlotta D'Ameri," she said, pointing to her solar plexus and then reaching for the map he'd forgotten he was clutching in his hand. Their first touch came with a spark of static, a minor electric shock that caused them to recoil at the same time.

A frowning man, apparently the woman's boss, appeared and spoke to her in a tone that made it clear she needed to get back to work. Sol did everything short of charades to indicate that he was lost and looking for help. "Marco D'Ameri." The frowning man said his name as though he were concluding a conversation, not beginning one, and directed Sol toward an exit sign.

Sol mingled with his fellow radiologists for a short time and then went back to Carlotta's booth on his lunch break. Later, after his conference ended, he snuck her out of the Sierra Milano and across the street to a sandwich bar. She ate prosciutto and finished with cherry gelato she made him taste off her spoon and, later, her lips, when she turned her head so the kiss intended for her cheek became the real thing. When Sol went back to his hotel room, he smelled her perfume on his shirt, or maybe it was just memory enveloping him, making him want to reexperience every detail of her. Sol felt sick, a desirous, can't-eat kind of sick. He had to see this girl again. He had to know everything about her.

Sol extended his stay in Milano and was undaunted by Carlotta's warning that her family would not approve of her dating anyone who wasn't Italian. He could handle Marco D'Ameri; he was an MD, top of his class at Harvard, an all-around stand-up guy. At least, this was the argument Sol made to Cici's stepfather in the cavelike darkness of his library. Marco D'Ameri poured him a tumbler full of brown liquor. Without understanding a word of Marco D'Ameri's terse, rapid-fire Italian, Sol understood exactly what he was saying.

It was 1959, and Sol was no stranger to anti-Semitism. Although they hadn't lost family in the Holocaust, Sol's parents adopted the "never forget" mentality of survivors. Sol, however, was pragmatic about religion. What was the point in arguing about God when you could never prove or disprove His existence? And while his parents assumed that he'd marry a Jewish girl, religion was the last thing Sol thought about when it came to women. He would never have guessed that it would become one of the major issues of his life.

It should have been easy for Sol to return to America and

forget about an eighteen-year-old Italian girl with a fascist step-father. He'd known her for only a few days, and he wasn't a thrill-of-the-chase kind of guy. He pursued women in a haphazard, unfocused way; if they said yes, Sol just didn't say no. But Carlotta D'Ameri was different. She vexed him. He might have been able to dismiss her as a limited, if beautiful, distraction, but her innocence was spiked with a sensuousness that made him feel off balance. The very act of his wanting her said yes, and while it made him feel out of control, he wanted to say yes again.

Upon his return to the States, Sol took on more hours at work in order to negotiate more vacation time to get back to Milano to see Cici. From their first cherry-laced kiss, the connection was strongly physical. The language barrier intensified the need for touch, and Cici moaned, she sighed, she giggled. To her, it was all play; she wanted to explore, to discover, to wander in their sexuality like a garden. She'd nip and lick his nipples, ask him to roll a cold bottle of wine up and down her back and over her calves to see if it felt good-cold or bad-cold.

Sol was overwhelmed at first. Thrown off by her contradictions—a girl who was scared to get into an old elevator because it creaked but would defy her parents and sneak into a near stranger's hotel room? A girl who wept if she thought her hair looked bad but who had not an ounce of self-consciousness about her naked body? A virgin who was rapacious, so open to anything pleasurable as long as they avoided the Vatican's dreaded "penetration" that it made him feel prudish by comparison. Cici would surrender completely to him, to his touch; "Tell me," she would say and he would look into her eyes and tell her to come, and she would, again and again. It made him feel like the most powerful man on earth.

If Sol was shy, Cici was encouraging. She told him she loved his feet and that his red pubic hair was like the Olympic flame over his big "generals." She laughed when anything struck her as funny, often something he said or did. When they were again in the thrall of geography instead of each other, Sol worried that the novelty would wear off and she'd wake up one morning and say, "What was I thinking?" When she didn't, when distance only intensified their yearning, Sol saw *Fortunella* and *La Dolce Vita* six times each and developed intense cravings for risotto. During their long separations they wrote near incoherent letters back and forth, and on occasion he could telephone Cici at her cousin Paulo's for a few expensive but tender minutes.

Sol didn't tell his colleagues at work about Cici but had every intention of marrying her as soon as possible. His time frame accelerated because it became harder and harder for him to leave Italy, and he spent more and more time when he was apart from her thinking about how he could lose her. Sol had made Cici tell him about her other boyfriends: the altar boy, the Moto Guzzi guy in high school who felt her up; an artist friend of cousin Paulo's who took her to see Piero Manzoni's work and showed her how to give a hand job. Sol couldn't bear the thought of another man going where he'd gone or, worse, where he'd yet to go. Sol wanted to wake up in the morning and smell her hair on his pillow. He was tired of waiting. He had to do something to placate her parents.

Both Sol and Cici were certain that her stepfather would never allow them to marry. And Cici couldn't bear the thought of causing her mother pain. Catholicism was a borrowed dress Cici had worn for so long, it conformed to her curves. It was what she knew, thrust upon her by Marco D'Ameri. He would lecture the girls on the value of developing the habit of worship. By participating in the external rituals, he said, they would foster internal belief, which was but a step away from the carrot of all carrots: faith. Regardless of the depth of her faith, one thing was certain: she had to be married in a Roman Catholic church.

Sol had converted without telling her, sure that Cici's family would accept him as a Catholic. If he'd stayed a Jew, Sol wonders now, would she still have married him? Would she have said, *To hell with my anti-Semitic fascist family, I'm taking the radiologist?* Then he would have been able to call his parents. Or not. They might have reacted the same way because he'd married a shiksa. Regardless, his conversion was the ultimate expression of his love, the sign that Cici needed in order to leave her mother, her sisters, and her country for him.

It took eight months for Sol to become immersed in Catholicism, which required believers to embrace strange, mystical views such as resurrection, virgin birth, and accepting Jesus Christ as the Son of God. Sol was trained to think rationally, and these notions defied reason. Sol had long felt that, great writers and thinkers aside, believers were, in general, stupider than nonbelievers. It followed that Jewish intellectuals were superior to non-Jewish intellectuals. But Christian writers had a profound understanding of human behavior, much better than the nihilism that was popular when Sol was in college; Nietzsche and Marx were depressing. But there was something about the Roman Catholic Church that appealed to the last bastion of his nonpracticing Jewishness—his liberalism. It strove to rise above ethnic differences, attempted egalitarianism.

If Sol had told his parents he was converting, at best they'd have seen it as a complete betrayal of them. At worst, it would have sent his mother into the hospital with a nervous collapse— something that hadn't happened since after Sol was born, precipitated by the constant criticism of her live-in mother-in-law and her belief that her baby was ugly and needed to be taken out facedown in the baby carriage. She reminded anyone who'd listen that she was too young to be a mother and how having Solomon ("Red hair's not from my side of the family") had almost killed her. If he ever showed anger toward his mother she would lash out at him and then dissolve into tears, precipitating an apology and reinforcing his fear that his actions could cause her to break down again. From an early age, Sol was taught to proceed with caution in matters of bad news. He hadn't discussed his personal life with his mother since he was stood up for the prom; he was waiting for the right time. Of course there was never a right time, and the longer he waited, the easier it was to put off.

Sol was aware that he fit the stereotype of the self-hating Jew. He would never deny that he was Jewish, but he didn't offer up the information either. Why should he? He considered himself an American first and foremost. He liked cultural aspects of being a Jew, things like rugelach and Lenny Bruce. But he cringed at his family's brand of Judaism; his mother treated going to temple like a competitive sport, Grandma Minnie kept the Passover carp in the bathtub, and the family's favorite game was Who's Jewish, as in "Did you know that Abraham Lincoln was one-quarter Jewish?" He loathed how his father made him glue down their Pontiac's hubcaps so they couldn't be stolen and guess how much his steak would have cost in a restaurant. The Judaism Sol learned in Hebrew school wasn't any better. His teacher, a bald man who wore a Moshe Dayan eye patch, steered all lessons to the Holocaust, and constantly discussed how the Nazis had made lampshades and soap out of Jews.

In Bridgeport, Connecticut, Sol's father, Bernard Matzner, was considered a natty dresser; he wore rum getups, and people in the neighborhood called him Flash. He had an abiding faith in DMSO ointment—a remedy for joint ailments of horses—proclaiming it a wonder drug. Sol had to rub the stinky stuff on his chest for colds, slather it on cuts and bruises, even gargle with it for a sore throat. In sixth grade, Sol broke down the chemicals in DMSO and proved that it had no effect on humans. The project won the state science fair but did nothing to convince Bernard Matzner, even when his son brought home a blue ribbon and a check for twenty-five dollars. Sol's father believed the Chosen Son should lay off the science experiments and spend time in his women's-wear shop learning the physics of how to fold a sweater so it didn't crease.

At least Sol's mother believed in higher education. She knew her son was smart, and just because she'd settled for a man in the schmatta business it didn't mean her son had to follow in his footsteps. "You don't have my Buxbaum looks," she'd say, "but women will want you for your brains." She stood up to his father for him, but her support had its price. Sol had to listen to her complaints: Flash's breath stank from his false teeth; she had to put bed pillows between them because his constant erections bothered her; how did she, the star of the Derby community theater, end up like this? In making Sol her confidant, she cemented him as her ally against his father, a position that made Sol uncomfortable. She also tried to beat into him a sense of obligation not just to his parents but to the Holocaust, to the redemption of debt. If a Jew raised his children out of the faith in the middle of the forest, she heard it and declared it a posthumous victory for Hitler. "If every Jew goes off and raises gentile babies, pretty soon there'll be no Jews left," his mother would say.

For all Sol knows, one or both of his parents could be dead now. This is the thought that crosses his mind as he's standing in front of the closet in his bedroom looking for a clean shirt. He sniffs the armpit of a shirt he pulled from the laundry basket and puts it on. It's been over a year since he's spoken to his parents. He'd written, but the letters came back marked *Return to sender* in his mother's handwriting. His mother had been devastated that he'd married a shiksa—his converting meant he'd renounced his birthright. He told himself he didn't care, but in truth, he cared, although he loved Cici more.

On impulse, Sol picks up the phone.

"Halloo..."

Sol is oddly comforted by her familiar vibrato. "Mom..." There's no answer. "Mother, don't hang up. Mom?" He listens until he hears her faint breathing. "I just wanted to tell you..." Here his voice catches; he's a six-year-old boy with a bloodied knee. "The thing is...we...lost the baby. There were complications. Cici's going to be fine, but...Are you there? For God's sake, just say something so I know you're listening." There's an exhalation on the other line. "You knew Cici was pregnant—you sent back my letter with tape on it. You didn't seal it very well; the paper was folded differently. Mom?" He swallows. "The funeral is today at three o'clock. St. Clare's in Montclair, right off the New Jersey Turnpike, the Cedar Grove exit takes you straight there. Dad can figure it out on the map if... Mom...Mom?"

"I'm sorry." The voice comes out like strained soup. "You must have the wrong number."

"Would you like to go for a walk?" Sol asks. It's crisp outside, a perfect Sunday for apple picking or taking a drive to see the changing leaves. Cici sits in an armchair by their bedroom window—he has no idea if she's looking at something outside or lost in her thoughts. He's grown used to seeing her in this position, like nonsensical modern art. When he awoke at five this morning, she was already in the chair. Cici's been home for six weeks and her sorrow doesn't seem to have diminished. Sol thought that she would eventually reach for him to pull herself up and out of grief. Instead, she's gone deeper within the shell of her suffering and Sol's starting to fear she may never come out. One night he'd found her in the middle of the backyard standing like a lost statue, her arms torn and scratched. He hasn't been going out on the weekends, even to run errands, so he could be near Cici "just in case." He retreats into the steam of a hot shower and focuses on the day ahead. At least at work he can be productive.

Cici stares out the window but doesn't notice the tree branches bowing from the wind. She doesn't register that the leaves on the circle of oaks have turned the color of marmalade and are starting to crisp on the lawn. For a moment she thinks of bathing but the sight of the scars on her abdomen, raised like train tracks, are too great a reminder. She closes her eyes and drifts back into memories of being pregnant. There, Sol brings her lilacs and espresso and nothing bad happens. "The world is your oyster," Sol had said when he'd carried her over the threshold into his Gramercy Park apartment. She laughed because she ate oysters with one gulp. She'd asked him what would happen if you swallowed the world and there was no more left.

But now, it was too horrible to think about what was no longer possible. With the truth came hatchling thoughts, scary, desperate feelings that made her want to hurt herself. She ran into the woods behind their house one night, letting the trees scrape her until she bled. The pain felt good and she could prolong it for days by picking at the scabs as they formed. This was what the monks had done with their flagellating sticks, this was what was meant by atonement through pain. She needed to atone. For her desire, so desperate that she had insisted on sex the whole time her baby was growing inside of her. Surely this is what the priests had always warned them about. God even showed her how to atone further by making fresh cuts on the inside of her thighs with Solomon's razor blade. She goes to the bathroom and crouches, blade poised in that exquisite moment of hesitation. The first drop of blood cleanses, the sting of pain follows, sharp and sweet like absinthe. It stops her from thinking of her punishment—never being able to have children—and the certainty that she will be abandoned by Solomon because of it. What man would want her like this? She pulls her nightgown down over her legs when she hears her husband coming and gets back in bed.

"I'm going into the hospital for a while," Sol says, stroking her cheek. Cici knows her hair, which hasn't been washed in weeks, must feel like dead hay. He thinks about putting on one of her favorite records—*La Cenerentola* or maybe something by Massenet—but he doubts she'd get up to turn it over and it would scratch and scratch until Cookie came in this afternoon. He stares at Cici's ankles, the curve of her bone so white and exposed, and he wonders where she got the slippers she's wearing. He hadn't noticed them before; they're dingy and flat, so unlike anything he's ever seen her wear.

Sol is hovering. Cici wishes he'd leave. She's relieved when he says, "Get some sleep, *chérie,*" and gently closes the bedroom door.

It's not until Sol comes home late that night that he discovers the strange object that will propel him into an action that's so drastic, it changes the course of three lives. He undresses in the bathroom because he doesn't want the light to disturb Cici. When he fumbles his way to the bed, he notices something odd sticking out from underneath her pillow. It's round, like a bicycle horn. He can't see more without moving her head. She can be restless at night, but her breathing is regular and even—which makes him think she's taken a sleeping pill. He slowly pulls the object out from under her pillow. She sighs and rolls away from him.

Sol sits on the closed toilet, examining the object. He hasn't a clue what the hell this thing is. It has a cone that's taped to a handle that splits into a black bulb on one end and a tube on the other end. Could it be used to administer a drug by squeezing the bulb? If it were for that, he'd know about it, because he filled all of Cici's prescriptions. It looks handmade. Where did Cici get it? He could ask her about it, but if she wanted him to know she wouldn't have hidden it in the first place. What the hell? At least it doesn't look dangerous. He'll have to do some research at the hospital library. Sol goes back into the bedroom, puts the bicycle horn–thing under Cici's pillow, and tries to sleep.

The next day is a Monday and the radiology department at St. Vincent's is swamped with patients. When Sol looks up, it's dark outside. Cookie will be long gone and he hates leaving Cici alone late into the evening. He's racing to pack up and get to the train station when an intern runs past him. "You coming? It's about to start." Everyone on his floor is gathered around the small TV in back of the nurses' station. "This government, as promised, has maintained the closest surveillance of the Soviet military buildup on the island of Cuba. Within the past week, unmistakable evidence has established the fact that a series of offensive missile sites is now in preparation on the imprisoned island." President Kennedy speaks slowly and deliberately. "The purpose of these bases can be none other than to provide a nuclear strike capability against the Western Hemisphere." Sol is as paralyzed by the dire news as his colleagues. For the next seventeen minutes, no one moves, no one speaks. Sol watches as President Kennedy tells Americans that they are in the Soviets' crosshairs.

When the speech is over, everyone stands frozen around the television, as if there will be further instructions. "This is America," the doctor standing next to Sol says, "nobody can bomb us!" Sol nods noncommittally, but suddenly his companion seems to forget his anger at the Soviets and snaps his finger in recognition. "Wait a minute—Sol Matzner? I'm Don Tremont, Mo Lubitch's partner. I remember when Mo was recommending potential OBs for your wife. You must be a father by now. Congratulations." Tremont offers Sol his hand. Sol stares at it, not knowing what to do. Words like *ballistic missiles* and *nuclear warhead* from Kennedy's statement reverberate in his mind before he realizes what Tremont just said.

"We lost the baby," Sol says before he can censor himself. Later, he will wonder what prompted him to confess so blatantly. In the moment he is rattled by news so unexpected, so large, that instead of shaking Tremont's hand and going home, Sol finds himself in Tremont's office spilling the whole, sad story. The baby, Cici's hysterectomy, his fear for her mental health, and, finally, the strange round object under her pillow.

"What do you think it is?" Sol asks.

Don Tremont considers, then says, "When your wife was in the hospital, did they give her the shot to suppress her breast milk?"

"She didn't want that."

"With no baby to stimulate production, her milk should have dried up within two weeks. But the only thing that comes to mind is that it might be an old-fashioned form of breast pump."

"A breast pump? For breast-feeding?"

"Well, of course you know physicians don't recommend that women breast-feed, but in some ethnic communities it's still done. And if, say, the mother has to be away from her baby, or if the woman is a wet nurse, there are devices that can be used to express the milk."

"But the baby died. Why would she be..." Sol's voice trails off.

Tremont gives Sol a pat on the shoulder. "I wish there was more I could offer. My sister lost a baby and I know she had a very hard time of it. Your best bet might be to consult someone in psychiatry."

Sol feels like he's been sucker-punched. He gets himself to the train station and on the train home, but he can't recall exactly how. He's alone in the compartment, staring off without really seeing anything. Tremont had to be right; it was a breast pump. The only person who could have given it to Cici was Cookie. That much made sense. But why was Cici using it? Expressing milk to give to her dead baby? Pretending that he's still alive and giving Cookie the milk to, what—take to some other baby? It was all too bizarre; he didn't need to consult a psychiatrist to know his wife was wading into some very dark, uncharted waters.

Unbidden, he thinks of his wife's breasts. He hasn't touched them since Cici came home from the hospital, hasn't dared, it isn't right. He's wanted to. He's thought about it, desired her, ached for her to touch him. At first he was ashamed. He would get hard in the mornings and want to roll over and press himself into the seam of her ass. He didn't want to masturbate, thinking eventually she'd respond to his tickling her foot or caressing her back. But she didn't, and weeks passed. He focused on work; he masturbated.

The back-and-forth of the train jostles him and Sol can't help thinking, *What if this is it?* What if nothing ever changes and this is his life? He has been so worried about Cici that he hasn't factored himself into the equation. He wants to have children—his own flesh and blood—but he's willing to accept that he never will. What he can't accept is the idea that he'll never make love to Cici again. He misses her raw, sensual mouth. Their intimacy became his touchstone. *I'm home,* he'd think when he entered her. Without that . . . well, there cannot be a without that. He had never felt truly alive until he met Cici. She gave herself so fully, so freely—it liberated him. During their courtship he'd told her that he was ruined; after experiencing the ecstasy of their connectedness, there could be no living without it, or her, ever again. He needs his sexy young wife back.

When Sol gets home, he pours himself a tumbler full of vodka. He drinks it in one gulp, standing over the kitchen sink. The liquor makes him warm and woozy. Although it's not that late, he knows he'll find Cici asleep. He sheds his pants and lies down on top of the covers.

Staring at the ceiling, Sol remembers Cici draped across her cousin Paulo's couch, naked except for high heels. He's fully dressed, kneeling in front of her on the couch. Watching as she circles her nipples with the point of her lipstick, making them hard and red. She takes his hand and puts it over her mound and he feels her heat on his palm. Her legs are open and he can see the folds of her labia through her forest of blond pubic hair. He leans down and inhales her scent, brushing his nose across her hair. She's liquid, musky. He reaches underneath her, cupping her bottom in his hands, and she presses herself into his face. She is undulating slowly, moving the lipstick down her stomach. His tongue parts her, finds her, hard and quick. She moans and pulls him up, loosening his pants, saying Italian words that roll with her mouth as she takes him in, tracing her tongue up and around until he sees white spots behind his eyes. Then, when he's close, so close, she stops, pulling him up and pushing him toward the mirror on the wall. Her damp hair clings to her face; her body is soft and round, with lipstick marks like tribal paint. She brushes her breasts against his back, her slender arms reaching around to stroke him. She folds his hand over hers and they watch her hand and his hand together, moving up and down and up and down.

Sol gasps and comes into his fist.

Now he lies in bed next to Cici feeling an ocean apart. There is nothing to do except wait to be released into sleep.

⚭

The following morning, Sol sits in the kitchen listening anxiously to the newscast on the radio while he waits for Cookie. The world, which seemed relatively safe just twenty-four hours ago, is now unpredictable and rife with crisis. By the end of the day, the Organization of American States is likely to approve of the quarantine against Cuba. Cookie arrives two minutes early wearing a coat that's three sizes too big. "Morning, Mr. M. How's she doin' today?"

"Why don't you tell me," Sol says, holding up the breast pump. "This is yours, right? You gave it to her."

"Yes, sir."

"And...?" Sol waits. When it's clear Cookie's not going to say more, he says: "It's a pump, so she can milk—but you already know that! Are you making her believe she can have another baby? Don't tell me she's pretending... our baby—" He sputters to a stop before shouting, "I hired you to clean the house, not to put delusional ideas in her head! What on earth were you thinking? Are you crazy?"

"I may be a lot of things, Mr. M., but I ain't crazy."

"Well, then, explain it to me, because I don't understand."

"No, sir, I don't suppose you would," Cookie replies, looking down.

Sol realizes his anger won't get results. "Why don't you sit," he says, "please, sit."

"Thank you," Cookie says, but remains standing. Sol runs his fingers through his hair. Composes himself. "As you can imagine, I'm very concerned about my wife. And... I'm just trying to understand. I'm trying to understand what a woman who doesn't have a baby is doing with this."

"Ain't you a doctor?"

"I know *what* she's doing with it, for God's sakes, what I want to know is *why*?"

"All right," Cookie says, leaning on the kitchen chair as if to brace herself for another outburst. "Sometimes people, they want to feel something they don't got," she says quietly. "Maybe they had it once and they lost it. Like a man who lost his leg, had it cut off, he still feel that leg. It's like that with your wife."

"What does she want to feel?" Sol asks, sensing that, whatever the answer, he will have no cure.

"Like she's a mother."

Cookie's words hang in the air. Sol looks down at his hands, not knowing what to say. "Thank you, Cookie," Sol says after a minute. "But you can't be planning on doing this forever. It'll have to stop eventually."

"Yes, sir. But there be plenty of room between now and forever."

"Taper off, however it's best for her to do it, but do it now."

"Oh no. I can't do that."

"Excuse me?"

"I can't be taking that away from her. It'd be taking away the one thing that gives her hope, and if you do that, you're in for a heap more trouble than you already got. Don't mean to be rude, Mr. M., but given what y'all been through, that saying a lot." Sol puts on his coat and grabs his keys, picks up the pump and shoves it in his pocket. He's almost out the door when he turns around. He never thought he'd take advice from Cookie, but maybe she has a point. He walks back and lays the pump down on the table.

At St. Vincent's, the television set on Sol's floor is always on. All day, news reports detail the showdown between the superpowers; no matter how Kennedy framed it, a quarantine against Cuba was an act of war and Khrushchev's anger shows no sign of abating. The staff is transfixed by the reconnaissance photographs of Soviet missile sites in Cuba. Sol, not usually prone to fear, tries to rationalize it as just a high-stakes game of chicken. But this was for all the marbles and Castro was unstable enough that who knew who would blink first. The world certainly felt like it was on the brink of collapse; could a nuclear bomb already be aimed at New York? Sol thinks of his life with Cici, what it is now compared to what he imagined it would be. What could he possibly do to give their lives a glimmer of the promise and meaning he'd felt the day he married her?

Later that afternoon, Sol tentatively knocks on the door of Dr. Tremont's office. He finds Tremont is sitting behind his desk, a messy mahogany affair that's covered with framed photographs of his golden retrievers.

"I appreciated our discussion last night," Sol begins stiffly. "I won't take up much of your time, but I'd like to ask you about something that could help my wife." He blunders on, despite his embarrassment. "The device we spoke about—it occurred to me that as illogical as it is, she's been using it to give her hope. She needs something real, something she can hold on to."

Sol looks at Tremont, silently asking him to understand the words he cannot bring himself to say out loud.

After a long moment, Tremont nods. "You're talking about adoption. Of course, if you're prepared to do this so soon after your loss, there are many good agencies."

"Given her circumstance," Sol says, "I believe soon is essential."

"No waiting. No questions. No checks." Walter Pembroke, Esquire's accent, is vaguely Canadian. He sits at his desk across from Sol. "If you're not interested, there are three other couples I represent who are." Sol looks at a picture of a baby. Indiscernible sex, unfocused, bluish eyes. He'd get better odds in Atlantic City. "I'm interested," he says.

Don Tremont tried to talk Sol into taking his time and working with an adoption agency. He warned that it was dicey to proceed without Cici's involvement, that given how unstable she was, she could potentially reject a new child. But Sol's desperation prevailed and Tremont confided that he knew a lawyer who could "cut through the red tape" and who was very discreet.

So what if the logic of a rushed adoption is dubious; so what if Mr. Pembroke's "Esquire" was most likely bought through a mail-order course? Sol has to do whatever is necessary to make his wife whole and happy. As shocked as he is to find himself in this position, as distasteful as it is to have to negotiate with Pembroke, Sol has to come up with four thousand dollars to buy his wife a baby.

Jersey National Bank closes at five, and Sol floors his Olds to get there in time. He financed his house with that bank and has a relationship with the branch manager. He reviewed Mr. Carlton's mother's X-rays and had gotten her in with a top orthopedist, so he hopes that will help. Radiology was a prime choice of specialization for Sol; still, he'd had to moonlight weekends at Mount Sinai's ER to pay for Carlotta's canary-yellow two-carat diamond ring, even though he got it wholesale, and the down payment on the house has used up almost all of the money he'd made on his real estate investments. Crappy garages, vacant meatpacking warehouses in the far West Village he bought for almost nothing then sold to local hospitals to use as storage for their old medical records. Sol figures if he has to, he'll run another line of credit with his percentage in the Bailey, Halpern, and Matzner practice for collateral. Which, it turns out, is what Mr. Carlton suggests in response to Sol's fib that he needs the money to pay for Cici's continuing home care.

The very next morning, Pembroke calls to confirm a time and place for Sol to pick up the baby and hand over the money. Even though he chose Pembroke based on the man's reputation for "efficiency," Sol assumed the process would take a few weeks.

Panicking, he thinks about all that needs to get done in the next few hours. Does he need to buy anything? Or are all of Cici's careful preparations still there in the neatly organized baby's room? He hasn't been inside that room for weeks. He still thinks of it as his son's room, and now another child—a girl, Pembroke told him—will grow up in it. She will have the life intended for their boy and never know the difference. Will Cici ever be able to forget their son? Will he? But he can't allow doubt to creep in now; it's far too late for that.

Sol needs to get out of the house. He feels uncomfortable being around Cici and not disclosing his plan. Even though it's hours before his meeting with Pembroke, he puts his four thousand dollars in the glove box and backs his Olds down the driveway. But the drive proves to be all the more unsettling; bomb talk dominates every radio station, and the news seems to be getting worse. With a click and a twist, he settles on something banal. "Duke, Duke, Duke, Duke of Earl, Earl, Earl."

Bird shit hits smack in the middle of the windshield. "Goddamned birds," he says and flicks on his wipers, making a streaky mess. "The whole world is going to shit." He can barely see and thinks, *Great, all I need is an accident.* The closest place to pull over is Dick Shelton's Cadillac dealership. The lot is festooned with American flags and there's a curvy brunette standing out front in a short, checkered jumper who offers to wash his window for free, and, by the way, would he like to take a look at the new Eldorado convertibles while he waits? Sol doesn't think of himself as a Caddy man—they are too ostentatious—but what the hell, why not check out a convertible? This could be their last day of—what? Freedom? Safety?—before going up in a mushroom cloud, so why not spend it enjoying a little luxury. The least he can do is try to make things right for Cici while there are still things to make right. Sol pictures Cici smiling in a way he hasn't seen for months sitting in the passenger seat of a new Eldorado, hair streaming out of control like in *La Dolce Vita*. If his love alone can't make her happy, then a baby in a red 1963 Cadillac Eldorado has to do the trick. Anyway, he still has two hours before he has to be at the HoJo's parking lot off the highway, plenty of time to take a look.

Billy Beal arrives at the HoJo's parking lot early. He thinks about the past few days, how so much happened so quickly. It was only last Tuesday when they were all watching game seven of the World Series on the black-and-white Zenith. Moms with the baby sleeping on her shoulder; Pops pacing, yelling at Ralph Terry to strike the batter out. It was another World Series title for the Yanks, and the Beals were all on their feet, nobody louder than Moms, who caterwauled like an overgrown cheerleader. Pops tackled his sons and they banged into the coffee table, knocking empty bottles of beer into a couple of discarded BB guns on the floor.

Later, when Moms came around for her good-night hug, she sat on the corner of Billy Beal's bed and shook her head. "I tried," she said. "Look at me, son, it's important that you hear this right." Billy Beal stared at the ceiling. "We can't keep the baby any longer, no ifs, ands, or buts about it." The week before, he'd heard Pops hollering bad at Moms and he'd discovered Pops sleeping on the couch the next morning. So Moms's news didn't exactly come as a surprise. Billy had also heard what Moms had to say about orphanages and state services; the baby deserved better. Billy Beal had touched the girl's pendant, six times front, six times back, and asked the universe for an answer. He asked and asked until he remembered the man who'd come to the clinic.

"Walter Pembroke, Esquire," was how he'd introduced himself. He'd come to the clinic right after the Fourth of July and spent a while talking to Syl behind the check-in window. Afterward, he'd walked up to Billy Beal and explained that he was a lawyer who represented good families who were looking to adopt babies. Billy Beal had never seen a man whose briefcase matched his shoes. He had no idea why this person was bothering to talk to him. "You look like a sharp fellow," Esquire said. "I help people in difficult situations; you understand what I'm saying, son? You call me if you know someone who needs my help. A lady who, for whatever reason, can't take care of her baby herself. I help. And if you help, there's something in it for you too." Just before the lawyer reached the exit, he trotted back to Billy. "Did I mention they should be white? White babies only." Billy took the man's card.

After Moms said good night and left his room, Billy leaned over the baby's crib. "Don't worry," he said, "everything's going to work out fine, you'll see." Walter Pembroke, Esquire, was the answer.

※

But Moms had caught wind of what was going on with Esquire—Billy was lousy at keeping a secret—and insisted on speaking to the lawyer-man to see if he and his potential clients passed her sniff test. Then and only then would she get in touch with the agency she fostered for and put them in touch with him. Moms further insisted that she personally deliver the baby to the new parents. Pops got in the game and said, "Make it farking sooner than later," and before Billy Beal knew it, Moms had her coat on and the baby packed and was saying if he didn't step on it she was leaving without him. Moms had a hinky feeling about meeting in a parking lot and wasn't about to let the baby go to some kook. So Billy Beal's standing outside of the station wagon in the HoJo's lot, chewing a wad of Bazooka, waiting for Moms to come back with some clam rolls and soda. Billy Beal peers into the backseat and wiggles his fingers at the baby. He checks the parking lot for Esquire but the place is dead.

Sol's palms sweat as he turns the leatherette steering wheel to make an illegal U-turn. Pembroke said to meet at the HoJo's near his office but Sol must have taken the wrong exit off the Garden State, because he doesn't see the familiar orange-and-turquoise sign. It must be the next exit up. Does he see a cherry top in his rearview mirror, a few cars behind him? Did a cop see him make the turn? What if the police pull him over? How will he explain riding around with four thousand dollars in cash, enough for a down payment on a house around here? He's a doctor, a good citizen; he doesn't even have any points on his license. What if he's busted for involvement in some left-of-the-law adoption scam? Sol relaxes when the car pulls into the next lane—the red placard on its roof advertises the E-Z Driving School. Sol looks at his watch. He hopes Pembroke isn't late; he might lose his nerve if anything deviates from the plan.

Sol pulls into the HoJo's lot at exactly the appointed time and parks at the end that's farthest away from the restaurant, as instructed. He turns off the engine and looks around: nobody in the lot except a teenager in a leather jacket who gets out of a rusted station wagon parked a few spots away from him. Sol will have to wait. He rubs the back of his thumb against his cuticles, feels antsy, has the impulse to flee. This is for Cici, he reminds himself as he switches on the new radio, twizzling the buttons— but it's just more about the missile crisis, so he quickly switches it off. That is the last thing he wants to think about right now. In the rearview, the boy is staring at the Caddy. He's about fifty feet away; close enough so Sol could read the expression on his face if it weren't totally blank.

The boy juts his chin out in a way that reminds Sol of the Irish kids he grew up with, the types his father labeled "goyish hood-lum delinquents." Sol checks his watch. Where is Pembroke? The kid has lasers for eyes and it's making Sol uncomfortable. What's he thinking, that he's going to rob a man in a new Caddy? Sol would lock the car doors but that would only make him feel more claustrophobic.

A heavyset woman emerges from the restaurant carrying some bags of food. The boy says something to her and now they're both looking over at Sol, who is about to sweat through his shirt when a Dodge Dart pulls in and parks next to the station wagon. Pembroke gets out, flaps his hands in front of the kid and the woman, then trots over to Sol. "Dr. Matzner. Terribly sorry I'm late. You weren't supposed to meet like this." Sol gets out of the Caddy and sees that the woman has put her bags in her car and is starting to walk toward them.

"We haven't met," Sol says coldly. Pembroke takes Sol's arm but Sol shakes it off. "You didn't say there were going to be other people here. Who the hell are they?"

"It's the foster family. They've been looking after the baby, and, uh, insisted they be here . . ." The woman is now only a few feet away and she abruptly thrusts out her hand.

72

"Margaret Beal, this is my son Billy, and you are . . . ?"

"The adoptive father, Mrs. Beal, I can take it from here," Pembroke says. Margaret Beal's eyes don't leave Sol's. She bulldozes ahead.

"I told Mr. Pembroke here that my son and I needed to meet the people who were going to take the baby." In response to Sol's quizzical look, she adds, "We didn't want to name her, it's usually better that way. Do you and your wife have a name picked out? Is your wife here with you? I expected to meet her too."

"I didn't realize this was an interview," Sol says.

"We're very fond of the baby, especially my son Billy here. He's the reason we took her in the first place. We wanted to meet you, face-to-face. You see where she's been; we see where she's going. Your wife?"

"Is at home," Sol says.

"Excuse us," Pembroke says, pulling Mrs. Beal away. They talk quietly on the far side of the station wagon while the son stands across from them looking into the window of the backseat. Pembroke told Sol the adoption would be anonymous and now there's Mrs. Beal to contend with. She's pushy, but well-meaning; the baby could have done far worse. Now Pembroke's raising his voice, spouting legalese. If Sol doesn't want this all to go south, he's got to get involved.

While the son wolfs down two clam rolls, Sol goes into doctor mode with Mrs. Beal. He diagnoses and then allays her fears with natural authority; soon she's asking him for advice about her sister Mab's gout and Pembroke's ready to close the deal. Mrs. Beal talks quietly about nipple flows and burp cloths while the boy gets a white wicker bassinet out of the car. Sol can see the baby's face peeking out of her blankets; she's filled out since her picture was taken and she has apple cheeks. Pembroke is pulling off the blanket to show Sol that the baby's got all her fingers and toes and confirms that Sol has reviewed all the medical records. He notes that she was vaccinated. It's like he's buying a horse.

Suddenly Pembroke is handing Sol the basket. It is heavier than Sol expected and more cumbersome. He doesn't know how to hold it. Just as he begins to readjust, Pembroke motions that it is time for the cash.

Sol doesn't want to hand Pembroke the envelope in full view of Mrs. Beal. It feels too mercenary, tawdry. He motions for Pembroke to open the passenger door. Once they're both in the car, they discreetly exchange the envelope for the signed adoption papers. "You took care of everything with the state?" Sol presses. "My wife and I have the baby free and clear?"

"Of course," Pembroke says. "All the paperwork from the foster program is there, signed and in order." Sol prays Pembroke doesn't have the bad taste to open the envelope and count the bills. Pembroke runs his hand over the dashboard. "Nice," he says. "Congratulations to you and Mrs. Matzner." Sol wonders if he's referring to the baby or the Cadillac. Pembroke doesn't really seem like a baby person.

When Pembroke's gone, Sol takes a deep breath. The air is redolent of new car and something else he'd smelled when he'd picked up the baby in her basket. Not soap or powder, he'd recognize those; this was organic and sweet. For the first time since he started this venture, he feels a moment of peace.

He placed the baby in her basket in the backseat but then decides to move her up front where he can keep an eye on her. He gingerly moves the bassinet to the passenger seat, taking pains not to wake her. Her skin's so white it's practically transparent and he can see her eyes moving beneath her closed lids. Her hair is black, and there's a lot of it, he thinks, not really knowing how much hair an almost three-month-old should have. She's also bigger than he expected. Just as he's settling himself back into the driver's seat, there's a sharp rap on the window—Mrs. Beal is standing on the other side of the glass. Her face has lost its composure; traces of sadness pull at the corners of her mouth. Sol searches for the button to lower the window.

"Sorry to bother you, but my son wanted to make sure I told you one more thing. Billy wants to let you know she likes baseball. The Yankees, of course. During the season, let her listen to a game, she'll light right up like she's rooting for them. Billy there is the star pitcher for the Trenton Tigers, look out because soon you'll see him in the majors." Sol nods politely and she waves and returns to her car. Sol fixes his own seat belt and now it's just him, his new sleeping baby, his new car, and a world still on the brink of collapse. "All right, then," he says to no one in particular.

THREE: THE LONELIEST NUMBER

Cici's face is wet with tears. Sol can't tell if they're tears of joy or pain. He'd left the baby, who was still sleeping, in the car and gone upstairs to get Cici. She refused to come downstairs, even after he said he had a really, *really* big surprise—one she was sure to like.

Even before he opened the front door to return to the car he heard it: a wail that began to crescendo and showed no signs of abating. The baby hollered when Sol took her out of her basket, she screamed and kicked off her blankets—it was all Sol could do to carry her up the stairs and into the bedroom. The baby gulped and sputtered and Sol bounced her a little but was having no luck calming her down. Cici must have heard the crying because she was standing at the window, locked in place, facing away from Sol. Waiting for Cici to turn around felt to Sol like an eternity. When she did, her gaze was lowered and he could see tears wet her face. She took a few steps toward him and when she met his eyes it was as if she was seeing him, again, for the first time. Her expression so tender, so grateful, as she reached out toward the baby in his arms. *"Per favore,"* she said.

Sol had assumed they'd talk a bit. He'd explain his decision, leaving out certain specifics, but in his mind, talking occurred. But now, there was no talking. Cici took the baby in her arms and began cooing and murmuring softly. "I'll just be downstairs, waiting," Sol mumbled after watching the circle close around his wife and their infant. "I'll leave the two of you alone, give you time to get to know each other."

⁂

Get to know each other? Sol feels like a galoot. He thinks it's going well, though, because every time he goes upstairs to check on them, they're clucking and cooing, and now the baby's quiet. He makes Cici a sandwich and brings it up along with the bag of bottles and formula and diapers Mrs. Beal had given him. "I thought you might both be hungry," he says. He lays down the care package, filled with things he isn't quite sure what to do with. The baby's in bed next to Cici, curled like a lima bean. Sol puts the sandwich down on the table next to Cici's side of the bed. She looks like a child herself. "Shhhhhhhhh," she says, pressing her finger to her lips and closing her eyes.

Sol spends the night on the sofa and the next day Cici and the baby sleep until noon. Sol tunes in to the Voice of America, which is broadcasting President Kennedy's response to Khrushchev. "I think that you and I, with our heavy responsibilities for the maintenance of peace, were aware that developments were approaching a point where events could have become unmanageable." Kennedy sounds so calm, so restrained. Listening to his voice makes the fact that the world has just been teetering on the edge of nuclear war seem unbelievable. The Soviets are going to stop building bases in Cuba and will dismantle their offensive

weapons; they had blinked. High noon appears to be over everywhere in the world, including in his own home. Sol is greatly
relieved. Why, then, does he still feel a sense of disquiet, like he's
forgotten to do something but can't remember what?

———

Cici and the baby stay in their bedroom for three days and nights,
until both are exhausted from the struggle to feed and be fed,
until Cici's milk is flowing fully and the baby is sucking from
her breast. Cici refused to use a bottle or formula, determined to
nurse this child as she would have her own. Love starts to form
underneath the crust of Cici's grief, and she is hungry to protect
and keep close the new object of her affection. "I am your mama,
and you are *mia bambina*," she says to the baby. "I am mama,"
Cici whispers until she can no longer picture the gray face of her
son. "You are my baby. Mama will not lose you, *tesoro mio*."

Sol feels like a stranger in his own home. The closed bedroom
door is a barrier between him and what is distinctly female. Sol is
excluded from whatever is going on behind that door, and after
days of it, he feels a mounting anger. Then again, shouldn't he
just be happy that she's taken with the child, that they're forming a bond? Isn't this exactly what he wanted? But Cici is young
and inexperienced, and what she needs is the advice of a more
mature woman, like one of her sisters. Certainly not uneducated
Cookie. He doesn't trust that Cookie, not anymore.

Sol has noticed that Cookie has a spring in her step since the
baby arrived. Maybe because she has a free pass into their bedroom and he doesn't. Sol watches her disappear into the room
and reappear with dirty diapers and dishes. Cookie makes trips
to and from the baby's room, fetching clothing and ointment

and rattles and returning with applesauce, corn pudding, mashed potatoes, yams. Sol has teeth he'd like to use and the rotation is getting tiresome. It's obvious that Sol isn't needed at home, so he calls the hospital and says he's coming back to work. He had another radiologist cover for him for a couple of days, but now it is time for life to return to normal.

By the seventh day of Cici's sequestration with the baby, Sol's back is tied in knots from sleeping on the living-room sofa. Rather than knocking softly on the door and speaking to his wife through a baffling of wood, this morning he barges in, unannounced. Cici is sitting up, a pillow under her arm and the baby nestled at her breast. Her hair is clean and pinned up and she wears no makeup. Sol can't remember ever seeing her look more beautiful. Without taking her eyes off the baby, she motions for Sol to come around beside her. All the words he planned to say— that she needed to snap out of this ethnic nonsense and feed the child some proper formula, that he would be coming back to their bed tonight—are silenced. A breeze from the open window releases the faint scent of powder and something buttery, almost like caramel. "Come, *amore mio,*" she says. He sits next to her on the bed as she turns the baby toward him. The child has the strangest eyes. They are two distinctly different colors; one blue and the other hazel, heading into green. The baby is alert, locking right onto him. Is he supposed to hold her? He hesitates and Cici puts the baby over her shoulder and pats her back for a burp. She's cooing in some version of Italian baby talk, making round circles on the baby's back. "Shhhhh, *cara mia, tesoro mio, chérie, cara.*" Cici looks so peaceful now; except for the scars on her stomach there's no outward sign anything bad has happened. Sol feels uncomfortable perched on the edge of the bed; should he slide his legs up, spoon into the family? He picks one leg up and slides an arm around Cici's shoulders. Is he supposed to watch her and the baby making eyes at each other in wonderment? He tries. The baby has spit bubbles on her mouth and Cici blows on her face, laughing her delicious laugh. But this new position is no more comfortable for Sol than the other, and he waits for Cici to notice and readjust. But she is too busy sniffing the top of the baby's head. Is Sol supposed to sniff it too? Is he supposed to feel something immediately toward this child that bears no resemblance to him, that is not his flesh and blood? Clearly Cici does. Cici squeezes his hand and tells him to breathe, right there; she kisses the baby's downy head. Sol realizes the baby is the source of the caramel smell, the scent he couldn't describe mingling with new car. Sol has a dawning dread that he may have made a mistake, one that can't be undone. They are now three. He feels the unevenness of the number, the potential for gaps, for triangles.

"Don't you want to know her name?" Cici says. She sounds fragile and terribly lovely. It makes Sol want to inhale her voice and sail away. When she finally looks up at him, her gaze fills him up. It feels like forever since she's done that. "It is Cherie," Cici whispers. "*Ma chérie amour. Is perfetto,* no?"

She's named the baby their term of endearment? The name she calls him when they make love? "Perfect," he says weakly as he walks out and quietly closes the door.

⌘

And what of the baby in all of this, the newly minted Cheri (without an *e* because Sol wanted there to be at least a letter of difference between his pet name and hers)? She inhaled the soft woolly smell of blankets, the powdery, sticky scent of white cream, and vanilla from the long hair that she grabbed as it tickled over her face. And there was the smell of something else that was put into her mouth, wet and soft, not like the salty-tasting fingers that touched her lips. This thing that was pressed into her mouth, that made her cough and choke and was dry at first and then became liquid that tasted sweet and slightly bitter. Sometimes it tasted different, it made her sneeze; she'd smell it on the cloth that would wipe her face or on the front of her when she spit it up. The source of the smell, the liquid, had big soft lips and big soft hands that sometimes pressed her hard into the smell, wanting her to drink more when she was full. The source of the smell clutched her and made noises that she'd heard before but that sounded different, like they needed her to respond. Like they were waiting. The smell would sometimes be so close she felt she couldn't breathe and then she'd cry and get pulled closer and closer so she stopped crying to get away. The smell opened its lips and closed them over and over again making "Mmaaa," and then "Maaaa." "I am your mama," so that one day she would know the smell was Mama, so the smell had a name.

Cheri sleeps with Mama and dreams of things she'll soon forget. A woman in a blue dress dances barefoot on the moon. "I'll fly you to bliss," she says, twirling to a chorus of voices spoken in words she doesn't yet know; "Terry's on the mound at the bottom of the ninth and the pressure is on"; "If I'd wanted another kid I'd go knock up Mab." "Cheri, *amore mio,* I am here. I will never leave you," she hears as she opens her eyes, as the smell reaches to embrace her, to take her in, grasping tight, too tight. "Never, ever."

PART II

chicago, 2002

somewhere in the middle

EGGS

Monday morning is the cruelest time for undergraduates, especially when they're sitting in the dark, and she suddenly knows she's lost them. Cheri Matzner stands in front of a projector while the ancient fertility idols and horned goddesses shown in the slides flow over her like a traveling tattoo. She can practically hear her students' heads dropping onto their desks. She can't wait to be free of these baby birds with their mouths and laptops open, partially because it's her last semester teaching and partially because her dine-and-drive breakfast of fried dough and coffee is repeating itself in new and unusual ways. Where did she put all those antacids she just bought? Not in her pockets where she needs them. Cheri always said that forgetfulness was for amateurs and the elderly; if she lost track of something, it was on purpose. She'd blame it on the hamster wheel of fertility treatments she's been stuck on for the past year but this is an off-month. A break from hormones, injections, and, thanks to the threadbare state of her marriage, sex.

The filled lecture hall confirms her worst fear: she's become an academic, someone who tells people the answer is in books; worse still, in books written in dead languages. She's a long way from who she was when she came to the University of Chicago six years ago as the rebel in Ancient Near Eastern Studies, that radical professor with the tattoos, piercings, and past career as a cop with the NYPD. Blame it on the looming brass glow of tenure or on the erosion from all the loathsome paperwork and departmental service hours, but any idealistic notion she had of shaking up the dusty status quo of academe through teaching undergrads is long gone. But Cheri doesn't like to lose at anything.

"Who's been to a prostitute?" she asks, flicking on the lights. "Has anyone been to a prostitute, used an escort service, Internet hookup? Anyone?" The students look at each other quizzically, wondering if Cheri is serious. Some shift in their seats. "I won't tell your significant other—it's a purely sociological question." A guy with facial hair like Jesus finally says:

"In Vegas for a cousin's wedding there were hookers."

"Okay, weddings, good. Anyone else?"

"A kid I knew in junior high got a blow job at his bar mitzvah. His big sister's friend came up to him and, you know, did it. She was in high school so it was a big deal."

"Did you all line up and watch?" a neighboring girl snaps.

"We were horny boys, what do you think?"

"The point is," Cheri says, "in both the wedding and the bar mitzvah, there's a ritual. Let's take Riley's example. A bar mitzvah marks a passage into manhood. The initiate receives a sexual favor from his big sister's friend. What do we think of this ritual? Yes, Rachael?"

"The girl was degrading herself; she was probably doing it as a dare, not because she wanted to. It shows how women are brought up thinking they have to worship the phallus and they get nothing in return."

"Why is everything about degrading women?" Riley says. "The girl was the one with the power. She was older, she approached him—she had the control."

"Oh, please," a girl wearing a beanie says. "The girl was a slut."

"Okay, in about a minute, we've called this girl powerful...a victim...and a slut." Cheri writes the words on the chalkboard. "Who knows what she would have been called in ancient Sumer?"

Rachael raises her hand. "A sacred prostitute?"

"A priestess. In the third millennium Riley's friend would have gone to the temple where a *qadishtu*—sacred woman— would initiate him sexually. Sexuality wasn't disconnected from religion. It's not until the sixth century that the priestess is thought of as a sacred prostitute and then, as the role of the goddess diminished, a harlot."

"Finally, we're back to prostitutes..."

"Riley, since you're eager—define *prostitute*. As we know it today."

"A prostitute has sex for money and it's illegal, except, I think, in Vegas. Although there are other ways to prostitute yourself, for power or grades, for example."

"Let's say, 'to offer sexual intercourse for money.' From a Judeo-Christian perspective, the holy woman becomes a prostitute, the powerful woman a slut. When we use the word *virtue*— the virtue of a woman—it's immediately linked to virginity. But imposing one concept of virtue on another isn't what we're supposed to do in a democratic society—that would be like having a national religion, right? So how we define words is affected by the prevailing point of view." She calls on a reedy kid who has had his hand up for a while.

"It comes down to what's moral. That's not something that shifts based on the times. I'm Catholic and I believe there is something wrong with prostitution. Back then *and* now."

"Mesopotamian families didn't have the structure and assumed relationships of Western society. You need to put your judgments and personal beliefs aside—"

"But it's not a personal belief—the Old Testament makes it very clear that being a prostitute is forbidden. A prostitute is someone's daughter. That's about family structure and values." Cheri feels increasingly dyspeptic—is it the kid, the lack of antacids, both?

"As I was saying, this class is not about a literal or religious interpretation of the Bible. If you're interested in that, take a course in the divinity school." Cheri moves behind her lectern to get the class back on track. "In the Abraham cycle—the original dysfunctional family story—we have polygamy, concubines, surrogacy. All legal in Mesopotamian law. Hagar was like the sacred prostitute, performing a vital function. In a tribal culture it was a numbers game; the more wives and concubines a man had, the more chances for children. The bigger the tribe, the greater chance of survival and nation building. Your next paper will be on Abraham's sons Isaac and Ishmael. Examine their two paths. Do you stay at home and inherit your father's kingdom, where his shadow looms long, like Isaac did? Or, like Ishmael, do you heed the call, either by circumstance or by choice, and leave home and become, like your father, a builder of your own nation?"

She can't make a clean exit. A few students lurk around the lectern after class, trying to get her attention. There's gifted but unlikable Rachael who wants to talk about Cheri's book, which linked the advent of writing to the decline of the goddess. The

Catholic kid, hugging his backpack like someone who never lends his books, and Riley. "My office hours are posted," she says, walking past Rachael and the backpack kid, but she can't shrug off Riley. "I'm serious about applying to the Near Eastern language program for grad school. I was thinking—"

"Based on how you do this semester, I'll consider writing you a recommendation. Now can I walk in peace?"

"Thanks, but that's not what I wanted to ask you. I heard you're going on leave to work with Professor Samuelson on that new Mesopotamian find? I want to apply to be your research assistant."

Cheri is surprised undergraduates have heard about Samuelson's project. She certainly hasn't been able to pin down the details. First, there's Bush's "axis of evil" rhetoric and accusations of WMDs, all of which make it impossible for Western archaeologists to collaborate with their counterparts in the museum in Baghdad. But there's also the black hole of McCall Samuelson himself, Cheri's department chair and head of the Oriental Institute. Samuelson has yet to specify for Cheri—a mere mortal scholar—any details of her job description and critical path until they are able to get into Iraq. "Not now," she barks, and heads up the stairs to her office.

"They say it's a cache of cuneiform tablets, that it could be as important as the Dead Sea Scrolls. Is it true, they could trace back to the Old Testament?" Riley tags after her. "No job would be too small. I'll be your temple prostitute. Not funny?"

In a few seconds she's alone at her desk, popping an antacid. Her office is anarchy. Scholarly books commingle with beach reads stacked randomly in teetering towers. There's a poster for *Rock 'n' Roll High School* signed by the Ramones; one shelf is home to the upper portion of a llama's skull and an aqua hookah worthy of Alice's caterpillar. Her coat is buzzing. She has several messages, most from Cici. Oh, for the freedom of the cell-free days when everyone wasn't available 24/7. Ever since Sol died, five years ago, her mother war-dials her if she doesn't answer right away. Then there's a message from her editor in New York, chirping, "How's that next book coming?" Her first book, an extended version of her doctoral dissertation, *The Rise and Fall of the Goddess: Dicks, Chicks, and Mythological Cliques,* reached what her publisher called the "upper mainstream," a segment of the population Cheri knew well from Montclair—urbane professionals who thought being open-minded was listening to NPR in their luxury vehicles on their commute to work. How ironic that the people she fled from turned out to be her most receptive audience. In academic circles, her colleagues had denounced it as "populist," likely because it didn't have enough obscure, dense footnotes, and resented its success. Cheri sits back in her chair as the last message begins to play. It's from McCall Samuelson's secretary, saying he has to cancel the meeting that was scheduled for this afternoon. Again.

It's gray and dreary outside. Hyde Park looks particularly New England-y today, its brick homes and tree branches dusted with weekend snow. Cheri has just enough time to try to track down Samuelson before heading back to the land where twins are made in petri dishes. At thirty-nine, any time off from fertility treatments counts in dog years. Her life has been co-opted by the microscopic of egg and sperm for so long now that she's forgotten what it's like *not* to think about it. She's burned out on more than baby birds, and her career has suffered because of it. She needs to get her head back in the game and would love nothing more than to be in the thrall of something bigger. Piecing together the puzzle of humanity's ancient past is what drew her to Mesopotamian studies in the first place. Teaching was never Cheri's passion. It was research and translation that thrilled and sustained her. Nothing compared to holding a clay tablet in her hands, knowing she would be the first person to read it in thousands of years. Translating known languages was a cakewalk compared to the linguistic detective work of deciphering cuneiform. She's always dreamed of being first in on a new discovery, having her translation become the benchmark for every subsequent generation of scholars. Now that she's part of Samuelson's team translating tablets rumored to be of biblical importance, this kind of lasting contribution is within her grasp. But first, she has to break out of the fog of infertility and pin down Samuelson about her job description.

Cheri walks past a row of Thai restaurants on Fifty-Fifth Street, heading toward the lake. She's heard Samuelson has been meeting with someone from the British Museum but she was supposed to be his primary—and only U.S.—cuneiformist. Her husband's words return to her: "You can't trust someone with two last names. Pace yourself; if you get caught up in every perceived slight, you'll run out of energy for the real heartache."

From their accidental discovery in 1991 by a Sunni villager digging a ditch near the ancient city of Ur, the Tell Muqayyar tablets have been a tangled web of happenstance and politics. The clay tablets—most in fragments—were no sooner found than separated and dispersed on the black market. Over the years, some were confiscated and returned to Iraq's national museum; others landed in the British Museum. They would have moldered in basements, along with thousands of other undeciphered tablet fragments, were it not for a plot twist. A cuneiform scholar from the British Museum stumbled onto one of the illegal fragments in a London antiquities shop and noted that its seal impression corresponded with a stone cylinder seal on documents he'd recently cataloged. Now it was a tale of two institutes, each with broken pieces of related texts and its own ideas about how to assemble and translate them. Neither could proceed without the other's fragments, so a third party was needed to mediate. Last year, when it looked like Iraq was opening back up, McCall Samuelson, as the United States' most experienced Mesopotamian archaeologist, was tapped to lead an international team of scholars in reconstructing and interpreting the tablets. Rumors swirled that the ancient documents could trace back to Abraham. Proving that the original biblical patriarch was a real historical figure was, indeed, the holy grail of archaeology.

Cuneiform scholarship was a small and rarefied field and one that was not immune to the petty politics and social climbing that was the blood sport of academe. Many of her colleagues were vying for a spot on Samuelson's team, and while Cheri knew Peter Martins—the scholar who had found the fragment at the London antique shop—and knew he'd put in a good word for her, it was both a relief and a triumph when she was named last month to his team. Involvement in a project of such prestige qualified her for the leave of absence she was desperate to take. It also stopped the clock on her tenure review while pretty much guaranteeing she'd receive it upon her return.

Her ears sting from the lake-locked chill and she needs nicotine. She turns her back to the wind, cups her hand, and lights up. Delicious. She tells herself she'll quit when she's pregnant and heads toward a green canvas awning that says *The Woodlawn Tap*. It's an old journalist's hangout, a dump known for its grilled cheese sandwiches and collection of reference books. She steps inside, walks around the horseshoe-shaped room, and spots

Samuelson in his usual back booth, reading the *Tribune* and the *Wall Street Journal* in tandem. His back stiffens and he pretends not to see her. A man who functions from the neck up, he has the incongruence of the hands and thick frame of a butcher.

"Am I interrupting?" Cheri says.

"Oh, Professor Matzner," he says, putting down his papers then clasping his sausage-like fingers together.

"I wanted to check in and see how things were progressing. I know Dennis Donohue was in town last week."

"I'm working with quite a few parties on this, as you know."

"And is there any news on how we might proceed? Obviously, nobody is getting into Iraq at the moment, given the current politics."

"Fits and starts, my dear. We've dealt with worse blows from UN sanctions in the past. Whatever happens this time, the prudent course is to take the long view. I believe we'll resolve the situation, just like we did in Nippur."

"That was before 9/11. Who knows if Tony Blair has any real evidence of weapons of mass destruction, but it's pretty clear that he and Cheney are building a case for invasion."

"Governments may enact all sorts of Sturm und Drang, but much can slip twixt the cup and the lip. One thing experience will teach you is—know enough to know when you don't know. Leave it to those who do."

A waiter appears, bearing iced tea.

"Sugar, please," McCall says, "the real stuff." The waiter looks at Cheri, but before she can order a drink, Samuelson waves him off. "In any event, while nobody wants bloodshed, one could make an argument that a regime change—if it's done with the framework of an international coalition and blessed by the UN—would be in the best interests of the Iraqi people as well as archaeology." He sits back and nods, seemingly satisfied at the wisdom he has just bestowed on Cheri.

But, to the evident annoyance of McCall, Cheri charges on. "Politics aside, I'm sure you must be considering how you'd like your team to proceed until we can get access to the tablets in Baghdad."

"There are many moving parts to consider and, rest assured, we are considering them all."

"I understand," she says, trying to sound calm as she clenches her hands under the table. "I'm bringing this up because, as you know, I've cleared my teaching schedule in the fall to be fully available to you. My publisher is waiting on my second book and I'm trying to plan my time."

Just then, a stately man walks up to the table, holding his coat in his hand. "Professor Matzner, Dr. Donohue," McCall says. "Professor Matzner is a cuneiform scholar and one of our professors. She was just leaving."

"Nice to meet you," Cheri says with a too-firm handshake, and with that, she is dismissed.

Cheri presses the gas pedal of her Jeep, listening to the engine cough and then die, cough and then die. Samuelson's condescension infuriates her. Her hand trembles. It's a tic, an old hangover from her love affair with amphetamines. When the engine finally catches, she drives west on North Avenue to get to the Kennedy Expressway.

"Men can't handle women being direct. You have to appeal to his ego," her oldest friend, Taya, had advised when she'd complained about Samuelson. "Or, better yet, make a donation. He

probably chairs some archaeology foundation that needs fund-
ing. You may live like you don't have money but you inherited
a boatload from Sol so fucking spend some of it to help yourself
for once. Or if all else fails, you could always fuck him." Unfortunately, Taya's only knowledge about the pressure points of
academe came via an affair she had with a visiting professor from
Russia when she and Cheri were undergraduates at NYU.

The direct approach with Samuelson had failed her before.
Last March when Saddam Hussein held an international conference in Baghdad and invited leading Western archaeologists
to attend, Cheri made it known that, if Samuelson was willing
to break the U.S. sanctions, she'd be on board to join his staff.
The official purpose of the conference was to mark five millennia
since the advent of writing. But the gathering was a flashing yellow light to international scholars saying, *Come back in, the water's
fine.* American archaeologists knew that if the U.S. didn't lift its
embargo soon, they'd be the last in and lose the best sites. Going
to the conference ensured McCall Samuelson and their university a place at the table. When her name didn't appear on his
staff list, she confronted him. "My mistake," Samuelson said, "I
presumed you would understand the politics. The Iraqi government reviews the staff list. Do you think they won't vet and veto
someone with a Jewish last name?" She pointed out that she
wasn't Jewish. Her parents were registered Catholics and she was
an agnostic. "If you think that matters to Saddam Hussein and
his Baathist cultural committee, you have no business being involved," he'd answered.

Samuelson was part of the archaeological establishment. He
had a long history of good relations with the Iraqi authorities
prior to the 1990s sanctions—they protected his sites, gave him
logistical support, helped him achieve professional fame. And as

repulsive as it was, Cheri had to admit Samuelson was right. They wouldn't have let her in for an event at Saddam's invitation. Now, as a scholar on Samuelson's team and with the British as a key element, it was different. She felt worse than idiotic; she felt naive.

Cheri was no stranger to being mistaken for a Jew. In her prior life as a cop in the NYPD, she'd been subjected to sniggers of "bagel bitch" and worse but refused to use the "I'm not a Jew" defense, since it implied that their anti-Semitism was wrong only because they'd made an incorrect assumption about her. She had no love for the name Matzner or the man it came from, and she had considered changing it when she married Michael. But who wanted to live her life as Cheri Shoub?

Cheri gets on the expressway bound for the suburbs. The irony is that she'd never had an affinity for babies. She didn't know what to do with small, helpless creatures. As an adopted child, Cheri was intimately aware that some people should never have children and she was afraid she might have inherited the propensity to abandon her young. So it was a shock to her when, as she was heading toward forty, she started thinking, *Well, maybe.* When maybe turned into yes, she assumed reproduction was an inalienable right—you didn't need a permit to have a child like you did to have a handgun—and her body would comply.

All roads lead to donor eggs. Cheri knows Dr. Morrison will push this as the only viable option. She's tried everything else: four failed rounds of inseminations with FSH injections and two in vitro fertilizations that didn't implant. Using eggs from a twenty-something increased her risk of multiples. Giving birth to and caring for a litter? Out of the question. She likes to think she has an open mind, but does she want another woman's child taking root and growing inside her? What twisted strands of lineage and dysfunction would she nourish and would she be able to love whatever she pushed out of her vagina as much as if it had had her own faulty strands? Then again, she was genetic mystery meat and could have any number of unknown hereditary conditions to pass on to her child.

As she nears the exit for the expensive Fertility Gods, Cheri's cell phone vibrates. She steadies the wheel with her knee and fishes around in her purse for her phone, almost rear-ending an old Saturn station wagon that suddenly decides to switch lanes. From the insistent buzz, she can tell it's Cici. She finally retrieves the phone and pulls over.

Cici seems to be midsentence already by the time Cheri answers. "Where have you been, *cara*? You could be dead on the street, bleeding. *I* could have been dead and bleeding on the street."

"Then there would be nothing either of us could do, so what's your point?"

"What if I need something, what if I need a check, or money?" Cici shouts, just in case there's a bad connection.

"That's what banks are for. Or any of your bookkeepers."

"I do not like speaking to those people, you know this, and the pug, he have diarrhea, on the Persian rug in the hallway. And Gristedes on Park, they no want to deliver, it is impossible, they deliver for fifteen years and now they say no?"

"Mom, what do you want me to do about it from here? Ask Cookie."

"She is so smart she can change the mind of Gristedes? Why you not pick up the phone when I call? What is wrong? You sound like you are not paying attention."

"Nothing. I'm fine."

"You think you may be pregnant? Is not too late. It is five in one hundred who become pregnant once they are forty, and the

Down's, there is the Down's, and the retardation...but we get the best doctors for that and of course help for you."

"I'm getting off the phone now."

"*Aspetta,* I am with Marcella at Berg-a-dorf's: aubergine or crana-berry?"

"What are you talking about?"

"Towels. Yes, she has sheets they are a *schifo* blend, and no linens for the table, can you believe? Marcella cannot believe. Aubergine or crana-berry?" Cici *uffs* and then mock whispers:

"You and Michael, you are still trying, *sì*?"

"Thanks and hanging up now."

As Cheri pulls the phone away from her ear to hit End Call, she hears Cici prattling on. "*Aspetta, cara,* we need to discuss your big birtha-day. For the party, I am thinking—" Cheri pushes the button before she can hear what, exactly, Cici is thinking.

For her entire sexually active life, Cheri worried about getting pregnant. When she was sixteen she tricked Cici into taking her to the gynecologist by saying it burned when she peed, then she asked the doctor to give her a diaphragm. He had shown her a plastic vagina, wearing it like a hand puppet as if she didn't know her own anatomy. She wasn't having sex with anyone in high school, but Taya was, and Cheri wanted to be prepared. She couldn't have imagined that now she'd be worried about *not* getting pregnant.

Michael asked about birth control on their first date. They'd met at Yale; he was a rangy director with cult status and packed film-studies classes, and she was a rising postdoctoral candidate twenty years his junior. They'd met at a screening of his famous exquisite corpse documentary, *Disco, Doughnuts, and Dogma.* After the Q&A, Michael wove through the crowd of genuine acolytes and poor undergrads there for the free booze and asked Cheri out for a drink. They spent the first part of the date wrapped up in each other's words, and by the end, they'd shifted to mouths and as many body parts as they could possibly touch in public. She was on the pill, she'd told him. "Do you want kids?" he'd probed. "Not at this instant, just in general."

"You're getting pretty personal pretty quickly."

"You know this is not just any first date, right?" He held eye contact. She knew.

"Well, to be honest, I've never had the desire to have a baby and can't see that changing. Guess you could say I'm not a kid person."

By the time Cheri was leaving her toothbrush on Michael's sink, they'd agreed they weren't kid people, group people, pet people, morning people, organized-religion people, suck-up-to-the-dean people, or joggers—though they didn't agree on everything. If Michael had known Cheri was a gun-toting NRA member, he'd never have dated her. But by the time he found out about her past as a cop, he was in too deep. Despite a twenty-year age difference, they were similarly independent and valued the freedom to go anywhere without the burden of dependents. They were far more interesting than couples whose lives had been swallowed whole by their kids. The kind who let Legos colonize the coffee table and yelped, "Oh, don't move that! It's Jimmy's Death Star. Isn't it amazing?" Grown-ups who moaned about how they hadn't seen a movie in a year and didn't have time to F-U-C-K.

But something happened in their marriage after the first five years of nonprocreative F-U-C-K-I-N-G. Was it their age difference, which didn't seem to matter at first? Was it because her academic career was on the rise while his career stalled in endless revisions to an already-years-in-the-making documentary? Because Michael wasn't earning any money and, unexpectedly, she had a large inheritance? She'd eschewed her parents' world of privilege and hadn't taken a penny from them since her junior year in college. She acted as if her trust fund didn't exist. But maybe it reminded Michael of what he didn't have. Whatever the cause of their estrangement, Cheri noticed Michael's age more and sought his advice less; where they used to be selfish with their time together, they became more selfish with their time alone. Cheri knew that if they didn't change something soon there would be nothing left to hold them together. She always hated it when her friends with kids felt the need to point out that having a child was the true experience of unconditional love. *You'll never get that with just you and Michael,* they might as well have said. Maybe they needed to add not subtract in their equation. "And why would I want to do that?" was Michael's reaction.

As time passed, Cheri became certain of *yes* while Michael's grasp on *no* loosened ever so slightly. As a self-described JuBu—New Age parlance for Jewish Buddhist—he tried to remain unattached to outcomes. Fine, she agreed, no birth control, no expectations. Let's just see what happens.

As soon as Cheri threw away her pill packet, things started to change. Whereas she had gotten used to inwardly recoiling from Michael's advances—how he would graze her breast with his untrimmed nails while she was in bed grading papers or sidle lazily up to her first thing in the morning—his hand tracing the curve of her spine now felt strangely arousing. Was it the sense of purpose, the thrill and fear of the unknown, the potential to perform the ultimate act of creation? The more sex they had, the more they wanted. Intimacies that were the first victims of familiarity and had long been forsaken—like making out or looking into each other's eyes—made their way back into the fold. They smoked weed together and watched porn. They were lovers again.

A few months later, still feeling no reason for alarm that she hadn't gotten pregnant yet, Cheri bought an ovulation kit. She was only thirty-seven. She had regular periods. There was plenty of time. Little did she know that once the sword of infertility was hanging over their heads, the same procreative drive that reconnected her and Michael would end up unbinding them further, pushing them back into their old, distancing habits.

Cheri sighs. Conversations with her mother always exhaust her. An ambulance goes screaming by, followed by police cars. There must be an accident up ahead. She checks her watch. With this gridlock, it could take hours to reach Dr. Morrison's office. She pulls a thick sheaf of papers from her briefcase. They're the donor-egg profiles she'd been given at her last appointment. Each profile is several pages long and contains details on everything from the donor's ethnic background to favorite music to body type. Donor 157 is getting her master's in music theory. Her parents breed dressage horses. She likes nature and can hear stones sing. Number 258: Harvard grad, diplomat brat, pole-vaulter, likes dogs, allergic to cats, no cavities. Where's the box for daddy issues, bulimia, low self-esteem, leaning toward nymphomania, Cheri wonders. Do any of these girls have a sardonic sense of humor that would remotely resemble her own? Or will it be a repeat of the *Sesame Street* "one of these things is not like the other" dilemma she experienced with Cici and Sol? Was it so wrong to want to see herself in her child? To want her child to have the automatic sense of belonging that Cheri never felt? She'd like to be able to say that having a child is more important than having a child of her own. But maybe she's not that good of a person.

Cheri looks up. The expressway is a parking lot. Her chances of making it to Dr. Morrison's office on time are roughly equal to the one-in-a-million chance of Michael's elderly sperm reaching one of her middle-aged eggs. She pictures Number 157's fresh young egg, winking: *Come get me.*

Not today. She doesn't have the stomach for it.

MERRILY WE ROLL AROUND

Lincoln Park is the whitest place in the world. That was her
reaction when she and Michael started house-hunting.
Leafy streets, safe park, upscale stores; far too vanilla. Until they
saw the old Victorian house with purple shutters and odd angles,
sloping hard oak floors and hidden compartments installed during Prohibition. It was long on charm and short on practicality—
perfect for them.

Michael is not in the kitchen making dinner. Cheri crosses
the backyard to the guesthouse that is his editing bay and office;
the plaque she made to look like a ship's insignia reading *HMS
Bay* hangs over the door. "Michael?" His office smells of weed
and nag champa. It's a delicate ecosystem and only he knows
the correct balance. Everything looks randomly placed, but if
she were to move something, he'd have an aneurysm. He's got a
framed Spanish titled version of his cult classic *Disco, Doughnuts,
and Dogma* over his "napping bed." On the bed are half-finished
New York Times crossword puzzles and a beading tray. Beading is
Michael's latest distraction. Cheri thinks of it as craft rehab for
artists who have fallen and can't get up. It's no worse than his

previous distractions: building shelves that tore up a wall in the process, making Moroccan lamb ten different ways, or trying to play Eric Johnson licks on his old Stratocaster.

Michael's computer screen is filled with beetles burrowing their way into glutinous dung, rolling around until they gradually become a living lozenge of excrement. He must have forgotten to hit Pause. Cheri doesn't come in here often, and she's never seen this footage before. How it figures into his documentary on drug addiction called *One World Under the Influence* or *Everybody Must Get Stoned*—the title teeters between the two—is anyone's guess. She can't help thinking that Michael's like the beetle, rolling around and around with his obsessive fiddling, revising and reshooting.

"Hey, babe. You're in my chair," Michael says, coming up behind her.

He's still wearing the same sweatpants and shirt he rolled out of bed in. "Your mother called," he says, motioning for her to get up. "On my line. Can you tell her for the millionth time not to do that?"

"Sure."

"Okay, then. Back to work." He hunkers down over his editing software. Tap-tap-tap. The beetles rewind. It takes several seconds for them to become denuded of dung. With his back still to her, Michael says, "There's nothing for dinner. My stomach's been acting up so I'm not hungry. You'll have to forage."

"I saw that. So...how was your day?" she ventures.

"Like any other. I worked. Oh, and your mother was putting a bug in my ear about your fortieth. Months away but no time like the present to plan for something I'm sure you won't want."

"I can't even start with that."

"Forewarned is forearmed. Maybe you can head her off at the

pass. Listen, I have to get back to this—is there something you need?"

"I guess I just wanted to see you."

"Well, here I am." Cheri notices a small Chinese apothecary cabinet next to Michael's desk. Its drawers have Post-its stuck on them with labels like *Doesn't hit you over the head, just lowers the ceiling; Don't take sitting down.*

"Is this a joke?" Cheri asks.

"Research. Also, fans send me their favorite stuff. I'm finally cataloging it."

"Fans send you drugs?"

"Yes, fans. Also biochemists, aborigines, people I've interviewed; that's what the film's about."

"And you're keeping all this in the house?" Cheri thinks: *How many counts of possession?*

"Just a few samples. A lot are classified as plants and medicinal. Don't look at me like I'm Timothy Leary."

"Doesn't look like a few samples..."

"I'm trying to work. Did you come in here just to bust my balls, or did you want something?"

"I just had a hard day."

"Well, why didn't you start by saying that instead of taking it out on me?" Michael says, not bothering to stop clicking and pausing the beetle footage. "Get some rest, babe. I'll be up later."

Cheri has cereal and two large tumblers of scotch for dinner as she grades the last of her students' papers. She doesn't have a home office per se; she rotates between a table in the bedroom and her old college desk squeezed into the corner of the den. She notices a necklace in Jamaican colors hanging over her desk lamp. Encroachment. Is Michael going to start hanging them everywhere, like the milagro bean trees? She looks out the window at the corona of the John Hancock Center, lit against the ink palette of sky. It's a sight she's seen hundreds of times before, unremarkable. Except when she imagines it seen through the eyes of her would-be child. She used to do that last spring when Oz fair was in full swing in the park, the sailboats along Lake Michigan making their lazy circles. She yearns to experience that sense of childlike wonder, when everything seems possible and the world has yet to teach you otherwise.

When she goes upstairs to the bedroom, she finds Michael already asleep. He's on his side, pillows flanking him for his back. She crawls underneath the covers. Her mind pivots from the debacle with Samuelson to the umpteenth fight with Michael. She wants, *craves,* another cigarette. She's had fewer than ten today. She goes back downstairs to the kitchen, where she exhales smoke out the window, wishing she could expel the heaviness of the day.

She gets back on her side of the bed and tries to remember the last time they had sex. Weeks ago, early, quickly, lazy spoon position; she was in the fertile zone and he had a morning hard-on. In their semiconscious states, there was less chance of them fighting. Sometimes she'd use her imagination: a faceless man in a dark alley grabs her and presses her up against the wall, his hand reaching into her blouse, pinching her nipples while he whispers what he's going to do to her. That's what she thinks of now as she breaks through the pillow barricade and curls against Michael, pressing her hips against his back, her foot sliding against the arch of his foot. He jerks away. "I'm tired, Cheri," he mumbles. "Can't you see I'm trying to sleep?" Lately Michael's complaints of tiredness feel near constant. The other night, after he could barely summon the energy to get undressed for bed, he had rolled over and asked Cheri if she thought there was something wrong with him. *Laziness,* she had thought to herself. She crabs over to her side of the bed and stares at the ceiling. Hating him.

"Do you want to talk," she says, not really meaning it.

"I'm not a machine; I can't fuck on command. Wait a minute, we were taking a break—you can't even be ovulating yet."

"It doesn't have to *only* happen when I'm ovulating."

"You're kidding, right? You are telling *me* this?" After a while he adds: "Did you even notice the necklace?"

"The one hanging off the lamp by my desk? That was for me?"

"No, it's for Elijah. What do you think?"

Cheri thought it looked like something you'd buy from a Jamaican guy at the airport. "It's cute, thanks."

"Cute? That's real buffalo horn," he says gruffly, pushing the covers off and swinging his feet over the side of the bed.

"Where are you going?"

"I'm going to take a piss if you don't mind and maybe a shit because my stomach's been messed up. And then I'm going to meditate."

Cheri listens to the on and off burst of his pee, the dribble at the end. She listens to the opening and half closing of the closet door, the rustle of fabric against carpet, the small crack of his neck as he settles on his cushion. He's perfected the art of using meditation as a passive-aggressive weapon. He belches, yawks at the back of his throat. Sounds that make Cheri feel like she's living with an old penguin named Milton. Without opening her eyes she knows he's in the lotus position on the floor by his side of the bed. She hears Michael's loud, heavy exhale, the sharp rise of his inhale. Namaste. She turns away and puts her pillow over her head until all she can hear is the hum of her own frustration.

SCHOOL'S OUT FOR SUMMER

It's only the beginning of June and Cheri can already feel the humidity socking in. She's sitting outside at the patio table, darting between news sites on her laptop and smoking. So much for quitting. Or being pregnant. Or, much to the dismay of her editor, making progress on her new book. Every time she tried to focus on ancient burial customs, her mind, like a dog that sees a squirrel, would turn to Iraq. True to form, gauging the chances of war in Iraq is squirrelly.

"There's nothing like the smell of impending war in the morning. Bush talking about preemptive strikes? Or is that just the carcinogens you're inhaling?" Michael has emerged from the kitchen with his usual breakfast of oat-bran flakes and soy milk. "Don't tell me the news is any different from what it was an hour ago."

"It's always different on Al Jazeera." She doesn't know what's more annoying, his crunching or his riding her about her self-interest in the fate of Iraq.

"Different perspective, same prediction. What are the odds now of an invasion—fifty-fifty by the end of the year? Who cares that thousands of young men could lose their lives in a trumped-up war? It's what will happen to the artifacts—that's the question."

She's not taking that bait.

"If you look away, it's not like you'll be able to get into Iraq any faster," he says, putting his hand on her shoulder. "Hard as it is for you to accept, maybe a little downtime wouldn't be the worst thing. I can't get away but maybe you could do something with your mother so she gets off your birthday bandwagon?"

Cheri gives a vague grunt and doesn't look up until she knows he's crossing the weedy, mess of a yard, heading toward HMS Bay. Even after his longtime producer Bertrand told him they'd lost their distribution deal, Michael continued to carry himself with artistic entitlement; he's indignant if anyone questions all the time he's taking with this documentary. Bertrand has always reminded Cheri a bit of Father Christmas; nobody had seen his chin since the sixties. It's covered with a full but always neatly trimmed white beard. He's put up with Michael's ego far more patiently than she has, and for much longer. Cheri watches Michael tramping up the stairs to his office. She knows better than to ask when he'll be finished. All the F-words are hot buttons: *film, finances, fucking,* and, the worst—*failure.*

Cheri was not supposed to be at home, staring down the barrel of a hot, muggy summer in Chicago without a project. Ordinarily, summers without teaching obligations were the best perk of her job. They allowed her to dive deeply into research, to write and devise new curricula or to travel to the Middle East as a visiting scholar. She lived for those transcendent moments when she was lost in her translations, ordering and reordering ancient symbols, unable to glimpse their story until they suddenly clicked into place, revealing a new custom, law, or, as was the case with the first tablet she helped Peter Martins translate, the world's oldest recipe for beer. "We are here to commune with ancient ghosts," he told her, "we liberate them so others can hear."

Archaeologists were known hoarders of information, so Cheri was grateful to have an ally in Peter. He had been a mentor to Cheri ever since her time in London conducting research for her graduate thesis. He was seventy now but had the enthusiasm of a twelve-year-old boy exploring a pond, pulling out tadpoles. He told her that his counterpart in Iraq, Dr. Irene Benaz, was far behind them in the painstaking first step of identifying and cataloging which tablet fragments among the tens of thousands in the basement of her museum belonged to Tell Muqayyar. Dr. Benaz was short-staffed and sure to be under government scrutiny. Despite the news online, Cheri has not lost all hope that there's been some progress. In fact, she had gotten a call from Samuelson's secretary that morning, requesting that Cheri come in to speak to Samuelson later that afternoon. The meeting is in three hours and forty-two minutes—not that she's counting.

Summer meant that Cheri had to make arrangements with her mother. A trip with Cici was not what she had in mind. Cici hadn't left the tristate area since Sol died; she always had excuses, like the annual meeting of the co-op board she'd never once attended or that she has to light the shivah candles. Cheri informed her that she was confusing shivah with Shabbat and neither custom applied to Sol, who was nominally Catholic and had actually started going to church with Cici in his last few years. But Cici insisted she needed to light the shivah candles every Friday and said, "We must remember," as if Sol's death should be commemorated like the Holocaust. Cici's memory had somehow reconstructed Sol as the perfect husband and father. "He worked so hard his whole life for us. He leaves money for the hospital. He leaves money for you to buy a nicer house, not with so many cold drafts to give you the pneumonia. Why you no want this?" Talking to Cici forced Cheri to bite her tongue until it was numb. The irony of Sol having made a considerable fortune, not as a radiologist but as the inventor of an easy-to-swallow coating for pills, called Entercap, may have been lost on Cici, but it certainly wasn't on Cheri. Sol was honored as a humanitarian for making the world's medicine go down, but Cheri well knew the price it paid to do so in her family. She had borne the ugly secret she shared with Sol for so long it was a part of her, like a deformed toe she forgot she had until she went to try on someone else's shoes.

Unsurprisingly, Cici picks up after the first ring and immediately launches into a play-by-play of a recent trip to Cartier in which a rude saleslady dared to imply that Cici didn't know the difference between the scintillation and brilliance of a diamond. Cheri gets hit with a wave of guilt. "You need to get out of the apartment to do more than shop," she says to her mother while she's refreshing the American Federation of Scientists webpage for the tenth time, seeking further confirmation that Saddam's WMDs don't exist to bolster her argument that war can be averted. "What about going to the opera?"

"There is no opera in the summer, are you thinking I go in the park to hear opera? I am no sitting on the ground."

"Then go see Zia Genny for Ferragosto and go to the opera in Milan. You love that. I'll deal with the tickets—you don't have to call Rosa; nobody uses travel agents anymore."

"How can I be in Lago di Como when I am giving you a birthday party? We can do it at Le Cirque or we open the house in Montclair but I have no redone the gardens and will need to start right now."

"Who do you think would come to this party? All the old high school friends I don't have? You'll be throwing it for yourself."

"Oooffff. You pretend you no care about this birthday, *cara,* but this is a turning stone and you should have family and friends at your side. Put on a dress and wear some of the jewelry I give you. Would that be so bad?" Even after forty years of failure, her mother still thinks she can mold Cheri in her own glamorous image. "You are smoking still?" Cici accused, clearly picking up on Cheri's nearly inaudible exhalation. "It bad for making a baby!"

Cheri is reminded of the birthday parties her mother had given her when she was too young to protest. Cici handed out invitations at the park and the market—wherever she saw a *bella ragazza* with a *bella mamma.* All of these strangers would descend on their backyard—which Cici transformed into a fairyland with ponies and ducks and bunnies where the little girls could be festooned in princess costumes. Cheri didn't want to be a princess; she wanted to be a pirate and wear an eye patch. "Girls can no be the pirate," her mother insisted, forcing her into a poofy costume. Cheri ran and hid in her room and came out and dressed up only because Cici was so desperately sad, so worried about social failure. Cheri remembers patting her mother's hair, and how heavy Cici's head felt against her small chest.

"I'll look into a ticket to Italy for you," she says again, checking her e-mails and finding one from Peter. Given the standoff in Iraq, he says he is going to start photocopying the tablet fragments that he's cataloged and promises to send a set of copies to Cheri. They both know it's virtually impossible to assemble this ancient puzzle without having all the pieces, but perhaps they'll get lucky, stumble across one or two contiguous fragments. "I've got to go now, Mother," Cheri says, cutting off Cici's birthday blather. "I've got a meeting."

The nape of Cheri's neck is damp from her walk across the quad to Samuelson's office. She thinks that whatever he has to say may be based on Peter's mentioning that they were scanning their fragments. If this is the case, maybe Samuelson will send her to London this summer to see what Peter has identified so far. While scholars often started transliterating cuneiform texts from photocopies, there was no substitute for spending time with the real thing. Even given the divided and unconquered state of the Tell Muqayyar find, Cheri feels a frisson of excitement picturing herself finally getting her hands on the tablets and actively engaging with Peter. And, although Samuelson's fifteen minutes late, she has a genuine smile when Dolores says, "Please go on in."

"Nice to see you," Cheri says as he motions for her to sit across from him. "Thank you for reaching out." She will let him lead; she won't mention anything about communicating with Peter Martins.

"I've had a complaint," Samuelson says, peering at her over his reading glasses, then leaning back in his chair and crossing his arms.

"A complaint. About?"

"Discrimination. One of your students says that you were biased and it was reflected in his grade." Cheri's stomach drops.

"*Biased?* Against what? Who is this student?"

"He claims that your presentation of material and your manner of leading the discussion conflicted with his religious beliefs and when he expressed this, you gave him a lower grade. Apparently he came to you to discuss this several times."

"This is the first I'm hearing of it. Nobody came to me. Does this student have a name?"

"Anthony Richards."

It takes Cheri a moment to place Anthony Richards as the kid who insisted prostitution was wrong because the Bible said so. "If I remember correctly, he got a C in the class. If he has an issue with my grading, he should have discussed it with me."

"He said he tried to do just that. And according to him it was a C minus."

"I can check the grade. He never came to me or tried to discuss anything outside of class. The criteria for grading is clearly laid out in my syllabus, and his work was evaluated in exactly the same way as all the other students' in the class. Biased about his religion in a course that deals with polytheism? I'd like to speak to him face-to-face. Where does he live? Can he return to campus?"

"Not appropriate," Samuelson says, leaning back even farther in his chair and tapping his fat fingertips together like he's able to gain power from his own superhuman touch.

"Why not?"

"We have to tread lightly. Mr. Richards's father is an alumnus and a significant donor to the university. Any contact at this point would not be advisable. Did you tell him that he should leave your class because he's Catholic or because he doesn't share your views on prostitution?"

"You can't be taking this seriously."

Samuelson exhales and picks a nonexistent piece of lint off his jacket.

"The entire point of the class is to look at texts without any contemporary or personal religious points of view—Catholic, Muslim, Jewish. I state that to all students and it's also in the course description. I would never tell a student to leave my class based on religion or race or gender."

"Mr. Richards has stated that he intends to file a written complaint. Given that his family is important to the university, I'm trying to resolve this. Informally."

"And that means?"

"The Richards family is upset. I want to find a solution that will avoid embarrassment for everyone, most of all for you, Professor Matzner. In the event of an official complaint, per university regulations, I will have to appoint an independent review board. Who will then give you a copy of his written complaint and outline the process and materials they need from you."

"Fine. I welcome that; anything they need from me, they'll have."

"I'm glad to see you being so cooperative."

Samuelson stands up as if to dismiss her but Cheri refuses to go gently: "I hope *you* realize that this sets a very dangerous precedent, especially where religious studies are concerned. If professors have to walk on eggshells and answer to any student who is dissatisfied with his grade and makes up bogus charges of discrimination, we'll be unable to teach. I take it this is all you wanted to talk to me about, not further developments with the British?"

Samuelson meets her gaze. "This is the only development you should be concerned with. Now, I did you the courtesy of informing you of this matter as soon as it came to my attention. And in return, I'd like to ask a courtesy of you."

"Yes?"

"Please take this to heart," he says. "Did it occur to you that you will be placed on academic suspension if this goes before a review committee? And you know as well as I do that if it comes to that, I'll have to remove you from the team."

"Temporarily. Until I am cleared, which I will be."

"My point, Professor Matzner, is that pragmatism, in situations like these, cannot be overrated."

⸻

Back home, Cheri pulls and yanks on the lawn mower she's dragged out of the garage, trying to get it started. She managed to still her hands while she was sitting, like a chastised child, across from Samuelson. Now they won't stop shaking from anger and adrenaline. The lawn mower yowls like a sick cat. As soon as she pulled into the driveway and noticed the weedy, over-grown lawn (yet another task Michael was too busy or too tired to bother with), she thought, *Good, a living thing I can raze.* If she can get the motor to run for more than ten seconds. She might have been brusque with Richards that day, but extracting *You're a Catholic, get out of my class* from that is absurd. She's had students like Richards before, advocates of creationism who tried to hi-jack discussions with it's-the-word-of-God-so-it-has-to-be-true. She steered those students to a theology class or they dropped out on their own, but this little fucker spent the entire semester with her and then had the gall to put her career in jeopardy because he got a C minus. She'd looked up his grades and recalculated his 71.2 percent just to make sure. Pissant motherfucker. Of course his father is a high-profile donor; if that weren't the case, would Samuelson even be trying to negotiate a peace treaty? Part of her thinks if it didn't reflect poorly on his department or him, he would have a glint in his eye that this was happening to her.

"Enough already!" Michael storms down the stairs from his editing bay, yelling. She motions that she can't hear him over the noise of the lawn mower. "Stop it, you're fucking up the ma-chine. Stop!"

"Then call the guy, because this is ridiculous!" she shouts.

He shuts the lawn mower off. "You're being totally inconsiderate. If I said I'll do it, I'll goddamned do it. Did it occur to you that I'm getting some work done up there?"

Did it occur to you that you will be placed on academic suspension?

Samuelson and Michael are the same age; is this a generational style of condescension? A gender issue? She wonders if Samuelson ever employs this sneering tone with Cheri's male colleagues. She hates dwelling on this line of thought. It taps into her prior experiences of persecution, the constant harassment she survived every day at the Ninth Precinct by pretending it didn't hurt and humiliate her. Michael stalks off, back up the stairs to the editing bay, and she feels twice stung. Hasn't she done enough to prove herself worthy? It's an echo of Sol's *You're not good enough.* Even when her father didn't say it, he said it. She's breathing hard and sweating; she puts her trembling hands on her knees. Her body hasn't felt like her own ever since she started trying to turn herself into a brood hen. Popping hormones instead of lifting weights has made her weak and soft in all the wrong places.

That's something she can change.

BODY SHOTS

For the past week, since her meeting with Samuelson, Cheri has favored the proletarian gym close to the house over the university facilities where she could run into someone from her department who might have heard of Richards's complaint. Insular environments breed buzzardlike reactions to the whiff of a comedown and while she hadn't heard back from Samuelson, she also doesn't want to be tempted to solicit information. Today, she's doing intervals of incline push-ups, kettle-bell swing lunges, and two-minute sprints on the rowing machine. Her body is responding, just not as quickly as it used to. Her cardio is lagging, but she's making progress. She pushes through her last round, panting from the effort.

Cheri showers quickly and is getting dressed when she glimpses her naked body in the mirror. She catches herself thinking like a cop, noting her distinguishing marks, the things Michael would use to identify her body at the morgue: the mole above her right breast, her tattoos—cherry bomb on her left shoulder, handgun on her hip, tiger crouching his way up her back toward the ouroboros between her wings. For a long time she was "that girl with the tattoos." Back up and give her room, people. Now her stomach has a slight middle-aged pooch and recently she'd detected a few threads of gray at her temples. But her legs are still long and straight, her face is what a boyfriend in college described as *jolie laide,* to which she responded, "Fuck you and fuck the French." But on any given Sunday, depending on the light, the angle, or her mood, her face does veer between ugly and striking. Her features are at odds with one another; near-black hair and white skin, mismatched eyes, small nose that leads to a full, heart-shaped mouth. One benefit of getting older, she thinks, is that she now takes "beautiful-ugly" as a compliment.

Cheri makes her way out of the locker room. As she's crossing the main floor of the gym to the front exit, she hears, "Matzner? Cheri Matzner?" A muscle-head guy standing beside a girl running on a treadmill is waving at her. He combs his hand through his hair and checks himself out in a mirror before trotting over. It's so out of context that it takes a minute for it to click. "It *is* you!" he says with a smile, then points to his chest. "Bobby Godino, you remember?" Godino, who begged to be in a mounted unit because chicks loved guys on horseback. "Pussy" Godino from the NYPD Sixth Precinct was now a personal trainer? "Yeah, can you believe," he says, reading her mind. Bobby flexes. "Bod's looking sweet, right? No shit, Cheri Matzner. I wondered what happened to you; you just disappeared. And *bam,* all these years later, here you are."

"Small world," Cheri says.

"So how you doing? I figured you went back to school and stuff."

"You called it, Bobby. I'm teaching at the university... and stuff."

"Cool. You married? You know, if it weren't for Eddie I'd have gone for you myself. You always seemed different, and I like a little flavor." Cheri holds up her left hand; her ring finger sports a gold band.

"And you?" she asks.

"Divorced. She got custody of the kid, moved out here—I followed so I could see my boy. You know, it's wild running into you like this. It's like people dying in threes, you know, because I heard from Eddie, out of the blue, what, it had to be before Christmas."

"Really," Cheri says, eyeing the girl on the treadmill eyeing her. "I think someone needs you."

"You're doing great, Sharon. Two more minutes," he says, checking his watch. "Sheila was friends with my ex, Angela, and when we busted up it was a kind of choose-your-side thing. Eddie checked in on me now and then, but, you know, we were never tight. Sheila's cooking on their fourth kid. And she's still on the Job. You knew he married Sheila?" Cheri didn't. "Eddie's Secret Service to some muckety-muck at the Pentagon—he's high up. No shocker there; we all knew Eddie Norris was going places."

"Well, I'm glad to hear he's doing well, and you too..."

"Yeah, I'm not usually here—it's only because my client is redoing her home gym—so let me give you my card. In case you want to work out or whatever."

Cheri sips a Jameson and Coke at the neighborhood bar where she often grades papers. She hadn't felt ready to go home to Michael, especially after that random encounter with her past.

Cheri hasn't heard anything about Eddie Norris in years. Of course he married Sheila the cop, a good Catholic bunny, and they have a litter of kids now. He was a cop of the Irish lead-with-your-fists breed, the type who believed real men don't cry. They retreat under the hoods of cars, speak softly, carry through on wicked practical jokes, drink only Coors, and kill any son of a bitch who tries to mess with their sisters or mothers. Eddie Norris standing in her apartment on East Ninth and Avenue A, naked, his head covered by a dish towel, leaning over a pot of boiling water and Vicks VapoRub. "Id it working yet?" Eddie Norris presenting her with his grandpa's cocobolo police baton, noting it had met plenty of flesh in its time. She carried it with her every day, out in the war zone and rubble of Alphabet City with its skinheads and squatters, crackheads and dealers with sawed-off shotguns underneath their coats. Venturing into the burned-out labyrinth of booby-trapped tunnels, the shooting galleries with *Clean up your blood* spray-painted on the walls, knowing anything could come at you at any time, Eddie Norris was the eyes in the back of her head. What fueled them wasn't the danger of being shot at; it was the heightened sense of being alive that came with hyperawareness. Their world was ultravivid and the high was better than any drug.

She was deeply in love. That stupid-and-crazy love that songs are written about. She'd wear Eddie's wifebeater under her Kevlar because he was her good luck. Was it because she was young, the cliché that the first cut is the deepest? Was it a cop thing? It was true that cops dated other cops or nurses because nobody else could understand the daily trauma that comes from witnessing the depths of human depravity, suffering, and violence. But it was more than that. Eddie Norris had done something for her no man ever had. He'd stood up for her, and he did it when he had a lot to lose and nothing to gain.

Why, they all asked. *Why* was the resounding question when Cheri announced she was dumping Yale grad school for the police academy. She knew her choice to join the NYPD would alienate her family and friends. Even though Sol and Cici knew nothing about Near Eastern languages and religion, they had liked being able to say, "My daughter's going to Yale." While they'd never come to terms with her appearance—she'd been adding piercings and tattoos steadily since high school— and they hated that she lived in the East Village with all the weirdos, druggies, and Mohawked punks who Sol said made "hate-crime" music—their unconventional daughter was still on track to have a respectable white-collar career. "Why would you throw that all away?" they wailed. To become a *cop,* of all things.

Of course, Cici panicked that she'd get killed. Even more typical, she demanded to know why Cheri would agree to wear a uniform and look like a janitor. Sol was convinced it was all for shock value. He said if she followed through he'd never give her another dime. But Cheri had never felt at home in their bubble of privilege and she was certain that wherever her birth parents came from, it was more trailer park than Park Avenue. But there was more to it than that. Festering beneath her bravado was something too painful and complicated for Cheri to acknowledge, even to herself. Cheri's relationship with her father had always been distant, complicated, and, in the storm of her teenage rebellion, volatile. They'd stumbled along the frayed edges of their imposed family bond until, in her junior year of college, Cheri pulled on the one thread that would unravel it permanently. She'd cemented herself into complicity the day she confronted Sol about his secret, and after that, the thought of ever accepting his money made her feel dirty.

"What the fuck, CM? A cop?" brayed Taya when Cheri told her the news. "Are you going to start busting your friends, arrest me for smoking weed? There's a reason they're called pigs—not to mention they're all bridge-and-tunnel." Cheri didn't expect for it to make sense to anyone except Gusmanov. Her family's Russian handyman had been her secret-sharer growing up; she owed her expert marksmanship to his tutelage. Gusmanov always smelled of talcum and tobacco. Cheri never cared that he was even older than her father. He showed her how to throw a pocketknife into the trunk of a tree and taught her Russian words. Best of all, Gusmanov had a gun. "Only for protection and sport," he'd told her when she saw it sticking out of his waistband as he crawled under her sink to fix a pipe. When she pinkie-swore that she wouldn't say anything to her parents, he let her examine it and explained the parts and how important it was to always keep it safe. Maybe one day he would let her hold it. When he eventually deemed her ready, he patiently taught her how to use it. She was a quick learner and a naturally great shot—at fourteen, she was an NRA double-distinguished marksman. But while Gusmanov acknowledged she'd be a good cop, even he had reservations. "Why you don't listen to me and go pro sharpshooter? It will make wallet much fatter."

But becoming a police officer made sense to her, and, for the first time in her life, she felt she could make a difference. Sol didn't buy it. "Now you're going to save the world? The people down there are degenerates and junkies who don't even try to help themselves. Doctors save lives! If you want to 'make a difference,'" he said, mimicking her earnest tone, "go volunteer in a hospital near Yale while you get your degree." There was no way

Sol could comprehend that Cheri specifically wanted to help the "people down there." She'd lived on the Lower East Side during her four years at NYU. The neighborhood was like her— gritty, rebellious, dangerous, and teeming with diversity. She not only didn't stick out, she belonged. And was deeply affected by random acts of violence that destroyed the lives of people she cared about, like her friend Yure's grandson who was jumped by a street gang and had to spend the rest of his life in a wheelchair. Yure was one of the Ukrainian immigrants who hustled playing speed chess in the park and he reminded her of Gusmanov. Her parents wouldn't understand that she missed Sweetie, the post-op tranny who worked the door at Eileen's Reno Bar and threw out acerbic comments about everyone who walked by. Sweetie had been killed on her way home from work by neo-Nazi skins. It made sense to Cheri and that's all that mattered. She was making the leap into the thump of a life lived on the outside.

Of course she didn't disclose to anyone in the NYPD that she'd come from ritzy Montclair and had a college degree. It wouldn't have mattered to Eddie Norris. He wouldn't know a doctorate from a doughnut. He only cared that she was the best shot in her academy class, that she was fast, reliable, and a quick study. Then there was the sex.

It started as a smack-down of passion in his Mazda hatchback, replete with adolescent pawing, fogged-up windows, bra-hook complications, and the discomfort of handguns pressing into sensitive places. They didn't break lips even when Cheri performed a near-contortionist move to straddle him. He fumbled to get inside her, one hand on his cock, the other on her hip, pushing a little too hard, a little too fast, but once he'd hit the mark, he cupped her face in his hands. "You okay?" he said, looking her right in the eyes. She nodded and started to move her hips, but he held her chin and said, "I want you to tell me if you're not." They fucked again in the vestibule of her apartment building, ignoring the persistent stink of urine. Her back was up against the wall next to the mailboxes, her legs were around his waist, his jeans were snaking down around his ankles; a down-and-dirty fuck on all counts. And not. Because while they were fucking they were kissing and while they were kissing their eyes were open. Cheri had never had a man look at her while they made love. Or if he did, she didn't know about it, because her eyes had been tightly closed.

If they'd had sex before she'd become his partner, it would have worked out very differently. Everyone would have thought he chose her only because he was fucking her. She might have thought so too. But she and Eddie hadn't gone "over the side" until well after they'd become partners, and by then they both knew it was going to be more than a onetime thing.

Just as Cheri starts to lose herself in another memory of Eddie coming up behind her in the precinct's file room late at night, whispering exactly what he was going to do to her as his hands clasped hers behind her back, the bartender asks if she wants a refill. "Not yet," she says. How long has it been since she's had an open-eyed kiss? She remembers the electricity that shot from her groin and lodged itself in her chest whenever she inhaled Eddie Norris's clean, masculine scent—a mixture of soap on a rope and sweat that lingered in her hair. Another filament of memory floats up and, with it, the phantom weight of a .38-caliber Smith and Wesson handgun against her left hip. Back then, and for a long time afterward, she couldn't imagine not carrying a gun. And now she's married to anti-gun Michael, sitting on a bar stool playing what-if. That's an insidious game, inevitably leading to that night with Red Hood, the look in Eddie Norris's eyes that sent her running from the NYPD, barricading herself in Cici's Eighty-first Street apartment in a drug-induced tailspin of heartbreak. You have the right to remain silent. She certainly did that. It's dark and deep down there, a chasm of shadows and regret.

PUNCH-DRUNK LOVE

You have a house for guest, that is where the guest stay. Your husband does not want me as a guest anymore," Cici wails into the phone. Three weeks since their last round of pin-the-tail-on-the-birthday, Cheri has been sucked into another. Cheri had been trying to convince herself that she could get some work done while jammed into the table in their bedroom, but so much for best-laid plans.

"The guesthouse is Michael's office, he works in there, at all hours. You complain that the pull-out couch in the den hurts your back and the air conditioner—"

"The thing in the window makes so much noise and does nothing. I tell you to get the build-in and you do not listen. Why you no spend the money?"

"I just think you'd be much more comfortable in a hotel," Cheri says, thinking of her mother's tendency to mix white wine and Valium and wander around at night in the nude. Cici reacts to this suggestion like she's Napoleon being forced into exile on Elba. "Besides," Cheri adds, "we're *not* having a party."

"*Whaaat?*" After more back-and-forth, Cici finally gives in.

But not without adding, in a wounded voice: "You really want me to make you the birthday wish from a thousand miles away? Like not looking a person in the eye when you make a toast, it is not good luck." That's a stretched analogy, even for Cici. But hearing the lingering hope in her voice gives Cheri a pang of guilt as she assures Cici that this is, indeed, what she wants.

They have this fight every year around Cheri's birthday. Usually Cheri would say fine, don't come here, I'll come to you. Cici lived in their Upper East Side apartment, and despite her penchant for constantly changing interior design, she kept it exactly as it was when Sol died. As if that would somehow cement the happiness of their last few years together and faux over everything that came before. The house in Montclair, Cici complained, was too big for a woman all alone, without company. She kept threatening to sell it, happily ignoring the fact that Sol's will provided that their holdings transfer to Cheri with Cici as the life beneficiary but with no signing power. It was an unexpected turn of events for Cheri, but it wasn't the only surprise in Sol's will.

After hanging up with her mother, Cheri attempts to get back to work—if she could really call it that. For hours, she's been fiddling around on Baghdad.com and obsessively checking her e-mail to see if Peter Martins has dispatched the promised photocopies of his fragments to her. Not that she could accomplish any meaningful work on them at this stage, but at least she'd feel close to the actual starting point. Everything she cares about is in plain sight but out of reach, like the toys in one of those claw vending machines. The Tell Muqayyar tablets remained hidden behind a cloud of increasingly hysterical WMD rhetoric, Samuelson has been incommunicado since putting her on suspension, and even Michael, perpetually in crisis mode over his never-to-be-completed documentary, was desperately seeking a shaman. When she walked into the kitchen this morning, he was venting on the phone to Bertrand, his producer, that the shaman he absolutely must shoot was coming to the U.S. but he'd been co-opted by an environmentalist in Sedona. "That guy caters to celebrities and woo-woos," Michael exclaimed. "His workshops are bullshit. We're making documentary art." For someone who had never left the Ecuadoran jungle, the shaman was certainly in demand. After twenty more minutes of aimless clicking, Cheri realizes she needs to leave, having promised Michael she'd meet him at the Biograph. The house feels like an Ecuadoran jungle and she cares more about the theater's air-conditioning than about the movie itself—all she knows is that it's by a director with three names, one of the rare Hollywood types Michael has blessed with his seal of approval.

As Cheri's walking out of the door, her phone buzzes. Samuelson's name flashes on the screen. Cheri takes a deep breath before answering. Shockingly, Samuelson's voice is buoyant. "Good news. After considerable effort, I've prevailed upon Mr. Richards to dismiss his complaint. All you need to do is write a letter of apology, and we can put this matter behind us."

"Apologize?" Cheri says, veering from relief to indignation in a second. "For what?"

"We can craft it along the lines of an acknowledgment. You apologize for your lack of sensitivity regarding his personal and religious beliefs and admit that this may have led you to make an oversight regarding his final grade. You say you're willing to revisit his grade based on a third party's review and recommendation."

"You want me to admit to something I didn't do. I don't take issue with my work being reviewed by a committee. But I do take issue with apologizing for being unprofessional or unethical when I was neither. If a committee finds that I did something wrong, that's one thing, but right now all we have is the student's word—and feelings." Cheri wants to add *And I'm not changing his grade* but thinks better of it.

"Don't let this be your hamartia, Professor Matzner. This letter is informal and not subject to the committee's review. Yet."

Cheri hesitates. He's backing her into a corner, one she's been in before. The familiarity is visceral; her fight-or-flight mechanism is in overdrive.

"I know the Richards family is important to the university. I appreciate this fact puts you in a difficult position. I will cooperate with anyone and everyone. If I made a mistake I'll admit to it, informally or formally. But I cannot—and will not—apologize for something I did. Not. Do." She thinks she hears him tsk her.

"That's very disappointing. You understand, Professor Matzner, that it's now out of my hands? Without an apology, I cannot hurry things along. This will be a drawn-out, deliberative process, and I have no influence over the findings. You will hear from the committee chair as soon as one has been appointed."

"I understand," Cheri says with a confidence she no longer feels.

"As I told you before, academic suspension applies to everything associated with the university, including participation on my translation team." Cheri feels punctured. All the air is leaking out of her. "If you want to reconsider, I'm telling you: now is the time."

It takes a second for Cheri to respond. "I cannot do that, Professor Samuelson. You know where to find me."

By the time Cheri walks to the Biograph she's pressed her nails into her palms so tightly they've left angry indentations. She's being blackmailed. Again. She pictures Eddie Norris's face, tight, shifty, unable to look her in the eye. Her heart is racing. Michael's pacing in front of the box office. He throws his hands up. "What the fuck? I texted you three times."

"Don't," she snaps. "Just fucking don't."

"Now there are only shitty seats left," Michael grumbles as the lights dim in the theater. They stumble past a dozen knees—"Sorry, excuse me"—to get to the only two seats together. "Evidence, not emotion," Michael offers after she whispered a rushed recap of her phone call. "Don't get sidetracked by how fucked up it is or by asking yourself why your boss is listening to a kid over you—stick to the evidence. You didn't do anything wrong, right?" She is pissed off that he asked. She doesn't want platitudes. She just wants him to take her side.

It's only when *Punch-Drunk Love* starts that Cheri realizes she's in for two hours of tedium told through the claustrophobic lens of a typical Adam Sandler man-child. It doesn't help that the large man on her left is taking up both armrests and that the smell of melted jalapeño cheese mixes with his BO whenever he moves an arm to dip a chip. She starts to ask Michael to switch seats with her, but someone behind her shushes her. She hates being shushed. Suddenly, everything is closing in on her. She's sweaty and antsy; her mouth is bone-dry. She needs air. It feels like someone is squeezing her heart in a vise. Really bad heartburn? Does she have her Tums? No, this feels different. Get it together. Now. She needs air. Her chest is constricted and her breath is shallow. She leaps to her feet, flails past the dozen knees again, gulping for air, mouth opening and closing like a hooked bass. Somehow she makes it outside and sinks to the pavement. Michael appears beside her, asking questions. "Can't talk." She gasps. She's massaging her chest and someone asks about her arm. Is she having a heart attack? She's in a Magritte, a forest of pant legs; they threaten to smother her, she's buried in pants.

Michael's holding her shoulders. "Breathe, in and out, close one nostril and then the other." Her chest feels like a buffalo is standing on it. "It must have been the movie, it stunk so bad," a teenage boy says, walking past her.

The paramedics arrive. "Who called them?" Cheri rasps when she sees the ambulance. "I don't need them." Then, to prove her point, she gets up. "Whoa, not so fast," says a trained medical professional. Two paramedics sit beside her and start checking her vitals, running through their list of questions. "I just couldn't breathe," she repeats over and over, "but I'm better now." Is she on drugs, under stress, any known medical conditions?

"It's likely a panic attack," one paramedic says. "Nothing cardiac. I suggest you follow up with your physician, and if you haven't had one recently, get a physical to rule out anything else." Michael starts to ask questions about panic attacks but Cheri interrupts. "I'm good, so let's go, okay?"

When they get home, Michael goes into his medicine cabinet and gives Cheri a pill. "Ativan—it's good for anxiety. Take one now and another one if it doesn't bring you down in an hour or two."

"We don't know if this had anything to do with anxiety," she says. Ignoring her, Michael pours her a glass of water from the kitchen sink and hands it to her. "At least you picked a historical place to collapse. Dillinger was gunned down coming out of the Biograph Theater with the Lady in Red on his arm."

"Let's not say *collapse*. I was conscious."

"I noticed you didn't tell them about the fertility drugs."

Please don't make this about my ovaries, Cheri thinks. "I'm not on them now—it can't be related. It's not about that."

"Hello—infertility is a major cause of stress. Look what you've been going through for the past year, even longer." He looks at her, concerned. "What's going on right now? How are you feeling?" She's speedy, flushed, tired, dizzy, embarrassed, muddled.

"I'll be fine."

"If you push yourself too hard, you're going to collapse; that's how it goes. You laugh at me but meditation would be good for you. I know how you feel about my shrink too, but talking to someone couldn't hurt." Cheri exhales angrily, and Michael takes a step back, hands raised. "Okay, I won't make any more suggestions. But that was scary for me, and I know it was scary for you. Don't do that to yourself again, okay? Please. Call a doctor."

"Okay."

Michael approaches again and mushes her into a hug. "Relax, let me hold you." Standing there in the kitchen, Cheri feels trapped, pinned. Michael senses it, and she can tell by the way he pulls away he takes it personally.

"Listen, I'm still wired," she explains, "I just need to hang out for a bit, try to unwind, wait for the pill to kick in. I'll be fine."

She is not fine. At three in the morning, she decides she needs banana bread. She goes into the kitchen in her T-shirt and underwear, throws ingredients in a bowl, and starts mixing with aggressive strokes, thinking, *How do you get the banana lumps smooth?* They had only one egg; maybe it needs two. She takes the other pill with a shot of rum and splashes some into the batter to thin it before it goes in the oven, but her body keeps surging. Her mind, however, is glazed. It's a good combination for doing things like cleaning out the top drawer in the kitchen, the one where they throw rubber bands and parking tickets and business cards of plumbers. When she remembers to check on her banana bread, it's charred on the outside and raw in the middle. She eats it in hot fistfuls; it's leaden and tasteless.

Whatever it was that Cheri experienced that night, she knew this much: it was not fine. *Panic* and *anxiety*—not words she associated with herself. She'd survived far more stressful times at work without getting so much as a cold. While she was still hormonally out of whack, attributing it to hormones was akin to saying she had PMS.

"For someone so smart, you are totally dumb!" Taya tells her the next day when Cheri recounts the episode. "Of course this has to do with stress. And hormones. When I was pregnant I had a million nervous breakdowns! Fertility drugs are worse than going through menopause. Fuck meditation! Hold on, hold on. Shut up back there right now or I'm going to put you both on the sidewalk! You want to walk home? You don't need Michael's New Age shrink, you need an MD who does meds and will load you up with Xanax."

Besides mandatory evaluations on the police force and a drug counselor she'd seen during her breakup with speed, Cheri had never been in therapy. But being that out of control, her heart clenching so unrelentingly, scared the hell out of her. She had a hard time filtering her thoughts; every time she got stuck in a loop of Samuelson's voice, telling her to apologize for a transgression she didn't commit, she'd get that buffalo feeling on her chest. She had to admit, the Ativan helped. She'd used up Michael's prescription and wanted more. "Fine," she told Taya, who promised she'd get back to her with a referral via her vast network of friends who knew the best of everything in every city, "I'll see a meds doctor."

Dr. Marlene Vega's office looks like the place where sixties art goes to die. The doctor herself is the kind of woman who calls pants *slacks,* wears pearls and blouses with bows at the neck. Cheri answers her questions with the minimum amount of detail necessary, quickly pointing to the factors leading up to the *Punch-Drunk Love* incident: bad eggs, marriage in the netherworld, the Richards complaint.

"You don't have to just stick to the facts," Dr. Vega says, "you've led an interesting life, and we have plenty of time left."

"I've never had anxiety issues. I'm used to functioning in high-stress situations and I haven't exactly shied away from them."

"They produce a dopamine response, which is adrenalizing. You didn't say what led to your career change, which was quite a significant one. Did it have to do with the stress of the job? That's very common for law enforcement."

"No, it wasn't that," Cheri says, wanting to get off that topic. There is no way to enter that dangerous territory without betraying or being betrayed. "Listen, I just want to prevent this from ever happening again. I'm sure there's something I can take..."

"There's no magic pill for the ups and downs of life," Dr. Vega says. "I can give you some Ativan, but all benzodiazepine drugs are highly addictive." Fortunately, Cheri opted not to mention her history as a speed freak when she filled out the patient-intake form. Dr. Vega hands her a script. "Don't take it for more than three days in a row. We need to do talk therapy as well. You have a lot on your plate right now. You can set something up with my receptionist."

Cheri walks out of the pharmacy into the shank of the late-July day, pops open the bottle of Ativan, and swallows a pill. She slaps on her dark sunglasses and merges with the Gold Coast denizens who walk in and out of buildings drinking their coffees, some leading dogs, others being led by various desires. Cheri catches a whiff of perfume—light, citrusy—and it reminds her of the Jean Naté bubble bath her mother used on her when she was a kid. It gave her a terrible rash. Cici became so distraught all she could do was cry. She had to give Cheri oatmeal baths for weeks afterward and swathe her in Saran Wrap. Cheri's throat aches at the trust of a child, any child, her as a child. How young her mother was then, how insecure; it fills her with a sadness that's close to love, but more akin to pity—the kind of pity that eventually provokes cruelty.

40BDAY 1.0

Cici's silk blouse is wet under the armpits, and, *porca miseria,* she forgot to put in those pads. The stain will dry like a Rorschach test inkblot with a chalky outline from her deodorant because the air-conditioning in her closet is never cold enough. She retreats to her walk-in jewelry vault and plops down on the ottoman. It's soothing in here, with the white marble floor and the gleaming wood drawers from floor to ceiling; like a museum. She surveys that *stronzo* Cookie, who is slow and shrunken with arthritis nibbling at her bones; a little wind could snap her in two. Sol arranged for Cookie, who's spent forty years with them, to get her salary for life whether she worked or not. But Cici hasn't told Cookie that, although it's painful to watch her straining to do the simplest task, like going up the ladder to get the boxes down. And that wrinkled old black-and-white uniform.

"I pay you now the whole year of salary if you throw that away and wear real clothing."

"Last week you said two years, so I guess you like it more this week. Is this the damn thing already?" She holds out a black felt jewelry box.

"No, no, no. That is for the tennis bracelet, not a ring. Put it down, put it down!"

"All look the damn same to me, crazy woman," Cookie mumbles under her breath. Cici directs her to the other side of the vault and sips her Sancerre. Cookie comes down the ladder, moves it over a few rows, goes back up.

"Why is it your Choo-Choo, she never talks to you like Cheri, she talks to me? It has to be trouble with that husband, Michael. Why else is there no baby? And he is not giving her a party for her birth-day!"

"With Cheri, you always up in her business. Didn't work when she was little, and it doesn't work when she's big."

"It hurts when she is mean to me. I think we get older, it doesn't hurt so much, but it still does."

"Nothing stops hurting. Something else just hurts more and you forget. Now, what exactly are we looking for?"

"We have to make the list so it is up-to-date what is in here. Sol, he always said without lists, they cut off the insurance."

Cookie almost loses her footing on the ladder. She hates listening to Mz. M. getting misty over that dead fool.

"What are you trying to do? Kill yourself? *Basta,* Cookie, *basta!* Come down from there."

Cookie shakes her head in disgust, then slowly descends.

"I go up myself." Cici totters on her heels like a glittering catcher at the bottom of the ladder, trying to figure out where to grab Cookie to help her down.

Cookie waves her off. "I can do it my damn self."

Cici dispatches Cookie to get another bottle of Sancerre, knowing she'll take a pull off their liquor bottles while she's downstairs, like she's been doing for decades. Cici clicks on the intercom and asks for profiteroles as well. There's some muddled answer. Cookie pretends she doesn't know how to use the inter-com so she can later say, "I didn't hear you ask for that."

It is less than two weeks before Cheri's birthday, and Cici hasn't decided yet on the piece of jewelry she will send her. A ring? It's a tradition, to give something of hers to her daughter each year—why save it all until she dies? She'd gladly give Cheri anything she wanted, but her daughter doesn't want any of the things she has to give. No matter what she picks, Cheri won't wear it or like it. But perhaps one day it will have meaning for her. After their last conversation, she's tempted to skip the ritual this year. Family stays together, not in a hotel!

Cheri was never a warm child. She didn't like to cuddle or be hugged; she was hard to get to know and even harder to under-stand. Sol simply treated her coldly in return, but Cici wasn't the kind of mother to pull away, like her friend Charlotte Detemeirs, who never once spoke about her son after he was in the newspa-pers for taking part in a money scandal.

Looking through her vault is like spending time with old friends. Without opening the box, Cici remembers when and where she got each piece, the carat size, country of origin, the luster, brilliance, dispersion, and scintillation of each gemstone. They speak to her in different ways and different tongues. Like this jabot pin that somehow got mixed in with the cocktail rings. She immediately recalls: 24K gold, tenth-century, made from horse-bridle ornaments. Solomon purchased it at an an-tique shop in East Hampton and gave it to her when she came back from her first trip to Italy with Cheri. It was an apology for the fight they'd had over the portrait. Looking back, it was more her fault than his. Cici had meant it to be a nice surprise for him, a painting of his two girls, Cici and Cheri. She didn't think he would want to be included; he was so busy with work, and men did not want to sit and pose for hours. But she had used the wrong words to describe it. "This isn't a *family* portrait," he kept saying, accusing her of leaving him out of his own family. She was so upset that all she saw was his anger and not his hurt. Even after she had the artist redo the portrait, Solomon insisted she hang it in the guest room where he would never lay eyes on it. When she goes to return the pin to its rightful drawer, she spies a heart-shaped black velvet box all the way at the back. Indian ruby Bulgari ring in 24K gold setting, June 6, 1981, Lutèce in New York City. Ruby: preserves chastity, kills poisonous snakes, can cause water to boil, declares love. Well, it was a declaration. Whether it had anything to do with love and happiness was another matter.

She thought Solomon was happy when he gave her the ruby ring for her fortieth birthday. His patents for the special coating on pills were making him a lot of money; he'd just bought a pied-à-terre in the city. Providing for her, buying her beautiful things, he said, made him happy. He was rarely home before seven thirty. But on her birthday that year, it wasn't even six when she heard the crunch of his tires on the gravel path and saw his headlights sweep up their driveway. She sipped her negroni.

She smoothed her skirt while standing at the kitchen sink and rubbed a cut lemon under her nails to remove any traces of garlic. She had been making pasta sauce that day, freezing it to give to Cheri, now at NYU, so she'd have something decent to eat. Solomon promised to spend the weekend in Montclair to celebrate Cici's birthday. She'd wanted Cheri to come home too, but Cheri, as usual, preferred to stay in the city with her friends.

Cici could tell by the way Solomon was whistling "Just the way you look tonight" as he walked through the front door that he was happy. She heard him place his keys on the hallway entrance table, listened to his footsteps, the slight drag of his left shoe. His legs had become swollen and stiff from phlebitis. He had always been so strong, with such beautiful legs in his white tennis shorts. But she tried not to let it bother her. "Nothing else for today, Cookie," she heard him say.

They went to their favorite restaurant, Lutèce, and sat at a table by the fireplace, next to the wall with elegant paper that looked like yellow flowers and green leaves on trellises. In the sophisticated quiet, they heard the clink of silver, the clearing of a throat, the sound of an aged port being poured into heavy lead crystal. He kissed her hands and put the pigeon-blood ruby ring on her middle finger. As she raised her champagne flute to toast Sol's gift, the large gem slipped to the side. But Cici twisted it back with her thumb before Sol could see that the ring was much too big for her finger.

They ate ginger crème brûlée and profiteroles and drank too much. It was rare that they were alone. She spoke about her concern for their daughter, wearing torn clothes, piercing her body, and looking so thin. He told her about how he managed to scoop up the new apartment and recounted with pride his outmaneuvering of the co-op board, how there were many people who'd wanted that apartment. Now Cici had a new design project; there would be architects and plans to coordinate and she could spend more time in the city, more time with him.

He touched her back. She shivered; was it from his touch? She would like to feel sexy with him; maybe tonight she could. He steered her out of Lutèce into the drizzle of the street and helped her into their waiting town car with its purr of classical music.

"*Buon compleanno,* Carlotta," he whispered in her ear, "you are more beautiful to me at forty than you were at eighteen."

When they got home, she peignoired herself, put her hair up, lingerie and pearls beneath. She browsed through *Architectural Digest* because it was on her nightstand and she didn't want to appear too eager. It was a sensitive situation. Would he want to make love? Ever since her hysterectomy, even when she craved his touch, intercourse was painful for her. She'd tried the olive oil her doctor suggested, but it made a great mess; she'd tried the breathing exercises and reading sexy stories. Once, they'd watched an erotic movie together. She *had* tried. But it never felt the same again and she could not have an orgasm. And Sol could always tell when she was just doing it for his sake. She felt ashamed and guilty. They slept like spoons, kissed hello, good-bye; he did not often try to do more. He never came home early.

"I have news, sweetheart," he said when he slid next to her in bed wearing his green silk pajamas. His face was smooth and she could smell the warm cashmere of his aftershave. "I've decided to go to law school." He announced it like a boy bringing home a blue ribbon. She didn't know what to say except "But you are a *dottore.*"

"And soon I'll be a lawyer. Goddamned lawyers—they always travel in groups, three on a call, three at a lunch, and three per hour on your bill. I added up what I've been spending on lawyers for Entercap—it's ludicrous. I could prosecute my own patents with what I've learned in the past decade. This just means I'll have more control over my business, sweetheart. I'm still a *dottore.* But I'm also a businessman." Cici had been so proud of her husband, standing tall in his white lab coat, inventing something to change the world. "I'm doing it for you and for Cheri. And for the children she might have one day."

"Of course she will have children," Cici replied. She imagined herself posing with them on a family Christmas card.

Sol had already given her such nice things; their house with the lilac trees in Montclair had been plenty. But once his pill coating had been adopted by every major pharmaceutical company in the United States, there was more money. Yet the more money Sol made, the more he felt he needed to make. Now he was always traveling, working, meeting, can't talk, late business dinner, *He's unavailable right now, Mrs. Matzner.*

"Are you no too old for school?"

"I'll certainly be the world's oldest law student." He laughed. "You're right about that." The more questions came to her, the more anxious she became. Would he still be a doctor? Cici liked being a doctor's wife. She knew what it meant. "I don't need to practice anymore, but I'll still run the research facility," Sol reassured her. "I know this is unconventional, but law school will be easy compared to med school. I'm doing all of this now, while I still can. Entercap is my legacy—and yours."

"Where is this law school, is it out of the state?"

"Here, Cici. Of course, right here in New York. I'm looking into a few accelerated programs in the city so I'm close to my office. NYU has a good one." Cici sat up straighter.

"You go where Cheri goes? Would you, Solomon?" More than anything, Cici wanted Cheri to have a good relationship with Sol. The kind that had been cut short with Cici's papa and that she had never had with Marco D'Ameri. "It would be wonderful, you can see your daughter more."

"NYU is a big school. And I'll be taking mostly evening classes. I'm not sure she'd be so happy to have her father going to her same college. She's not very receptive, at least not to me."

"No say that, Solomon. She is almost an adult now. It was difficult for me as well, with her so dark, so hard, nothing I did was good enough. But you fight with her and then you just give up. She is her own person. Maybe she is not as we want her to be—I pray that she can look pretty again, she is so pretty and smart. *Ma,* please, if it is not too late for school, it is not too late to try with your daughter."

"It's not like I don't want to try, Cici," Sol said with a sigh. "She just puts up so many walls. But NYU does have the most flexible program."

Sol went downstairs to his office to make a call, just for a minute, he swore. Cici looked at her ring, the color of an unripe pomegranate, of pigeon blood. "The best rubies are pigeon-blood red," she remembered her mama telling her. She would call Bulgari in the morning and get it sized. She slipped between the sheets of their marital bed and fell asleep waiting for Sol to return to her side. Her fortieth birthday ended as quietly as a ruby dropping onto a jeweler's felt.

The next day, Cici called Bulgari. It was such a simple request.

"I need to get a ring sized. Yes, it was purchased by Dr. Matzner." Cici was in her kitchen in Montclair, talking into the phone and making hand gestures at Cookie, who was staring into a pot on the stove, confused about what to do. "No, I don't have the receipt, but you should...what? He bought two rings? Yes, I hold."

"Come on, Mz. M., are you saying stir or pour? The rice is jumping around."

"All these years I teach you how to do the risotto, you no listen? Yes, I am here," Cici said into the phone. "Am I calling about the *emerald* ring?" Cici turned her back to Cookie. "Yes, that's right. Dr. Matzner's emerald ring...in eighteen-karat gold setting? Yes, that is correct." Cici pulled out a pad of paper and Cookie gave her a questioning look. "I would like to know the address you have for me. Also the telephone number, yes, to make sure you have the correct information." Cici's hand trembled as she scribbled on a piece of paper.

Ms. Catherine Webster, 5521 Forest Drive, Rye, New York, 555-0139

Cici was in her bathroom. She traced the name and address, going over each letter with the point of a fountain pen until the paper started to tear. She felt every loss rise up in her, the pain was so deep she could not bear it. She scratched at her arm, clawing at her flesh. It was not enough; she needed to cut all the way down, to hit the quick. She took the point of the pen and stabbed at her arm until she broke the skin. For a moment, she felt the relief of physical pain.

Cookie had been pounding on the door, and now she said: "I'm calling Mr. M. if you don't give me a sign you haven't slipped on the bathroom floor and split your damn head open like a ripe tomato."

Sol had had to go into the city, citing unexpected problems with the new apartment. He would be home late that night before he went on his business trip, or he might stay over. She thought of all the nights he'd stayed in the city, how she'd worried about him being there alone. She thought of how he always took a shower when he got home late. She thought of little things and big things; there was no size chart for lies.

The fountain pen had leaked all over her hands. Blue ink stained her skin and dripped onto the marble floor. Her white slip too; she'd bunched it up to get at her stomach, to dig at her scars, but they were too resilient, wouldn't be opened. How would she clean up the mess? She took her toothbrush and started scrubbing the floor.

"I'm calling him," Cookie shouted, still pounding on the door.

"No," Cici said, her voice surprisingly strong.

Cici leans back in her chair in her jewelry vault, her muled feet propped up on the ottoman next to the unopened Bulgari box. The empty bottle of Sancerre lies on the oriental carpet, next to the profiterole plate that's clean save for a few coagulated drops of chocolate. Donizetti's *Lucia di Lammermoor* plays softly from the speakers; candles diffuse cardamom and bitter-orange scents.

Her right knuckle is swollen with age; the ring might fit her now. The skin on her hands is still soft, but she hates the sunspots and veins. She had her jewelry, and Sol had his wine cellar. Sol taught her about wines, how to look at the color with the glass tipped. If it was thick, almost blood-dense, it was a Big Red, and Sol loved his Big Reds. If jewels are the patron saint of the guilty, then the ruby is the Queen of Hearts.

Once she knew about the emerald ring, Cici couldn't stop picturing her husband and Catherine Webster, their naked bodies rising up to meet each other. She had sat for a long time in their bedroom, looking at the piece of paper with her husband's mistress's name on it. Then she'd searched the house for scissors. She was sure she had some in her sewing box.

The first cut was easy. Cici almost wished Sol were there to witness it. She was a little tipsy; she'd been drinking the best of his Big Reds. Her right hand held the scissors while her left hand riffled over the rows of Sol's pants, jackets, and ties. She'd taught Sol how to dress. Had picked out all of his clothes, had his monogram sewn on the sleeves of his custom-made shirts. She thought about the weather where Sol would be going for a conference in California, he said—day wear, evening wear, maybe something a little sporty for afternoons. She color-coordinated the ties, shirts, and suits and grouped them on the floor. Then went into her closet and got tissue paper. Once she had everything organized, Cici cut. She started with the pants of his favorite blue suit. The leg came off with several satisfying snips.

She cut arms, toes, crotches, ran the scissors over the compression socks Sol used for his phlebitis, and they curled like ribbon. Threads scattered across the floor like spring pollen. She folded his clothes and packed them with tissue paper, like she always did, so they wouldn't wrinkle. She layered the items carefully, concealing the cuts. When it was all nice and neat, she closed the suitcase. For a moment, she was not sure she could follow through with this. It is amazing the things we think we cannot do and then when the time comes, it is so easy. As easy as a kiss on the cheek to say good-bye, travel safely.

When Sol got back from his trip, he called from the airport to say he'd be staying over in the city.

"How was the weather?" she said, gazing out the window of her Montclair kitchen at the lilacs in full bloom.

"Fine," he said, "it's always nice in Southern California."

"So they say." She heard the bustle of the airport, someone being paged over the loudspeaker. "You sleep well in the hotel?"

"Everything was fine. The driver is here, I have to go, darling."

"But was the weather too warm? Did you have the right clothing?"

"Perfect," Sol said, "and the thing about travel is . . . you can always buy what you need."

Tears were dripping down Cici's face when she hung up the phone. She went into Sol's closet and grabbed an armful of the Brooks Brothers and Armani suits off their wooden hangers. She curled herself into a ball on the floor like a child and would have fallen asleep like that if Cookie hadn't interrupted her.

"Twenty-five dollar." Cookie was standing straight and tall like a Miniature Pinscher with an agenda. "I ain't deaf, dumb, *and* blind—I know what's been going on around here." Cookie picked up a pair of Sol's pants. They're now shorts. She put them back on the hanger. "It ain't none of my business, but I'm here to tell you there's something you can do about this situation. Now get on up, you shouldn't be rolling around on no closet floor."

Cookie handed her one of Sol's handkerchiefs. "Blow good and hard, now." Cici sat up and blew her nose like an obedient child. "All right, I'm only going to say this once." Cookie took the handkerchief, folded it, and placed it back in Sol's drawer on top of a stack of clean ones.

"Twenty-five dollar. That's what it cost you."

"Twenty-five dollar for what?"

"Come on, Mz. M., you got Mafia in Italy, don't you? Just about the only thing That Nigger is good for is knowing folks who know folks, and yes, you know what I mean."

"You're not saying it is twenty-five dollars to—Cookie! God, He hears you. *Ossia la Madonna!*"

"Like God don't hear Mr. M. when he's doing what he's doing? He don't like that much either. It's always us women who suffer. I don't care what the Bible says, it's not right."

"But...twenty-five dollars, is so nothing..." Cici couldn't help thinking that Sol's life was worth more than that.

"To you, but to some folks—"

"Shhhhhht! It is a sin to even think like this."

"A'right, Mz. M. I just wanted you to know that you could do something constructive instead of drinking and cutting up clothes. That Nigger can work it out so nobody's the wiser. You know what he gone and done? He bought himself a Cadillac; how he got the money I do not know—you think I saw any of it? No sirree. And you know what? That damn Cadillac sits in front of the damn house because he can't afford to put gas in it. So I told him, Go live in it, fool, go get your money's worth." Cookie chuckled. Cici laughed as well, not because it was funny but because she was now a little afraid of Cookie.

"Thank you, Cookie. But I could not do that." Did Cici consider it, even for a second? She crossed herself and thought she'd have to go to see Father Padua immediately.

Who would think that a human life could cost so little? Cici had no idea Cookie knew those kind of "folks." Cici didn't even know the name of Cookie's husband; she called him only That Nigger. She thought she should send him a present; maybe he was angry not to be included at Christmas when she'd sent presents home for Cookie's children. Would he like a nice Burberry raincoat?

Cici's thoughts are interrupted by the sound of the pug scratching at the door. John Paul III doesn't like to be alone. Cookie's proposition had made her wonder how well we ever know other people, even the ones we see every day, even the people we love.

Sol certainly had his sins, but there were also her own. She had been so passionate, so hungry for every pleasure the body offered. She should have gone to church while she was pregnant, confessed her sin of placing her desire over the safety of her baby. Wasn't it a just punishment that after her surgery, she could not make love without pain or fulfill her husband's desire? In some deep unarticulated place, Cici knows this is what led him to Catherine Webster.

40BDAY 2.0

The more Cheri looks at the black-and-white card showing a winsome boxer in a birthday hat, the more it resembles Eddie Norris's dog. The birthday card is from Suzanne, the secretary of the Near Eastern Civilizations Department, who sends one every year. The generic Hallmark card is the first communication Cheri has received from anyone in her department in a while—her colleagues evidently thought it best to distance themselves from her in light of the recent allegations.

Suzanne's card was waiting for her on the kitchen counter, along with a growing pile of FedEx packages from her mother, who insists that Cheri celebrate this damn fortieth birthday, despite her demand that Michael *not* throw her a party and regardless of the fact that Cici has remained in Montclair and is not ensconced in the guesthouse to oversee the festivities. It was just as well, after the interrogation Cheri went through at her first meeting with the review committee earlier this morning. Only to be told, at the end, that they wouldn't be reconvening until school recommenced in September.

"Keep your powder dry"—that's what Eddie Norris would

have advised. Eddie schooled her in how to have her deposition taken for a case that went to trial: answer only exactly what is asked of you, don't offer more information; when in doubt say, "Can you repeat the question?" And that's exactly how she'd treated the academic gestapo. She had turned over all her grade books, her students' tests and papers. She'd studied her lecture notes from the discussion of sacred prostitution and prepared answers to the committee's likely questions. She'd felt a wave of *Punch-Drunk Love* anxiety cresting over her, and she'd popped a pregame Ativan.

Eddie's boxer. They called her Trooper General Hole-in-the-Tongue Gonzales because her bottom fang tooth kept getting caught in a hole in her tongue, exaggerating her underbite. When they found the dog, Cheri had been at a low point in her new career in law enforcement. She'd expected hostility from outside—civilians on the Lower East Side hated cops. But their jeers were nothing compared to the onslaught she'd endured *inside* the Ninth Precinct. She expected the hazing that came with being a rookie. She was used to having to prove herself. What blindsided her was the rage directed at her because she was a woman.

Maybe she'd overestimated gender equality in 1984. She was of the generation of women who were told they could bring home the bacon *and* fry it up in a pan. Or maybe she just thought that she could conquer any obstacle through sheer force of will. It wasn't the first time she'd been called a dyke because of her short hair and the multiple holes in her ears. Her firearms instructor at the police academy took her aside one day and said, "Guys will want to do you. If you won't, they'll say you're a lesbo. And you're a hell of a shot, better than most of the men. Might want to tone it down just a bit; Jewish, educated, female—they're going to hate you. Their wives will hate you. Not because they're worried you'll fuck their husbands, but because they don't trust a broad to have their man's back. You'll have to put up with that shit for years. Your career, your pension will depend on it. Maybe now's a good time to think about going back to school with the rich kids."

There was no way Cheri was going to be that girl. His suggestion only spurred her on, inspired her to prove him—and Sol and everyone else who assumed she'd fail at the NYPD—wrong. So she kept her mouth shut, didn't protest being relegated to desk work, was determined to survive the daily harassment, the bloody tampons in her locker, having guys walk past her like she didn't exist. Endure. She'd go to the gym and punch the heavy bag when it got to be too much and if a tear spilled, she could say it was sweat. She'd cover her face and scream into her pillow at night so that in the morning she could saunter in again like nothing bothered her. The worst thing she could do was let them see it got to her. How it bored into her like a parasite, the knowledge that they were all saying, "You'll never be good enough to belong." Cops were a family. When you were in the fold, no matter where you came from, you were blood. She yearned for that kind of family, for that feeling of belonging. Withstand.

One morning, nine months after starting with the NYPD, she'd gone to the gym early and noticed in the shower that something was wrong with her conditioner. She couldn't dry her hair; it looked like greasy vinyl and smelled like mayo. Someone's idea of a practical joke. The wood-paneled wall in the muster room had a row of official photographs and plaques inscribed with the names of members of the Fighting Ninth who'd been killed in the line of duty. Cheri had had one of those taken after her graduation from the academy. One of the photographs was of a man who looked barely twenty. She stared at the name on the plaque—PTL Timothy Rocco—searing it into her mind. It was as if a sponge blotted up all the noise, the humiliation, even her desire to keep wiping at her hair. And then the room was full again and the sergeant was pointing to her, saying she was in the rotation. They were short-staffed. Somebody had to take Cheri in his car. She waited like the last kid to be chosen on the ball field. And that's when Eddie Norris walked in late and, without looking at her, said: "She's with me." Everyone knew that if Eddie Norris tapped you, it meant something. There were protests and guffaws but Eddie Norris gave no explanation and made no apology. All he said to her was "If you fuck up with me, you won't fuck up again."

It wasn't until their last call of the day—a complaint of a foul smell coming from an apartment off Avenue C—that they found the boxer. The stench of the apartment made bile rise in her throat. But Cheri wasn't going to pull a rookie move and throw up in front of Eddie Norris. The dog was severely emaciated and dehydrated, barely able to lift her head. On the floor next to her was the decomposing body of a woman still holding a crack pipe—the coroner had to break her fingers to get it loose. The dog went nuts when they started to move the body, sinking her teeth into Eddie's hand.

Eddie saved that dog just like he saved Cheri. He nursed the dog, cooked her rice and chicken, and eventually her eyes brightened and her fur grew back with a new luster. For months, she smelled like chicken soup, and Cheri joked that it was from Eddie's being a Jewish mother. Eddie took the boxer everywhere and the precinct adopted her as one of their own; she even slept for hours under Eddie's desk while

he and Cheri were on duty in the projects of the Lower East
Side.

It's funny what Cheri remembers. Trooper General had a
thing for toes. She liked to go after Eddie's feet, especially
when he and Cheri were having sex. He'd swat her away, but
she'd get excited and turn in a circle like she was chasing her
tail, her tongue hanging like a wind-blown necktie. She was
comic relief from the assault of the Job, and Cheri went from
tolerating the dog to looking forward to seeing her. Trooper
General had the unnerving habit of staring at them while
they were sleeping; if Cheri woke up, there she'd be, her eyes
trained on them. "She just wants to make sure we're still alive,"
Eddie said.

"Your mother's gone crazy again with the presents," Michael says
as he walks into the kitchen. "Are you going to open those packages or just let them pile up until the day of? You'll have to move
them before our company comes."

"What company? Tonight?" Cheri instinctively slides the
birthday card back into the envelope.

"Next week. I'm waiting on the exact date. We finally got
that Sedona prick to let the shaman come here for a few days.
You wouldn't believe the negotiations with customs and immi-
gration. They're treating him like he's a terrorist because he's
brown-skinned; talk about racial profiling. I don't know how he
did it, but Bertrand got the U.S. consulate in Ecuador to help
with documentation to verify he's a tribal elder so he can bring
in the yage."

"Yage?"

"Plant medicine, DMT—aka ayahuasca. You know the footage we shot with Del Rio—you should really look at what I've done with it before he comes. Can you do that, please?" Cheri remembers that footage: initiates in the thrall of the hallucinogen, wailing, retching, the shaman walking among them making a high-pitched, keening sound like an aboriginal cantor.

"So, wait, is the shaman coming *here* to do a ceremony?"

"Well, I have to interview him again." Michael shakes one of Cici's packages. "More towels?"

"Is he coming alone or does he have an interpreter?"

"Yeah, they're giving me the second-string interpreter. The main guy is staying in Sedona. Can you believe it? Everything is a fucking battle."

"Okay, just let me know soon." The last thing Cheri wants is more people she can't communicate with in the house. Tripping on yage or not tripping. "Taya's coming to town and I'm trying to plan my birthday."

"You'll know as soon as I know. And don't worry, they'll bunk in my office." Cheri gives him a look: It's okay for the shaman to stay there but not her mother?

"It's work. And only for a few days," Michael insists as she grabs the package away from him and holds it protectively.

"I told Taya we're going to get together with her and her new guy; we were all going to do something for my birthday."

"You said you didn't want to do anything for your birthday. I took you at your word."

"I said I didn't want a party," Cheri says measuredly. "Remember, I told you she's dating that artist. Von something. He's around your age—he was big in the seventies. He does nudes..."

"Sorry, darling, but sometimes we have to accommodate other

people's schedules. I know Mezzo America's not your field, but I thought you'd appreciate meeting a Shuar medicine man. He's the first to come to the States ever; some people would consider it a blessing. Can we talk about this later? I'm exhausted. I was just on my way upstairs to take a nap." He's almost out of the kitchen when he turns around.

"You had your meeting with the review committee this morning. How was it?"

"I kept my powder dry," she says, relishing that the context is lost on him.

"I found a genius place for your birthday, CM," Taya says. Cheri has answered her cell in the locker room at the gym after getting a few sets of weights in. The lady changing next to her is giving her a dirty look, which Cheri pointedly ignores. *This isn't a fucking yoga studio,* Cheri wants to say.

"It's an authentic country-and-western bar with a real mechanical bull. My old guy is in if your old guy is in." Taya thinks all old guys will like each other, kind of like babies; just throw the oldies in Barcaloungers with bottles of whiskey and they're happy.

"Don't think that's going to work," Cheri says. "We have a shaman coming into town."

"A shaman?"

"Michael's got him staying with us for his film. Don't ask me. But you can't do anything that would embarrass him, he's very into this."

"Like I don't know how to behave? I've hosted a fund-raiser for the Dalai Lama, and he's a hell of a lot more important than a shaman. But it's your birthday, so you get to decide the venue.

Tell Michael to bring his camera. A shaman on a mechanical bull is too brilliant! He can call it *Slammin' with Shaman.*"

The venue, Cheri learns in the morning, will be their house. The only day the shaman can come to Chicago is on her actual birthday and Cheri slides into acceptance. For the next few days, Michael is buzzing with shaman prep. The yage arrives in an envelope—add that to the list of misdemeanors. Michael is calling homeopaths for a root to ferment into a beer the Shuar men drink; cooking a vegetarian meal although nobody's a vegetarian and Cheri is a carnivore who likes her steak blue. All she's been hearing from HMS Bay is atonal whistling and rattling. The news headlines are more of the same: war looming; economy crashing; environment collapsing; priests molesting; and the president's at his ranch in Texas taking a "nonworking" vacation. Deforestation in the Amazon—that's a good subject to bring up with the shaman.

Cici's packages continue to pour in daily. Her mother is extracting her pound of guilt by sending pounds of gifts. Cheri can't resist opening the boxes from Dean and DeLuca. Cici always gets the best of the best, but she excels in all things pig. Half the boxes are filled with cured meats, including a whole leg of imported prosciutto di Parma, Cici's homemade mozzarella, and *torta di noce.* Cheri stands in the kitchen eating slices of buttery-soft prosciutto. "The Shuar don't eat pork! Get rid of all that," Michael bleats as he walks through the kitchen carrying blankets and sheets to his office.

"I will not. It's not like they keep kosher."

"It doesn't matter if it's a religious thing or not, we can't have pork in the house."

"In whose rule book? They eat guinea pigs—they're not going to pass out at the sight of prosciutto."

"It's a simple request—just pack it all up."

"I'll stash it in the extra fridge in the garage. Problem solved. We've had Muslims over for dinner and I didn't clean out the refrigerator."

"That's because your mother hadn't just sent us a passel of pig!"

"No, I'm certain we had bacon and those sausage patties you like in the freezer." Michael's starting to get his aneurysm look. "It's delicious, want some?"

On the morning of Cheri's birthday, she wakes up to find that Michael's side of the bed is untouched. He'd cordoned off most of the downstairs with his party prep and must have fallen asleep in his office. She walks downstairs and finds a huge bouquet of tea roses that could only be from Cici and a plate of her favorite sprinkle doughnuts and fresh coffee awaiting her on the kitchen table. But this pales in comparison to what Michael has accomplished outside. He's straightened and cleaned and had his way with the backyard. He rescued the kiva from the ignominy of the garage and he's sectioned off an eating area with bamboo poles strewn with colorful paper lanterns. She walks into what is now a Zen garden; Michael's collection of large crystals and minerals jut up from the grass, seemingly rising out of the earth; flowers bloom, citronella candles ward off stinging insects, Chinese lanterns sit on tree trunks. Michael has covered their old plastic table with batik fabric and he's brought his speakers outside.

It all looks beautiful. She realizes how long it's been since either of them made this kind of effort. She lingers for a moment, feeling wistful, then turns around to go back upstairs.

Cheri sits on the bed with her plate of doughnuts and Cici's final box. Cheri knows this small box is part of a ritual. The handing down of a family idol that she doesn't worship, at least not as her mother might want her to. This year's offering is in gold paper with a white ribbon; Cheri tears it open unceremoniously to reveal a heart-shaped velvet box containing a heavy ruby ring. A virtuous woman is worth more than rubies. The proverb pops into Cheri's head, but she's never seen her mother wear this ring. The note, written in Cici's elegant cursive, says: *From my forty to your forty.* Cheri tries to remember her mother at forty. She seemed a lot older then than Cheri is now, but in some ways much younger. Her mother lived such a protected, simple life. Cheri tries the ruby ring on her middle finger; it's far too big and fancy for her, but it is beautiful. It's a shame, she thinks as she returns it to its case and puts it in her drawer, to keep something so precious in the dark.

Not to be forgotten, Sol has also left her a birthday gift. His will provided that Cheri would get all the keys to his patent castle when she turned forty. The fruit of Sol's labor resides in Citibank Land, guarded by dark-suited denizens, quietly growing. She's never touched her trust fund—she's doesn't even know exactly how much she's got—and has no plans to do so now. Did Sol think that Cheri would become more like Cici, blithely using his money to wallpaper over the holes he'd made in her life? And to think it all comes from sugarcoating. She knows of a far better way to swallow the pill of forty.

She blasts the Ramones as she forages for a decent bra. Most of her undergarments are stretched out and crappy except for the Wonderbra she bought when she was all sexed up to make a baby. She puts earrings in her piercings and a stud in her nose. Eddie Norris said she looked like a bull in the ring. Eddie's probably on a lake right now with his cop wife and four cop kids, on their summer vacation. Not like the time she and Eddie went camping and she convinced him to eat magic mushrooms and they laughed and had sex and marveled for hours over dead leaves that morphed into starfish. The image of Eddie Norris pinning her arms over her head while he slowly traced the indentation of her collarbone with his tongue flickers on and off in her mind like a lamp with a loose wire.

"Cheri! Cheri!" Michael's standing in the doorway. "Can you turn that down? They're here." She lowers the volume on the CD player. "Sexy." He nods approvingly at the Wonderbra and suddenly she realizes she's got doughnut crumbs in her cleavage. "You might want to put something more on, though. Happy birthday," he adds, already heading back down the stairs.

"Welcome," Cheri says a few minutes later, extending her hand to the shaman. She's red-lipped, studded, wearing a black dress. "Michael and I are honored to have you in our home." The shaman is a short, slight man with skin the color and texture of beef jerky. His face is like a fine engraving, and his eyes are clear and bright; he could be a hundred years old or fifty. His hand is surprisingly large and rough and he talks in an indigenous language she's never heard. She focuses on the sounds of his words, looks to see how they're formed in his mouth—front to back? What about the tongue, teeth, jaw, and lips? These are the clues and classifiers she uses as a linguist, but even applying the little she knows of American Indian languages, she's at a loss. The shaman keeps talking and the second-string translator, a young man with a thick black mustache and watery eyes, sums it all up as "'Hello, my name is Ramon.'"

They sit in the garden at a table under an umbrella Cheri didn't know existed. Michael's beverage tastes like malted dirt, but they sip it while he talks about his film and his plans for interviewing Ramon again. The translator is lagging behind Michael significantly. Ramon's attention seems to be focused on Cheri, to the point where it makes her uncomfortable. She smiles and renews her focus on Michael. When the translator finally stops, Ramon speaks and holds his abdomen. The translator looks at Cheri, then turns back to Michael.

"He says a grain grows inside of you; you must pay attention. No. Please, excuse...no, my mistake." He addresses Cheri: "He says *you* are the one with emptiness inside. It is...inhospitable. This gives you hyperactivity, restlessness, and despair." Cheri feels like she's gone through a metal detector and been caught packing. She doesn't know who or what to look at. There's an awkward silence.

"Or," the translator adds with a nervous laugh, "he is saying he is hungry and looks forward to your meal. The Chicago summer is hot, is it not?"

Taya arrives fifty minutes later, hair blown out, high-heeled, juggling her overflowing purse, bottles of champagne, presents, and, as promised, an old guy in cowboy boots whom she quickly introduces to everyone as Van. "Happy birthday! You look great," she shouts at Cheri as Michael relieves Taya of her packages.

"I'm so sorry we're late. It's all my fault, of course. We had to go to the Museum of Contemporary Art for this Frank Gehry opening. Aren't we all getting sick of Frank Gehry? He's everywhere, with all his weird shapes and crazy angles." Van gives her a cynical look. "He's become a deconstructionist showman, you know I'm right. Van knew him early on; he was part of the Venice artist group in the sixties."

"Everything was better in the sixties," he mutters, "including me."

"I'm with you there," Michael says.

"Don't listen to him," Taya says to Cheri. "His work keeps getting better." She gives Van's hand a little squeeze. "You have to see his show, it's absolutely brilliant." This moment of tenderness is not lost on Cheri.

"What's your poison, Van? I've got a whole bar set up." As the men go outside, Taya lags behind with Cheri.

"Speaking of showmen, where is the shaman?"

"He's in Michael's office. He'll be down in a moment. But, please, try to speak slowly. I'm not sure how much of anything he's getting because his translator isn't that quick off the draw."

"I think you're the one who needs a drink. Or three." Taya puts her arm around Cheri's waist. "Come on! Let's get this birthday started!"

Outside the lanterns glow and world music plays. Michael and Van share a joint; Cheri watches the ember going back and forth like the point of a laser. She knows by his hand gestures that Michael is telling his story about the Museum of Sex, the dwarf, and Andy Warhol. He'd interviewed Warhol for *Disco, Doughnuts, and Dogma*. Van strokes his beard and seems amused. The champagne is dry, Ramon and the translator have emerged from HMS Bay, and Taya's not yet said anything inappropriate. *This is not such a bad little party,* Cheri thinks. *It's actually turning out fine.*

Everyone loves the food. "It goes well with lightning," Michael says as a fork of electricity flashes across the sky, followed seconds later by a thunderclap. He's served vegetables grilled, curried, and stewed with goat milk, along with a mixture of grains and dried fruit and lots of crusty bread and salad.

"I'd try ayahuasca," Van says. "I've done plenty of peyote and shrooms, got some interesting paintings out of it. Does he work with frog venom? That shit's supposed to be a hundred times stronger than morphine. Makes you puke your guts out for days."

"You're thinking of the Mayorunas. Different tribe, another part of the Amazon," Michael says. "Medicine men like Ramon— they're called *uwishin* in the Shuar tribe—they've performed thousands of ceremonies with the plant, or Mama. She takes you very deep into the psyche, even to the point of simulating death."

"Like DMT," Taya says. "Not for me, but in LA there's always a market for anything mind-expanding. If the shaman wanted to leave the rain forest I'd be happy to connect him with people." The translator, whose name is either Samit or Samil, smiles at Taya and then goes back to eating.

"Aren't you going to translate what we're saying?" Taya asks Samit. "I don't want him to think we're rude."

"Ah, well. I am not really a translator, you see."

"What do you mean? You know the *uwishin* dialect," Michael says with some concern.

"This is true, but my knowledge of the language comes via taking care of their teeth. I am a dentist. I must travel often to their village. One must learn to communicate or there could be a big mistake."

"You're a dentist," Michael says.

"Yes. I am considered to be very gentle." Michael's getting his aneurysm look. Taya leans in and whispers to Cheri:

"Let's hope he's a better dentist than a translator."

"How much of this aren't you getting? We've got a shoot tomorrow and it's important that Ramon understand my questions."

"I do my best," Samit says, his round eyes getting rounder. Michael takes him aside for a moment. Ramon looks surprisingly unfazed, drinks his malted dirt.

Can't this all wait until the morning, Cheri wants to shout. Michael's hijacking the evening and it pisses Cheri off. She needs to either drink a lot more or stop now. "Toast!" Taya says, tapping her glass with a spoon. She prepares to take the stage but Cheri says, "No, I'm going to toast all of you for being here." She twists the cork of the nearest champagne bottle, resting in a bucket of ice by her chair, and it flies off, missing Ramon's left ear by a fraction of an inch. Van catches the errant stopper, holds it up like a baseball caught off a pop fly. As Cheri refills everyone's glass, she notices that Michael's is barely touched. She puts her hand over his. "I'd like to thank Michael. For this amazing dinner and the care he's taken to make the night...just right." Her husband tips a nonexistent hat to her and mouths, Thank you. Taya claps, is again about to leap to her feet, but the shaman rises and extends his arms to Cheri. He motions for her to come to him and takes her hands in his. His gaze is penetrating but kind. He smiles at her as if they've shared a secret.

"In honor of you, Ramon wishes me to tell the story of how the Shuar came to respect women. I do my best to make it as Ramon wishes." The translator smooths his mustache. "Long ago, it was the Shuar men who had breasts and nursed babies. Women gave birth and then were killed. One day a pregnant woman was tending her garden of nuts. She was crying because she knew that once the nuts were ripe, she would give birth and die. A rat approached her and said, 'Do not cry, I will help you. Female rats have many babies and we do not die afterward. Do as I say, and you will be strong and live.' The rat gathered the nuts and fed them to the woman, who ate them and became stronger. Then the rat said, 'Go home to your husband. Tell him the nuts are ready to harvest and come back to me.' The woman was afraid but did as the rat told her. The next day, the rat was waiting for her in the field. 'Do not be afraid,' she said and twisted the woman's belly until the baby came out. The rat wrapped the baby in leaves and told the woman, 'Take the baby back to your husband, and do not fear for now you are as strong as a rat.' The woman returned home, where her husband had built a big fire and was sharpening his machete. When he saw her with the baby he was furious. In a rage he cut off his breasts with the machete and flung them at the woman. This was the moment that everything changed forever for the Shuar people. The man instantly knew that women were to be honored and respected, and ever since that day it has been the duty of the Shuar men to revere their women. The end."

A few droplets of rain spatter the table. Michael has been moving around them with his camera and is now behind the shaman. "Well," Van drawls, "that's quite a story." The rain starts really coming down, giving everyone something to do besides dwell on the meaning of nuts and lopped-off breasts.

Later, when the Ecuadorans have retired and it's just the four of them in the living room, Michael sequesters Van in front of the TV, showing him the footage of the Shuar using shrunken heads in a religious ceremony. "Taya, come check this out! I'm sure Cheri has seen it already, but it's fascinating stuff," Van says.

"Cheri hasn't seen it," Michael says tightly. Cheri knows it's the footage Michael had asked her to look at. She would feel guilty if he weren't putting her on the spot.

"Not this version," she says.

"It's new," Michael says pointedly.

"Guys, let's get back to the rotting flesh later," Taya says, jumping up and doing her best Donna Summer impersonation: *"Someone left a cake out in the rain."* She runs outside and comes back bearing a slightly soggy birthday confection with two candles, one in the shape of a four and one shaped like a zero.

"I'm turning in. It's all on you to make a dent in that," Michael says.

"You can't leave now!" Taya says, lighting the candles, but Michael's already doing the man-hug with Van, and by the time Taya places the cake with the now-lit candles in front of Cheri, Michael is heading up the stairs.

Wishes are heavy, horrible things. Cheri is more than ready for the night to end but dreads being left alone with Michael. *To seeing the tablets before my next birthday,* she thinks as she blows out the candles. Van makes a big to-do about signing a copy of his catalog and presenting it to Cheri. "It was swell meeting you," he says, kissing her forehead. "C'mon, cowgirl," he says to Taya, "we've got another road stand to hit before it's all over."

"I'm so sorry, CM. Whatever's going on between you and Michael, he shouldn't treat you like that. Call me later." Cheri watches as Taya runs out into the rain and Van gallantly meets her with an umbrella and holds it over her head. "Thank you," Cheri shouts and then turns into the stillness of what's left over.

Dishes. Food to be wrapped and put away. Cheri grabs her cigarettes and opens the door to the porch. When she lights up, she sees a lump in the corner under the awning and moves to investigate. It's the shaman, curled up like a pill bug on his sleeping mat. He sleeps like a child, innocent, indifferent to his surroundings. She bends down and adjusts his blanket.

When she goes back inside, she is surprised to see that Michael has come back downstairs and is in the kitchen, doing the dishes.

"Do you know our houseguest is sleeping on the ground outside, getting wet?" Cheri asks.

"He's never slept in a bed; he's from the rain forest. Rain and forest, get it?"

"Just leave that stuff. I'll do them in the morning," she says.

"You don't do them right. You stick the silverware in the basket without scrubbing the tines and it's a waste of water to run the dishwasher twice."

"You know what? I can't do this anymore," she says before she can think not to say it.

"Then don't," Michael replies, still fiddling with the forks. "I said I'd do it."

"Not the dishes. This. *Us.* You're so angry all the time. Calling me out like that in front of everyone. For what? Not kneeling at the altar of five minutes of new footage?"

"I asked you to do one thing, Cheri. One thing. You couldn't be bothered." Michael drops a few more knives into the dishwasher, then pauses. "I'm not going to do this with you now. I just want to go to bed."

"I know that's what *you* want. And that's what we've been doing for years now. But I can't breathe here, and it started way before I was panting for air on the ground in front of the movie theater. There's all this anger in what you say, what you don't say, it just hangs over everything."

"So, wait, now I'm to blame for your panic attack? Is that what the goddamned shrink is telling you?"

"Meds doctor. Nobody told me anything or has to tell me. You and I don't communicate anymore, or maybe we stopped trying to. I don't know who I am here or what this marriage is about anymore."

"For the first time in your life you're not busy, every minute, all the time. Who are you without your tablets to translate or a book to write or your degrees to define you? Your problem, Cheri, is that you can't stand to spend time with yourself. You're always running but you won't ever admit you're afraid. Like it will make you seem weak. So instead, you shut down and push people away."

"Why is it that every time I try to bring up issues in our relationship, you make it all about me? Look, I have my shit, we both have our shit, but what I'm saying now is we're stuck. We have been for a while, and I don't know how to get unstuck."

"Did it ever occur to you that you create the situations you get stuck in? You take such an extreme stance, you don't back down or compromise, and you end up hurting yourself."

"Oh, so I created the situation with Richards and Samuelson? It's my fault I've been wrongly accused of some PC bullshit? Are you saying that I should just bow down and admit to something I didn't do? 'Please, sir, I'll do anything to keep my job.'"

"I'm saying you had a choice. You could have apologized, worded it in a way that you could live with. But no, you always have to go balls to the wall. You think *I'm* stubborn? You put yourself in a corner and then you blame it on our relationship. Just like you did with Sol."

"This has nothing to do with Sol! You want to talk father issues? You don't want to have a baby. You never did."

"What's that supposed to mean?" His tone is icy.

"Exactly what I said. You like being the center of attention; it's a role you've played your whole life, so why share the spotlight now?"

"You know what, Cheri? Your disappointment has nothing to do with me. In fact, the whole misguided journey to having a baby has had nothing to do with me all along. It's always been your agenda."

"Agenda? Since when is being a mother an agenda?"

"How do you want me to respond, Cheri? Script it and I'll say it. I've tried to be as compassionate as I can and listen to you go on and on about this, but there's only so much I can take."

"On and on? I won't let you make me into the needy, grasping female just because that image suits *your* agenda. This whole fucking party was about you! But good news: It's over. I'm lopping off my breasts and throwing them back at you."

Michael slams the dishwasher closed. "Go fuck yourself!" They stand there, breathing hard.

"I don't want to live like this anymore," Cheri says. "We both deserve better."

"So what do you want to do? Divorce?"

"I don't know. A break. Separation."

"Well," Michael says, turning his face away from her, "do what you need to do." Cheri doesn't notice that her cigarette's burned down to the filter until her finger registers the heat. She drops it in a glass of water. Michael is sweaty, not just drunk and stoned sweaty, but sickly in this light.

"Are you okay?"

"After this fucking fantastic conversation? No, I've told you I haven't been feeling well."

"What is it?"

"Upset stomach. I need to get some air."

"Should you see a doctor?"

Michael puts on his jacket. "I'm getting a physical next week. I'm going for a walk; don't wait up."

Cheri opens the curtain and follows the form of her husband as he crosses the street and heads toward Lincoln Park. His gait is comforting in its familiarity; shoulders weighted, head bent slightly, he walks with a tall man's lope. He could have said, *I want to fight for you, for us.* He didn't. The street lamps illuminate the mist, the edge of his coat, the profile of his nose. She imagines he'll venture a couple of loops, if that. She stands on tiptoe to watch him as he moves deeper into the park, walking until the night swallows him up.

PART III

different people die

FAMILY PORTRAIT, SUMMER 1970

The painting sits, covered in a velvet cloth, on a gold easel in the middle of their living room. Mama's made a huge fuss getting everyone ready for Solomon's big surprise. Gusmanov is due in a few minutes, to hang the portrait above the fireplace. It's a Saturday and Cheri is bored waiting for her father to come home, listening to Mama tell Cookie to watch out for his car, did she just hear it pulling into the driveway? Her father was only going into work for a few hours this morning, and Mama has made a special lunch.

"It's not a damn surprise party," Cookie says, rolling her eyes. Cheri is just glad her part in this is over.

Every Saturday for weeks Mama had been dragging her to her font of inspiration—Cecil's House of Fabric—so Mr. Cecil could paint their portrait. Mr. Cecil was a decorator but had paintings in a Montclair gallery "and Manhattan," her mother said proudly. He stank of BO and cologne and invited his favorite clients to the back room—his art studio—to smoke, drink, and eat cheese that looked like it could crawl across the plate on its own.

Cheri hated sitting for hours, frozen in place, on the sofa that smelled of stale tobacco with Mama's arm around her. She hated wearing a dress. Mama's efforts to girl her up stopped in kindergarten when Cheri had taken scissors to the bows on her dresses and then to her hair. She was almost eight now, but Mama burst into tears and said, "You are crushing my heart, for this one time, *please* look like the pretty girl."

"The eagle has landed," Cookie says ominously, and Mama sends Cheri to wait in the living room. A minute later, Mama trots into the room, leading her father by the arm. He's still in his white lab coat. Mama shimmies behind the easel and dramatically pulls back the cloth: "Your family portrait!" Cheri thinks the portrait looks the same as it did last time they saw it: Mama is glamorous in her pink satin dress, her long blond hair in a "do-up." Her arm is a little too tightly around Cheri, who looks uncomfortable, posing with a weird, fake smile.

"Is beautiful, yes, Solomon?" Mama stands by Cheri's father, who is staring at the painting. He shakes his head and closes his eyes, clearly disappointed. "What is wrong?" Mama looks crestfallen. Gusmanov has arrived in the doorway with his tool kit but pauses at the sight of Cici's distress.

Sol pulls Mama aside and speaks quietly. Mama is talking with her hands and her father shakes his head and says, "Family portrait," like the words don't make sense. Mama puts her hand to her heart and then glances over at Cheri. "Go to your room, *cara mia,*" she says.

Cheri feels the heaviness of her father's disapproval. For what, she's not quite sure, but she suspects that it has to do with her, as it usually does. Once upstairs, she becomes absorbed in her book of Greek mythology, imagining herself as Athena, turning her foe into a spider. When Mama calls her down for lunch, Cheri sees that the table is set for two. Mama's eyes are watery.

"Where is Dad?" Cheri asks.

"He had to go back to the office. He'll be home later." Mama puts pasta on plates and brings them to the table. They eat in unusual silence.

"I guess he didn't like the painting," Cheri finally ventures.

"Oh, no, *cara*. Is the misunderstanding. Cecil will fix everything and your father will be very happy." The corners of Mama's mouth turn up but her eyes are still turned down.

"Are you okay, Mama?" Mama nods and gives her hand a little pat. It makes her feel unsettled and angry at her father. Why can't her family just be normal?

Two weeks later, the curtain was about to be torn off yet another version of the Matzner family portrait. And just in time for her eighth birthday, Cheri learns she has living relatives. It wasn't as if she thought her parents had sprung fully grown from the head of Zeus, but they had always been silent on the subject of their families. Like all children, Cheri knew only what the grown-ups told her. When she was old enough to understand that everyone had grandparents, she asked where hers were. When "gone" wasn't the right answer on the family tree Cheri made in second grade, a note from her teacher shamed her mother into further explanation: Belle and Bernard Matzner had died in a car wreck before Cheri was born, and the D'Ameris, back in Italy, had gone to "a better place," save for Mama's sister Alida, who ran off and married Christ. A logical child by nature, Cheri had more questions about how you could marry a dead person than she did about the untimely demise of both sides of her family.

But Cheri learns about her mysterious forebears the day Cici marches into the kitchen while Cheri is eating breakfast, criticizes whatever jobs Gusmanov and Cookie are doing at the time, and announces:

"Is time for my daughter to make her roots." She plunks two airline tickets down on the table in front of Cheri and taps them with a long, polished nail. "In the premier," she says, as if traveling in first class explains everything.

"*Ooof.* I tell you this is food for pigs. You will see in Italia nobody eats the crunchy captain cereal. You will not find it at the table of my family. I tell you, Cookie, to toss the pig food." Cheri cradles her cereal bowl like a convict.

"Family? What family?"

"My sister Genny, you will say Zia Genny, her children—what do you call them, Cookie, the children of my sister?"

"But your family is dead, Mama. You said so."

"Niece if she's a girl, nephew for a boy," Cookie says.

"You told me they were all in heaven," Cheri insists.

"No-no-no. They are in Lago di Como. Is very nice, but heaven? No."

Cheri glances at Cookie in disbelief. Cookie shrugs: *You know your mother.*

"So you have family at a lake and I have cousins?"

"What is this cousin? Cookie says it is *nice.* You have three nice."

"They're cousins to me, Mama."

"*Nieces* like *pieces,* that's how you say it," Cookie mutters.

"Does this mean Papa's family is alive too?"

"*Porca miseria,* no!" Mama laughs so hard she snorts.

———

Just like that, Cheri's world expanded. She'd always been jealous of kids with big families, like her neighbor Stacey Walthers. Stacey had relatives at every end of the globe. Her house was always brimming with cousins, brothers, and Rottweilers. Cheri's lack of extended family was another thing that set her apart from most of her friends, along with the fact that she didn't look anything like either her mother or her father. Nobody ever told her, "Oh, you have your mother's eyes," or "That's your father's chin." When Cheri got separated from Mama at Saks, a saleslady took care of her while they announced a lost child over the intercom system. When her overdressed mother ran to the sales desk, jewelry a-jangling, the saleslady didn't believe that this grubby little boy belonged to Mama. Incensed, Mama unfurled a wallet full of photographs of her *daughter* and stormed off, gripping Cheri's hand so tightly it hurt.

Cheri was thrilled to learn her family might consist of someone besides her mother and father. But if her father wasn't coming with them, then something was wrong. Did this have to do with the portrait?

That night, her father comes to the door of her room. He rarely gets home before Cheri's bedtime; Mama has told her that he's working on something that will change medicine. "Are you still up?" Cheri sits up in bed holding Bippy—a square patchwork pillow with eyes and a tongue she won at a fair. Mama keeps throwing Bippy in the trash because he is *schifo,* but Cookie always rescues him. She can just make out her father's silhouette in the doorway. "Dad, why aren't you coming to Italy with us?" Her father makes a throat-clearing noise. Not an *ah-hem,* but farther back in the throat, two clearings, one-two. At night, when she can't sleep, she can locate her father by that sound.

"Too much work right now," he says, "get some sleep."

Cheri lies back. "Dad, would you tuck me in?"

He pulls her blanket up under her chin, pats it down awk-wardly. He's never tucked her in before so he doesn't know to pull the sheet tight. She closes her eyes and hears his *ah-hem, ah-hem* going down the hall.

Cheri knows there is more to her father not coming to Italy than work. She overheard him telling Mama, "You're not only a mother, you're a wife. I came first and I should come first." They've had this argument before. When her father wanted to take Mama to the Greek islands, she said no-no-no, they couldn't leave Cheri. Cookie had her own children to take care of and Cici couldn't possibly leave her child with a stranger. Cheri loved staying at Cookie's; she liked playing with baby Choo-Choo and was comfortable in Cookie's little house—practically everything in it came from their house anyway, but it all looked cozier at Cookie's. She wanted to tell them that, say that it was okay, please don't fight. But when her father came out of their bedroom and saw her standing there, he seemed mad so she just looked down at the floor.

Cheri doesn't want her father to be mad at her, but if he came to Italy she knows Mama would be different, more anxious to please, more critical of Cheri. The harder Mama worked on bringing everyone together, the more forced it seemed. The rare times Cheri was alone with her father, it was easier. If Mama was out getting her hair done on the weekend and Cheri heard the Good Humor truck down the street, her father would buy her a chocolate éclair ice cream bar. They'd walk back and she'd give him a bite because it was his favorite when he was a kid. But even then, he never seemed comfortable with Cheri—or with any other kids. He always spoke to them in a loud, formal voice, like they were miniature village idiots. Mama was more fun alone, except that she made Cheri sleep in bed with her. Mama would say, "How about you have the special treat and sleep with Mama tonight, I make the discretion." But Mama's "discretion" often became the rule rather than the exception. Would the relatives make her sleep in the same bed with Mama?

Cheri had a million other questions too. "Will my cousins have black hair like me?" Cheri asked. Mama said, with a touch of pride, that Zia Genny was not so blond. So Cheri imagined her cousins as brunettes, and, as Mama said they probably wouldn't speak English, she studied her Italian/English dictionary extra hard. Mama used to speak to Cheri in Italian all the time. Then one day, she stopped. Cheri asked why and Mama said, "Your father no like it. It makes him feel bad that we speak and he cannot understand. We speak, just not in front of him. *Sì, cara?*"

<hr />

Cheri's first thought when she sees her cousins standing behind the security gate at the Milan airport is: *Normal.* Zia Genny and her three older cousins Maria, Donatella, and Lucia are groomed and polite and have mousy brown hair. They try not to stare at Cheri's mismatched eyes, but she catches Lucia checking her out. They have presents—a book of Italian fairy tales and a box of chocolate drops—but nobody squeals, "Oh my, look at you," like she'd seen with other families. Zia Genny resembles a greyhound; she is thin with close-cropped gray hair and a taut, alert air. She kisses Mama on both cheeks and then Mama drops her suitcase and holds Zia Genny's hands. They both start crying.

In the car, the sisters talk like Zia Genny drives: speeding ahead and then stopping suddenly. They slip back and forth between Italian and English. Between the luggage and the number of people in Zia Genny's matchbox of a car, Cheri winds up in Donatella's lap. Nobody talks except for Mama and Zia Genny. Zia Genny asks what happened to Mama's tongue, she sounds like a foreigner. "Screw yourself," Mama says.

"Screw yourself twice, in the ass," Zia Genny says. Cheri is used to Mama cursing but didn't expect it from another grown-up.

Many hours later, Cheri finds herself waking up on a cot in an attic room. She can see the sun setting through a lozenge pane of window. She follows the sound of voices and a piano downstairs to a great room that serves as living room, dining room, and, on one side, a kitchen. Maria is practicing on one of the two baby grand pianos that face each other; her fingers move like spiders across the keys. The walls are filled with oil paintings: portraits, still lifes, hunting scenes, a few of the Virgin Mary and Jesus on the cross, His crown of thorns dripping with blood. The great room has high, wood-beamed ceilings. The tall glass windows look out on snowcapped mountains that soar up from a vast, deep blue lake. Something pungent and garlicky is bubbling on the stove. Zia Genny holds a large rabbit by its ears and skins it with a knife in long, scraping movements. When Cici sees Cheri at the foot of the stairs she leaps in front of Zia Genny, as if to block her daughter's view of something indecent. "How was your *pisolino, cara?*" Cici cries out, too cheerfully. Her cousin looks up from the piano and Cheri is embarrassed. Why does her mother treat her like she is a baby, asking about her nap?

Rabbit, it turns out, is delicious. Cheri eats and eats and then has a stomachache all night. The next day, Zia Genny sends the girls to swim at the lake. Her cousins dip their toes and adjust their bathing suits while whispering things Cheri can't understand about the skinny, tan boys who punch each other in the stomach and scrabble up the rocks to see who can dive from the highest point. Not to be bested by boys, Cheri climbs up to the apex and jumps without hesitation, making a huge splash and getting water up her nose because she forgot to hold it shut. The cousins seemed unimpressed and she is pretty sure they are now talking about her because when she returns to where they are sitting, they all shut up.

Maria is eleven and the best bet for a comrade. In mangled English, she asks Cheri if she knows Donny Osmond. Maria provides a second ray of hope when she suggests throwing the knife in their picnic basket against the knot in a tree. Coincidentally, this is one of her favorite games to play with Gusmanov, but when she gets overconfident and proposes that Maria stand in front of the tree to make it more challenging, Donatella announces it's time to go home.

Zia Genny takes Cheri into the library and tells her to wait while she hunts for an Italian grammar book. Cheri peruses the shelves, looking at a few framed photographs of Zia Genny's family and finding one that is clearly Mama and her sisters. Mama looks like a beautiful little doll, not much older than Cheri is now. Behind the girls is a tall, stern man linking arms with a woman wearing a veiled hat and pearls. "Are those my grandparents?" she asks shyly.

Zia Genny walks over and looks at the picture. "This was at Chiesa Brunella. Marco D'Ameri is our stepfather and, yes, this is your *nonna*. She passed three years ago next month. May God rest her soul." Zia Genny crosses herself.

"And Marco D'Ameri?"

Zia Genny waggles her finger. "Do not talk about Marco D'Ameri to your mama. They have not spoken in many years and it is best left that way. *Va bene,* come, let us work on your diction."

Zia Genny's English is better than Mama's, despite her fifteen years in America, and Genny's a more patient teacher. Cheri sits at the butcher block in the kitchen with her dictionary and workbooks while Zia Genny cooks and Mama *uuffs* around them, pointing out that nobody in America speaks other languages or travels, like Europeans, so why bother? Zia Genny ignores Mama and holds forth, especially since Cheri has proved to be not only an eager student but also a mushroom aficionado.

Zia Genny becomes another person when talking about mycology. Wild porcini, she explains, are a national treasure and the finest specimens are hiding right on our hillsides. "They wait, sheathed in darkness, yearning to be wet and moist, to push out from the earth with a firm stem. Oh, the joy—the thrill—to touch their smooth, brown caps. I know all their secret hiding places." Zia Genny grins, leaning into Cheri. She teaches Cheri the biological names of all the local species of fungi, bemoaning the fact that her children don't share her love of the hunt, and she is aghast that Cheri doesn't know Latin. "Your America," she says to Mama.

One night before bed, Lucia grabs Cheri's arm and twists it like a towel. "I give you a warning: you eat the wrong mushroom and your tongue, it will swell up. You will vomit blood. The intestines will come out of all the holes in your body. You will be black and stinking. Then you shrivel like a leaf and die." Apparently, she speaks English.

Soon the days begin to pass in a comfortable routine: scrabbling the rocky hillsides, swimming, fresh sunburn, fresh pasta, and Italian studies. In the evenings, when the other grown-ups are smoking hand-rolled cigarettes and drinking grappa, Zia

Genny plays Chopin and the girls take turns playing Für Elise and tarantellas. Even Mama sings along. Here Mama is fun, even a little funny, not embarrassing like she so often is back at home. Maria tugs on Cheri's hands—come, sing. They are like the Von Trapps; they are a family.

The easy routine that has quickly developed is interrupted on the weekends by the arrival of Zio Ettore, Genny's husband, who works in Varese during the week. *Finally,* Cheri thinks, *a relative with dark hair like mine.* She's never seen a man with so much hair. Not just on his head but in a forest of a beard, sticking out of his dark silk shirt—even on his knuckles. Zio Ettore makes a big fuss over Mama, kissing her cheeks until Mama giggles and says, "Stop, just stop." There is a noticeable change with a man in the house; priorities shift. Mama wears red lipstick, mealtimes are fixed, children lower their voices. The great room smells of cigars and gun oil. Ettore often goes hunting with friends on Saturday and spends most of his time deciding which shot to use in which gun. Zia Genny spends her time cleaning up the black marks his boots made on the floor.

That night Cheri dreams about mushrooms with sharp teeth chasing her through the mountains. She wakes up and looks out the window to try to tell the time; she sees mountain shapes beneath a veil of gray light. Ettore is trudging to his car, carrying guns and supplies. It will be hours before the rest of the house is up, but Cheri feels wide awake and she suddenly remembers the leftover chocolate torte in the pantry.

The stone floor is freezing and Cheri wishes she'd put on socks. She stands in the kitchen eating torte, licking its residue off her fingers. Distracted in her rapture, it takes her several minutes to notice a man standing in the doorway. He has a cap pulled over his eyes, is dressed in forest-colored hunting gear with a wood-barreled shotgun at his side. Cheri freezes. The man comes toward her. He's much older than her uncle or her father and he smells of tobacco, dark and mossy. He looks her over like she is a horse and starts speaking rapidly in Italian. Cheri can't translate quickly enough to know exactly what he is saying but can tell that he was expecting something and she wasn't it. He curses and shrugs. And then he's gone.

Before Cheri can go back upstairs, the man returns with a rucksack and several shotguns. He barks questions at her. She struggles to answer as quickly as she can: "Cheri Matzner. Eight years old. I..." He pulls out some clothes and a pair of muddy boots from the rucksack and thrusts them at her, indicating she should put them on. Then he breaks one of the shotguns noisily and holds it to the light to inspect the condition of the bores. She can now see his face and she recognizes the stern man from the photograph. "Marco D'Ameri?" He grunts.

"*Frette!*" He shakes a box of ammunition and glares at her impatiently. Cheri goes into the bathroom and changes. The clothes are itchy and cut for a boy, but luckily the boots almost fit. She knows her mother wouldn't approve of any of this. Maybe that's why her heart is racing with excitement.

Her grandfather is on the move, guns at his side, two spotted dogs trotting next to him. Cheri runs to catch up, hiking her pants up with one hand. They head to the hillside, away from the bridle path that leads to the lake. The path is dim in the early-morning light; she has to keep looking down at her feet to make sure she doesn't trip and fall. Her grandfather doesn't glance back to see where she is, which makes Cheri wonder if she's misunderstood that he wanted her to follow him. It's hard enough to understand people when they want to be understood. Her grandfather isn't a talker, but he makes himself clear. Like when he stops and she thinks, *Whew, he's waiting for me,* but instead he gives her a gun to carry. It's smaller than his gun. Later, when she knows about such things, she'll realize it was an open-choked 20-gauge shotgun clearly outfitted for a child. She can't believe he is letting her hold it and remembers what Gusmanov taught her about safety. She carries it snugged up against her shoulder like a soldier, hoping that's right.

As they climb higher into the mountains, the air is damp from the lake and smells like firewood. Cheri is thirsty, and the gun is growing heavy and awkward to carry. Her grandfather has a canteen, but he doesn't suggest stopping for a rest. *Buck up,* she tells herself. She doesn't know where she heard that expression but it seems like something this grandfather might say, if he spoke English.

She's lagging farther behind now and no longer catches glimpses of her grandfather or the dogs through the trees, which all look the same. The floor has the same brown needles, the same mossy patches, the same reddish dirt. It's scarily quiet. Cheri breaks into a run, clasping the gun, then stumbles on a rock and falls on her side, *whomp.* Her hip hurts and her eyes burn like she's going to cry, but she needs to get up. She sees a low area ahead that leads to a pond and courses through the shrubs and branches.

Suddenly, her grandfather appears from nowhere, grabs her by the arm, and motions to the dogs, who are behind him. *You wait for the dog! Stupid girl, you scare them.* As if on cue, there's an ominous flapping of wings and she sees birds flocking out of the bushes, gray noisy streaks in the pale sunlight. He has his forefinger against the trigger of his gun, tracking the birds as they swerve and flare and go higher in the air. The dogs are on point, bodies taut. In one fluid motion, the grandfather swings his barrel ahead of the birds' path and squeezes the trigger. *Bam-bam-bam.* It makes her wince. The gun is like an extension of his arm; he doesn't stop swinging as he fires again. *Bam-bam-bam.* Cheri feels as alert as the dogs, her pulse thumping in her temples. A bird falls out of the sky. *"Uccello!"* the grandfather commands. *Bird!* The dogs run into the clearing, their strong hindquarters pumping. They sniff and disappear in the tall grass by the pond and then come racing back. One dog gently deposits a bird at her grandfather's feet. Tan with brown and white mottled feathers, nearly perfect except for a broken wing. It doesn't look like roadkill or like the rabbit Zia Genny was skinning. It looks like the still-life pictures in the great room, with fruit and cheese and a bird with a raspberry patch of blood on its breast. Marco D'Ameri's eyes are dark shields. He praises the dogs and pours water for them from his canteen into his hand.

For the rest of the hunt, Cheri stays close to him, but not too close. It's thrilling to watch the dogs tracking the birds; they cross left and then right, darting through the underbrush on the perimeter of a clearing, sniffing out the birds' hiding spots. When the birds are flushed and airborne, Cheri studies her grandfather's movements. He doesn't aim where the bird is but where it's going to be. How does he figure that out? He stops only once, to drink from his canteen. He sees Cheri eyeing it and thrusts it in her direction. She drinks greedily, but he grabs it back before she can down too much. He caps it and sets off again.

Cheri has lost all track of time. One of the dogs sniffs around a tree, lifts his leg, suddenly reminding Cheri she has to pee. She doesn't want to stop and get left behind. Now her grandfather is turning around and coming toward her. Is he going to yell at her? He takes her gun and snugs the stock tight against her cheek, then positions her right index finger softly on the trigger and points to a bird in the sky. He guides her to do as he did, starting with the gun muzzle behind the bird, catching up to it, then passing it, then pulling the trigger. She lifts her head up but he pushes it down, gesturing that she should keep her head level. They repeat this movement a couple of times, practicing. Then he takes the gun, loads it, and shoves it back at her.

Loaded, the gun feels even heavier. Heart pounding, Cheri crouches in the brush with her grandfather. The dogs are on point and suddenly she hears the thundering beat of wings. She raises her gun quickly and her grandfather holds his hand up—*Wait*—pointing to wait for the birds to get into the air. Everything but her breathing has slowed down. The moment lasts only a second or two, but she distinctly feels the hot sun on her neck, a bead of sweat drip down her face. She blinks. Moving her gun like they did in practice, sighting ahead of the flock. She squeezes the trigger. Nothing has prepared her for the force of the kickback; it knocks her on her heels. "Wow," she says, as she repositions and fires again, "wowza." When they've made their shots, her grandfather gives her a slight nod. *"Uccello!"* he says to the dogs.

Cheri's shoulder throbs from the throwback, and she is breathing like she's run a marathon. One of the dogs has a bird in his mouth, waiting for the command to release. Her grandfather takes the mangled quail from the dog and holds it up so Cheri can see countless buckshot holes dotting its breast. His brow furrows in derision—nobody will be eating this. Cheri wills herself not to show any emotion over the dead creature. She focuses on the fact that she hit a bird on her first shot. She can't wait to tell Gusmanov! They trudge through the woods for a while longer, her grandfather carrying his long string of birds over his shoulder, Cheri tagging along with her one bird banging against her leg.

Cheri's face is flushed as she bursts into the kitchen. Where is everybody? Zio Ettore's car is gone and there's no sign of the women. Cheri wants to shout: Look what I got, come see what I did! The clock on the wall says it is ten fifteen, so they've been gone for hours. Mama is going to be insane with worry. But it doesn't matter. This has been the best day of her life. Her grandfather throws his string of birds on the butcher block; Cheri copies his action. He sets to cleaning his guns, his fingers dexterously working with a cloth and oil. Cheri is filled with pride. Marco D'Ameri is Zeus to her, the most powerful man she's ever met, and she is a member of his family. It doesn't matter that he is her step-grandfather and she doesn't literally share his blood. It doesn't matter if he doesn't love her. She loves him and will always love him.

Mama flings open the kitchen door, holding one of her ruined shoes in her hand. She has clearly been in the woods this morning, frantically searching for Cheri. She assesses the damage inside: dead birds on the kitchen table, shotguns disassembled for cleaning, her daughter's face scratched, hands cut and covered with black powder and blood, Marco D'Ameri calmly oiling his gun. She rushes toward her stepfather like a harpy. "You kick me away like I am dirt!" she cries. "You say if I go to America I can never come back. And now . . . you dare to take my child, without permission . . . with a gun. You could have killed her!" Marco D'Ameri doesn't look up during Mama's tirade. She uses words so bad that Cheri doesn't even have to know what they mean to know she must never repeat them. But it is the look—a narrowing of the eyes, a puffing of the chin like a lizard makes when it's threatened—that makes her mother so fierce. That look would have earned Cheri's respect had it not been directed at the object of her newfound adulation. Mama grabs a bird from the table and holds it up like it's the devil incarnate.

"No, that's mine. I shot that one, don't touch it!" Cheri snatches at the bird but her mother lifts it higher. The dogs are in a frenzy of barking. Mama grabs Cheri by the collar with her empty hand.

"Stop, Mama, let me go."

Marco D'Ameri silently picks up his birds, whistles for his dogs, and walks out the door. He doesn't look back, not even when Mama throws Cheri's quail at him. She misses. The bird thumps on the wall and lands on the floor, its neck twisted at an impossible angle.

"I forbid you to ever speak with that man again. You will not see him, talk to him, nothing, ever. You will not fool with guns—ever! Never again will you go anywhere, *anywhere,* without telling me. Understand?" Mama shakes her violently. "Say you understand. Say it! We will stand here forever until you say 'I understand.'" Cheri fights to free herself.

"I hate you!" Cheri yells. She doesn't see Mama's hand until it has smacked her across the face. She tastes the iron of her own blood and pushes her mother away as hard as she can. She wants to run outside but is badly positioned for an escape. The best she can do is race upstairs and lock herself in the bathroom where, at last, she is finally able to pee. Her shoulder still aches from the recoil of the rifle and her lip is bleeding. The pain is nothing compared to the hatred and confusion she feels. It courses through her body and comes out through her trembling fingertips. Cheri is silent when emissaries from downstairs come knocking, asking if she's okay.

Hours later, the gurgling in Cheri's stomach wakes her up. Judging from how dark it is outside, she's been sleeping on the bathroom floor for quite a while. The last thing she ate was the chocolate torte early that morning and she's starving. On her way downstairs she sees Mama's bags lined up outside her room. The muffled, conspiratorial voices of her cousins are floating from Donatella's bedroom. *Did you see what she was wearing? I heard she had blood all over her face.* Cheri tells herself to keep walking, but she has to know what they are saying. *She was holding a gun. She looks like a boy so he treated her like a boy. Don't you know that in America, women burn their bras?* They speak so quickly it's hard for Cheri to get it all, even with her ear against the door. Like listening for a bad heart, she waits for the skipped beat that confirms a malfunction. *You're a stupid idiot! Open your eyes. Can't you tell she's not one of us?* There is one word they toss back and forth like a ball: *adottata.*

Cheri's stomach drops at the sound of the word. Somehow, she already knows what it's going to mean. It's going to explain why she doesn't look like her parents or her cousins. It's going to explain why she has the funny feeling that she doesn't belong in Montclair, with its fancy china and crystal and silk curtains. It's going to explain why Sol always looks at her like he can't quite figure out where she came from or what she's doing in his family. She races to Zia Genny's library and looks it up in her dog-eared Italian/English dictionary. "Adopted." Given away because your parents didn't want you. *Not one of us.* The only person Cheri knew who was adopted was a Vietnamese girl in her class, Mary Frances O'Leary. On the first day of school, Sister Agnes kept calling her name because she refused to believe it belonged to the girl who was raising her hand. There are not many Vietnamese people in Montclair, and they weren't named

Mary Frances O'Leary. Cheri was the same as Mary Frances? How could Mama have kept this from her?

Cheri hesitates before she goes into the kitchen, feeling like she's got an arrow pointing to her saying exactly why she's the thing that's not like the others. But she's starving. The floor of the kitchen is swept clean of all traces of bird and grandfather. Bread, olives, cheese, and cured pork are set out on the butcher block, and Cheri forgets her manners and grabs at whatever is closest. Mama appears at her side, saying, "Slow down. Here, use a plate, you're making crumbs on the counter." Zia Genny gives her a lemon soda and waves Cici off. "Let the child eat."

"You. You told him we were here."

"Shhhhhhht," Genny says. "How was I to know he would show his face? I could not have known he would take your daughter—"

"Donatella says I'm *adottada*," Cheri blurts. The women fall silent. Then Mama looks up at her sister and hisses, "How dare your Donatella say—" Zia Genny quickly interrupts her. "For the sake of Jesus on the cross, don't put the blame on Donatella; you are the adult, start acting like it for once in your life." "It's true then," Cheri says to Mama, "you aren't my real mother."

"It is true that you did not come from my body," Cici says gently, bending down so she is at Cheri's eye level. "But I love you just as much. I love you even more because I could not have children any other way. Being a mother...it does not come because we have the same blood or the same face. It comes from having your heart live outside your body. That is how I felt from the day your father brought you home to me."

Zia Genny goes upstairs to have words with Donatella. A little later, Donatella comes downstairs and, within earshot of the grown-ups, apologizes to Cheri in loud broken English. Zia

Genny looks sad and tells Cheri that she is sorry that her sister is so bullheaded and insists on leaving tomorrow. "We will have our mushroom hunt another time, yes?"

⁕

Shortly after they get back from Italy, Mama comes home with the family portrait and Gusmanov hangs it above the mantel in the sitting room. It now includes her father, standing stiffly behind the couch, with his arms on either side of Mama. Everyone looks even more awkward. Nobody looks like they go together; how could Mama not have told her the truth? "There, see, we are a happy family," Mama says, giving Cheri one of those big hugs that gets tighter when she tries to pull away. Was it because she was adopted that her father was mad about the painting? She tries to picture her parents going into an orphanage and picking her out, like in *Little Orphan Annie*. Mama clearly told him what happened with Donatella because, about a week after their return, he stops in her room and says, "I know your mother has said this, but I want you to know that you are our daughter and we are your parents. No different than any other family, and don't let anyone tell you otherwise, okay?" *Okay,* she'd nodded.

If something bad happened and Mama wanted to make you feel better she'd say it was a "blessing in the skies." The grown-ups keep telling her nothing has changed, her parents are still her parents, and Mama's family is her family. But something *has* changed. Somewhere out there, she has a real mother and father. They were like the gods and goddesses in her book of Greek myths. They had her pale skin and strange eyes and must have had a very good reason for giving her away. It might just be a matter of time before they come and take her back.

THE BAD SEED

Gluten is the devil. For the past few weeks since his physical, Michael has been seeing a gastroenterologist and is convinced that gluten is what's been wreaking havoc with his digestive system. He's performing an exorcism in their kitchen. Cheri walks in on his sorting and tossing—mostly of her main food groups, carbs and sugar.

"What the hell? This is perfectly good stuff. What's wrong with licorice and ketchup?" Cheri pulls the items from the trash.

"Hidden wheat repositories."

"You've been eating wheat your whole life and now it's suddenly poisoning you?"

"Celiac disease can manifest over time; it's often overlooked or misdiagnosed. Don't start putting stuff back, it needs to be segregated. Can't you see I've got a system going? Everything on the counter goes on the bottom shelf."

"Meaning I get one shelf and the rest is for millet—isn't that for birds? And oatmeal doesn't have wheat, why is that in this pile?"

"It has to be gluten-free oats. Plus, I do all the shopping. I get to organize the food according to what my system can digest."

"You don't even know if you've got this condition. You don't even have a diagnosis."

"I will today," he says.

"You get the test results today?" Cheri knew that Michael had recently had a battery of tests done, but he hadn't offered details and she hadn't probed. "I'll come with you."

"Thanks, but I've got it under control."

"I'm sure you do," she says. "But I'm coming."

Cheri doesn't want to fight; it seems any subject can make one of them start foaming at the mouth. Since she'd thrown down the separation gauntlet the night of her birthday, they've retreated to their own corners, cocooning themselves in avoidance. Her corner is now the den; she's stacked boxes from her office to stake her claim but hasn't unpacked them yet. She tries to distract herself by looking through some late Bronze Age Ugaritic texts, sniffing at a thesis for mourning rituals that traces cutting and tattoos back to ceremonial pagan rites. But all she has are filaments, nothing for a full-fledged book.

It's back-to-school time and, for the first time in her whole academic career, Cheri has no school to go back to. She wakes up with the thump of *I'm late for class* only to realize another long day stretches ahead of her. Still, fall is her favorite season: crisp air, fresh start, new notebooks. The review committee did nothing in the August doldrums but she's heard that they will soon start interviewing students from Richards's class. The thought of her peers questioning her former students about her work is demeaning. Does her entire career really all hinge on the interpretation of her questions about prostitution? Every act of translation is interpretation. How many times did she say that to her students, never anticipating that one of them would turn the idea back on her. Unlike when she was in college, kids like

Richards feel entitled, as if merely showing up means they should get good grades. And the university certainly doesn't dissuade them from that notion.

All she can do is hope that the wheels of the academic gestapo churn faster than those of international consensus for a war in Iraq. It's not exactly a consolation, but progress on the Tell Muqayyar tablets is as stalled as she is. With talk of UN inspectors returning, it's possible that Saddam will acquiesce to Western demands for full transparency of nuclear sites rather than risk war. In a perfect world, the sea would part on both fronts, and they could be able to get into Baghdad. She has the urge to e-mail Peter Martins to ask once again how the photocopying is progressing. Samuelson didn't mention her suspension to anyone at the British Museum, but, in stark contrast to her own wasted summer, Peter has a museum's worth of projects on his desk—ones that aren't bogged down by external events. She gnaws on a pretzel she rescued from an untimely demise and thinks it's time for her luck to change.

The car ride to the doctor is thick with what Cheri and Michael leave unspoken. Cheri relegates herself to duckling status, silently following him into the waiting room and, once the doctor beckons, into his office. She's about to introduce herself since Michael hasn't bothered when the doctor abruptly announces, "It's not what we'd hoped for." Michael's ass hasn't even hit the chair and the doctor barrels on: "Your biopsy results indicate pancreatic cancer." The doctor's mouth is moving and he's talking about early detection, surgical options. Michael holds up his hand. "But what about celiac? All my symptoms."

"Pancreatic cancer is hard to diagnose because the symptoms are so vague; it's often mistaken for something more benign. That's why we did the endoscopy and took a biopsy. Now, if you'll look here, I can show you what we're talking about." Michael is clearly blindsided. All Cheri knows about pancreatic cancer is that it's one of the bad kinds. This is all happening too quickly.

The doctor displays images of Michael's pancreas, then fans out laminated diagrams of the organ and points to the salient features like he's a car salesman.

Cheri stares at the diagram of the pancreas like it's a Rorschach test. "You're positive? No test is one hundred percent accurate, is it?"

"Tissue doesn't lie. You're welcome to get a second opinion, the faster the better. It's imperative to stage the cancer so you can form a treatment plan. I'll refer you to an oncologist at the cancer center here. Likely he'll do a pancreatic-mass CT to assess the tumor for size, location, and involvement of the surrounding organs."

"Fuck me," Michael says. His left eye twitches like it does when he's overtired or lying.

"But we've caught it early. He hasn't been feeling sick for that long. It's in the early stages, right?" Cheri asks, grasping to put this into some kind of perspective.

"That's what we're hoping for, which is why it's important to move quickly and aggressively. This is a very tricky kind of cancer, and we won't know if the tumor is operable until we see if it's contained or if it's spread to other organs."

The doctor's voice sounds like the teacher in the *Peanuts* cartoons, *Wah-wah-wah*. Michael's lost in the fog of news too bad to absorb. "Can you hold on a second?" Cheri fumbles through her purse to get a pen. "Sorry, so sorry." She writes: *Ampulla vedar (sp?) spread to lymph nodes? Exocrine system. After staging determine if ressectable—pancreatoduodenectomy, Whipple procedure. Can't give chances of survival until tumor is staged.* Her handwriting is loopy and her hand is shaking.

"Is this a death sentence?" Michael's hand covers his face. "Is that what I'm looking at?"

"Michael, no, nobody is saying that," Cheri says emphatically. Who is she trying to convince, she wonders. Herself or Michael?

"It's far too early to speculate; there are new treatments and if you're a candidate for surgery and the cancer is contained to the pancreas, it can be successfully eliminated. The oncologist will go over all of this with you." With a loud scrape of his chair, Michael is up and out of the room.

"It's quite common to feel overwhelmed. It's too much information to process all at once. Here's a handbook with treatment options, support groups, et cetera—I'd stay off the Internet, as there's a lot of misinformation and worst-case scenarios. Call Dr. Perry right away. My nurse will give you his card and can help you schedule an appointment. He's very booked up."

"I appreciate that, Dr. . . . I'm sorry, I didn't catch your name."

"Fishman," he says, handing her his card.

"I meant first name."

"You can just call me Dr. Fishman."

Cheri looks at the card. "Thank you, Karl."

If there was one thing Sol had taught Cheri about doctors, it was that you needed to level the playing field. She imagines her father had the same lack of bedside manner as Karl.

When she walks into the waiting room, Michael isn't there. Cheri gets Dr. Perry's card from the nurse. "My husband, did you see him leave? Tall guy, salt-and-pepper hair?"

"Just got here, so no, but he can't have gone far," the receptionist chirps, giving her a big smile. What a job, Cheri thinks. You'd have to be a cheerful idiot to survive.

By the time Cheri reaches the elevator bank, she can feel the edges of panic nibbling at her chest. She has the car keys but Michael might have taken off anyway. He did it once before, after a fight outside a restaurant. She'd driven around for hours trying to find him because he wouldn't answer his cell. She eventually went home and found Michael already there—he'd taken the bus. The thought of him right now taking a bus, surrounded by strangers, makes her throat catch.

Following a full check of the main lobby and the downstairs men's room (she had a janitor go in to call his name—"Michael Shoub, anyone in here named Michael Shoub?"), Cheri races to the parking lot, which now seems nothing short of Kafkaesque. Didn't she just walk past that gray Toyota? She knows she parked on level four, green, so where is the goddamned car? Her hand shakes as she takes an Ativan from her purse and swallows it dry. Cheri briefly wonders how many she has left before Dr. Vega forces her back onto the couch in exchange for a refill. Cheri wanders up and down the aisles, holding out her keys like a divining rod. "Fuck," she says. "Fucking fuck!"

"Where the hell have you been?" Michael suddenly appears, stomping down the middle of a ramp from the level above. "I've been waiting for you for thirty minutes. You insist on driving, you take the keys, but then you never remember where you parked." He turns on his heel and walks back up the ramp. "Green Four. How hard is that? Number-one rule of being the driver, note the signage."

"There's a West Green and an East Green, it wasn't clearly marked."

"It says Four West right here, with a green square. Hello? Now give me the keys." Just because he's scared, does he have to be even more of an asshole?

She hands him the keys. "We're going to get on top of this." She gets in the passenger side of her Jeep. "We'll get other opinions. Chicago has the best cancer facilities in the country, but if we have to go out of state, we'll go out of state."

"Duane's father went to Johns Hopkins, and we know how that turned out." Duane was Michael's accountant. It takes her a moment to remember—his father died of pancreatic cancer. After ratcheting his seat back as far as it can go, Michael struggles with the ignition, turning it on and off. She'd been meaning to fix the starter. "Give it some time," she says, and he lets out an exasperated sigh. He turns it off and then on and then he floors the gas pedal. The engine finally lurches to life.

When they get home, Michael takes his yoga pillow and mat and retreats to his office. An hour later, she goes to check on him. She finds him on the floor in the lotus position. She can tell he's straining to quiet his mind, and his exertion is clearly visible; his T-shirt is damp around the neck, his left eye twitches. When Michael was a kid his mother would tell him, "That's good but imagine how well you'd do if you tried harder?" Cheri can't imagine how hard he's trying now. What can she say to or do for him? She would like to take back the words, the horrible news of today. But she can't take back all of the moments big and small that led to disappointment and hurt until they were so deadlocked that they stood over the dishwasher, panting from anger. She had been slowly acclimating herself to the discomforting but liberating notion of an exit and now their lives were unalterably changed. She would like to bend over, wrap him in her arms, in spite of, because. But even in his newly vulnerable state, Michael seems unapproachable. He moves his neck from side to side, sighs heavily, eyes tightly squeezed shut.

Cheri roams the house like a dog searching for a comfortable spot. Of course she's going online. How could she not? Pancreatic cancer, she learns from her first hit, is Napoleonic. Nasty and short, it invades everything around it. Everywhere she goes, she's hammered with facts and statistics she doesn't want Michael to see. Her finger remains poised to close the browser at the first sound of his footstep. One website comes with a warning: *Some patients may not want to read the following.* Cheri reads it all: thirty thousand deaths per year, average one-year survival rate, only 3.2 percent of patients survive more than five years. She finds a few defeating-the-odds comment threads: a woman who says qigong healed her; a man who claims to have survived through diet and prayer; patients who were told they had three months left and had lived three years. She reads that the chances for five-year survival increase to 30 percent with a surgical procedure called the Whipple.

Cheri's stomach is gurgling. She reads that by the time pancreatic cancer patients are showing symptoms, the disease has already invaded other organs. It could have been lurking for months in silent invasion. She ignored his constant exhaustion, writing it off as laziness and disaffection. Now that she thinks about it, he *had* been complaining about his stomach after meals. She should have paid more attention. The struggle to feed and be fed is a battleground, per the website. "Enjoy your food," Milton the Penguin's wife says as she serves him kippers. How can she be the penguin wife? Hunting she could do, but Michael does the shopping. She hates grocery stores and will wind up getting the wrong things, and he'll say, "What the fuck is that, you know I can't eat that. It will kill me!" Only this time he won't be exaggerating.

Michael is in the den, sitting on the sofa, watching the news. "Do you want anything? Soup? I can order in." When he doesn't respond she says, "Listen, we can't get ahead of ourselves; we'll take it step by step. Make a plan."

"We? This isn't a group activity last I checked."

"I'm obviously not going to say the right thing now. Which is fine. I can't walk in your shoes, but I'm here. For whatever that's worth. You are not alone."

"I need to feel what I'm feeling without you trying to make it better. Can you respect that?"

Cheri had always believed she could do anything she set her mind to; it was a matter of will and perseverance. But she hadn't gone through a major medical crisis with anyone close to her. Sol's death was immediate and unexpected—he had dropped dead in the middle of the street, carrying a Thanksgiving turkey. She stands with the refrigerator door open and feels lost. Is prosciutto still edible after four weeks? Is it milk or water you put in eggs for an omelet? She pulls out what's left of her mother's cured pork and peels off strip after strip, hardened edges and all, chewing mindlessly until nothing is left but the wax paper.

The next days are a muddle of exam rooms, expectations, and fear. Waiting for doctors who assure them they are the best; for Michael to be inserted and extracted from machines; for insurance to preauthorize; for medical records to transfer; for the phone to ring with results. The hospitals feel like airports—transitory places with too many people, bad lighting, overpriced food, and chairs that hurt your back. A place you want to get out of quickly, but it's never that simple. *One in three.* One in three people will develop cancer in their lifetime, but who will be the one? She tries not to stare at the pretty young Asian woman sitting across from her in the waiting room. She's wearing a scarf to cover her baldness. What kind of cancer does she have? Cheri imagines asking her, *So, what are you in for?* As for Michael, he keeps looking like *Who is everyone talking about? I'm not sick. I don't have cancer.* He looks nothing like the gray, gowned ghosts shuffling down corridors trailing IV lines like mutant jellyfish.

Cheri and Michael are two planets traveling in their separate orbits in the same solar system. They intersect briefly, then return to their own paths. Michael meditates. It seems like whenever Cheri walks into his office or their bedroom, he is on the cushion, eyes closed, palms open or sometimes positioned in mudra at his heart. One night she woke up to a loud ripping sound. Michael was tearing his T-shirt so it fell off his chest, saying over and over, "Why, why?" Seeing him literally rend his garments was so painful, so private, she burrowed back under the covers. The ripping sound reverberated in her mind even when he'd calmed down and slid back in bed. As for her, she walks around, saying sometimes out loud but mostly to herself, "He will be the exception, not the rule."

News from the team at the cancer center isn't good. Michael's tumor is inoperable; the cancer has spread to the lymph nodes close to his liver. The lead oncologist, Dr. Perry—Randall, as Cheri insists on calling him—a humorless man with skin that looked parboiled, has assembled a team of experts to make their pitches. Michael is still healthy enough to be given a combination of chemo drugs, and the doctors are debating which protocol to use, weighing side effects from nausea to potential nerve and kidney damage. Cheri sees Michael's aneurysm look and feels his rage coming like a pressure drop.

"Let's just cut to the chase," he barks. "Are we talking a year?"

"Given the stage of the cancer and location, the prognosis is typically six months to a year after chemotherapy. With a clinical trial, maybe more." Dr. Perry moves into a hard sell on a combination of chemotherapy and radiation; the chemo guy holds up a port system for the administration of drugs at home. He pulls a tube out of the fanny pack, demonstrates how it will connect to a port Michael will have in his chest. Suddenly it all feels too real.

"You're not going to point to the exit rows and tell me to put my mask on first? I've got the picture, and no, I won't be trying this one on for size," Michael says, waving away the fanny pack. "I want to think this through—including alternative treatments. I know you guys aren't high on those, maybe because the drug companies don't make money off them, and the drug companies fund your research. It's to your benefit to push what they're selling. Even if it makes people feel even worse than if they did nothing. But you doctors have to do something so people feel like they've tried everything possible."

"That's an extremely cynical viewpoint," Dr. Perry says, "and misinformed. The statistics on chemotherapy clearly show that it does prolong life in many cases."

"I'm aware of the statistics. But unlike a lot of people, I'm not a sheep who will just follow the flock, not unless I believe it's right for me."

Cheri might have been proud of Michael for being true to his stance on Big Pharma if this didn't scare the shit out of her. "Let's just get back to the options. At least hear them out," she says.

When Michael asks questions about nontraditional protocols, Dr. Perry officiously recites statistics to show that enzymes, diet, supplements, and daily coffee enemas do nothing more than act as placebos, sometimes accelerating the course of the disease.

"This cancer is extremely aggressive and we've caught it late. If we don't make an offensive strike with chemo and radiation right now, you won't even get to the six-month mark."

"Other than that, Mrs. Lincoln, did you enjoy the show?" Michael says. "Thank you, gentlemen, and good night." Michael laughs ruefully in their faces. The odds are awfully rigged, but if you're going to fight, Cheri believes, at least have the right weapons.

In the car, Michael buries his head in his hands. They sit in silent deflation, and Michael's shoulders start to shake. "Oh, baby, I'm so sorry," Cheri murmurs, touching his back. He lifts his head up and she's shocked to see he's laughing. A big peal of laughter rises from his belly. "What?" she asks, confused. "What's so funny?"

Michael shakes his head. "I just realized the translator got it wrong. And not just because he's a dentist. It's the punch line to a bad joke, is what it is." Cheri has no idea what he's talking about.

"Let me in on it," she says, "I could use a laugh."

"Oh, man, it's too good. Remember Ramon talking about the grain at your birthday party? We thought it was about you not getting pregnant? The translator had it right the first time; it was *me*. Ramon was talking about the tumor. I'm the one who was pregnant; I have the bad seed."

Over the next few weeks, Michael starts a macrobiotic diet and researches alternative, natural therapies. Because Michael shows no outward evidence that he's dying any faster than anyone else, it would be easy to be lulled into denial. And perhaps denial *is* playing a role in his fuck-Western-medicine attitude. All the more reason for Cheri to be vigilant. Cancer requires an all-out attack, a data blitz. Cheri knows there are alternative weapons out there more potent than macrobiotic diets. She dives into the online swell and finds clinical trials in France, non-FDA-approved experimental drugs from China that could increase life expectancy by a year. Maybe.

The reality is that Michael's bad seed—as he now refers to it—is proliferating quickly and Cheri can't help but read further into the shaman's prediction. Maybe Ramon was seeing not only what was barren in her womb but also what was barren in their marriage. She was planning on leaving Michael. The terrible irony is that his cancer will give her an out she never would have wanted. The world was an unsafe place. She might have fled to the Ivory Tower after what went down with Eddie Norris, lived a life of only everyday risks, but nothing was safe. It makes her want to go out and buy a gun. Having a gun always made her feel safe. Why did she ever agree to give that up? She knows the answer, of course. Michael stuck to his proverbial guns when it came to establishing a ban as a condition for living together.

Everyone has an Internet vice: porn, eBay, dating or gambling sites. Precision firearms made of German steel are her weakness. As Cheri clicks out of her windows on pancreatic cancer research and onto the Heckler and Koch homepage she thinks: *No harm, no foul; I'm just looking.* But now, scrolling through pages of the latest, fully automatic nine-millimeter pistols, she has a primal desire to have and to hold. Thanks to Mayor Daley the only way she can legally have a gun is if she keeps it in one of the few suburbs that hasn't adopted his draconian ban. It's amazing to think that gun ownership was once the biggest issue in her marriage. She shuts it all down. Erases the site from her browser history. She wants to say, *I'll do whatever you want. If you let Michael live I'll never look at a gun site again. I'll give to the starving children, quit smoking, be nicer to my mother, stop thinking about Eddie Norris. Take back the word separation.*

A small miracle does happen. Suddenly the object of Michael's epic procrastination, now definitely titled *Everybody Must Get Stoned,* is declared finished. Seemingly overnight, HMS Bay becomes drug-free; gone is his old apothecary cabinet full of pills, dope samples, and hallucinogens. Jars of foul-smelling roots, herbs, powders, and liquids leave only dust to outline their existence. The documentary left Michael's grasp with little fanfare and an expired distribution deal, but he was decidedly upbeat and set out to gather his crew for a new project. Cheri can barely recognize this new Michael. He is buoyant, purposeful. He is living in the present. Today is a new day.

"The question is, can anyone tell you when you're going to die?" Standing before the five members of his longtime documentary team, Michael is animated, energized, charismatic. "Can a doctor? A psychic? A voodoo priestess? Given that I have a finite but as yet undetermined number of days, I've decided that I want to spend them taking a last stand. A filmic campaign across the U.S. where we uncover every roadside palmist, every neon psychic sign, every fortune-teller at every country fair from Coney Island to New Orleans to Santa Cruz. We'll talk to everyone who claims to have the gift and ask them about death—specifically, my death. It'll be called *The Palmist.*" He passes out T-shirts. A hand with Day-Glo-colored palm lines is on the front and on the back is *Last Stand. Michael Shoub 1945–?*

The team is huddled on the couch and on the frayed armchairs of HMS Bay. They glance up at Bertrand, leaning against Michael's desk, to guide them. He has long been the still center at the eye of Michael's creative hurricane. There's Jane, his production coordinator and assistant, a woman whose entire life has been spent midwifing other people's art. She doesn't even have a cat waiting for her at home. Giaccomo, a chameleon-like director of photography who seems to take on the aesthetic characteristics of whatever subject he's working on. There's Jonah, Michael's former student turned editor, and Papa John, a wiry Cajun soundman who doubles as a composer. "The palm is like the stop sign," Michael continues, "recognizable in any language. It shows up everywhere—in strip malls next to McDonald's, chicken stands in the South, off the highway, next to the rattlesnake museum in Albuquerque or on a beach shack in Venice. Imagine looking past the signs, through the windows with the cheap venetian blinds, into the faces of so-called American mystics. Remember the snake oil salesman in the beginning of *The Wizard of Oz*? Bertrand, you know who I'm talking about, right? Dorothy's on the bike with Toto and she stops to buy an elixir out of his horse-drawn wagon..."

"Yeah, of course, let me see what it will cost to use a clip," Bertrand says.

"You're talking about Professor Marvel; Frank Morgan played him," Jane says, her tiny face peeking out from her mass of gray hair. "They wrote it for W. C. Fields, but he wanted too much money. Morgan also plays the wizard and the horse-of-a-different-color cabdriver."

"Leave it to you, Jane." Michael smiles. "Call it an odyssey or a fool's quest; we're going on the road to find these people. I've started the research, but it'll be all hands on deck on this one—especially as I'm the subject. We'll get a rabbi and a priest saying mortality is in God's hands and we'll show my doctors being certain about their grim timeline. God versus Western science. We start on the East Coast and work our way west. This will be down and dirty, folks. And fast. This is the first and last time we talk about my cancer. I'm still the same stubborn asshole

I've always been. Don't treat me any differently because I sure as hell won't be any easier on you. Worst thing that happens is I pull through and take fucking forever to edit this one as well." Michael's tribe is in his thrall. Cheri is obviously the only one who thinks this is a crazy, morbid idea, the manic effort fueling it being the exact opposite of the attention on treatment that Cheri had been trying to get Michael to pay attention to. "Okay, as for tone, Bertrand, I'd like a landscape kind of like we did in *Disco,* but more Robert Frank."

"Screw Robert Frank. Best thing about *The Americans* is the car. You need a car. Vintage. American. With muscle."

"Get on that," Michael says. "I need interns yesterday; promise them college credit, whatever it takes. Get me visuals: ancient depictions of the lines in hands, art, architecture, where it started, how it spread. Jane: Locations, locations, locations. This will be one hell of a trip and there's no way I can do it without all of you. Is everybody in?"

Cheri observes the faces in the room. The concern and obvious discomfort that flickered across every face this morning is gone, replaced with a contagious excitement. The team would follow Michael almost anywhere. Everyone is in.

"I said it's a good idea," Cheri says cautiously as she sits at the kitchen table, surrounded by pancreatic cancer research, after Michael's troops have gone for the day. Michael is making himself some tea.

"It's a great idea."

"Okay, it's a great idea," she says. "But can we discuss how all this travel will work with your treatment? I'm not giving up on that clinical trial in France with stem cells; it starts at the end of the month. The timing is similar on the other two at Johns Hopkins. We should go over that now so there's still time to get you in." She opens a file and shows him a paper. "Here are the dates." He looks at her and shakes his head.

"I've decided that I'm going to give the natural treatment a chance."

It takes Cheri a moment to absorb the resolve in Michael's voice.

"Have you spoken to your doctors? What does Randall think about this?"

"It's not in his, quote-unquote, wheelhouse. I've already had my metabolic typing done to follow the Gonzalez regimen. The clinic is figuring out which enzymes and supplements I'll need on the road, and they can be freeze-dried and shipped to our various locations, cross-country. Jane can handle the logistics."

"The Gonzalez people don't know what your locations are like. You'll be going to Podunk towns hundreds of miles from a reputable hospital. What happens in an emergency?"

"I'll manage. I am managing quite well so far. I'll be checking in by phone, and Bertrand's setting up a video-call system. I can overnight blood samples as needed. If I need a hospital it will be a hell of a lot better in the U.S. than that pre-morgue waiting room we went to in Chiang Mai."

"But what about your schedule? You're exhausted from a shoot when you're healthy; it takes you weeks to recover. You're not thinking realistically. I know you can fight this, Michael." She clutches his arm. "There are people who have lived years beyond what the doctors told them. The clinical trial in France is extremely promising. Don't you think it's worth a shot?" He looks away, crosses his arms over his chest. When he looks back in her direction, she can see the certainty in his eyes.

"Bottom line: It comes down to how do I want to spend my

time, however little of it I have left. Do I want to fly to France and spend those moments with doctors in a hospital being monitored and observed, feeling like shit from the drugs they give me to combat the disease that's going to kill me anyway? Or doing something I love with people I love?" Cheri cringes inwardly at the implication of what he's just said.

"You're going to the extreme. Some people tolerate chemo better than others. If it were me, I'd do everything and anything—"

"But it's not," he says, cutting her off. "It's not you. You cling to the almighty chemo because anything that's not debilitating and invasive doesn't seem like fighting, and God knows, *you* love a fight! Get up, Michael, put your dukes up and fight; not how you do it, but how I do it." He takes a beat to let his anger dissipate. "And here I was, thinking you had an open mind."

"It's a big decision," she says, straightening her files and closing her laptop. "I thought we'd talk it through."

"We just did." He sighs. "You've made your point. I've looked at all the pamphlets you leave around like bread crumbs. And I appreciate the effort. Do you hear that? I appreciate what you've been doing for me. You may be right. You may be wrong. But this is what I'm doing."

Cheri feels defeat closing in. "You haven't told them everything, have you? Jane, Bertrand, the rest of your crew. They're not prepared for how bad it could be, are they?"

"Bertrand knows. There's no need to concern anyone else with the details."

"On top of everything else he does, Bertrand's now in charge of helping you remember to take hundreds of supplements? Bertrand's going to give you the coffee enemas every few hours?" When Cheri stops to think about it, Bertrand probably would.

Shouldn't this be Cheri's job? Whatever image she conjures up, it's all distressing.

"Jesus, stop fucking worrying, Cheri. I can handle most of the instructions myself. It's not like you to be so—"

"So what?"

"Forget it."

"Finish the sentence, Michael. It's not like me to be so what? Caring? Nice?"

"Fearful." The word sits between them like a fly ball they both called for and both missed.

"Someone has to be the voice of reason," she says quietly, angrily. "Nobody else is, so I guess I'm it."

"You know everyone showed up for me today; no questions, no second-guessing. That felt really good, and feeling good is what's best for me. I can only tell you this is what I need so many times."

Cheri's been the one chopping wood and carrying water, slogging through the minutiae of treatment options, but his crew shows up and suddenly they're the only ones supporting him? There's no way for her to win. She takes a deep breath.

"Taya will have some ideas about psychics," she says, "I'll call her."

"I already reached out to her; she sent me an e-mail."

Since when did Michael have that kind of a relationship with Taya? "So you don't need me for anything," she says, realizing how deeply the words cut her only as she says them aloud.

"What's that supposed to mean? Bertrand's mortgaged his fucking house so we can start shooting while he gets the investors together, and you're worried about being needed?"

"It came out wrong," Cheri mutters.

"What exactly is your fantasy? You and me in that funky little pensione we stayed at in St. Germaine with the duck cassoulet I can't eat anymore and you never had the palate to appreciate? You pushing me around in a wheelchair, wiping my ass when I'm too weak from the chemo to get up from the toilet? Good times. I'm not doing chemo or a clinical trial just so you can tell yourself that you did everything possible."

"It's called having hope," she says bitterly.

Michael's eye twitches and he rubs his face with his hand. "All we have is our ability to get up each morning and choose how we want to live, what we want to experience—good or bad. Without that we're nothing." Michael walks over and rummages in the refrigerator. "It's a fucking dairy in here, three cartons of milk, all expired."

"Bertrand didn't have to mortgage his house," Cheri says quietly. "We can pay him back."

"With Sol's money? Don't even go there."

"It's my money now."

"So you want to use his money—that you wouldn't take for yourself—as what? Absolution? For Sol or for you? Because I'm now a 'good cause'?"

"That's not fair," she says, "that is *not* fair and you know it."

Michael turns away. They've danced around the issue of her trust fund so many times it's exhausting and his voice shows it. "Okay," he says. "Let's not get into the money conversation. Bertrand knows what he's doing. We'll have no trouble rounding up investors. It's fine."

"Here." Cheri walks over to the fridge, reaches in, and hands him the almond milk. "Believe it or not, I'm trying to help. You don't make it easy."

"None of this is easy." Michael takes his tea and almond milk out to his office.

"For the record, it was duck rillettes," she calls after him, "and I loved them." The open fridge hums. She checks the dates on the milk—only one is expired. Should she offer to go with Michael on the road? She's never done that; she had her work and he had his. That's not an issue at the moment, but this Last Stand casts a long shadow. What would she be? Roadie, groupie, handmaiden, wife? As much as she wants to help, Michael would resist it coming from her. She dumps the spoiled milk down the sink and, in an act of defiance, throws the carton in the garbage instead of the recycle bin.

ON THE ROAD AGAIN

In the next days, Michael is a whirlwind of focused activity, energized by his palm-wearing loyalists. Cheri sits in her den/office and listens to the phone ringing and ringing, all on Michael's lines. She lights a cigarette, takes a deep drag, and doesn't bother to get up and blow the smoke out the window. Almost halfway into the quarter she won't be teaching, she's finally unpacked her boxes and made the den a working office. No photocopies have arrived from London, and she's yet to find a book thesis that's compelling enough to make her want to sit down and write. It's pathetic that all that's on her desk is a growing pile of papers that's exclusively on the Richardses' complaint.

She'd been so consumed with Michael's diagnosis that, for a brief moment, she's almost forgotten her righteous indignation over the review board's questions. They've spoken to her students about the in-class discussion the day Richards claimed she tried to kick him out because he was a Catholic. They asked, with what she thought was moral superiority, if it was her practice to query students about their experiences with prostitutes. Did they read her book? Contemporizing ancient subject matter was what she was known for and hers was among the most popular classes in the department. And what did any of this have to do with Richards's claim of religious bias? They asked to see her notes from the past five years, presumably to verify she'd covered this subject before. She'd given them everything. Meanwhile they'd given her no information on how quickly they intended to wrap up their investigation or what their verdict was likely to be. She hadn't told anyone at the university about Michael's diagnosis, although she soon learned that "dealing with family matters" conveniently shut down any well-intentioned, or not-so-well-intentioned, questions from her colleagues about how she'd filled her summer or what was occupying her time now. It was vague enough to suit Cheri, yet it didn't invite further questions. Now that she stops to think about it, what if people think she and Michael are getting a divorce; wouldn't that be ironic?

Cheri tries to rationalize: She's not in exile, she's in research mode. She should get back to the Ugaritic texts instead of staring out the window at the comings and goings of the *Palmist* base camp. If productivity had a scent, it would be wafting out of there. It pierces her tar haze. Damn Jane, that organizational freak of nature has given Cheri no opening to do even the smallest task, like ordering lunch. (Twin Anchors, anyone? Best ribs in Chicago.) And now there's also a young intern with the mile-high legs and lush red ponytail ready to meet Michael's every need.

Twenty minutes later, Cheri gets out of her car, bobbling two trays of Starbucks. She opens the door to Michael's office with her foot. "Jeez, Cheri, think you got enough? Let me help," Michael says, taking a tray.

"I also got you some matcha tea from the health store, it's this cup." She points with her chin then realizes Michael is alone. "Where is everyone?"

"They'll be back in a bit."

The room has been transformed with a galaxy of signs, photographs, and old posters of turbaned swamis, fortune-tellers, mystics, a map of the United States with various routes red-pegged like a Battleship game, a bulletin board spattered with images of tarot, multicolored symbols, and runes. Michael is the center of his universe, standing in his low-slung jeans, his hands in his pockets. Scrub-bearded, he is a man in charge. This is the man she'd once found irresistible, the man who knew things she didn't, the cynical rascal who charmed her while she was walking out on his film and made her want to fuck him right then and there. "I have to kiss you," she says, taking his face in her hands. If he resists, it's only for a moment. He's aroused by her sudden hunger; she can feel him pressing into her with a small moan.

"What are you doing? They're on their way back." Michael's got a lopsided smile. They scrabble to find footing, release the appropriate fastenings so that they're both depantsed, his hand under her blouse. "Watch the map," he says. Fuck the map. She's pulling him to the floor and maneuvers herself on top of him the way he likes, with his hands on her hips. She curls her chest toward his and he looks her in the eye. "Oh, baby."

A few thrusts and it's over.

"It's been a while," he says. He holds her and she can feel his body vibrating like a washing machine that's just been turned off. After a minute, he taps her to roll off him. They lie next to each other on the floor and she reaches for his hand, squeezes it. Michael breathes heavily. He's clammy.

"I can't let you go. It's too risky. It just is. Michael, please reconsider."

Michael pulls himself up and puts on his jeans, hands Cheri hers. "We've been over this. Please. Respect what I'm doing here."

Okay. Cheri nods. Okay. "I'd come with you," she says. "If you needed—or wanted—me to, I'd be there."

"Sorry, am I interrupting?" It's Bertrand, peering in the door. "I can come back."

"Come on in. Cheri got coffee, you might want to nuke it."

"Yours is cappuccino," Cheri says, discreetly buttoning her blouse.

"Thanks, Cheri," he says, holding up his cup to her. "Are you sure you weren't in the middle of something?"

"No, I'm ready, what have you got?" Michael sits at his desk and starts tapping his computer's keyboard. Bertrand gives Cheri a kindly look and starts unpacking his laptop and thick production notebook. Cheri feels like maybe she should leave. "Hey, you two didn't happen to talk about the car, did you?" Bertrand asks.

"Car, what car?" Cheri says.

"We need a car for the film, and Michael mentioned your mother has a vintage Caddy from the sixties?"

"I keep forgetting to ask you about it," Michael says. "Do you know what year it is?"

"You're talking about Cici's old car in Montclair? She's had it ever since I can remember, I don't know what year."

"I know it's early sixties and it's a classic convertible, at least I remember it that way, with the fins and whitewall tires?" Michael is on his computer, Googling away.

"I bet it's an Eldorado." Bertrand bends over to look at Michael's screen. "Is this it?" He beckons Cheri to look.

"Yeah, I think that's it. I'm surprised you remember it, Michael."

219

"It's in those photographs she has up on that one wall at Eighty-first Street, you know, of you as a kid? I pay more attention than you think. Knowing your mother, it's barely been driven."

"It's been covered in the garage for decades. It probably won't even start. If you want a cool old convertible, why not go with a Tiger or a Vette?"

"Too predictable," Bertrand says, smoothing his beard thoughtfully.

"I like the feel of the Caddy, it's retro and American from when American cars meant something," Michael adds.

"Out of all the cars you could get, you want my mother's car?"

"It's the right creative choice for the film, Cheri," Michael says. "And we don't exactly have unlimited time or money right now." Cheri looks at Bertrand and remembers he's already taken out a second mortgage to accommodate Michael's dream. He's being diplomatic but she can tell he's in favor as well.

"This is Cici we're talking about; she'll ask a million questions. She doesn't know anything about your diagnosis. Are you sure you want to open that can of worms?"

"She won't even notice it's gone. When was the last time she was in Montclair?"

"That's not the point," Cheri says.

"You asked what I needed from you," Michael says.

Cheri was snared. "Of course," she says.

The moment Cheri sees the stately Colonial rising up at the end of the long gravel driveway on Upper Mountain Drive she feels like she's ten years old. She hasn't been back here since after Sol's funeral. It's an elegant house, gracious in its ripening age, with its wraparound porch and rows of Italian cypress trees standing sentinel. The earth smells rich with fall rot; the oak trees have mostly flamed but still burst with yellow in places. Only her mother's beloved lilac bushes have missed the party and are faded brown. Birds. Amazing how she can hear the trills and the whistles in suburbia; it all gets lost in the city. Without even stepping inside, Cheri can picture the layers of Cici's decor: the earth tones, the gilt, the overstuffed armchairs, the antiques from various eras that smell of beeswax and lemon. Even before all of the additions, the house felt too big for just three people, maybe more so because they were always teams of two. *Okay,* Cheri thinks, *let's just get this done quickly.* Michael's traveling road show waits on the street below; his camera truck and van are parked and ready to roll as soon as they've got the Caddy.

Cheri joins Michael in the garage, watching as a white-coated mechanic who specializes in vintage cars revs up the Caddy's engine. Naturally, Jane managed to find an expert within a thirty-mile radius of their target. Michael walks around, looking it over, and then nods at her and grins. She has to admit it looks cherry.

"For a car that hasn't been driven in a decade, it's in pristine condition," the mechanic says. "She's all tuned up and ready."

Michael and Cheri linger awkwardly next to the Cadillac. Michael puts his hands on her shoulders. Sometimes she forgets just how tall he is.

"I'm nervous about this," she says.

"We'll take good care of it. Cici will never know."

"I wasn't talking about the car."

"I know," he says, giving her shoulders a squeeze. "I'll be okay." She wants to hold on to this moment, say, *Stop, go back. Don't move forward because looming there is an even greater good-bye.*

"Okay," she says.

"This house must have been quite the place to grow up in,"

says the red-ponytailed intern trailing behind Bertrand into the garage. "It's too bad we don't have time to see inside..." Cheri and Michael shake their heads simultaneously.

"Thanks, Cheri," Bertrand says, squeezing her protectively. "I'll keep my eye on him," he whispers, then he turns back to Michael. "You ready, O Captain, my captain?"

"I feel great," Michael says, "and this is going to be one hell of a trip." He turns to Cheri; his lips graze hers and they hug. She holds on to him for longer than both of them know is good. He pats her back, saying, "I gotta go now."

Cheri's hand is raised in a brief wave as the Cadillac wends its way down the long driveway then disappears into the oak trees and the skyline. She is filled with a deep longing, the profound sense of missing something she's never really had. It's young and primitive, this fantasy of family; the idea that someone is there for you no matter what. She looks down at the shape of the Cadillac superimposed on the dusty garage floor, like the chalk outline of a dead body. She should get going, but where to? Back to the airport and the specter of her empty house, a career endangered by the word *prostitution*? Or should she go inside this empty house, where memories she'd sought to avoid thrive and whisper to her through dusty curtains, slipcovered furniture, and shuttered windows?

The slanted sunlight coming through the small window makes the dark inside the garage seem darker, and Cheri finds herself feeling along the wall for the light switch. Somewhere in here there's a box with her junior rifle trophies and medals. Gusmanov once asked if he could take a trophy to put on his mantel, and she'd said, "Of course." When she was heading to college he'd helped her pack it all up, along with her first pistol, a Colt 911, and together they placed the box with the other flotsam and jetsam of her childhood way back on a high shelf here in the garage. She peers up at the stacks of boxes; she can barely make out Cookie's misspelled labels: *Baking staff, Cheri's colledge.* The shadows up there are nothing, she realizes, compared to what lurks in her mind. She decides to get a ladder and a flashlight and find whatever it is she's supposed to find.

CHERRY BOMB

Nobody asked Cheri Matzner to the Montclair High School prom and her only truly close friend was Taya Resnick, the socialite daughter of a Wall Street tycoon. It didn't matter to Taya that Cheri didn't look or act like any of her other rich-kid friends. As different as the two girls were, they bonded over absentee fathers, the belief that Dostoyevsky was very fucking funny, chain-smoking, and their burning need to get the hell out of Montclair. They were coconspirators who never got caught.

By twelfth grade, Cheri was a suburban subversive with a nose ring, multiple piercings, ripped clothing, and dyed blue hair she'd buzzed on one side with her father's electric razor. She wore her difference as armor against the cliques, the me-too forces that tugged on her adolescent impulse to find safety in numbers. She was in enough AP classes to qualify as a nerd and had the basketball skills to be a jock. But while Cheri had a foot in every camp, she didn't fit into any one category. Better put, no category could accommodate all of her conflicting parts.

And she was no more comfortable in the community at large. She walked through Montclair with the Talking Heads as her sound track; this wasn't her beautiful life with its beautiful wives kookookachu-ing over their electronic pool covers. She preferred to hang out with the blue-collar crowd, apartment kids who cut school and had jobs pumping gas or at the 7-Eleven. She smoked weed with the kids who got bused in from Plainfield, kids who dropped in and dropped out, kids who shoplifted gum and necklaces from Korvettes. They knew people in jail, runaways, decent garage bands, and which dealers didn't cut their drugs with baby laxatives.

The apartment kids turned Cheri on to uppers. She loved the euphoric, knee-jiggling turbo charge and hyperawareness that, somehow, evened out her frantically active brain. The pills were black and coated (ode to her father) or white with twinkly blue sparkles. In the morning, she'd pop a few black beauties, wash them down with free coffee she got from an apartment kid who worked at McDonald's, and by the time she got to school, she'd be buzzing.

Cheri was like every other teenager who wanted to believe that her struggle was unique, her malaise more desperate, and her soul more misunderstood than anyone before her. No wonder she related to the alienation and rage of punk and new wave music and cranked them up on her Walkman. While Taya dangled her lineage to get into clubs like Studio 54, Cheri was pounding it out in the mosh pits at CBGB's. She loved the East Village's hustling trannies, winos, and glam boys, tatted gangsters, and hard-core punks. She slammed into strangers pogoing at CBGB's while Joey Ramone sang "I Wanna Be Sedated." Years later, when she was a cop, she'd realize just how much danger she'd put herself in during her teenage years, but then she'd felt invincible, pumped up on the wild blue beyond of breaking all the rules.

One day in May as Cheri and Taya lounged on Taya's platform

bed, passing a skull-shaped bong between them while listening to The Doors, the subject of the prom lifted its ugly head. "I don't give a shit about that stupid dance," Taya said. "But to quote your man Jim Morrison, 'This is the end, my beautiful friend.' We can't go out with a whimper. We made it through high school relatively unscathed, and if that doesn't deserve a blowout, I don't know what does."

"What did you have in mind?" Cheri asked.

"How about Atlantic City?" Taya said with a wicked smile.

⸻

It turned out that Atlantic City was a little sad, a lot tarnished, and more crowded than they'd anticipated. But they scored mescaline and quaaludes from some Disco-Suits they met at a casino, so they didn't need arcades or Ferris wheels to see neon-color trails, to see cherries dancing out of the machines and becoming the waitress who brought them Long Island Iced Teas. They crashed by the pool in their clothes and returned home Sunday night with farmer's tans and tattoos they got from a biker named Papa.

"Thanks for taking me to the prom," Cheri said as Taya dropped her off in front of her house. She was expecting to open the door and collapse on an overstuffed couch. Instead she walks into . . . Thanksgiving? It's three o'clock in the afternoon in late May, yet her parents are at the dining-room table eating a very large roasted turkey.

"Thank God!" Her mother jumped up. "We were so worried!"

"Don't get up," her father said, grabbing Cici's arm.

"You're supposed to be in Europe," Cheri said.

"And you're supposed to be at the Resnicks'. But they thought Taya was staying here. We called them to let you know our flight had been canceled and we'd be back home for the night. Imagine everyone's confusion," her father said.

Cheri's stomach clenched; she couldn't believe she was busted.

"Solomon, let her sit and eat. I make the plate."

"Do not get up and serve her," Sol said calmly.

"You no look so good, you skin is all red. What were you doing in the sun, it makes wrinkles. I get some *crème*." Cici stood up.

"Cici, I mean it. Cheri's old enough to lie and steal and be a delinquent, she can damn well make her own plate."

"I didn't steal anything," Cheri said, shrugging her bag up on her shoulder.

"How about Mr. Resnick's car?"

"I no think they stole, only not ask to take it," Cici said, eyeing Cheri's arm. Cheri instinctively pulled her T-shirt down to cover her tattoo.

"Taking without permission is the definition of stealing. Let me handle this, sweetheart."

"So you called the Resnicks? That's great now that you're getting Taya in trouble. If you're going to ground me, can you just do it now? I want to go up and take a nap."

"And we wanted to be on the trip of a lifetime, but we didn't get to do that."

"Can we please be the civilized people and have a family meal?" Cici said to Solomon. "She is home. She could have driven off the road, bleeding from her eyes."

"How long?" Cheri said. "A day? A week?"

"Cheri, you are hurt!" Cici leaped up and grabs her daughter's arm, pushed up her T-shirt sleeve until she's exposed the patch of fresh ink and angry skin. "What did you do to yourself? Solomon, look!"

Before her father was able to clumsily maneuver himself up on his stiff legs, Cheri decided that her best defense was a strong offense. She defiantly rolled up her sleeve to show her cherry-bomb tattoo.

"Add this to my list of offenses."

Cici looked grief-stricken. "How could you? You already make so many holes in your body! This no comes off." Cheri knew this was serious but her reaction was to laugh, which pushes Sol past the breaking point, as she'd known it would.

"What is wrong with you?" he shouted. "Haven't you put your mother through enough? Defacing your body, showing no respect for yourself. You want to do that, you can do it when you're eighteen and supporting yourself. But while you're in our house, living on our money, you will show some respect for *us*, at least."

"A month? It's my final offer..."

"That's it. You're grounded for the whole damn summer: no money, no car, no Taya. And don't look at your mother like she'll save you. I'm sick of your manipulative bullshit."

"Whatever," Cheri said, turning her back to go upstairs.

"Where do you think you're going, missy?" Her father stood up; despite the expensive tailoring of his clothes, his legs looked like tree trunks in slacks. The word *elephantiasis* sprang to her mind, forget *phlebitis* or *gout*.

"You think you'll laugh when you have to pay for your own college?"

"Solomon, no," Cici said, standing in front of him.

"Fuck you and your money."

Sol stood like a soda can that had been shaken and was just

about to be popped open. He let out a sound, not quite a growl but close. Even Cici was silenced. Cheri slammed up the stairs. She was sleep-deprived, hungover; her emotions turned on a dime. She was suddenly overwhelmed with thirst. Going into her bathroom for a glass of water, she was infuriated to see her mother had fluffed—there were now expensive lotions, perfumes, and soaps on every available surface. Cheri hurled everything onto the floor with one sweep of her arm.

"You're going to pay for everything you break." Her father was suddenly by her side in her bathroom. "I'll keep a list."

"You've probably got a list of everything you've ever bought me since I was a baby. Do I get the bill when I move out?"

"You ungrateful..." Sol's hands were pressing into his sides like he was trying to stop himself from using them. "We have done everything for you. Do you think I can't see how you turn your mother against me? You've done it since you were a child and you're still doing it, even when you're old enough to know better."

"Why is it a competition? Why does it have to be a contest with you over who Mom loves more? I'm the child, you're supposed to be the adults! You think I don't see how you look at me? Like you don't want me here? Well, that makes two of us! I can't wait to get out of here. What's most fucked up is that you think I *want* her suffocating me. You're pathetic. A pathetic fucking freak."

He moved toward her surprisingly fast, given the condition of his legs, hand raised. She stumbled back and fell against the toilet, slipped sideways off its smooth surface, and smacked her head against the tub. Seen from this angle, her father looked enormous. She had a pooling feeling in the back of her throat. One of her ears buzzed and a throbbing pain began where she'd hit her head. She squeezed her eyes shut, waiting for the blow to fall. But when she looked back up, her father was gone. Suddenly she was retching into the toilet bowl. The last thing she heard before she falls asleep on the floor was Jim Morrison droning, "This is the end, my only friend, the end." She hates The Doors.

Without Gusmanov, the passion Marco D'Ameri sparked in Cheri might never have flourished. When she got back from Italy and told Gusmanov that she'd gone hunting, he was dismayed that she'd shot at birds without proper training. Gusmanov wouldn't let her fire one of his guns until she could identify all the parts and how they worked, determine the muzzle velocity, clean, assemble, load, and unload. He'd hold up his father's old pocket watch and time her taking the gun apart and putting it back together as he banged and clanged things in the garage to distract her. Then, when he felt she was ready to shoot, he taught her how to use her breath to keep her mind and body focused. He told her not to peek, but she peeked and saw the makeshift firing range he'd created for her at the old junkyard a few miles outside Montclair. He had her make her own targets, drawing circles or spattering paint, and he displayed them like artwork from school, being careful to take them down and hide them in his toolbox at night. When it was apparent that Cheri had talent, Gusmanov came up with the idea of having her don the green Girl Scout uniform because he knew Cici couldn't say no to sashes, pins, and an American Institution. It was the perfect cover for him to take her to shooting lessons at the 4-H and, later, to state junior riflery competitions. Gusmanov said he inherited his aim from his dead Russian mother, who hid from

Nazis in the forest, eating bark and squirrels she killed with a slingshot. "Where did I get *my* aim?" she'd wondered. Certainly not from Sol, who would never approve of Cheri's love of guns and didn't understand why she was always hanging out with "that handyman," as he referred to Gusmanov.

Target practice was her only refuge that summer, stolen under the guise of a project Taya and Cheri were doing for NYU. Just stepping into the 4-H firing range calmed Cheri. Precision shooting wasn't just her sport; it was her sanity. Even before she put on her ears, she tuned out the rest of the world and was fully focused. While Cheri found absolution in her secret sport, she acted as confessor to Taya, whose father was involved in what was soon to become a public scandal instigated by his secretary, who alleged he'd fired her when she broke off their long-term affair. Cheri preferred listening to talking, especially about herself, and never guessed that Taya's drama would cut close to her own father bone.

Cheri packed up her room, vowing to return to Montclair as infrequently as possible. She had two agendas upon entering NYU: to live in the East Village and to lose her virginity. Soon she was juggling a full course load and a bartending gig—making good on her vow to use none of Sol's money beyond the necessary cost of tuition—but it didn't take long to find her first real lover, a bass player who happily relieved Cheri of her burden.

"Well, at least one of us is getting laid," Taya said when Cheri called her from a pay phone at Washington Square Park. Cheri was sharing an apartment on West Twelfth and Sixth with an Israeli graduate student who had a grand piano and a seemingly endless stream of relatives who needed a free place to stay. *Look, here is Tamar's third cousin twice removed and his two friends who just happen to be in the neighborhood at three a.m.*

with their sleeping bags, hummus, and blind dog—no problem, we'll make room for them in the living room. Tamar's early-morning piano practice failed to rouse the crashed backpackers but drove Cheri to the great outdoors.

Washington Square Park became Cheri's de facto study hall/crash pad. It had some of the city's best speed-chess players, including an old Ukrainian man named Yure who reminded her of Gusmanov with his patience (he taught her to play chess) and stories of his war-torn life in the Old Country (in Yure's case, tales of fleeing the Cossacks). Yure gave her the lowdown on who was who in the park and brought her stuffed cabbage his wife made for their restaurant on the Lower East Side.

Cheri rarely saw her parents. NYU was far enough from the Upper East Side that, even if her parents were in the city, she could beg off getting together, citing her course load. And while Cici kept Cheri's room in Montclair exactly as she'd left it, the last thing Cheri wanted was to return to the place she'd spent eighteen years waiting to flee. So it was a great surprise when, toward the end of her freshman year, Cheri saw her father coming out of the library by the park.

"Solomon?" Since their fight, she's taken to calling her father by his first name because it irritates him. He is wearing a dark, pinstriped suit and a bow tie; his rusty gray hair raked across his head looks as if it might spring up at the slightest provocation. "What are you doing here?"

"I was looking for you," he says. "Your mother gave me your schedule. You've got a class in there at ten forty-five, yes?" Since when did his voice lilt like a Canadian's?

"What, you're thinking of auditing? Spending a little father-daughter time?" She lights a cigarette. Sol's nostrils flare in disapproval but he doesn't say anything.

"No to auditing and yes to the other," he says, resisting the urge to wave the smoke out of his face. "I'm a full-time student here. At the law school, right down the street by the gymnasium. Have you checked it out? Great tennis courts and the swimming pool—outstanding."

"Law school," Cheri says with incredulity. "Here at NYU?"

"It certainly disproves the adage you can't teach an old dog new tricks." He laughs uncomfortably. "I'm on an accelerated program. Should be a cakewalk compared to med school. It's not a career change, more like an expansion." Sol's eyes squint in the sun, making him look like a mole.

"And you're telling me all this because . . . ?"

"Because I thought we could spend a little time together. I wanted to tell you personally, and we haven't crossed paths at the house very much lately. Let me take you to lunch," Sol says. "After your class. One o'clock at Cicero's in SoHo?"

"Can't. I have to get to comparative religion. Sorry to ruin your reunited-and-it-feels-so-good moment but I'm late. See you around campus."

"Cheri," Solomon calls as she's walking away. She turns around. "I'd like to believe that it's never too late—or too early—to learn something."

But his overture was too little, too late. The last thing Cheri wanted to do was revisit the fallout of their fight. The idea of seeing her father at school infuriated her. It wasn't as if he needed another degree on his wall. How dare he follow her?

"Why, why, why can't you be nice to your father? Please, he came with the olive branch in his beak," Cici begged when

Cheri finally deigned to answer the phone one day just as she was heading out of the apartment. As Cheri suspected, her mother was behind all of this.

"Right. And if I sent him doves, he'd send them back stuffed with olives and capers and ask you to cook them."

"You are tearing my heart," her mother said.

Cheri finally agrees to let her father take her to lunch. That phrasing bothers her. She feels like she's a briefcase that her father carries into Le Cirque, throws down on the chair next to him. *The briefcase will have the snails.* Actually, he says, "Let's start with some snails for the table." Because the table really enjoys mucus-producing garden pests. Her mother thought her father was manly when he ordered for her. Cheri didn't.

"Well, then," he says after the waiter leaves. "Let's chat."

"About what?"

"Tell me what your life is like. What courses you're taking, other than the prerequisites. How do you like your professors? Who are your friends? Do you have a significant other?"

"Significant other? Who says that in normal conversation? You think you're going to catch me off guard so I'll admit I'm gay?"

"Okay, let the record be amended: Do you have a boyfriend?"

The waiter arrives with their snails and Cheri fixates on the garlic butter pooling in the indentations of the snail tray. The risk factor is at red. Her father has never met a condiment that didn't somehow end up on his face; sauces were also fair game.

"So, where were we?" Sol asks. "You were going to tell me about college life. You found a major yet?"

"I'm thinking about comparative religion. And yes, I have male friends, some of whom I've slept with."

Sol ignores the thrown gauntlet.

"Religion? Where did this interest come from?" A portion of snail butter drips out of the corner of Sol's mouth and dribbles chin-ward.

"Well, not from you guys or that Catholic elementary school you sent me to."

"But what are you expecting to do with a religion major? The job field after graduation has to be pretty narrow."

"Isn't a liberal arts education supposed to be about learning?" Cheri answers emphatically. "If I just wanted a job, I'd go to trade school. Religion is actually one of the broadest fields. It intersects with history, art, language, politics. Wars are always being fought over religion. People are adamant that one is better than the other but they're all kind of saying the same thing."

Sol nods. "Organized religion is just another political system, especially Catholicism. The whole point is to create a hierarchy that is sustainable over centuries and, of course, offer the promise of salvation if you follow A, B, and C. I always found the history of the church surrounding the Council of Nicaea especially interesting."

It's shocking, but Cheri thinks she may actually have something to talk to Sol about. "Since when are you so interested in the Catholic Church? Religion is Cici's thing. It always seemed like she was dragging you along at Christmas and Easter."

"I had to learn about it when I converted," Sol says, looking around for the wine steward. "To marry your mother."

"Converted? From what?"

"My family was Jewish. I thought your mother might have mentioned that."

"Nope," Cheri says, amazed, once again, at the lack of communication in her family. Sol looks relieved to see the wine steward appear; he puts on his reading glasses and makes a to-do over swirling the glass and savoring the taste of an expensive Montrachet. "And you can pour some for my daughter." Cheri had been drinking wine since she was a teenager, but her father acts as if he's bestowing a great favor on her.

"To continuing education," he says, holding up his glass and clinking it against hers. She takes a big sip.

"So why are you really going to NYU? Did you just wake up one day and think, *Man, I've really got to go to law school?*"

"Not at all," he says, stabbing another snail. "You sure you don't want to try one? They're delicious."

"Screw the snails. I'm being serious."

"Screw the snails. That would be a good name for one of your punk bands." Cheri slits her eyes. "It's a joke. Come on, Cheri, I know I'm an old fart but I can still make a joke."

"I answered your questions. You can answer mine." Cheri wonders if he's going to wipe his face before more butter settles into the cleft of his chin.

"My lawyers were costing me a fortune. I figured if you can't beat them, join them. Besides, it's good to have an intellectual challenge and the law school here is excellent." He pauses and sets down his fork. "I also thought I'd see if we might repair things. On neutral ground."

"I'm sure that's what Mom wants you to say. She called me too. But we don't have to play this whole game. We can wave to each other across the street and call it lunch. Tell her whatever you need to tell her. She'll never know the difference."

"But I will. I'll know."

"Sol," she says, because she can't stand it anymore, "you have butter all over your chin."

The father-and-daughter lunches and sometime dinners continued, about once every other month, up until her junior year.

The conversations adhered to well-trod paths: the legal machinations involved with Sol's patents, questions about Cheri's classes, and the occasional jab about her needing to figure out what she wanted to be when she grew up. And while they didn't Kumbaya afterward or take a stroll in Central Park to look at the stars, they found their sweet spot, surprisingly, in world religion. Cheri was passionate about her comparative mythology course and inspired by Joseph Campbell's *Hero with a Thousand Faces.* She even managed to audit a class Campbell taught at Sarah Lawrence that interwove threads from pagan and monotheistic religions, art, literature, and philosophy and introduced her to Sumerian gods and Mesopotamian studies. At first Sol pooh-poohed myth as the study of fairy tales, but Cheri overcame his objection by passionately drawing a circular diagram on the tablecloth (in pen, gasp) illustrating the stages of the hero's journey from his call to adventure through his return. Sol raised an eyebrow, intrigued. *I'm not as stupid as you thought,* Cheri felt like saying.

While Sol liked to hold forth, Cheri managed to have a few decent two-way conversations with him. In the process, Sol revealed surprising things about himself. If anyone was the archetype of the good son, it was Sol. A straitlaced doctor—he was the paragon of success, a Jewish parent's wet dream. He was everything Cheri wasn't. So why did Sol's parents disown him? Sol explained that he was a disappointment to his father because he chose medicine over the family schmatta business. His mother had supported his ambitions, but she was horrified by his marriage to a shiksa, and his conversion was viewed as a complete betrayal. Cheri had had no idea that religion played such a major part in her parents' relationship.

It was starting to dawn on Cheri that there was more to Sol than she had realized. And it seemed like Sol, who had always seemed either repelled by Cheri's tough exterior or totally perplexed by her, was recognizing the same thing about her. Still, they were safest when keeping their conversation strictly in the realm of the intellectual. When they veered outside of that, they were back to being two radically different people thrust into a biologically false role. Then they'd revert to their familiar pattern of anger. Anger was protective, safe. But even though Cheri would never admit it, she liked the attention Sol gave her at these lunches. She claimed that she went only out of obligation to her mother, but a part of her hoped that she'd find a sliver of something that would justify her relationship with Sol. She wasn't quite sure what she'd found, but she started to think she wanted to know more.

OUT, DAMNED FATHER

When it was all over, Taya dubbed 1982 "The Year of the Outed Fathers." Taya's father's sex scandal played out in gossip columns like Page Six and in the tabloid headlines, thanks to her father's wealth and her mother's celebrity as a former movie star. Many hundreds of thousands of dollars and half-truths later, the Resnicks' money and stand-by-your-man solidarity prevailed. The unveiling of Sol Matzner, on the other hand, had Cheri and Taya as the only witnesses.

It was in their junior year, after Taya's twentieth-birthday bash, that Cheri again ran into her father where she least expected him. This time, he was not alone.

Taya rented a gallery in SoHo for the party, and when Cheri has enough of tight leather, clove cigarettes, and angry art, she slips out the side door. It's late September and the Feast of San Gennaro in nearby Little Italy is in full swing. The scents call her like a barker: *Come closer, little girl, have a* zeppola, *some braciole; we won't tell your mother you ate street food with us lowly Italian Americans.* Her mother took her to the festival when she was little, but it was a pale imitation of how things were done in Italy. After years of complaining about the red sauce and bastardization of *la bella lingua,* Cici said *fanculo* to that patron saint of the barbarian southerners.

Cheri hasn't been to the festival in years, but walking under the green, white, and red banners, she's transported back to the loud, we're-one-big-Italian-family party she loved as a kid. What she most vividly remembers is the clown in the dunking machine. Whether you hit the bull's-eye—causing the clown to drop into the water below—or not, you'd get, "Fuck you, you cocksucker motherfucker, I'll yank you so hard I'll pull your balls through your mouth." Cheri was eight years old the first time she encountered the clown. "But I'm a girl," she said as Mama pulled her away from the booth, shouting her own obscenities. "I don't have balls." Cheri loved that clown; he was what being Italian was all about.

As Cheri strolls down Mulberry Street eating *zeppole* out of a paper bag, she glances at the entrance to the Most Precious Blood Church. Men who look like they could be extras in *The Godfather* are gathered outside, smoking cigars by the statue of San Gennaro. And there, behind a lady with her three kids squeezed into a stroller for two, is her father. For a second, Cheri's view is obscured, but then her father reappears with his hand on the shoulder of a blond woman, ushering her through the crowd, up Broome Street. The woman has her mother's stature and her hair length and looks around her age. But on second glance Cheri knows it definitely isn't Cici. This woman is wearing flat shoes and carrying a functional black briefcase like she came here straight from work; she also looks distinctly American. She has a gelato in her hand, and her face is turned to Sol. Before Cheri can move closer, they are swallowed up by the flow of revelers, reduced to dots in a pointillist painting.

It takes Cheri a while to digest what she's seen. Her father has never gone to the Feast of San Gennaro with them, so why was he here today with this woman? There was nothing illicit about their behavior. The woman was probably a business associate. But something about the way her father was shepherding her seemed a little too familiar, bordering on possessive. Cheri dumped the rest of the *zeppole* in a trash can and ducked into the nearest subway station to head home.

What she saw that night gnaws at Cheri over the next few weeks. If their lunches had taught her anything, it was that there was a lot about her father she didn't know. She vows to forget the incident, wall it up like asbestos. But one night, as she heads to the White Horse Tavern to meet Taya for a few beers and a ride home to Jersey for the weekend, she is struck by an insatiable desire to know more. She calls Taya from a pay phone: "Change of plans. Can you pick me up at Mercer between Eighth and Waverly in about twenty minutes? That's eight o'clock real time, not your time." While she waits, she realizes it was a bad idea to cut the fingers off her gloves. Cheri blows on her hands for warmth, then hugs her thrift-store coat closed as she heads down Eighth Street and toward the garage where her father parks his car.

She knows Solomon will be in his evening class, after which, Cici informed her earlier that day, he is staying in the city for the weekend to attend a medical convention. That was why Cici had begged Cheri to come home for one of her rare visits.

Cars honk and swerve to avoid Taya as she pulls up in her purple Camaro and tries to park, almost hitting Cheri in the process.

"I'm going to assume that wasn't on purpose," Cheri says,

plopping into the passenger seat, shutting the door, and holding her icy hands against the hot air vent.

"First: What are we doing here? Second: What are we doing here? And third, I've got pot and there's a pipe around here somewhere, so whatever we're doing, let's get stoned first." There's a boot poking Cheri in the ass, makeup spilling out of the glove compartment, and something that looks like a plumbing part under her seat. "Give it here," Taya says impatiently, then she packs the plumbing part with weed. Cheri stares out of the window. What if Sol walked into the parking lot while she was dealing with the pipe, what if they missed him?

"My grandparents are in Montclair right now expecting me for dinner. I bagged Chandra Beekman's book signing to aid and abet you. You're not getting any of this"—she wiggles the bong—"or going anywhere until you tell me what we're doing."

"There he is!" Cheri says, pointing in the direction of the garage's entrance.

"Who's *he,* the parking guy?"

"My father." Cheri grabs the bong and takes a hit. "He's going to pull out in a big silver Mercedes any second."

"So what do you want to do, follow him?" It takes only a beat for Taya to catch on. "Oh, fuck. Now your dad too?" "I don't know. But I saw him with some blond woman. Walking, not doing anything," Cheri looks out the window again. "It's probably nothing."

"But enough of a something that you want to follow him." Taya takes a hit of weed. "I can't believe our fucking fathers. Mine kept saying it was all a lie, and me, like a dumb idiot, I believed him. I'm sorry, CM. I wish I'd never learned the truth. Maybe you're better off leaving it alone. Call me insensitive, but it's not like you like Sol anyway. Why find more reasons to hate him?"

In the darkness of the car Cheri feels something tugging at her heart. She and Taya always seemed to know where they were going even when they didn't. But in this moment Cheri feels like Dorothy following the yellow brick road. She's in touch with a childlike innocence she didn't know she had—a belief in the union of her parents. Dysfunctional as their threesome had always been, there's never been a doubt that Sol and Cici were devoted to each other. Cheri has lived for so long feeling that she hated Sol, but now it's more complicated to use that word or want to believe he'd give her more reason to use it. Taya chews on a cuticle and mutters, "Fucking fathers."

Just as she takes another hit, Cheri sees the grille of the silver Mercedes poking into the street.

"There he is," Cheri says. "Let's go!" When Taya hesitates, she adds, "Come on. If the situation were reversed, you know I'd do it for you."

"I'm just thinking about you," Taya says with concern, pulling into the street. "Let's just hope it really is nothing."

They almost lose the Mercedes a couple of times as they follow it to the Cross Bronx Expressway. But swerving taxicabs and traffic lights do not deter Taya, who is as intrepid as she is reckless.

The Mercedes takes the Midland Ave. exit and winds its way into the town of Rye. A smattering of snow hits the windshield and melts on contact with the defroster's heat. Rye looks like Montclair or Scarsdale or any other affluent community, with its imposing driveways, stately brick houses, and oak trees that seem to stand up and scream as Taya's headlights swept past them. Cheri cautions her to stay farther behind the Mercedes. "Who can see anything in this weather?" Taya says. "If this snow keeps up, we could get stranded here."

Sol's Mercedes pulls into the circular driveway of 5521 Forest

Drive. The snow is lighter now, and the stone Tudor house looks like something out of an English storybook, with trees and topiaries in large pots lit up with small white lights. "Go behind that van; we don't want him to see us." Cheri motions for Taya to park two houses down.

Sol gets out of his car and walks, briefcase in hand, to the front door of the house. He goes inside as the little white lights on the trees blink on and off, on and off. Did he have keys? Was the door left open for him? It's dark out and the distance between Taya's car and the front door is far enough that Cheri couldn't tell for certain. They sit listening to the hum of the heater and the *flip-flap* of the windshield wipers.

"Maybe it's someone he works with, and your dad is bringing him papers to sign."

Cheri lights a cigarette and cracks her window.

"So now what?" Taya asks.

"I guess we wait. What else can we do? We can't knock on the door." Cheri rubs a spot on the windshield, making a hole like she's ice fishing. Taya reaches into the backseat for more layers of clothing. She wraps a few sweaters around her. "Riding jacket or evening gown, your choice." Cheri rubs the window to keep her spot clear.

"Fine, more insulation for me," Taya says. "Are you hungry? I think I have a Slim Jim in my purse." Cheri finishes her cigarette and rolls the window back up.

"When you say wait, do you mean for a little while? A long while? What if he doesn't come back out? I've got a full tank of gas but we can't keep the car running all night. And if we turn it off, we'll fucking freeze."

"I don't know. It's not like I've done this before," Cheri says. "Let's just see what happens." Cheri doesn't take her eyes off her ice hole. The picture she sees through the patch in the window is like a snow globe after it's shaken and everything is settling into place.

"This calls for getting way sober or way stoned and I'm neither." They light up another bowl to forget the cold, then another. Eventually, the twinkly lights on the house next door flicker, then go dark. The last thing Cheri remembers is looking up at the sky and thinking, *It's like a giant black tongue, capturing the snowflakes.*

With no one to maintain it, Cheri's ice hole closes in on itself.

Certain sounds immediately evoke a sense memory. The rhythmic sound of a shovel scraping the pavement says *Snow day, snow day,* and Cheri's dreaming mind conjures the image of her young self, dressed in her red parka and rubber boots, excited to see the world covered in white. Cheri bolts upright. It's light out. Taya's in the backseat buried beneath clothes and magazines. Cheri reaches over and turns the key in the ignition. She flips on the windshield wipers and the snow is swept aside. There he is, shoveling the driveway of 5521.

Sol wears his pants tucked into boots Cheri has never seen. She's also never seen him hold a shovel or a rake or do anything that Gusmanov could do. But her father is fully engrossed in his task, shoveling with determination Then Cheri notices a young boy, maybe five years old, sitting on the front steps of the house. He's dressed in a snow outfit, the kind that makes a crunchy rustle when you walk, watching Sol intently. When Sol motions to him, he comes running. Sol bends down and puts the boy's hands on the shovel's handle, on top of his; together, they are a great big machine for moving snow. The boy laughs, but his legs wobble and he takes a tumble in the snow. His hat falls off and his hair is a halo of strawberry curls, his little fists are at his eyes. If there had been any doubt in Cheri's mind before, there is none now. It isn't just that the boy has her father's red hair and fair complexion; it's the way he's looking at Sol, lifting his arms: *Pick me up.* Sol sweeps him up immediately. She experiences a frisson of that same primal need. She suddenly remembers falling, finding herself at the bottom of the slide at the park, in her favorite red parka: bright, loud, now dirty. Reaching toward him: *Pick me up, pick me up.* Her father looking at her like a package he doesn't know how to unwrap, then turning away. Cici's arms reaching in.

Sol sets his son down and brushes the snow off him. The blond woman from the Most Sacred Blood Church opens the door, smiling. She waves at them: *Come back inside.*

Cheri has glimpsed an alternate universe, one that apparently exists alongside hers. What would happen if she blinked? Would she be in Montclair, walking in the snow up her driveway to find her mother waiting in the doorway in her bathrobe, her father behind her with a shovel, ready to clear their path?

"Oh, shit," Taya says softly, leaning over Cheri's shoulder, seeing what she's seeing. Taya has raccoon eyes from last night's makeup and a sweater wrapped around her head. She puts her arm softly on Cheri's shoulder. "Let's get out of here," she says.

Cheri doesn't see Sol for weeks after her secret trip to Rye. He is out of town on business; she has exams. It's easy to avoid him until there he is, standing outside her lecture hall, saying, "I'll walk you to your next class," like they're in high school. She isn't prepared for the bile she tastes when she makes eye contact. She imagines him just a few hours ago handing his kid a Superman lunchbox. *Thanks, Dad,* she hears the mop-headed little boy say as he hugs Sol good-bye.

Sol leads her down the crowded hallway, making small talk. "There's another storm coming in; looks like we could get more snow."

"A snow day, how perfect." Cheri can't contain herself. "I saw her. I saw you and your kid playing in the snow."

"What?" Sol stops in his tracks.

Cheri looks at him with contempt. "Forest Drive. Your other life. Which you couldn't even manage to do in another state. You disgust me."

A kid wearing a backpack gives them a look, then brushes past.

Sol is flustered, tries to take her arm. "Let's go somewhere and talk," he says in his best I'm-the-grown-up voice.

"I'm not going anywhere with you."

"There are things you don't know, Cheri. A compendium of things that all affect each other. This is not the place to do this." Sol's tone is becoming defensive, which only angers Cheri further.

"A compendium? A fucking *compendium?* Take your hand off me. I said I'm not going anywhere."

Sol backs off, waits for an arm-in-arm couple to go around them. "I understand how this looks," he says, grasping for a phrase that might calm her down.

"Is that all you care about, appearances? Fuck how it *looks!* How could you do this? To us, to her? You're a fucking lying bigamist. I could have you arrested." She turns to storm off.

"Whoa," he says, grabbing her arm again. "The only woman I'm married to is your mother. And keep your voice down."

"Oh, great. You're only married to one of them. I guess that means you're in the clear!"

"Please," Sol says, relaxing his grip on her arm. "I don't know what you were doing there or what you saw. Were you following me?"

Cheri laughs ruefully. "I don't think you're in any position to be questioning me."

Sol lets out an exasperated sigh. His shoulders slump for a moment, but he quickly returns to his full height and clears his throat. "What do you want me to do here, Cheri? Tell me and I'll do it. I'll tell you the truth."

"You know, the irony is that I thought I was actually getting to know you. Why did you even bother when everything you do is a lie? Does your other family even know about us?" Cheri pauses, trying to grasp all the implications. She hasn't, until just this moment, considered that this little boy is her half brother. "Forget it, I don't want to know." Cheri wrenches her arm out of Sol's grasp and barrels her way outside. Sol is behind her.

"I can understand that." He pants, struggling to keep up.

"You don't understand anything about me and you never have." Cheri halts, lights up a cigarette, watching as her hands shake. "You never liked me. Can we get that out in the open? I was never enough for you. Would it have been different if I were your own flesh and blood? Well, now that's a moot point."

"That's not true. I may not always like how you behave, but you're my daughter. I love you."

"You might love me out of obligation, but you never *liked* me. I know the difference."

"You're wrong," he says adamantly. "You have a right to be angry. But this is not about you—"

"It never is!" Cheri says angrily, exhaling smoke in his face.

"And that's part of the problem! But forget about me. What about Cici? You didn't just do what Taya's dad did, fucking a secretary and then dumping her. Oh no. You've got a whole other wife, a kid. A whole other fucking family!"

"Jesus Christ, I told you she's not my wife." Sol's face is growing red.

"And I suppose he's not your kid?" Cheri knows the little boy is just another victim of her father's lies, but she can't access sympathy for him, or for the blond woman. She can't calculate how many lives he's hurt, but all she cares about in this moment is Cici.

Sol can't look at her. "Cheri, it's not that simple."

"No, it's not." Cheri feels the weight of what is now their shared secret get a bit heavier. Of course it's on her, not Sol, to make the choice about whether to keep it. Cheri looks down at her shaking hands. "As much as I hate you," she says icily, "I'd hate myself more if I ruined Cici's life. Telling her . . . would ruin what she believes is her life. "

Cheri sees Sol's shoulders relax. His obvious relief makes her hate him all the more. She needs to get away from the woody smell of Sol's cologne, his semi-tearing eyes, Washington Square Park. Nowhere could be far enough.

"Just stay away from me. You're not a part of my life anymore."

THE END OF THANKSGIVING

Ever since Sol died on the day before Thanksgiving, both the bird and the holiday were verboten by Cici. It's only three p.m. but Cheri's neighborhood market is jammed like people are getting ready for the Siege of Leningrad and she's thinking, *Wasn't it just Halloween?* There are cardboard cutouts of turkeys everywhere and too many carts for the narrow aisles; it's claustrophobic. This is why she avoids grocery stores. She snags toilet paper and paper towels and heads to the deli, where there's a sign about ordering your holiday birds. But with Michael on the road for *The Palmist,* she'll likely settle for commemorating the holiday with a turkey sandwich.

Her favorite sight when she was a kid was the foil-wrapped bundle Cheri would pull out of the fridge and pick on for days after a holiday. Her fridge is currently a wasteland dotted with old takeout containers. The woman at the head of the line orders a pound of corned beef. Sol loved his corned beef on rye. "If only he'd gone out for a corned beef," her mother had been known to lament.

When Sol died, it had been fifteen years since Cheri had

agreed to keep his secret. Since that day, Cheri had avoided him whenever possible and when—for Cici's sake—she went back to Montclair for obligatory holidays like this one, she kept her sarcasm to a minimum. It was hard enough for her to handle the pretense in her conversations with Cici, but seeing it up close and personal challenged her resolve to stay silent.

Cheri was told that it had been a crisp fall morning. Sol decided to walk to Citronella's to pick up the Thanksgiving turkey. Cici had debated between an eighteen- and a twenty-pounder. It was just the two of them, but Sol liked plenty of leftovers and Joe the butcher had picked out a lovely hen for Cici. Sol was in a wonderful mood; he had a spring in his step because he'd lost a little weight and was getting his tennis game back. Sol had had a mini-stroke three years earlier, after which he had re-prioritized his life. He started eating healthy, exercising daily, and working less. His phlebitis was finally under control; by all accounts, Sol and Cici were enjoying a second wind in their marriage, happily ensconced in their Eighty-first Street apartment. Semiretirement also rejuvenated Sol's humanitarian interests and he volunteered a few hours a week at a free health clinic.

Cici had told him to take Cookie's grocery cart to collect the turkey, but he scoffed; it wasn't right for a man to be seen wheeling a cart down Fifth Avenue. He felt the same way about a man being seen in public walking a small dog. Joe the butcher said he was surprised to see Dr. Matzner that morning, as they'd scheduled the turkey's delivery for later that afternoon. But they joked around and Sol looked in perfect health. "Happy Thanksgiving to you and the missus," Joe remembered saying.

The police report quoted witnesses who said they saw a well-dressed older man carrying a large package on Eighty-first Street suddenly fall to the ground. They thought he'd tripped but on closer observation, they realized he was clawing at his chest, unable to breathe. When the EMS team arrived, the man had lost consciousness, and they quickly packed him in the ambulance. Apparently, a bystander had thought to put the package in with him.

Cheri got a garbled call from Cici saying her father had been hurt carrying a turkey and was in the hospital. Come home immediately. Sol died of sudden cardiac arrest at 3:47 p.m. while Cheri was in seat 23C of a United airbus. During her three and a half years as a police officer, Cheri had often been in the position where she had to tell people a loved one had died. She knew it was important to look them in the eye, keep it brief and neutral. The doctor who told Cici the news no doubt adhered to those rules, but Cici was so distraught she'd needed to be sedated and was sleeping when Cheri checked in on her. The hospital administrator gave Cheri a plastic bag filled with Sol's belongings: clothing, watch, wallet. And then he handed her the sodden turkey, wrapped in once-white paper blotched with pink juice. "Can't you throw it away for us?" Cheri asked. She was told she'd already signed for it; staff could not take personal effects that had been signed for and released, and disposing of raw poultry in the hospital trash was a health hazard. So Cheri carried the dripping turkey out to the street and dropped it in front of the first homeless guy she saw. "Do I look like I have a stove?" he protested.

The images are so vivid, as if it all happened yesterday. Later, Cheri would hear every detail of that day recounted over and over by her mother, and she'd listen and nod and say, "Yes, it's shocking." And it was. Because no matter how she felt about her father, his absence loomed as large as his presence ever had. He was the white space around words.

On the first anniversary of Sol's death, Michael and Cheri flew in from Chicago. Cici prepared a rib roast while Cookie fussed. "Now, don't you be crying into the food, Mz. M., that meat's too expensive to blubber in it. Why you can't make turkey like usual I'll never understand."

"I should eat what killed my husband?"

They ate prime rib and mushroom risotto and Cheri went to Mass with her mother. That was the last Thanksgiving Cici would ever celebrate.

THINGS I HATE ABOUT HER

When Cheri gets home from the grocery store, she logs on to her computer to see if Michael's online. He's not. But Jessica the intern answers his phone. Cheri was used to Jane or Bertrand picking up his calls, but lately, it was always Jessica, with her offhand way of acting like she knew everything about Michael. "He's in a pre-interview, but we should wrap by midnight if you're still up," she says in her cartoon bubbly voice. It was hard to tell how Michael was really doing. He said he was maintaining weight, on track with his regimen. They were on schedule and getting great stuff for the documentary. Cheri knew he'd never admit to anything less, but the last time they video-chatted, his eye was twitching, and she knew the grueling pace on the road had to be taking a toll. Whenever he checked in, it was from another noon-struck little town, a new motel room, always on the move.

She calls to video-chat later. Jessica Rabbit with her red ponytail is on Michael's computer in the van. It's just after midnight and she's whispering. "It was a really long day. He's sleeping." She looks over her shoulder. "Yeah, he's out. Do you want me to wake him?" If Michael's sleeping, what is she doing there?

"I guess not," Cheri says. "Just tell him I was looking for him."

"Will do. You should have seen him today. It's amazing how he gets people to relax and say these incredible things like it was rehearsed. I'm learning so much from him." Jessica leans into the camera. "You know, Cheri, your husband's a genius."

"That's why I married him, Jessica." Cheri closes her computer and feels like a snarky ass. Back when she met Michael, there was always a *Disco, Doughnuts* groupie in the background, a young production assistant who hung on Michael's every word. But there's something about Jessica that gives Cheri pause.

Cheri can't sleep. Fretting over Michael's health, Jessica's devotion, and the infuriating ongoing silence from the university, Cheri gets out of bed and crosses the yard into what's now HMS Base Camp. It smells like Michael is still there: Indian blankets, nag champa, and marijuana. A notecard with *Sit with your fear and find your love* is tacked up above his big computer screen. The last time they were in here together she and Michael had sex on the floor. Maybe he's having sex on other floors with Jessica Rabbit. Longer-lasting sex. He's telling her the story of how he almost died when they ran out of gas in the Ozarks with his crew and didn't have any water or food. How he saved them by urinating in the gas tank to get enough fumes in the carburetor so they just made it to a gas station. He's explaining the Tyndall effect, how to see light in shadows and shadows in light. Cheri loved his black-and-white photography; he'd once taught her to see through the shadows. Is it inevitable that the oxygen runs out in every marriage, each person consuming the other's air until both are left gasping? You pledge allegiance to a united state and with that comes compromises, adjustments, a snip here and a snip there until you are more alone together than apart. Did she think that her suffocated feelings would all disappear because he had cancer? She'd wanted to face it with him, to be united in the battle. But now he's so far away. Spending his remaining time with someone else. A younger someone who doesn't argue with him or make demands or challenge every decision he makes. *And why shouldn't he have that,* she thinks in a rare moment of selflessness. *Doesn't he deserve a few moments of happiness now?*

Cheri had never been tempted to open Michael's diary before. He'd kept a journal for as long as she'd known him. It was on his bedside table or on his desk, never hidden. He has his current journal with him, but at the bottom of his bookshelf there's a stack of black, hardbound books filled with his lefty scrawl. She's sure there's plenty she doesn't want to know in there, but she feels so disconnected from him she's willing to risk that to feel—what? Close to him again? She takes a journal off the shelf and skims through quotidian complaints and confessional thoughts on fear: that he won't finish his film, that he won't make money, that he's getting older. But one sentence jumps out, cries for her to stop: *I want to fall in love again.* Her throat catches. She wasn't even looking for Jessica, she tells herself, but there she is. But it's not about Jessica. It's not about infidelity at all.

It's all about Cheri. Michael's bemoaning their lack of intimacy. Although this is nothing new, seeing it in writing feels like a spotlight is being shone on her failure. She wants to look away. She's about to close the journal when she notices a list at the bottom of the page:

Things I Hate About Her

1. has stopped kissing
2. won't recycle
3. incapable of intimacy
4. Sol's money thrown in my face
5. no maternal instinct—how long to continue the delusion?
6. RM suggests separation—look to rent an office outside of the house

Michael wrote about how he secretly hoped she wouldn't get pregnant, as it would only make separating harder. His words had oceans of glare. There is more, but this is more than enough.

Her mind is churning, restlessly circling back to a sick realization: Michael wanted to leave *her*. Long before she'd brought it up, he'd spoken to his shrink, Robert Meirs—RM—about separation. While she had harbored a belief that they'd either get pregnant or split up, her thoughts were blunt knives rendered harmless by her single-minded focus. The notion that he'd been sitting on this for so long cannonades what was left of her defenses. She tells herself it's high school semantics—who cares who wanted to break up with whom first?—but a crushing sense of abandonment overwhelms her anyway. He wanted to leave her first. He was thinking of leaving her the whole time they were trying to get pregnant. Or rather, *she* was trying. How had she not seen through his patina of acquiescence?

But just as bad was Michael's doubt about her maternal instincts. This echoed her deepest fear: Did she have the ability to nurture, to love unconditionally? Or was something irrevocably wrong with her? Michael couldn't understand what was driving her to such lengths to have a child. Maybe she'd just been trying to prove to herself that she was better than the woman who'd given her away. That she was better than the woman who suffocated her with her love.

Cheri wakes up with the same gnawing sense of dread she'd gone to bed with but a new resolve to regain some control— at least of herself. On one of her pilgrimages to the suburbs to see her fertility doctor she'd noticed signs for Pro-Maxx Sports, Illinois's premier gun store and shooting range, but she'd resisted the temptation to go out of deference to Michael. She drives there now and hands the clerk her firearm owner's identification card. Even after all these years, a gun club feels like home. She says she's looking to demo a few handguns and selects a Kimber, single-action, semiautomatic chambered in .45, an HK P95 9 mm, and a Beretta PX4. "You know your shit," the clerk says admiringly, his dentures clicking like a snapping turtle.

The shooting range has the usual mix of weekend warriors, but once Cheri puts on her hearing protectors and eyewear, everything gets quiet. She tunes in to her breath, focuses on her front sight. She notes every detail of the HK: the weight of the trigger, the crispness of the pull, the softness of the recoil. After her initial bout of self-criticism—she is out of practice—she centers on one moment, and then the next. *Steady the body and the mind, don't anticipate,* she tells herself. *Let it happen.* Soon she's made a tight cluster of bullet holes right in the center of each target, so she increases her distance. The trick is to exert only as much energy as she needs for each shot. Michael had his meditation; she'd forgotten how much this was hers. For the first time since his diagnosis, Cheri feels herself relax.

When she's back at the front desk, the clerk says, "I was going to come get you, we're closing—holiday hours this weekend." She hadn't even looked at her watch and, like her mother, had opted to ignore Thanksgiving. Cheri buys the HK and the Kimber and gives the clerk instructions on how she wants them adjusted. She pays for a year of locker fees. Despite her temptation to conceal and carry, she won't break the law or her promise to Michael. She's already violated his privacy and paid a painful price for it.

When she walks in the door, she's hit by the resounding stillness. In the past, Cheri loved having the house to herself. But now she keeps the news on in her office at all hours—is she turning into a little old lady, watching TV to keep her company? Or just a bad-news junkie? While there are still a few hoops to jump through with UN inspections, an invasion of Iraq is looking imminent. She imagines Samuelson firing off impassioned e-mails to Washington, making a list of sites that need to be protected, warning about the antiquities that could be destroyed in the event of a war. In a normal world where Michael didn't have cancer and there was no Richards, Cheri would have been adding her name to those e-mails.

At least now she has a little something to occupy her mind. The package from Peter Martins finally arrived—the photocopies of the tablet pieces he'd identified, along with his notes "for your edification and eyes only." Two-D representations go only so far; Cheri knows she needs to have and to hold all of the fragments, including the ones in Baghdad, to determine how they fit together before they could be translated. Peter wouldn't attempt a transliteration without the pieces in Baghdad. *And neither should you,* she tells herself as she hunkers down in her den and spreads the copies out on the floor.

Translating a dead language that scholars could approximate only phonetically was the kind of maddeningly complex work that appealed to Cheri's type A personality. Precision. Control. Working with cuneiform put her in the same zone she achieved at the shooting range. There were six hundred signs that the Sumerians used regularly; knowing which code words went with which symbol was the easy part. Even a slight directional change in one character could alter the meaning. Words and sentences would collapse, change, emerge as something different, then disappear again. That was for an assembled tablet. This was a tease, an unsanctioned taste, but it was a welcome distraction, far better than pawing through Ugaritic texts for the umpteenth time.

What are you without your work? She hears Michael in her head and starts to panic; is he okay? Rather than risking getting Jessica on the phone, Cheri calls Bertrand, who goes on about Michael's "indefatigable spirit" but confides that he looks thinner. Bertrand says he's forcing Michael to take naps; they can afford to slow down the pace. It's upsetting that everyone on Michael's crew knows more about what is going on with her husband than she does. They're enclosed in the terrarium of their road show, and whatever's outside of it reanimates only upon their return. She's experienced this on his other shoots, but this time the question he's tracking is about his own life and death. Cheri knows that as long as Michael is on the hunt, he can be the predator and not the prey. She understands it perfectly and knows that she can't really claim to understand how he feels at all.

THE LAMPPOST SURVIVES

It's always nighttime when the voices come prodding. As Cheri's lying in the dark, trying and failing to stop her lazy Susan of a mind from circling back to "Things I Hate About Her," the phone rings. Michael sounds panicked. "Bertrand's daughter was in a car accident. It's bad and she's in the hospital—" Michael's voice is breaking up due to a poor connection. After hanging up and calling back, all Cheri gleans is that Bertrand flew home yesterday as soon as he got the news. Karen is in the ICU at Northwestern Memorial. The last time Cheri saw Karen, she was in their kitchen with Bertrand, proudly showing off her baby bump. Cheri feels ashamed that she'd felt an ugly twinge of envy at the time. When the connection is better, Michael tells her that eight-and-a-half-months-pregnant Karen was driving home from Whole Foods when she swerved to avoid a raccoon in the street and drove smack into a lamppost.

Cheri is haunted by if-onlys. If only Karen had left the house a few minutes later; if the counter man had kept her waiting for just a few seconds longer; if she'd bought an SUV, because who gives a shit about carbon footprints when this can happen? The

lamppost survived. So did Karen, albeit with extensive injuries—
four broken ribs, internal bleeding, and a serious concussion—
but the baby did not.

Michael tells Cheri that a memorial service will be held for
the baby tomorrow afternoon, at the hospital chapel, since Karen
is in no condition to travel yet. He's coming home for the service, arriving at O'Hare in the morning around eleven thirty.
Of course he'll be there for Bertrand at a time like this, though
Cheri can hear in his voice the anxiety over completing the shoot
on schedule. "It's only one night," he says, more for his benefit
than Cheri's. "Let's meet at the chapel."

The death of a baby destroyed the natural order of things; the
parent should always die before the child. Parents should fly on
separate planes so if one goes down in a fiery crash, the children
aren't orphaned.

The next day, as Cheri contemplates what to wear for the
memorial of an infant, she's struck by the irony: when she was
trying to get pregnant, all she saw were pregnant women. Now
that Michael has cancer, she's immersed in grief. After nine
weeks apart, she will spend her first minutes with Michael in the
company of mourners. How many days did he have until his last?
This was the question Michael was trying to face by making this
documentary, but Cheri didn't want to know. Nor did she want
to count how few she was going to be sharing with him. She's
suddenly leveled by the reality of time. How little Michael may
have left; how much of it was wasted these past few years in moments of lost connection.

Cheri picks her most conservative black dress and places one
demure gold hoop through each earlobe despite her profusion
of piercings. At the last minute, thinking of Jessica, she puts on
lipstick. The hospital chapel is filled with Bertrand's family and

friends, some of whom Cheri recognizes from Karen's wedding. The room is like a yoga studio: candlelit, scented with lilies and patchouli, a guitarist to one side playing James Taylor songs. People mill about, sipping herbal tea. "Karen, I'm so sorry for your loss," Cheri says, bending to hug Karen, who is in a wheelchair with a rose-colored scarf wrapped around her hospital gown. Her face has a purplish bruise on one side, and she's clutching a small bouquet of wildflowers.

"Thank you," she says, her eyes blurred with tears. "We're choosing to look at it as a celebration of life." Cheri isn't quite sure how to respond. Bertrand comes up behind her and gives her a hug. It's devoid of his usual papa-bear warmth.

"Michael's plane was delayed; he's in a cab now," he says. "Thank you for being here." Cheri nods and starts to offer her condolences to him, but Bertrand, ever the producer, notices an elderly man with a walker and goes to help him find a seat. It's then that she notices the small white casket on the dais. Cheri is taken aback to see that it's open. People are going up to pay their respects; some put in a flower or a note. Other than for one of her former professors, the only funeral Cheri had ever attended was Sol's. He had wanted a closed casket. As well versed as she was in ancient rituals, she hadn't participated in many modern ones, but she slowly makes her way up to the pulpit. Inside the casket, the baby is perfect; uncreased, pink-hued, seemingly sleeping peacefully. Moon kissed, still blessed. It reminds Cheri of the Victorian photographs of dead infants posed to look as peaceful as cherubim. Those were creepy, but this is just sad. *Where is Michael?* she wonders with a tinge of impatience. Cheri feels slightly self-conscious without him, as well as overdressed. For this "celebration of life," she's one of the few people who chose to wear all black. Cheri takes a seat by the door and drapes her coat on the next chair to save him a spot.

A female minister with a gray bob steps up to the podium, and the musician puts down his guitar.

"Josephine's parents and family wish to express gratitude for her brief presence in this world. Let's take a moment to let in the joy she brought to everyone who anticipated her arrival. Who is to say that this child didn't lead a more impactful life in the few short hours God granted her than most of us do in our entire lives? It is not time that determines the quality of our existence."

Cheri cranes her neck to look for Michael as people stand up and read poems in wavering voices and speak about how moved they were by this little girl's fight. Cheri's underarms dampen and she feels her throat closing like she's swallowed pepper. How many more platitudes does she have to hear? When Michael slips in next to her, her heart drops. His clothes hang on him and he's got the prominent Adam's apple of a very old man. Everything about him seems to have diminished. "Hey, kiddo," he says.

"Hey, you."

"It is hard to comprehend why God would do this," the minister says. Cheri is looking at Michael, trying not to stare. His color is off, way off. "There are no answers, save that each life, no matter how long or briefly lived, is a precious gift. It's not about the amount of time we are here, but how we use it, how we love." She ends her sermon and people nod and close their eyes in silent prayer. Michael's face looks pained, and she doesn't think it's solely because of the occasion. Behind the wear of the road, the exhaustion, there's a searching vulnerability in his expression. Suddenly, what Cheri read in his diary feels utterly irrelevant. Jessica is utterly irrelevant. Cheri wants to leap to her feet and yell,

Life is fucking unfair, people! She can't believe she doesn't have an Ativan on her. The room is close and cloying.

The guitarist plays Joni Mitchell's "Woodstock." Cheri watches Michael make the rounds; he looks like a crane as he stoops to put his hands on Bertrand's shoulders. She'll give him a few more minutes and then she'll insist he come home and get some rest. Is she the only one not feeling the hippie vibe, the magical thinking? Cheri half expects someone to flick a Bic and start swaying. She's had enough. She locates Michael in the crowd and taps him on the shoulder, hoping to steal a moment of privacy. When he turns to her, focusing on her for the first time today, she sees the whites of his eyes are pale yellow. "Michael," she says, her voice betraying her fear. "Michael, something's wrong with your eyes."

She fishes around in her purse for a mirror.

"What's wrong with my eyes?" Michael pulls out his phone and looks into the camera.

"I think you have jaundice."

"Fuck me," he says.

CALL ME ISHMAEL

Disaster! We are robbed; someone stole the car from Montclair. I should call the police, the insurance? Tell me what to do," Cici shouts into the phone. Cheri thinks, *I knew it, I just knew this would happen.*

"Mother," Cheri says, interrupting her free fall of fretting. "Cici! It's not stolen. I know where it is."

"You know? Why you not say something?"

"Michael borrowed it. It's been sitting there for years unused; it's not like you need it, so just calm down." It takes a moment for this to register with Cici.

"Your husband stole my automobile? Why you no tell me?"

"It's not stealing, it's borrowing," Cheri says. "It's safe and you'll get it back, so whatever you do, don't call the police. I'll take care of it."

"He is a wolf in cheap clothing, always so nice to my face. What he uses it for? It is my property and I do not want anybody using it. Where is it, you tell me right *now.*"

"You're overreacting, as always. It's just a car, Mother, he'll return it in perfect condition, please don't worry."

"Who are you to say what is and is not important? You think this is funny? You no tell me where it is, I will tell the police and they will stop him."

"Cici, I can't take this crap right now. You're concerned about a goddamned car and meanwhile Michael's got cancer." Cheri stops herself from saying more. She knew she couldn't put off telling Cici forever but she hadn't planned on breaking the news this way. "It's in his pancreas. Which is bad, and he's not doing well."

"Cancer," Cici says quietly. "Where is this pancreas?"

"It's behind the stomach. I didn't want to tell you and have you worry," Cheri says. She also didn't want to have to answer her mother's endless questions or deal with her fear.

"Why he not get the surgery to remove the cancer like they did for Cookie?"

"It's not in a place where it can be removed. Look, just tell me you won't call the police about the car. Don't screw this up for Michael."

"What? I am in the city doing nothing and you take my property, you no tell me why or that your husband he is sick with the cancer, and I screw up? Why you no tell me? Your father, he would not like that."

"I didn't care what he thought when he was alive, so I certainly don't care what he might have thought now that he's dead. This isn't about you or Sol."

Cheri is angry that she allowed herself to be caught in the crosshairs of her mother's myopia. Cici's helplessness infuriates her and makes her cruel. It doesn't help that Cici's call came on the heels of her learning through a colleague that Samuelson was in Washington presenting a list of locations in Iraq that needed to be protected, number one being the Iraq museum. If she weren't benched, waiting on word from the academic gestapo, she could be adding her voice to the protest, taking part in something meaningful. Her heart feels like it's one of John Paul Whatever Number's squeaky toys, and she doesn't have any more Ativan refills left. She'd called Dr. Vega, who, true to her word, wouldn't give her more Band-Aids without seeing her for another session. Too bad that among Michael's cornucopia of new meds there wasn't anything Cheri could use.

Michael has been in the hospital since the funeral two weeks ago. They'd put a stent in to drain the bile and that had stopped the jaundice, but the cancer has metastasized to his liver. The doctors brought up chemo, but Michael's response was "Appreciate that it's never too late to nuke, but I'm still going to pass." The Gonzalez regimen had gotten him this far—the clinic would continue to adjust his enzymes and supplements—and he was sticking with it. With steadfast resolve, Michael insisted he would do things his way, and finally the doctors had no choice but to discharge him. But as he and Cheri approached their street, he let out a deep groan. "Are you okay? Should I pull over?" Cheri asked. Michael's face was painted with fear and he buried his head in his hands and began to weep. They sat in front of their house for what felt like a long time; she made little circles on his back until he pulled himself together. "Okay, I'm done," he announced. But they both knew a corner had been turned; Michael's homecoming was the beginning of the end.

<hr />

"If you can't go on the road, the road will come to you," Bertrand said, invoking his virile magic. Like Michael, he seemed to deal with his grief by throwing himself back into his work. It was as if he'd clapped his hands and the Oompa-Loompas converted HMS Base Camp into a set. Giaccomo, Michael's cameraman, was suddenly everywhere at once, subjecting every detail of their lives to his lens. His very unobtrusiveness made his work more insidious. Cheri didn't like to be photographed under normal circumstances; it made her self-conscious and provoked the half smile everyone thought was a smirk. Jessica had launched a website for the film and chatted with Michael by phone daily about their social media outreach. But the good news was she'd gone back to wherever she came from, most likely a college out of state.

"You wanted him to be working and not beading." Taya's voice blasted through the phone. "It took cancer to kick his ass into gear and turn him back into the man you fell in love with, that's why you're upset. Listen, go back to that shrink. You need to talk to someone who specializes in this kind of thing. You're *so* not a Jew."

In response to Cheri's silence, Taya continues on: "Cheri. Talk to the shrink. Because, unlike me, who does nothing but obsess and talk about myself all day, you actually have real issues you're dealing with. Hold on a sec, this fucking guy's about to take my parking space. Hey, no—"

Silence confirms they've been cut off. Cheri could have argued that her distrust of shrinks sprang from her being a cop and having to pass psych evaluations, some while amped on amphetamines, rather than from her not being Jewish, but Taya's point was made.

It wasn't as if Cheri shunned all forms of help. She'd had numerous online sorties with pancreatic-cancer support groups where people told one another "I'm praying for you" and swapped stories about how their husbands' testicles swelled up like grapefruits at the end due to a salt imbalance. So that's what they had to look forward to. She'd even gone with Michael to a visualization group for people with cancer at the hospital. She detested consciousness-raising, especially in a herd nobody would volunteer to join, but when Michael wanted to go, she went along.

She sat with Michael in a circle of strangers, eyes closed, imagining their diseased organs to the beat of a therapist's word drum. But instead of visualizing Michael's pancreas, she had an image of him from the first vacation they took together, Michael singing "My Cherie Amour" like Stevie Wonder, his gray chest hair matted with salt, holding a trail of silvery fish in one hand, a Cuban cigar in the other. *"Cherie amour,"* he croons as he sloshes out of the boat and wades to shore with long strides, a pair of local Portuguese fishermen in tow. "We got your breakfast!" He was her Diego Rivera, her Hemingway, her Marc Bolan. The memory made her bone-crushingly sad, but the exercise seemed to cheer Michael, which was the point. "You should try the caregivers' support group," the therapist had said afterward, handing her a flyer. "They have much better snacks."

She thought about calling Dr. Vega again as Taya had suggested. There was something comforting about her silk blouses with the bows at the top and her fernlike plants. Despite her frugality with the scripts, Cheri liked her. They'd have the same conversation about Cheri going on some daily antidepressant with a name like Relieva. The commercials featured people balled up in bed, then suddenly out in a park playing Frisbee with a cute puppy. Why not show a homeless guy sitting in his own feces saying, "Homelessness is no problem since I've been on Relieva"? The last time she'd seen Dr. Vega, she didn't even know about Michael's diagnosis. Even with the Ativan she hadn't been protected from emotional surges and she has to steel herself for what she knows is coming.

———

Dr. Marlene Vega leans forward in her chair. "Why did you come here today, Cheri?"

"Honestly, I need more Ativan."

"I can give you a script but that's not going to resolve anything, and I think you know that. Underneath the anxiety is loss. You've got to grieve; if you don't, it will keep showing up in other ways. There are no shortcuts. The only way to really address what's going on with you is to acknowledge it and talk about it."

Cheri hesitates, contemplating what lurks behind and beneath her usually impenetrable facade. Giving it form makes it more powerful. "I have all of this knowledge," she finally begins. "You want to know about ancient funeral rites—in any culture—I'm all over that. I can talk about death mythically, religiously, contextually. But when it comes down to dealing with it in a real person—my husband—I don't know where to begin."

"Your father died unexpectedly. How did you deal with his death?"

"On a literal level? Great. I identified the body, made the funeral arrangements, coordinated with the executor of his will. My mother was a wreck so I handled everything. Crisis brings out the best in me. What I couldn't figure out was what to do about his other family. I spent years keeping my mouth shut to protect Cici; I didn't want it all to blow up now. How would they even know he died?"

"You didn't tell me the details, only that your parents were happy together at the end. Do you think Sol ended it with the other woman?"

"I didn't know. How would I? After I outed Sol I wanted nothing to do with him or my parents' dysfunction. All I knew was that the last three years of their marriage was a glorious revival. Sol stayed home with Cici and served the Great Unwashed by volunteering at a walk-in clinic. I assumed he'd broken things off with Catherine. That's her name: Catherine Webster. I looked up the title of the house in Rye after Sol died— it was under her name. I thought about writing to her and her son over the years but I never did. Now, I had a real reason to contact them. I even paid to get their e-mail address; I thought it would be less invasive than a phone call. But what could I say? 'Hi, there, I'm your half sibling. I'm sorry to tell you but Sol Matzner just dropped dead carrying a turkey across Eighty-first Street.' Maybe they didn't even know him as Sol Matzner. These are the things you have to think about with someone who led a double life."

"So you didn't contact them."

Cheri flashes on the image of the little boy in his snowsuit reaching his arms up to Sol. "I cut out the *New York Times* obituary, put it in an envelope, but at the last minute, I didn't send it. Maybe if I had been a better person I would have, but I didn't think it was my burden to bear. I looked for them at the funeral. The boy would have been in college. Ironically, he'd have been twenty—the same age I was when I saw Sol shoveling snow that day. I knew I'd recognize him. They didn't come. That's when I felt this deep pit of... I don't know, longing. I'd never wanted to know them," Cheri says, "but suddenly I wished I did."

Dr. Vega gives a consoling nod. "You may have been an adult when you discovered Sol's secret but you were also his child. All children long for a sense of family. However fractured yours was, these people were connected to you. They were the other piece of the puzzle."

"I was really worried that Sol might have mentioned the other family in his will. I wouldn't have cared about the money, but my mother still didn't know anything about them—she's always lived in Ciciworld. She had her fantasy about our family; it was *all* she had. I wanted to protect her."

"And were they in the will?"

"No," Cheri says, remembering her meeting with Sol's attorney, how he chose his words with the discretion of a man used to carrying other men's secrets. "But he took care of them financially, in a separate arrangement, neat and clean so Cici would never find out. But Sol's lawyer clearly knew that *I* knew about the other family because he went out of his way to tell me that Sol had ended his 'other relationship' but had insisted on honoring his obligations. It's not like I wanted to know the details, but I was glad that he'd provided for his child. It wasn't that poor kid's fault that he was born to Sol any more than it was mine that Sol adopted me."

"So Sol provided for his biological son and he didn't provide for you? Only for Cici?"

"No, actually. His will was extremely complicated, but bottom line: Cici got all of his assets—the house, the apartments, the jewelry—but he left me his patents in a separate trust."

"That's interesting," Dr. Vega says noncommittally, "let's get back to that in a minute. You said you'd had a moment of wanting to know Sol's other family. Have you thought about contacting his son? Do you know his name?"

"Thinking about him is like thinking about my biological parents. If I contacted him, then what? I'm not going to get to know him as a sibling. What's the point? I can assure you that his version of Sol—the one I saw shoveling snow that day—would be very different from the version I grew up with. He'd say how loving and supportive a father he was, and I'd be like, Well, not really, kid. And what would that say about me? Plus, he won't know why Sol led a double life any more than I do. Truth is, we see our parents only as our parents—that one particular role—and whatever damage they do in that capacity is permanent."

"That may be true, but you're also suggesting that Sol's biological son would see his father in a purely positive light, as opposed to what you experienced. And that this would say something about you. What would it say?"

There is a long pause. Cheri looks down and takes a deep breath.

"That I wasn't good enough," Cheri says quietly.

"And this other child was?"

"That's what I felt when I found out about him. Jonathan." She rarely even thinks of her half brother by name. Nor does she wonder where he lives or if he's married or whether he has a family of his own. These things would all make him more real.

"But you also said that Sol left you his life's work, his proudest accomplishments. Not just his money, but his patents."

"His lawyer couldn't believe I wasn't thrilled. I'd never have to work again," Cheri says. "But it felt like a payoff for my silence."

"Maybe it was Sol's way of making amends."

"I don't think so. I think he knew it would piss me off."

Dr. Vega raises an eyebrow. "You were talking about how you'd felt as a child. It was very vulnerable. Then you went right to anger about the will. Anger's a lot easier for you, but underneath the anger there's a lot of sadness, the little girl in you who doesn't feel worthy of her father's love. Growing up, you didn't feel safe. You haven't known many safe places where you can be vulnerable, have you?"

There is another long pause. "No, I guess I haven't," Cheri says.

"Dealing with Michael's cancer puts you in a vulnerable place. You're safe here to be in that place."

"What if I don't want to be vulnerable," Cheri says, crossing her arms over her chest, her voice returning to its usual volume. "I feel like a child having a tantrum, but I don't want to deal with this shit. I. Don't."

"Our work is to forgive ourselves first. For all the anger, pain, and disappointment we lug around every day. For not doing enough or being enough. Then forgive others: Michael, Sol, Cici. You know the list. And take responsibility. We create our own reality with our choices in relationships, what we say about ourselves to ourselves."

"I can take responsibility for choosing Michael, but not for Sol. I didn't have a choice there."

"It has no bearing from a psychological standpoint, but you probably know there's a school of Buddhist thought that says we choose our parents before birth."

"It would be very screwed up of me to choose birth parents who gave me up, and then Sol and Cici—a real glutton for punishment," Cheri says with a smirk.

"It could also be a perfect lens through which to view the lessons you've learned, and are learning. We can look at everything we go through without judging it as good or bad but as an opportunity for growth. Our parents all leave us in the end; we start separating from them from the moment we're born. Forgiveness won't change the past, but it can change the future."

"'It is in pardoning that we are pardoned,'" Cheri says. "If only it was as easy as you and Saint Francis make it sound."

⊙⊙⊙

While Michael's engaged with Bertrand and his edits during the day, Cheri retreats into the solitude of her den, noodling with Peter's photocopies. Translating is an occult connection between worlds, a crossed wire that allows her to communicate with a scribe in old Babylonia, a man who, thousands of years ago, pressed his stylus into wet clay. What was he saying? She seems to have found a fragment of a letter that pertains to a funeral in the ancient city of Hebron. Genesis has Abraham born in the Mesopotamian city of Ur and being buried in Hebron. Since the discovery of these tablets eleven years ago, rumors swirled in archaeology circles that they could prove the existence of the biblical patriarch Abraham. The fragment mentions a funeral procession accorded to a man of great stature and respect with his two sons in attendance, though there are no name identifiers. Could this be the kind of evidence that fueled those rumors? The kind of once-in-a-lifetime find every scholar dreams of running across. Of course, it's all wild speculation and conjecture without the pieces of the Tell Muqayyar tablets in Baghdad.

Are you Isaac or Ishmael? It occurs to her that in all her years of posing that question to her students, she'd never applied it to herself. Cheri has always identified with Abraham's outcast son, Ishmael. But her conversation with Dr. Vega about Sol's will has made her rethink her family mythos. She heeded her call to become a cop. Like Ishmael, she couldn't have gone farther afield from her father's kingdom. She would have cast Jonathan as Isaac. She suspected he'd be a doctor, a chip-off-the-old-Sol block in his tennis whites. The Chosen Son. Biological progeny trumps adopted misfit. But then why *did* Sol leave her his patents? Was it atonement? She remembers their lunches when she was in college, how she'd glimpsed who Sol was before he was her father. Sol had also been an Ishmael. He heeded the call to marry Cici and was disinherited, exiled from his tribe. Did he leave her his patents so as not to do to her what his parents had done to him?

It's the afternoon and she hasn't even had breakfast. Is this the soiled linen of working at home? Too much time to think, wearing the same clothes for days, forgetting to do up her belt after going to the bathroom and then thinking, *Why bother?* Soon she'll be that woman at the post office dressed in black jeans and a work shirt, middle-aged with no husband or kids, just parcels to post. She looks out the window and is startled to see Michael at the far end of the lawn. It is sunny but cold, and he's wearing sweats and a wool cap. His arms extend above his head, palms facing each other, fingertips reaching toward the sky. He goes through a series of poses: bending over in a swimmer's stance, leaning on one leg, standing with his hands folded as if in prayer. She's seen him do yoga hundreds of times, has come to think of it as yet another practice that leads to avoidance rather than integration. Yet here he is, alone on a cold winter's day, saluting the sun. He stands in this moment, on this day, in gratitude, humility, in spite of. We are capable of such great acts. We rise up even when our legs are almost too weak to hold us. We claw our way out of darkness and isolation with just the memory of light to guide us. We find ways to practice our faith even when we're hunted because of it. We are all so vulnerable, so close to nothingness, and yet we survive.

It fills her with a reverence for the terrible and beautiful experience of being alive. She closes her eyes and thinks she can see the daisy chain of all beings, trees and wind and sea, sunlight and the reflected light of stars that burned out long ago. She imagines lines like arteries and veins, the spinning helix of DNA forming an infinite superhighway of energy running through her hands and into Michael's and up beyond space. Michael loses his balance and folds himself into the child's pose. Cheri is ashamed of how quickly she goes to judgment. She's ashamed of all the conceptions—right and wrong—she's ever had about this perfectly familiar and yet still unknown man. *Oh, Michael,* she thinks, *I'm sorry.*

MICHAEL

The thesis of *The Palmist* was turning out to be true. Nobody was able to tell Michael when he was going to die. He had proven his doctors wrong and outlived their prediction by three months without chemo or radiation. Whether this was due to the Gonzalez regimen, an act of sheer will, or a fluke of nature was anyone's guess. But it was getting harder and harder to manage his pain—the latest episode landed him in the ICU. A foul hospital patient, Michael was sullen and snapped at the staff. He turned his frustration on Cheri, yelling, "Just get me the fuck out of here." The doctors made it very clear that Michael had only two options: he could stay in the ICU with IV nutrition or go home with hospice care. Michael had already made his medical directives clear and given Cheri power of attorney. As much as it frightened Cheri to leave the safety net of the hospital, she knew she had no choice but to get him the fuck out of there.

Cheri was ill-equipped to be a nurse. As a child she'd fantasized about being a ninja warrior and leading underground revolutions against Orwellian forces. She was physically fearless, but being a nurse required facing very different enemies, the kind Cheri's time as a cop didn't prepare her for. Some people were natural caretakers, fluffing a pillow without disturbing the sick person, never saying things like, "Well, if I'm doing everything wrong, why don't you get someone else to wipe your ass?" But she was flummoxed by Michael's impatience and demands, all of which made her feel incompetent. In the hospital she was always in the way of someone else trying to do his job. She dropped ice chips on Michael's chest and had missed the lesson on how to properly apply a cool compress to the forehead. She wouldn't want somebody as clumsy and clueless taking care of her. So when the option of having a full-time nurse was raised by the hospice administrator "for an extra fee, of course," she said, "Yes, whatever it costs." Michael was right; perhaps she would have been a shitty mother. But at least she could make sure Michael had everything he needed to be comfortable. He had to know she was dipping into her trust fund for all his medical expenses, but he never asked where the money was coming from. Michael's silence on the subject was an undeniable sign of just how bad things were getting.

The nurse, Robyn, came with an electric hospital bed, an emergency kit, and a Japanese husband who was a paramedic and a former chef who worked alongside Robyn in his off-hours. Robyn told Cheri, "I've got five minutes to win your trust. That's an established fact in my line of work. I am here to make Michael comfortable and help him transition with dignity and peace. That means keeping him out of pain and managing his symptoms." She pointed to a small silver cylinder with a black button on top—it looked like the clicker Cheri used to use to move through slides while lecturing at the university. "This pump will deliver medication at higher doses than they give at the hospital; Michael will control how much morphine he gets and when. Now I want to set things up, so show me whatever room he's most comfortable in and we'll get started."

In no time, Michael was set up in his former office, which Cheri now dubbed HMS Sickbay. Cheri knew Michael would want to spend his last days in the place where he was the most creative, surrounded by his movie posters, *The Palmist* art, Indian rugs, *Sit with your fear and find your love* notecard, guitar, and photographs from various decades, including several of Michael and Cheri. With Robyn around and his finger on the morphine joystick, he and Cheri finally slept through the night. Robyn was Mary Poppins and Nurse Jane Fuzzy Wuzzy rolled into one six-foot-tall dreadlocked black woman. She briefed Cheri on the IV lines and the emergency kit filled with drugs to combat nausea, anxiety, fever, and pain, and told her what to expect in Michael's last days. Cheri was well aware that in other centuries people had rituals and customs for dying, written guides to *ars moriendi*. The Sumerians had a checklist of things to do before burying their family members underneath their homes; they had incantations to sing, grave goods and offerings to gather, rituals to perform. All Cheri had to rely on was *A Caregiver's Guide to the Dying Process.* She relished the irony that you would never be able to recall the two largest events of your life: your own birth and death. The descriptions of the most elemental transitions of existence were lost between worlds. There were near-death experiences of going into the light, but those sounded too much like alien abductions for Cheri's taste.

The house was now ensconced in the dome of illness; visitors—the few Michael wanted to see—seemed to automatically lower their voices. Cheri's world revolved around Michael's bod-

ily minutiae while the rest of the world spun on and had larger
life-and-death issues. The war in Iraq was days away.

***

Cheri has stopped waiting to hear from Samuelson about the review board's "findings"; their endless deliberations have dragged
on week after week. She is in the kitchen making herself and
Robyn coffee when her cell buzzes. "I only have a moment. But
I wanted to be the first to tell you." Samuelson's voice is laced
with self-congratulation and muffled by sounds from an airport.
"The review board did not find sufficient merit for discrimination. Your faculty suspension is relieved." Cheri can barely
process the news before Samuelson goes on. "However..." He
pauses, and Cheri waits for the other shoe to drop. "You will
be required to restructure your curricula and have it approved
by the committee before resuming your teaching duties. We obviously don't want further complaints of this nature. A detailed
report is forthcoming." As he is rushing off the phone, Cheri
just manages to ask about what's been done to protect the museum in Baghdad. "We have warned the DOD. I have told them
in no uncertain terms that the museum is the number-one site
they must protect. They have assured us that troops will be placed
throughout the city as soon as it's been secured. The museum
is closed so we aren't likely to get further communication for a
while. I will keep you informed."

This dire assessment takes a moment to sink in. What kills her
the most is the timing: she's been waiting for endless months to
be exonerated and now the tablets are in lockdown, behind the
doors of a closed museum, in a city being bombed and invaded.
But at least she was exonerated; she is not going to lose this career

ignominiously, as she lost the last one. She would have expected to feel not just relief but elation. Of course, her liberation comes with handcuffs. The committee's report would be voluminous, quoting the university's bylaws to justify the censorship they'd inflict on her. She can't begin to think about the implications this has for her future as a professor. No time now to think about the news, good or bad; Michael is at the end of the end. Relief, when it comes, is a whisper.

When Cheri goes into Michael's sickbay, he's sitting up in bed working on number three on Robyn's to-do list: put your affairs in order. "What do you want to do with this?" Robyn holds up a striped cape.

"Bertrand got me that for my birthday a few years ago. It's a Tibetan snow cape. Mark that with a red sticker to give to Bertrand, please." As Robyn puts a red sticker on the cape and sets it aside with a stack of other color-coded possessions they've sorted through that morning, Cheri remembers itemizing their wedding presents the same way. Back then they were deciding what to exchange and what to keep. Some of Michael's friends have already made their journey to say good-bye, leaving with boxes and wet eyes. Filming for *The Palmist* has concluded, so Giaccomo wrapped his visit by pulling Cheri aside and asking what Michael had done with all his drug samples from the apothecary cabinet. For a moment, Cheri wished she had a few baggies to hand out to Michael's loyal followers. Bertrand was the hardest one to watch make his final descent down the stairs. It made her throat clutch with sadness. "Thank you for taking care of him," she'd said quietly as he leaned on her for support.

"Okay," Cheri says now, turning to Michael. "What's next?"

Ever since Robyn arrived, Michael seemed to be doing better. Cheri had been reluctant to taper off his G-tube feedings, despite Robyn's explanation that Michael's body wasn't absorbing much of the nutrition anyway and stopping the feeding would decrease his bloating and make him more comfortable. But Cheri had done it, and Robyn had been right—the difference was notable.

Today Michael has color in his sunken cheeks, and his eyes look clear. He'd felt rejuvenated enough yesterday to sit at his desk and edit the final footage of *The Palmist*. He moved around his office holding on to chair backs and other objects for support, calling out, "Dead man walking," and he weakly suggested going out for dinner. "Twin Anchors," he said. "Maybe I'd have a bite of ribs just for the taste." Cheri smiled. Until Michael got sick, she hadn't realized how attached she was to the cycle of meals. His inability to ingest pained her.

"I'll go out for my dinner break now and leave you chickens to it," Robyn says. "While everyone's feeling good, this is the time to do number four on the list." Robyn taps her finger four times on the table. Cheri knows this is the number for funeral preparations. Years ago, when death was purely theoretical, they'd jokingly agreed that if either of them ever became more vegetable than meat, the other one would put him or her out to sea on an ice floe. "Careful, there, don't get any ideas about committing senilicide when I'm just plain old," Michael had said.

"Whatever you do, I am not going in Sol's plot." Michael settles his back against pillows and rearranges his IV pole.

"Wait a second. Do you honestly think, even in your wildest imagination, I'd suggest burying you in Sol's plot?" Sol's will provided for a family plot, with spaces reserved for Michael and Cheri; they had laughed at the notion of family members who didn't like one another in life being confined together for eternity.

Michael is about to say something flippant and then stops. "Forget it. I can't get it up to Sol-bash. One thing being a dead man walking teaches you is that none of it matters. The petty bullshit, the squabbles." He dismisses it all with a wave of his hand. "Burial is out. I don't want the whole pomp and circumstance of marble and headstone unveilings. Sign me up for fire."

"Okay. So cremation," Cheri says. "Do you want a rabbi or ceremony or any of that?"

"No service, no funeral. Nobody reading poetry or eulogizing. Throw me a party and screen *The Palmist*. I've gone over my cut with Jonah and Bertrand, so when they say it's ready, go with it. I made a list of the booze and food to serve; play Hendrix, and—it's all written down, along with a list of who to invite. Make it an Irish wake minus 'Danny Boy' and the other maudlin crap. People should get loaded and have a good time." Michael looks up at her. "That means you too, Cheri." Their eyes meet for a long moment. Cheri offers him a sad little salute.

Michael continues: "That's all I want. The instructions are in the yellow file on the desk, along with the name of the place to do the cremation. There is something, though, that I need you to do, to promise me."

"Sure," she says.

"I need you to make sure that my body is really cremated and not dumped in a storage unit. This place has its own crematorium so it's not outsourced. They all claim to be ethical, but who knows what happens when nobody is looking."

Cheri thinks that sounds a bit paranoid but bites her tongue.

Sensing her skepticism, Michael adds, "Remember that cremation scam in Georgia last year? They found bodies in an ex-con's garage, piled up like in the Holocaust."

"How would I check? It's not like I can go in with you."

"You watch," he says, "from behind a window or a partition. They let you if you request it in advance. It's also good for you, by the way. Helps with closure."

"To watch your body go into the furnace?"

"Since when are you squeamish? The door comes down so you don't see the whole crackle-crackle-crackle, pop, pop, pop. Bit of a mess if he's not quite dead." Michael does a fair-to-middling Monty Python impression. Cheri exhales. In theory, this is something she can embrace, but looking at Michael now, propped up in bed, the leap to picturing his trip into the fiery furnace is too disturbing. "You know how they do cremations in Tibet?" he asks.

"I think I know a thing or two about that."

"I don't mean in the ancient past, I mean now, modern day. The villagers put the body in a coffin they've knocked together out of planks they find, no lid; they put the coffin on top of logs in front of their town hall or along the riverbank and light it on fire. Everyone comes and watches. It's part of life, a continuation of the cycle. I'm dying, Cheri. That fact won't go away. It will keep getting your attention in other, bigger ways. Pebble, rock, brick. Anything you keep hidden, anything that you don't face, has power over you. Don't let it."

"I'm confused. Is this about you being worried that your body will end up in some ex-con's garage? Or is this about me not being as—accepting—of all of this as you are?"

"Both," he says, then pauses. "But I need you to know that acceptance is something I struggle with every day. There are times when I'm fucking terrified. Some days you eat the bear, some days the bear eats you."

"I'm sorry," Cheri says, searching for how to define all that she's sorry for. "I want you to know that I'm truly sorry."

"For what?" he asks.

"For not seeing you. For pushing you into the whole baby thing. For everything..." He reaches out and touches her arm.

"It's okay," he says. "I've forgiven you; I've forgiven myself. That was step one. You were right about how angry we'd become. Until you let go of your anger and resentment from the past you won't be able to truly move forward. We're stubborn fucks, you and I. Nothing comes easy. Whatever it is you need to find to live your life, go find it. And while you're at it, give yourself permission to spend *your* money—and not just in an emergency." Michael pauses, eyebrows raised, to make sure she understands. She slowly nods her head.

"Speaking of findings, I heard from the review board," she says. "I'm out of jail." Michael gives an ironic smile.

"Just in time. I'm glad for you. Now you'll be able to go to Iraq."

"If there's an Iraq left to go to," she says.

"But that's not what I was talking about," Michael says.

"I know."

"While I'm thinking of it, I have something for you." Michael points to his desk. "Under that stack to the right of the computer, the big manila envelope. Can you bring it here?" Cheri retrieves the envelope and returns to sitting on the bed next to him. "This is for you. I don't want you to open it until after I go up in flames. You're going to do what you promised, right?"

"I'll do it," she says, knowing however hard it is for her, she will follow through.

"Okay. This envelope isn't time-sensitive, so open it whenever you're in a good place."

Will she ever be in a good place again? He is releasing her. They have traveled such a long distance just to get to this end.

"Got it."

When the moment recedes, Michael says: "If we had a boy, I'd have wanted to name him Hank."

"Hank? You never said you liked Hank."

"He'd turn out to be a baseball player or a musician; either one is good in my book." Michael moves his leg to give her more room. "Is it scary to be this close to me? I'm pretty fucking scared to look at myself. These can't be my bony, veiny legs with the dry skin flaking off like Alligator Man."

"Oh, sure, it's fine for you to laugh," she says and lies down next to him, gently.

"It's okay. You don't have to hold it together anymore. We loved each other. Not always well or in the way the other one wanted, but there was love. There is love." She says, "Oh, Michael—" but he says, "Shhh. I want to lie here like this for a while. Just lie with me like this."

Does he reach to touch her hand or does she reach for his? It just happens. She listens to his breathing and thinks, *You're still you, Michael. Underneath the skin and bone and disease, you're still you.* On one of her support websites she read that one woman made love to her husband even when he was unable to talk or walk or eat. That had seemed far-fetched, but now she understands. She thinks of starting with a kiss, imagines parting his dry lips with her tongue, breaking into his mouth, inhaling the sour chrysanthemum scent of illness. She should be able to touch him, really touch him. What is she afraid of?

"Do you want a blow job?" she says.

"What? Did you just ask if I wanted a blow job?"

"Yup. I'd like to if you'd want it."

"Where did that come from?"

"Since we're in truth-telling mode, I've been contemplating if I should kiss you, if maybe that would startle you. Then I thought that maybe I should do something for you where you don't even have to respond."

"I can't believe the answer to that would ever be no, but...I don't think it's possible. How about a dance instead?" Cheri rolls her eyes. "C'mon, one twirl. Let's lighten the mood." Michael tips the IV pole, making it bow. He slowly gets to his feet. His body is reedy, and his pajamas slip down on his sharp hips. He doesn't notice. It's ignoble, leveling. She feels an inner welling, a sadness forming inside of her she doesn't dare show Michael.

"The tall guy stands! C'mon, just once around."

"You shouldn't," she says.

"Just let me lead. That's the only trick, baby, let the man lead."

His hands are chalky and cold and she's afraid he'll fall over and she won't be able to get him up. Of course they decide to get silly when Robyn's out of the house. Michael sways a little and she steadies him. Her head rests in the snug of his arm, up against his armpit; he is her basketball player, her big galoot, an apparition who is somehow managing a one-two-three, one-two-three with his feet. His head tilts back and he's calm. It's hard to tell from the angle—she's looking up at him, a position she remembers from the early days where they were in a constant embrace—but, yes, Michael is smiling. She holds on to him like he's a flower and she's the press, wanting to preserve him forever.

"I've got to sit down. Dizzy."

Michael tips and Cheri catches him just as the IV pole crashes to the floor.

"I'm coming undone." He paws at the IV catheter in his hand. There's blood in his line.

"Easy does it," she says, guiding him so he's sitting on the bed.

"It's all messed up. My hand..." His voice trails off.

Cheri rights the IV pole, does her best to straighten out the lines. Michael's face is gray, ashy. When is Robyn coming back? It can't take her that long to eat; why isn't she back? Should she call her?

Michael is fiddling with his hand, trying to undo the tape to readjust the line. "I can't get it back in; it's not working, Cheri, it's not working." His eyes are the color of streaked glass. She doesn't trust herself to fix the IV line; she feels inadequate, useless.

"It's okay," she keeps saying until she hears Robyn's reassuring footsteps outside HMS Sickbay. "We need your help!" She means to call calmly but it comes out as a shout.

Soon. Even the word, with its double *o*'s languishing like a hammock, lulls Cheri into expectation. It's the inevitable child's question: When will we be there, are we there yet? *Soon* means "not now. Not yet." Before Cheri realizes it, the end of the end has crept in on tiptoes. Robyn told her that a burst of energy was typical right before the end. It has been two days since their dance. "Promise you will take the envelope," Michael reminds her. "Do it for you, not for me. For you." Then the slim cord that connected him to the here and now retracted, and Michael went dark. He slept most of the time. Once, he thrashed about, clutching the sheets, his mouth gasping, yelling at someone only he could see.

"Troops have landed in Baghdad." Robyn recounts the headlines to Cheri quietly as she sits by Michael's bed. When Cheri's eyelids get too heavy she drifts off, but never for long. Robyn takes breaks to watch the war on the TV in the kitchen. Cheri half hears the sounds of shock and awe like ambient action-movie noise. Is this a sign? An augury?

Michael lies in bed, his hand loosely cradling a stuffed mouse that Cheri found among some old boxes in the garage. Robyn said that the dying often like to hold something from their childhoods and she'd fished this out from one of his boxes. She had no idea whom it had belonged to or if Michael recognized it. Maybe the way it felt or smelled evoked a memory? Is this what happens to all of us in the end—a return to our beginnings? Was he already crossing over, dipping into the other realm, part of his body already in the shade? People were dying every second—in Baghdad, Omaha, Basra, Darfur. Chicago.

Please don't take Michael.

She is waiting, hoping for a reprieve, just one more day, one more hour. The house is outside of time, suspended by Michael's rattling inhale and exhale, the click and hum of his morphine pump, which Cheri now controls. Is he agitated, showing signs of distress? She is an insect caught in the amber of waiting. All there is, is contained in this room, and everything—the musty air, the sunlight slanting through the window, the ratty mouse with its button eyes—is holy. She has promised herself that she will hold his hand until he dies. She will be there in his final moment as his shepherd, his guardian, his witness. She is vigilant, puts her head down on his bed to close her eyes, telling Robyn she's okay, really, not hungry. "You have to let him go," Robyn says, "tell him it's all right for him to pass."

Hearing is the last sense to go. Speak to your loved one with words of comfort, the guide advises. She talks. About everything and nothing. She says, "It's okay, you can go now," even though she's not sure she means it. Soon. She dreams she's saying no, she doesn't want to see the body and it's really a turkey carcass, not a body. It gets up to run away and the men with the black bag are at the door and she's forgotten her slippers. She wakes up confused, having to pee.

It happens when she's in the bathroom. By the time she gets back, Michael's eyes are open but vacant. She's furious at herself for leaving. Exhausted. Relieved. Almost immediately, Robyn begins to take the next steps: She unhooks and rearranges. She tells Cheri she doesn't need to be here for this, but Cheri doesn't move. She feels nothing. When she is alone with what's left—it is clear that Michael does not inhabit this body on the bed—she observes him as if in a dream state. He's someone she once loved, she knows that, but she can't quite recognize him.

The room survives. The objects on his bed stand are exactly as she left them, safe and silent: medications, syringes, a box of blue rubber gloves, and the big white bottle of lotion Robyn used to rub his feet. Nothing has changed. Yet everything is different. The bottle of lotion is perfectly ordinary; she'd never really looked at it before. It's white with blue writing. Baby colors, mashed potatoes, chipped porcelain white plates at Sam and Dave's, half-dirty silverware on plastic blue chintz tablecloths, the white fleece lamb blanket she'd bought when she thought she'd get pregnant. Remarkable. Ordinary.

Cherie holds the bottle, its pump at the ready. She knows what to do. She puts some lotion in her hands, rubs them together to warm it, but not so hard that her skin absorbs it. She moves to the side of the bed and unwraps the tucked-in end of the blanket, then the sheet, to reveal his feet. Sitting at the end of the bed, she gently puts the dry hub of his heel on her lap. She feels as if her heart is in her hands, and, like a stone, she uses it to polish, erase the cracks, smooth. Soon her hands are not her hands; they move in silent prayer. Much later, she will think, *If only I could have done this while he was alive.* But for now, she has her purpose.

PART IV

what's left

WHITE RABBIT

It starts with her picking up the dirty clothes that are scattered around the bedroom floor like fallen leaves; *Goddamn it, I'm going to do laundry.* But she can't find the basket and doesn't want to make trips to and from the garage, where the washing machine and dryer are housed, dropping panties and socks along the way. It has been almost three weeks since Michael died. Corseted by numbness, she has been on a get-shit-done tear, trying to carry out his instructions; laundry felt reasonable.

The home phone rings. She stopped picking it up after Michael's obituary ran in the *Tribune* because she'd been inundated with calls, as well as flowers, plants, and deli platters despite its stating "donations only." But she figures she can't ignore the outside world forever.

"Have you seen the news?" Peter Martins's voice is choked. "You must turn on the TV." The last time someone sounded like this on the phone it was because airplanes were crashing into the Twin Towers. This time Saddam's soldiers have entered Iraq's museum complex with automatic weapons and grenades. Staring at the television, Cheri watches in horror as looters swarm the museum like locusts, ravaging, pillaging, leaving destruction in their wake. Baghdad was bleeding antiquities. The museum director was saying he thought a hundred and seventy thousand artifacts had already been stolen; the common heritage of mankind was lost. All gone. It was April 13; it wasn't a Friday. In retrospect, she'll want to believe the first thing that crossed her mind on hearing the news was *What happened to Dr. Benaz and the museum staff? Are they alive?* But Cheri's first reaction had actually been *What happened to the Tell Muqayyar tablets?*

On the drive to the university, Cheri's mind kicks into crisis mode. Wartime looting is hardly novel, she reminds herself, and curators would have hidden the good stuff in the basement vault. While the museum housed items of far greater and more discernible value than the Tell Muqayyar tablets, given their suspected biblical link, Dr. Benaz might have successfully had them included in the vault. It dawns on Cheri that the last time she was on campus was for a meeting with the review board. Was that three months ago? In the haze of Michael's final weeks, Cheri hadn't even looked over the committee's report. And when she finally did feel up to the task, the restrictions were worse than she had imagined. Tenure was off the table; she'd be working in a fishbowl, censored and monitored by academic bureaucrats. Plus, the committee's findings were now part of her official record, her reputation marred by a claim deemed specious but damaging nonetheless. Her opportunities for research and scholarship were all tied into her professorship, so if she didn't teach, she lost access to the Oriental Institute. She hasn't even begun to think of how she could teach in those shackles.

The hallways of the Oriental Institute vibrate with how-could-this-happen ululations of professors and scholars. Her colleagues wander from office to office, poleaxed and teary-eyed.

The only benefit of the museum looting, she thinks, is that her colleagues are so ensnared by the enormity of the loss to mankind's heritage—a past they devoted their lives and livelihoods to studying—that they seem to have forgotten about her suspension. No one mentions the Richards case. "I'm so sorry to hear about your loss," Suzanne, the department secretary, says when Cheri passes by her desk. "I wouldn't have expected to see you...so soon."

"How could the U.S. military leave the museum without even one tank, totally unprotected?" Cheri can hear Samuelson's voice from outside his office. Dolores, his receptionist, waves her over, maneuvering her into a group of professors gathered in Samuelson's doorway. Samuelson acknowledges her with a nod. "I told the DOD this could happen. The museum was the number-one site on my no-strike list. Number one. They stood by and watched as the looting happened and did nothing!"

In the next chaotic days of speculation, rumors, and blame, Cheri and the rest of her department huddle in the faculty lounge like survivors of an earthquake, exchanging what little information they'd gleaned from contacts in Iraq or elsewhere in the Middle East. Dr. Benaz and the museum staff were safe, and when the looting was over, they'd returned to the site to sort and identify what remained. The number of stolen artifacts was already going down from the initial news reports of near-total loss. Recovery teams had even found one of the museum's most valuable statues, stoking the flames of hope.

But Cheri senses it is over even before it's official. Certainly before she hears the news unofficially from Peter and then officially from Samuelson. Somewhere in the hang time between the museum director's fluctuating accounts, she realizes it's lost. The tablet fragments belonging to Tell Muqayyar weren't fully cataloged and hadn't been flagged and stored in the vault pre-raid. There was no sign of them in the rubble.

This is the final straw. Cheri is broken.

She moves in a pattern: bed to bathroom, bathroom to bed, bedroom to kitchen, then back to bed. Like an ant, although she can barely summon the energy to lift her arms, let alone carry her own body weight. Slovenly and shredded by despair, she cannot envision a future. If she tries to project past this moment, she sees nothing. Neither black nor white; what is the color of absence? It's the color she feels when she wakes up on the floor of her closet, balled up in a heap of Michael's clothes. How did she even get here? She must have migrated like a bird in the wee restless hours. Just outside her window, people are retrieving the papers, going to work, knotting ties, saying good morning and meaning it or not meaning it, buying lamb chops for dinner.

Her neck is kinked, her tongue has grown a sweater, and she's scratching like a junkie, having helped herself to Michael's leftovers—pain pills washed down with codeine cough syrup—because she drank up all the booze. She envisions tugging on the corners of space, crumpling it in on herself until she's a black dwarf emitting no signal, no trace evidence, in the immense stillness. There's a bosky smell—the commingling of dust, stale cigarettes, and something with a sour tang to it, probably her and/or the pair of jeans she's using as a pillow.

Mustering all her strength, she makes her way to the bathroom. Looks like it will be OxyContin cut with Sudafed this morning. She chops up her DYI concoction with a razor blade on her hand mirror. She could walk to the liquor store down the street and get some vodka to throw in for good measure. But that would require going out of the house. Which would require pants. Pants were out of the question. She needs to get a fresh pack of cigarettes, but that also requires pants. Not going to happen. When was the last time she'd had something to eat? Oh, look: there are a few perfectly good butts in the ashtray. God provides.

It's amazing how sadness can make itself infinitesimally small so as to invade even the whisper of an opening. But once it enters, it transmutes into a vast, carnivorous beast, relentlessly gnawing through flesh and tissue, organ by organ. It had been waiting years, tick-like, for this moment. Despite her attempts to use drugs and booze as sealants to plug up the cracks, the sadness has found its way in. It's consuming her; she can feel its tundra breath on her neck. Buckle, wail in widowed anguish, rend garments like a normal person, for fuck's sake; give it what it wants. Take the pill to make you taller or stop running and take its grotesque head in your hands and kiss it on its open mouth. Then howl, Fuck you. Fuck you, U.S. tanks, fuck you, looters, fuck you, Michael, fuck you, Samuelson, and your academic gestapo fucks. And fuck this self-pitying, roll-into-a-ball-in-the-closet-and-play-dead crap. You've got a mouth, open it, and call for fucking help.

I can't, the dangerous sadness inside her whimpers. *I can't.*

The beast has her by the toe; it has succeeded in dragging her into the lair of regret. One loss brings up all the rest. What did she expect? She lured it, poking into the landfill of her past with a stick, pulling up snacks to toss into its open maw. Cheri surveys what's left of the pill powder on the mirror. She was a little too aggressive with her chopping and sent most of her product onto the floor. She gets down on her knees and hoovers it up with a rolled dollar bill. Her nostrils smart. The sensation is so familiar.

The drugs, the despair, the regret, the anger. Fuck you, Eddie Norris, and fuck you, NYPD. She remembers her younger self, barricaded in her old room at Cici's, on a Tilt-A-Whirl bender from speed laced with God knows what, sure that nobody from the job would ever find her in the privileged enclave of Eighty-First Street. Now she's over forty but back in the same fucked-up place she was in in her twenties. A million uncensored images skitter along her buzzing neural pathways like lines on a 3-D subway map, lighting up, flashing, all moving at a nauseating pace. "If she plays one more opera I'm going to bludgeon her to death with a frozen leg of lamb." "The back of my right knee itches." "That was an inferior Hitchcock movie." "You broke my heart, Eddie Norris. And I still love you." *"Cave canem."* She doesn't know if she hates herself more for indulging in misery or for snorting up every last white speck on the tile.

Suddenly she hears the sound of packing tape stretching and cutting. *Riiip.* "More!" A worker wearing overalls shouts to other workers making big cardboard boxes. *Riiip.* She sees Michael immobilized in a coffin-shaped box. His face is frozen, but he says, "Press the button." "But I already did that, exactly like you wanted." He's trying to say more but she hears only rasps. She turns and now Michael's on a conveyor belt going around and around like a piece of luggage.

"Press the button," someone says on the loudspeaker. She tries to tug him off the conveyor belt but his box doesn't have handles. She can't get a good grip. She's sweating. He's humming like he did while driving or making coffee in the morning and she'd say, "Stop fucking humming!"

"If you don't press the button, everyone is stuck. We must keep it moving," a disembodied voice instructs her. She's behind a glass partition watching as Michael is back on the conveyor belt heading into a furnace. A siren goes off, wailing, flashing lights. "Press the button." She wants to break the glass and looks for an ax. *Imagine an ax in your hand, think of it growing out of your hand.* But her hand is just a hand. Michael goes into the fire and suddenly lunges forward, sitting up, his hands flaming, hair burning. He looks right at her and smiles.

———

"We are sick from no news," Cici says into the phone, "nobody, not her work even, has heard from her." Cookie sits at the kitchen island, putting mozzarella balls in jars. She's been hearing Cici worry to anyone who will listen. Normally, Cookie rolls her eyes at Cici's hand-wringing, but this feels different, and it's making her worry as well. Her arthritic fingers lose their grip on one of the balls. It plops to the floor. Now she'll have to shimmy off the stool, which is too tall for her, like everything in this damned place, and get down on her hands and knees to wipe up the mess. With age she's gotten a lot slower and stiffer and is in need of fortification more frequently.

She can hear Cici in the other room saying, "Did I ever tell you she is smart enough to join Mensla?" She's always got to work that in and say it wrong. Damn woman can't even speak English after all these years. By the time Cookie has captured the errant cheese and put it back in the jar, Cici's calling out that her wineglass needs refilling. Which reminds Cookie that she might as well have another teensy nip of brandy.

"What you doing—you put oil first, then mozzarella." Cici's eyebrows are raised. Cookie didn't think it was possible for those eyebrows to go up any higher—they had hit an all-time high the last time Cici had returned from injecting blubber into her face or whatever it is she had done, but it seems Cookie was wrong. Why does she do it? The woman was a beauty when she met her, and at almost sixty-three, she still looks pretty damn good without all that nonsense. "You are too slow. This could be done by now."

"I'm too old, you gonna complain about that?"

"I will pay you double to not come in."

"Last week you said triple. I'm not retiring for less. Now just calm yourself down and address the problem."

"You are the problem. You do not listen."

"Oh, I listen, all right. And if it were me, if it were my Choo-Choo—like the time she ran off with that man who'd left his wife and three kids for her, then left her, broke, pregnant, with fifty thousand dollars of his unpaid gambling debts—"

"You think Cheri is pregnant, has the other man?"

"I think you should go to Chicago, that's what I think."

"She will not want me there. She will be upset."

"She's already upset. Her husband died, she's got reason to be upset. Although that's not always a bad thing, plenty of husbands better off dead."

"I do not know. What if she will not speak to me?"

"If she doesn't want to talk, then you just sit with her and be quiet. Children always be your children no matter how old they are. Don't go there making this all about you and waving your hands and worrying. Just go there and be her mother."

"What if she does not answer the door?"

"Come on now, you're not as helpless as all that. You can pull yourself together when you want to. Question is: Do you want to?"

On the plane, after a few glasses of champagne to settle herself, Cici realizes that she doesn't really know her daughter or what she cares about in her life. It's not so much of a realization as an admission, because she's always felt that no matter how hard she tried she couldn't understand what made Cheri do the things she did. She and Sol had brought her up to believe education and culture were the most important things in life. Why, then, did their daughter throw away Yale for no-makeup, a gun, and an ugly blue uniform? Why did she want to put herself with drug dealers and thieves who could kill her? When Cheri quit playing policewoman and moved back home, Cici thought she'd finally come to her senses. But she was angry and mean and locked herself in her room for weeks smoking cigarettes and drinking beer and playing headache music. "Look on the sunny side," Cici had said, "you can go back to school, you can become a doctor, a professor, be the smart girl you are." All she got back was "Life is not *La Bohème*. Leave me alone."

Cici was not educated like Cheri and Solomon, but she knew things. She knew it was not just beer making her daughter's mood black. Where she'd worked, in that park with the crazy tent people and trash, there were all kinds of drugs. Drugs going up the nose and in the veins to fill the dark spaces inside. She remembers the feeling of putting a blade on her skin, tracing the line and waiting for the first cut. After the blood came pain and with that peace; pain on the outside made her stop thinking of what was on the inside. She wore long sleeves in summer to hide the red lines and even when they faded to white, she was careful to cover them up in case anyone noticed. She did not want her daughter to be like her.

She remembers thumping on Cheri's door until her fists hurt, saying, "Open! Now, now, I am not fooling." But Cheri wouldn't even respond. *Whatever Cheri needed in a mother,* Cici thinks now, reclining in her seat, *I do not seem to have it. If she'd come from my womb, then maybe we would be able to hear each other better, to listen.* She cannot remember that feeling, the connection of blood and water and life inside of her. But she knows it existed many years ago. It makes her too sad to think about, so she stops and, despite hating reptiles unless they've been made into handbags, plucks a magazine from the seat pocket and reads a story about iguanas in Mexico.

Cookie had had better luck back on Eighty-first Street. "What do you think this is, a halfway house? I'm not soft like your mama. You either let me in there right now or next thing you know, the super's gonna be taking the door off the hinges and leaving it that way." When Cookie emerged from Cheri's room hours later, she had a trash can full of empty bottles but few details. "That girl has a broken heart. I can smell it on her. Only thing for that is time."

About a week later, the entire apartment felt like a bunker. Cici was pulling her hair out, yelling at Cookie that they needed to drag Cheri to a hospital. "I can deal with you. I can deal with her," Cookie said. "But both of you locked up in here together—ain't no way I'm going to deal with that." And then Cheri came out of her room. Skinny, disheveled, hair plastered to her head. Cici and Cookie followed her into the kitchen, where she opened the refrigerator, drank a Coke, and calmly announced that she had spoken to people at Yale and was moving to New Haven. Wasn't that what Cici had suggested, wasn't that exactly what she'd wanted?

When Cici gets to Chicago she wishes she'd brought her fur coat. Although it's spring, and fur in spring is almost as bad as white after the Day of Labor. She's standing in front of Cheri's house feeling chilly. It was painted purple when they bought it; she'd tried to convince them to repaint it in a nice neutral, an attractive ecru or eggshell, but they liked their purple house. So many stairs to walk up. What are all these newspapers doing on the porch? The robbers will think she is not home. Cici rings the doorbell and knocks, hard. Finally, she takes a few steps back and throws a small rock at an upstairs window like a child. Maybe Cheri is in her bedroom? It misses. Does that filthy black car across the street with all the tickets belong to her daughter? Would she leave town and not move her car? The last time Cici managed to get Cheri on the phone, Cheri was running into work because there had been a disaster at the museum in Iraq. But when Cici tried her at work, the secretary confirmed she hadn't been in since then—and that was more than two weeks ago. Panic rises in Cici like reflux. Maybe Cheri leaves a key—but where? Cici is about to walk around the back when she decides to try the front door. It's unlocked. A bad sign. "Cheri," she calls. "Are you here?"

Inside smells of stale smoke, must, and dirty diaper. Mail litters the floor. A faucet drips. The refrigerator door is open. Something inside is making the dirty-diaper smell. "Hello?" Slashed limes rot on the counter along with empty bottles of gin, dead plants, and vases with desiccated flowers still with the sympathy cards on sticks. She swallows her disgust—this is not the time to be thinking about her daughter's piggery. Empty chairs and stillness. Has someone broken in? Is she going to find her daughter bleeding? "Cheri, I am here," she calls. She remembers that movie with the knife and the shower curtain. She rushes up the stairs. No harm can come. Not to Cheri. Please, not to her.

The bedroom door is ajar. In the slate light, she can make out a lump on the bed. Has she taken too many sleeping pills, wanting to join Michael? Why didn't Cici think of this and come sooner?

The telltale lump. She recalls all the years of pulling back the covers above exactly such a lump, saying, "Wake up, sleepy-toes." She will never forgive herself if she came too late. She puts her hand on her daughter's back.

Cheri wakes with a start. She rolls over and sits up quickly when she sees Cici standing over her. "What the fuck?" Cheri says, pushing away her mother's arms and murmurs of gratitude. "What are you doing here?"

"Are you sick? Is this why you are not answering the phone?"

"I'm fine."

"I thought something had happened to you. You scare everybody."

"Sorry I scared you. You came, you saw...now go away." Cheri flops back down on her back and pulls the blanket over her head. Cici opens the shade and, in the light, can now survey the full extent of the chaos: paper cups half filled with water and cigarette butts, cans of half-eaten food, files, books, clothes belching out of the closet.

"Close the fucking shade! I'm fine, now turn around and go home."

"Fine?" Cici picks up liquor bottles that have overflowed from the garbage can. "This is no fine. You are a drunk. It is one in the afternoon."

"Says the person who pops champagne for breakfast."

"I am not the one living like this, leaving her door open for the world to walk in. I am not a drunk."

"First of all, I am *not* drunk. You can give me a Breathalyzer. I'm not on drugs. I'll even piss in a cup, if you can find a clean one. Second, you can't just barge in here and tell me what to do. I'm not a kid. I'm asking you nicely to get out of here."

"Are you sick?"

"Not going to keep saying it nicely."

"Please do not tell me you are pregnant and drinking like this."

"I am not pregnant, Cici. I am not sick." Cheri rolls over. "I'm going back to sleep now so shhhh."

"Okay, okay. You sleep."

"No longer listening."

"I will sit and wait for you to wake up."

All Cici wants to do is get a giant can of disinfectant and some rubber gloves and start to pick up the garbage that surrounds Cheri's bed. She can't even find a place to perch in the bedroom. There's clutter upon clutter. When she finds a chair, it's beneath clothes. She's got to throw everything on the floor, which she cannot bear to do, so she sits with it all in a ball on her lap. This is the wreckage of her daughter's life. She feels a pain that emanates from beneath her ribs where she draws breath. A specific pain that comes from knowing that her love—no matter how unconditional and strong—cannot solve everything for her child. "Put the seashell to your ear, *cara,* and wherever you are, you will hear my voice." All those years moving from house to house along the seashore, Cici never doubted her mother's words. She wishes she had the power to reach Cheri.

"I can feel you staring. You're like a dog."

"You said not to talk. I need to close my eyes as well?"

"Oh, fuck it. I'm up now," Cheri says, tossing back the covers. She rests her forehead in the palm of one hand. "Can you pass me the lighter, it's on the table." Cici goes to the bedside table, moves a filled ashtray on top of papers and bills, rifles through them. "Oh, for God's sake, Cici."

"What you doing with this?" Cici has found the package of razor blades underneath a bra on the table.

"Give me that." Cheri stands, reaches over to take the box.

The sudden rise to vertical makes her see spots before her eyes. "If I was going to kill myself, that's the last way I'd do it."

"Sit down. You are very pale," Cici says, touching her arm. "You will fall."

"I'm always pale. Please, just get off me."

"You need help."

"I'm fine, I can stand on my own." Cheri turns away from Cici but has to steady herself against the wall.

"You need help. I am here to help."

"What do you know about what I need? You live in your own little bubble completely removed from reality, never worked a day in your life. What's your daily drama? The shoes you ordered are too tight or the pug's shits are too loose—now it's, 'Oooh, Cheri's sleeping in the afternoon, and she's in her T-shirt and ratty old underwear,' and yup, I stink. Welcome to the den of iniquity, Mother! Go complain about it to Cookie or your friends who are only your friends because you employ them, but don't you dare show up here and judge me—"

"Do not talk to me about judging. I am sick of how you look at me, always with the hard eyes. Saying I am a stupid woman who sees nothing, hears nothing. How dare *you!* I have lived a life. You think I have had no suffering? There are many things you do not know about me. My life is not so full of cherries. I know what it is to lose. I lost my family. I lost my husband—"

"The great man that Sol was, yeah, I know. Spare me." Cheri turns her back to Cici, who grabs Cheri by the arm and wheels her around, a primordial anger rising.

"You think you are the only one with the right to anger? Plenty of things I have spared you." Cici allows the words to spill out. "Your father, he was not perfect to you, but he cheated on me. He had another woman. You think this does not cause me pain? Some things are so painful we must look away to go on. But when we turn back, we can be surprised. In the end, I was able to forgive. You think I am such a weak woman. Well, I am stronger than you think." Cici is puffed up like a lizard; she has stunned Cheri into silence.

Cheri sits on the bed. After a moment, she quietly speaks. "When did you know?"

"You were in college...it was over long ago," Cici says, wanting to suck her words back in.

"So you knew. And...you didn't do anything." Cheri is looking at her with hard eyes, and it makes her angry all over again.

"Nothing is so simple between men and women. Was it so simple with you and Michael? You had not seemed so happy together. In a marriage, who is happy always? In the end I let happiness back in and if that makes me the fool, then I am the fool," Cici says, talking to her daughter like she should have spoken to her when she was a teenager. "I do not care if you like it or no like it. I am here to help you. I am going to run a shower. You will get in it and get clean. Then we have a coffee. That is where we start." Cheri stands stiffly, but her eyes are softer. "You hear me," Cici says. It is not a question.

Cheri hears the water running. She's surprised she can make it to the bathroom without passing out. Her head feels like aliens are drilling a hole in it. The bathroom is steamy and humid. She wipes off a corner of the mirror with her fist. Her left breast is hanging out of the side of her tank top. She can't believe Cici knew. Then again, of course she can; it's all part of her fucked-up-family bullshit. She thinks about saying, *Thanks for telling me what*

I already knew. But Cheri doesn't know exactly how much Cici knows about Sol's other life. Does she know about the house in Rye? About his son? She's not about to open that can of worms. As if her own life isn't caving in, now she needs this? "Fuck," she says, stripping off her clothes. She steps into the shower and lets the hot water sluice down her back. Barely able to stand, she puts one hand on the tile wall. All she wants is to crawl back in her hole and be left alone. She thinks she still has some of her Sudafed-pain-pill powder. Just like in her twenties, she's too in control to go over the edge and become a full-blown addict.

When she's clean and wrapped in a towel back in her room, Cheri assesses what's left of her depleted stash. She decides that she'll do just one snort now and chase it with a swig of cough syrup. Her hand is shaking and she doesn't want to waste any of her product; she struggles to tip a small amount of powder from one of Michael's empty pill bottles onto the back of her hand. The last time she was like this, she cold-turkeyed her way back through sheer grit. The thought of doing that now makes her feel sick. And then there's Cici banging around downstairs, doing her infernal cleaning.

Cheri walks into the kitchen wearing the same tank top and underwear, her hair still wet. There are two full garbage bags lined up next to the front door. Cici is pouring espresso into two cups Cheri has never seen. Did Cici bring her own cups along with her damned espresso pot? Cheri was fortified enough to get down the stairs, but the smell of the cleaning products Cici was using mingling with coffee makes her want to retch.

"Sit and have an espresso," Cici says, bringing the cups over to the table that's now cleared. There's a box of biscotti on the table; Cici's taken a few out and put them on a plate. "I can put more sugar in if you want."

"This is your idea of help? Flying halfway across the country to make espresso and compare my marriage to your fucked-up marriage? Playing who is the biggest martyr?"

"That is not what I try to do, Cheri. The point I make is that I suffered too. I have felt as you are feeling now—"

"So let's stop everything and immortalize your grief about Sol," Cheri says, grabbing the box of biscotti and shoving it in Cici's bag.

"That is not what I am saying; you twist my words," Cici protests. Cheri fixates on the counter, where a pile of Cici's things has already accumulated. She starts scooping up whatever she thinks might have come from Cici.

"What are you doing? Stop." Cici is by her side, trying to take the coffee grinder out of her hand. Cheri turns around to avoid her and slams her leg into a trash can.

"Fuck!" Cheri's shin throbs; she's gnashing her teeth, and her mother is looking at her like *she's* the one who's batshit crazy. "Damn it, don't go moving things," she says, trying to push the trash can with her hip. It's full and heavier than she thinks. Or she's weaker.

"You cannot keep up like this. You hurt yourself. Let me have that," Cici says, taking the coffee grinder from Cheri's hand.

"I'm fine."

"No, you are *not* fine," Cici says forcefully. "Nothing is fine. You are in the depression; this is normal when someone dies. But it is not normal to shut yourself away from everybody for so long, to be hurting yourself, wearing the same clothes for days, drinking yourself sick."

"You really want to compare normal?" Cheri stares at Cici, who claps her hands together and waves them up and down in an effort to stop herself from saying the first thing that occurs to her.

"You want me to bite; I do not want to bite. *Cara mia,* when someone you love dies, nothing feels the same. A part of your heart is gone and never comes back."

"I'm afraid it's more complicated than that."

"Everything is always more complicated. And also always more the same," Cici says.

Cheri turns away and when she turns back Cici has put the coffee grinder and other things in her tote. "I don't know what you want me to say. I can't explain it myself," Cheri says. How could she describe to Cici that her pain was about more than Michael's death? That she'd lost him in the marriage and then, just as she saw him again, she lost him and everything else she cared about permanently. "I can't feel anything, and when I do, it's all too much."

"I have been in the shoes you are in," Cici says, sitting down at the table. "I shut myself away like you do. I could not get out of the bed. I had no reason to move forward. I wanted to hurt myself..." There's not a trace of the puffed-up lizard left in Cici. She looks all too human.

"You lost a husband too, I know..."

"I am not talking about Solomon." Cici takes a deep breath and pauses. "I lost a baby." The plainness and weight of the statement levels Cheri.

"You had a child?" Cheri asks, sitting down.

"I was pregnant before you." Cici's voice sounds distant. "There was an emergency. The doctors had to make an operation so I would not die and they got the baby out. But he was so small and so sick. He lived only a few hours. I could not have children after that."

"You had a hysterectomy? You could have told me," Cheri says, remembering the trip to Italy when she found out that she was adopted. Nobody told her anything in her family, but when she did hear something, it was dropped on her out of the blue. "Why didn't you say anything?" Cheri asks.

"Maybe I should have told you. But it caused too much pain to look back. Your father and I never spoke of it. But losing a child is something you can never forget." Cheri thinks of Karen, the funeral and the baby in the tiny coffin. For the first time, she thinks of her mother as a young woman, bereaved, emptied. Had there been a funeral for Cici's baby? Cheri's head is spinning and she doesn't feel at all well. Her mother is looking at her with concern.

"Enough talk of sad things. Sit. I make you something to eat."

Although Cheri wasn't hungry, she ate a few bites of the risotto that Cici miraculously threw together from the seemingly empty pantry. She drank water and napped, and when she woke up, Cici came into her bedroom and said, "I am going to help you pack up Michael's clothes. It is not good to sit with them there for so long. You are ready?"

Is she ready? To let the memories in, the images she'd kept at bay by sinking into the mound of overarching despair? Cici opens Michael's closet, takes something off a hanger, and approaches Cheri with it. Is she ready to feel the softness of Michael's favorite shirt, the one that made his eyes the color of blueberries in summer? He had this shirt when they first met and there was a time she would wear it when he was away, feeling protected and attached. Cheri has never been particularly sentimental, but she knows she's not ready to let that shirt go. Cici is sitting on a corner of the bed, looking at her expectantly.

And suddenly, moments that were commonplace float up in Cheri's mind. How he'd throw off his boots and then later ask, "Have you seen my other boot?" The boots with the caulking splatter from when he decided to put up shelves and made such big holes in the wall that they had to call the handyman to redo it. How he would run his hands over his face when he was tired. The day she caught him listening to mariachi music and actually liking it. She sits, clutching the shirt to her chest, until she feels her mother's hands on her shoulders. Instead of withdrawing, she allows herself to lean back. "We will keep this one for you," Cici says, gently taking the shirt. Cheri gets up and moves like a cluster fly, pausing in front of his closet, then circling to his chest of drawers, not knowing where to start. His clothing is stained with food and accidents that smell of indignity. She is looking at the remains of his last days and thinks she should have taken care of them better. The struggle to feed and be fed, worn on his sleeves. She can hear her mother exclaiming, *"Che schifo!"* Where to start?

Without uttering another word, Cici swoops in and picks up Michael's things from wherever they met their inglorious end weeks ago. Cici sorts and folds, making neat piles of clothes to be donated or thrown out. "We decide this one later," Cici says when Cheri gets stuck, which is more often than she would have thought. *Is she ready?* There is much more letting go to do, she knows, and not just of objects.

After all of Michael's clothes have been sorted, Cheri and Cici sit in silence on the edge of the bed. Cici puts her hand on top of Cheri's. They sit like this for a few minutes, until Cici says, "I will stay in a hotel. But you must promise me that you will not hurt yourself. No razor blades. No pills."

"I promise," Cheri says.

"I want you to remember that God is always here for you. I know you do not believe as I do, that you think I am simple...but this is what helps me. I know your father and my baby are in heaven. And so is Michael." Cheri quells her impulse to say, *Do you actually believe in this?* Cici continues. "Going to church, talking to Father Joseph—this helped me with my loss, with all my problems. When you make the confession, you put all your sin and sorrow at the feet of God. His forgiveness and love are so big, it makes your troubles feel smaller."

As soon as her mother leaves, Cheri regrets not asking her to stay. She wanted to be alone because she's jonesing and there's the last bit of chopped-up Sudafed-pain-pill powder to consume. But as soon as she cuts her last lines and inhales, she knows it's an empty gesture, like sex with someone you once loved but now can't stand. She wanders through the house. It feels too big. Like she's lost weight and it hangs off her. Who knows, maybe Cici and the millions of believers out there are right. Maybe Michael and Sol have reconciled in the Great Beyond. They're at the seaside chasing waves with Cici's baby boy and numerous vestal virgins, laughing. Maybe she'll just pop the last pain pill and take a bath.

The world might collapse, but as long as there is running water, Cheri will survive. She adjusts the water temperature. The yellow washcloth draped over the side of the tub smells of her mother's tea-rose perfume. She feels a deep longing; for what, she's unsure. The kind of painful sweetness that makes her want to call and wake her mother up and say, I'm sorry, come back, please come back. But it's one o'clock in the morning. First thing tomorrow, she promises herself, I'll get up and do things differently. Start small: Put on pants. Work my way up to being kind.

LILACS

Cici likes air travel. She finds it soothing to be in the capsule of neither here nor there. But first class isn't what it used to be. She's had to tap her champagne glass twice to get the stewardess's eye and decides to switch to vodka and orange juice. For the first time since Cheri was a small child, Cici feels like she was actually able to help her. She would like to have stayed longer but she knew she'd done as much as Cheri would allow. It doesn't get easier. She thought that maybe with age she wouldn't feel the referred pain that comes from seeing your child suffer. She was wrong. If she could, she would take Cheri's burden away, breathe in her loss and expel it like smoke. But she can't do that for Cheri any more than Sol could do it for her when she lost the baby. You were once my salvation, she could have whispered to Cheri, you gave me a reason to live and now you must find the same for yourself.

Why does she think of the right thing to say only after the fact? She felt she had said both too much and too little to Cheri. A child does not want to know the intimate things that go on between her parents. How could she tell Cheri that she was also to blame for the woman with the emerald ring? That after her baby died, she became numb to pleasure she knew Solomon wanted to give her but she could not receive. Or give to him. She turned her face away, pretended for so long that one day the mask she was wearing had become her face. She had put so much of her love and energy into being a mother, wanting to do better than her mama. She had only one child; there was plenty of room in her heart. But she had not left enough room for Solomon. She knows this now. But then, she was so young. She understood so little.

She could not tell Cheri about Solomon's confession. She would like to erase that memory and focus only on the fact that they found happiness again. Solomon had shown her that he was still the man she had fallen in love with. He'd awakened something in her that she had given up hope of ever feeling again. But she found herself able to speak of only the small things to her daughter. For such big things, she could never find the words. You did nothing. It might have taken Cici years, but she did do something. If I could forgive Solomon, so can you, was what she meant to say. "God forgives us so we can forgive each other," Father Joseph told her and Solomon when they sat across from him in his office at the church. "Are you prepared to do that, my children?"

She was not prepared when Solomon confessed. He had been on a phone call at work when his eyes suddenly went dark. She had raced to the hospital. He was sixty-six years old. His veins were bad; the phlebitis could give him a stroke and kill him. He was getting special attention, surrounded by doctors who said he was lucky—it was only a miniature stroke. A TMI, she was sure, but she was saying it wrong because Cheri corrected her. They did not want to worry Cheri; she had told her afterward, when most of his eyesight came back. She had seen him struggling with his gout, his swollen legs, but he was always so strong. "Doctors make the worst patients," he'd told Cici when she worried about his health. Now the man with all the answers, the proud doctor she'd married, was like a little boy in his hospital gown. She slept on a chair by his bed and would wake up in the middle of the night and find his hand searching for hers. She got in next to him; his arms looped around her waist and his head rested on her neck.

The next morning, his sight had come back in one eye and the doctors said he could go home. "I have to tell you something," he said as they were packing to leave. "It's over with her. It has been for a long time, but I needed you to know." Cici could not have said when, exactly, but she'd sensed Sol's attention was slowly returning to her.

"I made a mistake," he continued. "I'm not proud of it or of how I handled it. I never loved her the way I love you. But it wasn't just the two of us." For a moment, Cici could not breathe. He and the Emerald Woman had a son. And that boy was going to be a man; he was soon to be in college. "It wasn't planned," he said, and she'd snorted. She did not want to hear any more. Was it worse or better that he'd stayed with the woman because they'd had a child? She could not give him his own child. Was this why he'd sought out someone else? As much as she tried to block them, these thoughts crept in with cat's paws later. But for now, she needed Sol to stop talking. She held up her hand.

"If you don't want me to come home, now or ever, then I will have to accept that. But I needed you to know the whole story." How could her husband have a child that was not hers? In all her years of thinking about the Emerald Woman, she had somehow never imagined such a thing. Men wandered, had affairs. Not children. Because he had confessed, was she supposed to forgive? Was that what his eyes were pleading? She had to ask herself: Could she imagine a life without Solomon? "We are going home," she said.

Cici wraps the cashmere throw that she brought around her, glad that nobody is in the seat next to her. Never once had she considered a life without Solomon. They had the glue of their marriage: beautiful homes to run, food she knew to buy and cook for him, the suits she picked out and packed and unpacked, the daily calls, his always knowing what to do, how to fix things. Her papa had died when Cici was so young, but she remembered the look on her mama's face the day it happened, a look that said the world would never be the same, would never feel like a safe place again. Solomon had kept Cici's world safe.

It is hard to remember the gradual way the shoot of forgiveness surfaced. She had not gone looking for it. To celebrate the fresh start, he had bought her a gift—lilacs, just like the ones he'd planted for her in Montclair. He knew to get tight clusters with the purple buds just awakening. Where had he found lilacs in winter? "Nothing is impossible," he had said, but not about the lilacs. A perfect spray sitting there on her white plate at the dinner table. *Someday, when I'm awfully low, when the world is cold.* Frank Sinatra crooning on the stereo. *Croon.* Solomon had taught her that word back when his touch made her shiver as if with fever. When her teeth were white and her knees unwrinkled and her heart tender. "You are my home," he said. "I only ever wanted you, us, as we were." He poured her some wine, an excellent vintage. "I only ever wanted to make you happy, Cici. The houses, the jewelry, these were things I could give you when you didn't seem to want everything else I had to give. More than anything, I wanted to know that you still wanted me. When you cut up my clothes, I thought that you'd scream and threaten to leave me. A declaration would have stopped me in my tracks."

A declaration—where were the words back then for all the emotions she had held in? "It was not my duty to tell you to stop," she said. She thought of her mother and sister. "Men slow down when they are older," Genny had said about her Ettore when he had his women, "they come home again." A declaration. Now, that evening, she'd found the words. She shouted and called him a liar and a motherfucker, screamed that she should have taken a whack out on him when she could. When she was exhausted and about to call to Cookie because the dinner would be cold and she was probably drunk, watching TV, he stood up and took her in his arms: "We can't go back to where we began—we are both different people than we were twenty years ago. But I want to share who I am now with you. But you have to be willing to share yourself too." He touched her cheek with his hand. She could see the passage of time, reflections of all the men she'd known or thought she'd known in his face. He talked about how he would retire and become a doctor again, work in a clinic for no money. He was going to help the people who most needed helping. "I am going to be a better man, just let me show you." *And the way you look tonight.* And then his hand was on her back like a knife, cutting the buttons off her dress. His breath on her ear: "Forgive me. Please, forgive me."

"Are you all right, ma'am?" The stewardess is leaning over, handing Cici a tissue. Cici nods her head; she didn't even realize she was crying. She pats her eyes and then checks herself in her compact, fixes her makeup. There is still an hour left of the flight; she settles back to try to nap. "A woman is born with only so many butterflies," her mother had said when Cici told her she was in love with Sol. "When your heart is broken by a man, when he hurts you, he steals one. Don't let your butterflies go easily, Carlotta *mio*—one day you may be left with none." The last gift Solomon gave her was a gold necklace with a mother-of-pearl butterfly, tiny diamonds around its wings. It had been too painful to wear that necklace after he died, but now she thinks she can. And one day, when she passes it to Cheri, she might just find the courage to tell her a little bit more.

ASHES ARE HEAVIER THAN YOU THINK

Cheri hesitates outside the door to Michael's office. She's been back in there only once, to put the box of his ashes on his desk because she had no idea what to do with them. Michael, with all of his obsessing over her watching him go into the fire and detailed instructions for his memorial/premiere party—right down to the cocktail recipes—was mute on the subject of his mortal remains. She'd told the lady at the funeral home no to putting Michael in a columbarium, an urn, having him made into a ring, or hanging him in a portrait; she'd just take him to go. But now she has to reenter HMS Bay, since Bertrand wants her to send him *The Palmist* files from Michael's computer. She's been putting off the task for long enough, and she certainly doesn't have the excuse of being too busy. She'd said no to Samuelson's invitation to take back her classes "with modifications" and could no more listen to news about the Iraq museum's losses than she could revisit her book or write anything more than a grocery list.

She cracks a window to relieve the stuffiness. A breeze blows in, riffling a movie poster on the wall that's come untacked on one side. The afternoon light looks dusty. The plain brown box of ashes is right where she left it, by Michael's computer next to a vase of deeply dead lilacs. As a parting gift, Cici had filled the house with "new life." Cici's fluffing up HMS Bay felt like a violation, but Cheri has to admit that it's thanks to her mother that putting on pants is now an almost daily occurrence. The air no longer smells of nag champa or sickbay or, she realizes sadly, Michael. *Are you ready?*

When she sees Michael's face come to life on the screen, it startles her. Like he'll come up behind her saying, "What the hell are you doing on my computer? And by the way, did you read my journal?" She fast-forwards through *The Palmist* video files, catching bits of what he says. Images move in time-lapse; his eyes sink deeper into his face, he goes from sitting, to being propped up in a hospital bed, to lying down. His voice grows thin and raspy. "How do I live while dying?" The light is crepuscular; his face is partially shadowed. She lets it play: "The dirty little secret is that I had a fantasy that I'd find the answer *out there*. And I'd be healed. But whatever anyone said to me, it all boiled down to: believe. My rational mind wasn't having any of that. 'Fake it until you make it'...if I had a nickel for every time I said that. Then I remembered what I'd witnessed with this monk in Thailand. He was a meth addict dying a painful death on the streets, his face covered in sores. He had gangrene. I asked him how he had lost his way. He said that there was no way to lose, that everything— good and bad—was all experience. 'Nothing to do, nothing to change, everything is perfect as it is.' If we accept what is, then there's no conflict. No conflict, no suffering. No suffering and we are at peace. I could tell looking into his eyes that he knew this, not in his mind, but in his heart. Despite his miserable cir- cumstances, this man had dignity. And, finally, I got it. It's not about the mind; it all comes from the heart." Cheri has no stomach for this. She powers down the computer, then yanks every last tentacle from the wall. Bertrand can have the whole damn thing.

Her weekly talks with Marlene—she'd cut the *Dr.* crap—is her only social life. She is sick of herself, of being in this house.

As she lifts Michael's computer onto the counter at the UPS Store, she thinks she is done with inertia. Peanuts and bubble wrap—hell, yes. Insure it for the highest amount possible, and get it there as fast as possible. Why not say yes? She didn't have to stay in Chicago. She could start over, move to another state or out of the country because she had no ties and, for the moment, no job. Buy all the guns she wanted and go around the country to every three-gun competition there was and call that her life. Yes to telling Samuelson take your handcuffed job and fuck it. She has money and doesn't need to be ashamed of it or hide it from anyone anymore. Hell, if she could figure out something she was inspired to research, she could fund her own trips, or even become a donor, greasing the wheels on any number of projects. She walks home feeling the late-summer sun on her face like a warm slap telling her to wake up and get on with her life.

⸘⸙⸘

"It's okay to feel relieved. Even excited at the prospect of new beginnings. That's understandable, even necessary," Marlene says. "You're familiar with the pink-cloud syndrome, I'm sure."

Cheri is distracted by the ass prints on Marlene's faux-suede couch. Looks like there was a couple here before her. Shouldn't the good doctor rake the couch to clear it, like in a Japanese stone garden? "I'm sober and can conquer the world?" Cheri says. "And after the pink cloud comes the crash of reality. Not really into Big Book–speak."

"I wasn't referring only to your being sober. Loss isn't a cold that lasts for a few days and is gone. But I want to return to Cici's visit first," Marlene says. "It sounds like she showed some real emotional honesty. It couldn't have been easy for her to tell you she'd lost a child before she adopted you."

"No, it wasn't," Cheri says and then pauses. "Now that I think about it, my entire childhood was spent filling a void I didn't even know existed and could never fill anyway. It's ironic because before Michael died, we'd gone to a funeral for a baby. I was un-hinged. They all kept insisting it was a 'celebration of life,' that we needed to be grateful for the hours the baby was here on earth. What bullshit. If my math is right, Cici adopted me right after she lost her own baby. One puppy dies so you rush out and buy a new one?" Cheri meets Marlene's gaze. "It was like there was this shadow child the whole time I was growing up."

"A shadow child . . . that's quite common to feel when a child in the family dies and everyone must go on. Usually there's a lot of guilt. Especially if your mother didn't have time to process the death. Was her baby a girl?"

"A boy. It's funny—when I was a kid, people mistook me for a boy. Cici was always trying to girl me up. I thought it was to make me look more like her, but maybe it was so I didn't remind her of him? She put so much on me. I was her everything; it felt like she was stalking me with her love. Her happiness was all tied up in her being my mother—Sol was jealous of that. She told me that she got very depressed after the baby died. It sounded like she was nearly suicidal . . ."

"So you were her salvation."

"Or consolation prize. Maybe it was better I didn't know. You need a flow chart in my family to know who knew what about whom at any given point. Moments of emotional honesty are few and far between."

"Did it change anything, when Cici told you that she knew about Catherine?"

"They say kids of divorce secretly wish their parents would get back together. Well, it was the opposite for me. I always wanted them to get a divorce and be done with the lies."

"And why do you think they didn't?"

"Her whole identity was wrapped up in being the wife of a rich, important man and living on the Upper East Side. Bought off with baubles. I didn't exactly hide my feelings about her...choices." Cheri hesitates for a moment. "But what do I know about my parents' relationship? She said she was happy with Sol in the end; maybe he told her he'd broken up with the woman and they had a come-to-Jesus moment. Give all the credit, and the blame, to the Catholic Church. As much fun as it is deconstructing my family mythos, it doesn't change what happened."

"As an exercise," Marlene says, "what if you stepped back and looked at them not as your parents but just as two flawed people, doing the best they could at the time? If you can separate your expectations of them as your parents from who they are as people and see them in a larger context, then it's easier to let go of not getting what you needed from them."

"Does it all come down to not getting what you need from Mommy and Daddy?" Cheri doesn't hide her irritation. "I'm a grown woman. This is what I hate about therapy. It all boils down to whining about your relationship with your parents. I want to deal with *today*. I want to get over *this* patch."

"You know how to go out in the world and accomplish.

When you're ready to do that again, you will. And what you 'do' may look and feel very different when you've actually dealt with your grief. Past and present. Right now, your work is to let the empty spaces be empty."

Cheri sighs; another version of nothing to do, nothing to change. "Well, I'm thinking about doing that somewhere else. Getting out of town for a while."

"I'm going to point out that there's a pattern here," Marlene says. "When things get too tough emotionally—"

"I knew you'd say that. Taking a break isn't the same thing as running away. I haven't a clue what I want in any area of my life, but I'm not going to figure it out until I get some perspective."

"Do you have something in mind?"

"My friend Taya has a house she never uses in Malibu and is always saying I can come stay there. I hate the sun almost as much as I hate the West Coast, but it's far away from here."

"Sometimes you have to go to the least likely place in order to find what you're looking for," Marlene says, "especially perspective."

It had been years since Cheri had been to LA. She'd gone for a conference once when she was still a TA, and another time for Taya's extravaganza of a wedding. She'd had the typical East Coast aversion to it then but, to her amazement, finds it appealing now. Being in transition herself, why not go to a place where the very ground was unstable, where people were coming and going in various stages of hope and disappointment? Michael had had a brief flirtation with Hollywood in the early seventies and lived in Venice. It was before her time, when *Disco, Doughnuts, and Dogma* was the coolest of the cool and he was being courted to make features. He'd enjoyed a whole *Easy Rider* period prowling up and down the California coast. She pictures young Michael on his motorcycle, his Jew-fro bobbing in the breeze, wearing one of his many ponchos.

⟋⟋⟍⟍

"Thank God you're going to get out of that place," Taya says when Cheri calls to ask if she can stay in her beach house. "You should seriously consider selling it. I would have immediately."

"So that's a yes?"

"Yes, but I think it's insane for you to stay in Malibu. It's beautiful, but it's isolated." Taya's voice competes with blitzes of a blender.

"Sounds perfect," Cheri says.

"Two things, though. No smoking. Including on the deck; the smoke gets into the wood. And take care of Skipperdee." How could smoke penetrate wood and what the hell was a skipperdee, Cheri thinks. "Skipperdee, as in the turtle from Eloise," Taya rambles on in the face of Cheri's silence. "You know, the girl who lived in the Plaza?"

"Take care of the turtle and no smoking, got it."

"Cat," Taya says, "Skipperdee is a cat. Long story short, the dogs almost killed him so he lives at the beach house. Laura, the housekeeper, comes and feeds him but if you're there, it's on you. Shit, this fucking thing is stuck. I'm on a liquid diet because I'm so fat I can't see my vagina over my stomach. Gotta go."

LA is just like Cheri pictured it: brown haze squatting on the horizon, cars and more cars, rows of palm trees in the glinty sprawl. No, she doesn't want to pay a thousand dollars a month for a new Camry. She'll take a long-term rental on that Buick that looks like a seventies cop car and squeals when she pulls out of the lot. It's not until she gets her first glimpse of the coast unfolding like a party invitation that she's glad she said yes to coming here.

Laura, a short sunburst of a Latina, is standing in front of a white stucco house with turquoise shutters holding a fistful of keys and instructions for how to work everything from electronic shades and pool covers to the cat, a talkative Siamese look-alike with folded ears. "I am a house manager and organizer, not a housekeeper," she says briskly, "but if you have any miscellaneous questions, you can call my cell." She walks through the house with Cheri, pointing out its many features, most of which Cheri's sure she'll never use. "These are Taya and the kids' favorites," Laura says, putting a bag in the fridge, "tamales—cheese and chili and pork. My cousin makes them. Warm them in the oven, not the microwave." And then she's gone and Cheri is alone with a cat and a whole lot of white furniture.

She can't sleep that night. The sounds coming from the coast highway are too unfamiliar, the ocean with its unceasing pull and push. At least the repetition quiets the thoughts of Marlene's so-called empty spaces that snap and bite like fish at the water's surface. Just as Taya promised, Malibu is an insular outpost that shutters early and doesn't do delivery. She starts reading a book, puts it down and starts another, only to put it down too. She wanders through the house, pours herself a tumbler full of booze from the bar cart. Taya's become so grown up: the second home, professionally taken photographs of her and the kids beaming from silver frames placed just so, the bar cart. People Cheri's age are living such fancy lives and decanting.

Cheri sits on the bottom step of the deck, staring at the ocean like it's a fire. She prefers the beach at night, the oyster-shell moon, the way the sand is firm from the moist air. The ocean reminds her that there's something bigger than herself. She could walk Michael's ashes into the water one of these nights. Let the box float until it drifts out of sight. When she closes her eyes, she sees Michael's gaunt face toward the end, eyes vacant. She walks the beach. Her feet get cold and damp. She walks in no particular pattern, like a songline. The sun is almost rising by the time she returns.

⌘

"My life is insanity," Taya says, plopping down next to Cheri at the table. She makes desperate hand signals to the new nanny, like she's a baseball catcher and the nanny's the pitcher, as her kids hurl themselves into the horde of toddlers in the playground in front of the café. Cheri has been waiting for her for the past twenty minutes, watching nannies wipe snot and donkey diaper bags while casually beautiful parents check out the casually beautiful shops and wave at their progeny. Was there really a time when such a sight warmed the cockles of her heart? It all feels far away. She can't imagine what it would be like now if she'd had a baby with Michael. Yet there's a part of her that's still sad they didn't. "Sorry we're late," Taya rushes on. "The old nanny didn't show up to train the new nanny. Do you see who that is over there? She's adopted two more kids from Cambodia or Mali; I guess brown is the new black. Waiter! We need bread and butter immediately. I kept my poor friend waiting here forever. She's starving." Taya pulls up her shirt and grabs a roll of belly, which she shows off to anyone within eyeshot. "And, as you can see, I'm desperately in need of carbs." The waiter trots off. "So you are in trouble, CM. My friend Janet said she called you and wanted to take you to some wine event around here, and you didn't even call her back."

"Must have slipped my mind," Cheri says.

"I don't know why you came to LA if you're just going to stay holed up in Malibu—you could have stayed in Chicago if you wanted to be housebound. You have to call Janet back." Taya jumps up and chastises the new nanny for something, then makes a point of telling her to order anything she wants for lunch. "Oh, is Skipperdee okay?"

"Great," Cheri says, wondering if she's put out food in the last day or two.

"Waiter?" Taya signals to a harried-looking man. "We need to get one of those pizzas right away, what she's eating—what is that, peach and burrata? Yum." She turns back to Cheri. "Okay, sorry. Enough about me. I'm just glad you're here. And, listen, this is important. I've been thinking about the whole ashes thing. My friend Rick Gould had his first wife's ashes put into a book, like those hollowed-out books people used to put drugs in back in the day? When he got remarried, his new wife didn't want the dead wife's ashes around, so he gave them to his friend to keep for him until he could figure it out. Cut to ten years later, and the friend is moving, forgets all about the ashes, and donates the book with a bunch of other stuff to charity. Rick finds out that his wife is now in Rancho Cucamonga, of all places, at some Christian Science Reading Room, and their whole friendship blows up."

"Your point is?"

"You never know what you might find at a Christian Science center! No, but seriously, people should be buried, it's less complicated. Just bury Michael's ashes when you get home and be done with it."

"I'll put that into the suggestion box," Cheri says. Easier than saying his ashes are in the glove compartment of her rental car.

"I just want you to be able to get yourself a new career or a new man, preferably both. You're brilliant, CM. Forget the university, you wrote a book—which is more than I can say for myself. Write! Write about the museum looting. It's a total detective story—right up your alley. And you have the personal angle because of the tablets. Great for PR! Call it *Baghdad Boondoggle*! Don't look at me like that—forget the name; it's a genius idea." Thankfully, the tiny pizzas arrive at the same time as the frantic nanny and sandy toddlers. An older woman in too-tight jeans whom Taya introduces as Honey whisks Taya away to meet her boyfriend. One of Taya's kids puts french fries in his nose. The older one tries to wedge them in with her fist. Time for an adult beverage.

It's a revelation to Cheri how she can do nothing in a day and look up and the sun's gone down. How did she ever manage to work? It doesn't seem like anyone in Malibu works. They're all in organic coffee shops or going to or from yoga. Is this who she will become, a member of the gainfully unemployed, living off her inheritance? She'd found a way to say yes to get here. Her mind wants to lurch forward to *What if this is it?* Or go backward to the tipping point, to Richards and anger. But she's supposed to be here. What did she think would happen? It wasn't as if life comes along like the arm in the bowling alley, sweeping away the dead pins and putting in fresh ones nice and neat. Roll again.

She begins venturing out of the keep. Her rental car's got

old-school vroom, and if she travels at off-hours—it would be easier to decipher the Phaistos Disc than understand LA's traffic—she enjoys taking it out for sorties, listening to Johnny Cash because he's the best of Taya's CD collection and she's too lazy to download music. Johnny and June, along with Morticia and Gomez Addams, had always been her shining examples of true love. She gets lost and then found and then lost again. She gnaws on beef jerky as she winds through the canyons, descends the craggy coastline, purrs through streets lined with minyanim of gnarled oaks. She avoids the claptrap of suburbia with its prefab and McMansions, the malls and discount oases with inflatable air dancers. The road less traveled, the brackish water, this is what's always interested her. Instinct is the ultimate survival weapon— it leads her to an inn that declares it was Al Capone's love nest and a biker bar featuring drag-queen bingo but is silent on the question that crooks its finger everywhere she goes: *Does this say Michael?*

Besides a scattering place, Cheri is looking for a good gun shop. She stumbles across Walter's Second Amendment Guns, which proves to be ridiculously well stocked. A Texan array of fully automatic weapons is the big draw, but what catches her eye is a sweet .308 Palma rifle and a Benelli M2. She leaves with both guns, plenty of ammo, and the address of an outdoor rifle range, courtesy of the redneck salesman with an *Only God Can Judge Me* tattoo on his arm whom she talked into not charging her tax if she paid cash. Gusmanov's rules for being a gentleman: Always carry plenty of cash, mints, and an umbrella. "A man arrives without these three things...date over."

She drives to the gun range with the box of Michael in the backseat. Next thing she knows she'll be turning into her mother and talking to him. She's crossed over into crazy land; this is what happens when you have too much time to think. Thankfully, there's the turnoff for the range. It doesn't matter if she's in Bakersfield or Ireland; give her a target and a gun, and time telescopes. All worries slough off like dead skin. She focuses on nothing but her shot. And somewhere in the middle of it all, Cheri realizes that she was looking for something when she went out that first time to Pro-Maxx and she's looking for it again here. She wants to reclaim a part of herself she gave up for Michael.

Not all of her forays are equally successful. Sometimes the best of the worst is a Christmas Store open 365 or a dive bar with nothing but sad, bleached-out strippers and tourists in backward baseball caps. Cars crash into each other or into electrical poles along the Coast Highway, shutting down access to Malibu for miles. It's on one of those days that she decides to fuck taking a canyon in bumper-to-bumper traffic just to get out of the house, and she turns the car around and heads home. As soon as she walks in the door, she smells it. Shit. Cat shit, on the white carpet and dribbling along the kitchen floor. She narrowly avoids stepping in it. Fucking cat. That's going to take some scrubbing. While looking for cleaning products, she spies the fucking cat staring at the kitchen floor. "Hey, Skip, are you okay?" Are cats supposed to blink? Because he's not. His pupils are dilated. Catatonic. He won't drink water. She doesn't know jack shit about animals. No point calling Taya and getting her all worked up, and she's pretty sure that Laura, the non-housekeeper, said something about going out of town. Now Cheri does step on something. It's brown and vegetal, and what is that underneath the wine cooler? She kneels down and runs her hand along the bottom; it's moist, and she snags a few scraggly mushrooms. Out of the recesses of her memory she pulls up a genus and species: *Agaricus xanthodermus.* If her long-ago mycology lessons with Zia Genny serve her, they're poisonous.

⸻

"Say that again," the girl behind the desk at the vet clinic says. Skipperdee's head sticks out of the towel she's thrown around him so it looks like he's wearing a babushka. Cheri juggles him while she fishes a plastic baggie out of her purse.

"*Agaricus xanthodermus.* Here's the sample. I told the guy who answered the phone all of this already, and he said the vet would take him right away."

"You would have spoken to me, and I've been here the whole time. Are you saying you spoke to me without my knowing it?"

"We're not really going to argue about this, are we?" It's looking like they might when a guy with a shaved head and full-sleeve tattoos interrupts: "It's okay. I spoke to her. So this is the shroom eater?"

"Yup. I think I gave you all the info. Should I leave him with you and you'll contact me?"

"No, no. I can take you back right now."

"Animals are required to be on leash or in a carrier. She should have brought him in a carrier," the receptionist says, twisting her red kabbalah string.

"At ease, Jenna," he says, "I got this." The guy, who is dressed in a T-shirt and jeans, comes around from behind the counter and takes a look at the bundle of Skipperdee in her arms.

"He's my friend's cat—I'm just kind of visiting," Cheri says to the guy.

"It will be okay, little dude," he says, taking him gently from her. "He's in shock. Good thing you came right in."

Cheri follows the guy into a room, where he puts Skipperdee on a metal examination table. "Do you know how long he's been like this?" he asks. She's about to answer when a long-haired surfer dude with exceedingly white teeth and scrubs walks in, extending his hand: "I'm Dr. Rick. Nice to meet you. Let's take a look at Skipperdee."

"You're in good hands," the guy says, touching Cheri's shoulder as he walks past. Dr. Rick says he's seen it all—dogs who've scarfed a batch of pot brownies, a whole soccer ball, a bottle of antidepressants. The patient is whisked away to be hydrated, fed activated charcoal, and monitored for the next twenty-four hours. Cheri forks over her credit card and checks the boxes to say she authorizes and will pay for whatever is needed. "You don't have to call me first, just get him back to normal."

Outside, released from the smell of disinfected piss in the clinic, Cheri reaches for a cigarette only to find her pack is empty. "Impressive knowledge of mycology," says a voice over her left shoulder. She turns to see the guy with the tattoos proffering a cigarette and a light. "I Googled it. Think you nailed it." He smiles with just enough curve to be genuine but also to say there's more to him than being a whatever-he-is at the vet's.

"Thanks."

"Don't worry. Doesn't look like you'll need to go find another Scottish fold to pass off as this one to your friend." She can't deny that the thought had occurred to her.

"Good to know."

"It's pretty scary seeing animals so helpless."

"I'm not really an animal person."

"Okay, then. Drive safely, just-kind-of-visiting lady." He stamps his cigarette out on the ground. She notices just then that his eyes are the color of tide pools—she wants to jump in.

She's too wired to head home. She hits the firing range again, then an über-dank dive bar with wannabe punks (everything old is new again) called Sinners and Saints. By the time she checks her phone, she's three Jack and Cokes lighter. Dr. Rick informs her that Skipperdee is doing well. If he doesn't convulse overnight he can go home in the morning. A bullet dodged deserves another drink. She flags down the bartender, who says his name is Chad but everyone calls him Rico.

"You didn't say if you're coming or going," Rico says, pouring her drink.

"In between," she says.

SONNY

Someone is ringing the doorbell. It takes a minute for the sound to register and then Cheri thinks it's her phone. She picks it up. It's one in the afternoon. How did that happen? How many Jack and Cokes have there been? It's not her phone. It's the door. She's wearing one sock, underwear, and her shirt from last night. She throws on sweatpants. "Stop that fucking dinging. It's hurting my head. I'm coming." She swings open the door.

"Land shark."

"What?" Cheri is too blinded by the sunlight to determine what she's seeing.

"Land cat."

"Is this a joke?"

"Don't tell me you're too young to get an *SNL* reference." Cheri vaguely recognizes that this is the guy from yesterday with all the tattoos before he says: "It's Sonny...from the vet. You remember this little dude?" Skipperdee's face peers out from behind the grate of a cat carrier.

"Haven't you heard of the phone?" she says, realizing she's not wearing a bra.

"That was plan A. You might want to check your..."

She looks down at the phone clutched in her hand and discovers her ringer is off. "Oh, shit. I'm sorry. You didn't have to come all the way out here."

"I live right down the beach, so it's no big deal."

"Come in. I'm a bit disorganized at the moment. What do I owe you for this?"

"I don't work at the clinic. Dr. Rick's my oldest friend. I stopped in to see him yesterday and randomly picked up the phone just to irritate GI Jenna. That girl cannot get enough of me."

"So you deliver cats for community service?"

"Only tripping ones," he says, opening the carrier and letting Skipperdee out. "Go forth and multiply, little dude. Or not, given you don't have the equipment. He's probably going to be super-thirsty so put out lots of water. Oh, and don't freak out if his shits are black for a while. From the charcoal."

"Good to know."

"Nice place. Very white."

"Not my house."

"Or cat. Got that." He takes in her appearance; she knows he's seeing the crumbles of yesterday's mascara dotting the top of her cheeks, her hair in a knotted mess. He gives her a half curl of a smile. "Rough night?" Cheri straightens her shirt. Skip wraps himself around her leg; she makes a point of petting him. "Hey, I'm the last one to judge," Sonny says. Even while pretending to like the cat, she can't help notice that Sonny's got a great skull, marble smooth. She suddenly understands why bald men are sexy. His face is lined enough to say he's lived loudly but not so much that it gives away his age. Maybe he's younger than she is.

"You want coffee? I think I've got some of those cup things left." After leading Sonny to the kitchen, she reaches into one of Taya's mile-high cabinets to get the individual pods for the coffee machine and realizes she didn't tie her sweats. While her midsection is exposed, she thinks she catches Sonny checking out the tattoo on her hip. She sucks in her stomach as she discreetly pulls her pants up.

"No thanks to the coffee," he says, "but you can have dinner with me."

"Excuse me?" She spins around to face him.

"Tonight. You. Me. Red meat. You do partake of dead cow, don't you? I've got some beautiful T-bones and big Italian reds that need to be drunk before they go bad. If you can't think of a reason to say no by seven thirty tonight, come over."

"You want to cook me dinner. I don't even know you."

"Perfect way to get acquainted. It's just a walk down the beach, so you've got an easy exit if my grilling skills fail to impress. You can't miss the house; it's got a green-and-white-striped awning. Here's the address." On his way out, he turns and says: "Nice ink, by the way."

As soon as he's gone, she thinks, *Did he just ask me over for a date?* Back when dinosaurs roamed the earth and she was single, she'd played away games only. Going to a guy's place gave her freedom to get up and leave whenever she wanted with some excuse like having to feed the dog she didn't own. She has no idea what it would feel like now. She hasn't been with anyone except Michael for almost twelve years.

She takes her cup of coffee and sinks into the big purple paisley pillows on the huge bed that Taya had insisted she sleep in because it had the best view. Taya had gone on to add, "And do not, I repeat, do not hesitate to fuck in it. You of all people need to get laid." Cheri isn't sure she even remembers how to kiss someone. She hasn't had an inkling of sexual desire since long before Michael died and wonders if all of her parts still work. She'd gone into the bedside-table drawer looking for a pen one night and found a huge Rolling Stones tongue vibrator. In fact, sex toys turned up in virtually every cabinet she opened. Her hand wanders idly over her stomach. It always looks so flat lying down. Was her gun tattoo the only thing Sonny had been checking out?

"I like my animal flesh short of blue but far from black," Sonny says, brushing butter on the steaks. He's doing it with a bundle of herbs tied to a wooden spoon. "Hope you're not too cold out here. I should have warned you, it's a bit spartan. Fire pit's built in, so nobody can sell that." Cheri had noticed the For Sale sign when she parked in front of Sonny's gray concrete modern house. What's left of the contents of the house are either in boxes or labeled for auction.

"I'm fine," she says, sipping on a glass of red wine. "I thought you had to leave the appliances if you're selling a house."

"You do, but tell that to my sister. On divorce number two, I guess she figures, fuck it. She sends e-mail updates listing the indignities. Today's was how could her ex drive his new girlfriend around Brentwood in her beloved Jag? I'm not kidding, she used the words *beloved Jag*. Good to know she's got her priorities straight."

"What are you cooking in that?"

"Potatoes," he says, lifting a lid on a cast-iron pot. "Not much you can't do with a grate and fire. Can you pass me those tongs?" He puts the meat on. There's a way that he fully inhabits his body that makes her think he'd be good at just about anything he did with it. It makes her a bit nervous. The flames surge, then die down with a spit and sizzle. "So...how's our shroom friend doing?"

"Glad you warned me about what to expect in the litter box. Other than that, he seems fine."

"Animals and kids. Down one minute and up the next."

"Oh, no. I forgot to bring your cat carrier."

"No worries," he says, "I can pick it up later."

"Are you always so helpful?"

"This is an aberration. My family has accused me of being a selfish prick. They weren't always wrong."

"Packing up your sister's house sounds pretty selfless to me."

"It's payback. She's let me crash here since I've been between houses, so to speak. You like the wine? It's cheeky. Got that cherry bite, a bit of pepper." He holds up his glass.

"To cheeky wine," she says. His shirt grazes her arm and she feels her hair stand on end.

"You're cold, let me run inside and get you something. If it flares up again, just move the meat to the side."

"No, really, I'm good." He's disappeared behind the sliders. The air is a combination of sea, grilling meat, and damp night air. Delicious. She closes her eyes and listens to the lapping of the waves.

"You *do* smile," he says, returning and draping a blanket over her shoulders. She watches him press the steaks with his finger to test if they're done. "Almost there."

"So what exactly is it that you do?" she asks.

"Well, I guess you could say I'm in hiding."

"Hiding as in *out*? Like from the law or the IRS?"

"From myself, mostly. But I'm getting better at that. I'm a

Valley boy. Grew up in Van Nuys—went to high school with Dr. Rick. Dropped out of Cal Arts with a half-finished degree in sound engineering and worked my way through the music business. Last seen as a manager. Lived most of my life out of suitcases, catering to overblown egos, fueling my own sense of self-importance, and popping, snorting, and drinking anything that came my way. Until I crashed. I quit drugs thirteen months ago. And you, just-kind-of-visiting lady, what are you hiding from?"

"I didn't say I was hiding."

"You didn't have to."

They eat themselves into a meat coma spiked by wine and easy conversation. Although Sonny managed rappers, he knows his punk rock. He tells her stories about being a roadie for the Circle Jerks and about his first engineering gig, for the Dickies' *Killer Klowns*. "The Dickies were a bubblegum Ramones rip-off," Cheri says, and they debate West and East Coast bands. They both extol the virtues of Klaus Nomi, and Sonny goes on-line and finds a video of his performance with David Bowie on *SNL*. It's not quite as great as either one of them remembers. They easily confess to the trivial—she has never heard of In-N-Out Burger, and he admits to owning and wearing, on occasion, a kilt. "The last perk," he says, cracking open a collector's Macallan. He wipes out their wineglasses with a napkin. "God, did I love the liquor sponsors, especially these folks. I gave this to my sister and her now-soon-to-be-ex for Christmas one year and found it shoved in the back of a closet behind his third-best set of golf clubs. Can you imagine?" The taste, with notes of chocolate and tobacco, has her in a leather armchair in front of a fire. "It's pretty fucking good, isn't it?"

Pretty fucking good. And, wow, the moon is bright. It has an otherworldly halo that shines bright against the ocean's blackness. They sit on the bottom step of the wood deck with their feet in the sand getting cold. He lights two cigarettes and passes her one. She feels the warmth of whiskey and smoke in her chest. "You miss it?" she asks.

"Miss what?"

"What you used to do," she asks, thinking of her career, what she may be in the process of giving up. "It sounds like you were good at it."

"Price of admission ended up being too high. At first I barely noticed how much of myself I gave away. A little cut here; it's just a flesh wound. That's nothing. I'm still in it for the right reasons. You rationalize the things you do and the people you do it with as being the cost of doing business. After all, drugs and the industry go hand in hand. And when you're up, you're master of all that exists. Limits? That applies to other people. When I partied, I pushed the edge farther and farther. I actually broke in and stole doggie morphine from Dr. Rick. And people followed me, thinking they could hang. Until crazy shit happened." He looks at the ocean and then turns and looks at her. "Someone I actually cared about—not that I had done a great job showing I cared—a young, talented kid I was working with got killed. Ran into the middle of a busy intersection, high on drugs *I* gave him. And, somehow, I stopped myself before I went over the cliff. My toes were hanging off. I was doing one of those backpedal things with my arms, but I stopped. Other people were like, 'I'm fine...aaaahhhh.' They went over."

Cheri wants to say, I understand. More than you think.

"That's tough," she says.

He stops to stub his cigarette out in the sand. "Mistakes, I've made a few. But do I miss making music? Every fucking day." In the moonlight, with the smoke in his eyes, he looks like a damaged priest. Why is it that the broken are drawn to each other, grasping at one another like drowning swimmers?

"Here's some trivia for you: Did you know that whiskey comes from the Gaelic *uisge beatha*?"

"'Water of life,'" she says. He looks shocked. And pleased.

"Didn't take you for a Gael."

"I've got a knack for languages. Especially ones nobody uses anymore."

"And do you use them?"

"Sometimes."

"Other than to impress me?"

"You impress easily."

"No," he says, "I don't." He lights another cigarette and takes a deep drag. "My last vice. Really good whiskey and really good wine don't count."

The wind blows her hair in her face.

"Do you mind, I wouldn't presume to know to tuck or not to tuck." She goes to push it away and she's trapped in his eyes. He puts his hand on the side of her face to brush back her hair. The kiss is inevitable. Lips have memory. She feels the first parting then the surge from entwining tongues, gentle and deep. Her hand grasps the perfect dome of his head; it is, as promised, silken, cool from the night air. His lips, soft as ripe plums, kiss her neck. Her body shivers in compliance. When they've made out until they're breathless, and sand is in their hair and jeans from buckling to the ground, rolling on top and then beneath, he holds his hand out. She lets herself be pulled up. Feels the curve of his biceps as he holds her like he means it, no hesitation, no fear.

He leads her into the empty cavern of the house, their footfalls echoing. Everything that is on comes off. They explore each other's bodies like blind people. Each touch is a revelation of hard and soft, wet and cool, smooth and rough. His body is taut and more sculpted than she'd thought. He traces his tongue down her belly. Her animal body is awakened; she can leave her mind and rise in reaction. Their urgency makes them rough. She bites his shoulder as they grapple on the floor, first him on top and then her. Knees and backs chafe from the carpet. They rise together; her legs wrap around him; his hands cup her ass. He carries her like this, lips and hips locked, and releases her onto a platform bed minus the platform. His hand covers her face, his fingers redolent of her. Then they are in her mouth. She's in the curl of pleasure, riding it, no hands on the rail. He says something like, "God, you are lovely." Later she will think she imagined it. Time stands still or moves so fast they can't grab hold of it. It is as if their bodies have reached a singularity and everything else is left behind.

They end crumpled, damp, on the floor beside the bed, a sheet one of them must have dragged down snared around her leg like seaweed. His arm is draped over her shoulder. She can see the veins rising beneath the shadows of lines and ink on his arm. He tickles her shoulder with his fingertips; she shivers. It's raining. Hard. She listens to it *tip-tip-tip, tip-tip-tip*–ing against the roof. He yawns and stretches his arms over his head. What was it about the over-the-head stretch, the casual display of biceps and forearm that was so masculine it made her feel like Olive Oyl? "You got me good here," he says, touching his neck.

"Oh, sorry," she murmurs.

"Why? I'm not. I don't know about you, but I'm thirsty as fuck." He goes to the kitchen in search of an oasis. She hoists herself into the bed. She thinks: *I'll just close my eyes for a minute. Just for a few seconds.*

She wakes with the where-the-hell-am-I panic of a one-night stand. Sour breath, dry mouth. Sonny's on his back, one leg swung nearly off the side of the bed. She checks him out in the gray morning light: no drool, no snoring. His face looks younger at rest. She can't believe she passed out like that; sex was one thing, but actual sleeping with someone? She sees a bottle of water left on the floor for her; she grabs it and guzzles quietly so as not to wake him. She settles back into bed and realizes what's missing. For the first time since Michael's death, she didn't awaken to a sense of dread.

Sonny sighs and rolls over, his hand finding her breast, rousing her and himself into the half-life of not-quite-awake desire. They go easy; he enters her spoon-position, his fingers cheerleading her into the collapse of orgasm. She drifts, dissolving into vapor. When she wakes again the room is dark and she's alone in bed. She levers up a blind he must have closed. The ocean is whitecapped, the sky is gloomy, spitting rain.

She checks herself out in the bathroom. It definitely looks like she was fucked all night. The only thing she sees to put on is a sweatshirt hanging on the back of the door. It's missing a zipper. She dons it and pads to the kitchen, searches the space for her missing clothes. He's gotten a fire burning in the fireplace and proffers a mug. "Be warned: it's instant. I'd have done a Starbucks run but it's pretty gnarly out there. What—are you crushing on the djellaba? You are, aren't you?" He's wearing a white-and-blue-striped cotton tunic. It's not unsexy.

"Looks like a caftan to me."

"I got it in Morocco. Stole it from a hotel room. Admit it. It's turning you on." He's funny and knows how to build a fire, but where is her underwear?

"Have you seen my clothes?"

"I've got another one of these if you want," he says, referring to his caftan. "Super-comfortable. Although that's a good look," he says, taking in her near-nakedness. She runs a hand over her hair and feels sand.

"You're not good at accepting compliments." Michael always used to say that to her, but she tries to put that thought out of her mind.

"Not my strong suit," she says, sipping her coffee. Instant makes her nostalgic, something about astronauts and Tang and simpler times.

"Don't tell me you're shy? You weren't last night—"

"I'm autistic before I've had coffee."

"Got it. Look, can we cut past the awkward part now we're sober? You have anywhere you've got to be anytime soon? Because I'd like to hang out with you some more."

"Are you always this direct?"

"I'm not always anything." He's moved next to her and traces her neck with his finger. "You're cold. Get ye by the fire, lassie. That and a shot of *uisge beatha* will warm you right up."

They toast and drink standing by the fire. He moves behind her, his arms around her waist, and she wonders how he can still smell so good after a night of sex. She's seduced by the fire, relaxing into his steadiness. She can feel her lids getting heavy when it hits her: she's forgotten about the cat.

"If he was going to die, he would have done it already. It's true. If there were toxins left in his system, he's either purged it or is four-paws-up. In any case, there's no point rushing back."

"Says the volunteer vet?"

"You thought I was the vet? More like vet tech. If you're going to be facetious, at least get your semantics right."

"I should see for myself. Clothes, please?"

"Ah, what the hell, I'll drive you. We'll stop and get some food on the way. I'm jonesing for something ethnic. You like Indonesian? I know a place that makes killer crab *lada hitam*."

"Where do you get Indonesian food around here?"

"Well, it's not exactly around here. In case you haven't noticed, Malibu is a whole lot of bland and blander. I'm starving, aren't you? You have to be hungry—it's two o'clock. Your clothes..." He opens the door to the living-room closet, where they're hung on a peg. "Didn't want them to dry all wrinkled." Did she look like someone who cared if her jeans were wrinkled?

"I thought you were an animal lover."

"I love a lot of things. Spicy food isn't totally top of the list, but close. It's all about balance; I learned that the hard way. Come on, let's do this. It looks like the rain is slowing down for a minute. We'll take it to go. The faster we get there, the faster we get back to check on the kitty."

"Not exactly around here" is twenty minutes away in a strip mall off Pico in Santa Monica. Sonny's truck is filled with boxes so she has to maneuver to get in and out. He holds up an umbrella and they dash through a tiny market back to an even tinier restaurant. Who would even know this place existed? As a child she'd associated the scent of cumin with dirty underwear, but now the spicy smell makes her ravenous. The woman behind the counter recognizes Sonny and leaps up to help. She brings out a hot tray of banana-leaf wraps for them to try while they wait. They're like little Asian TV dinners. Melt-in-your-mouth, pop-of-spicy deliciousness.

"I told you it was worth it," he says.

Because you're worth it. Was that a shampoo commercial, some bullshit statement that was all Go, woman, go, but at the same time saying, As long as you cover those grays? You're worth it. Something Taya might say once Cheri tells her she hooked up with a random guy she met at her vet's. A guy who belts back the booze despite being self-proclaimed sober. She may be hungover but she doesn't miss a beat.

Skipperdee, it turns out, is exactly where she left him, curled up on a white pillow on the white couch, shedding gray fur. He meows when they call his name but doesn't get up. They peel off their wet jackets and Sonny sets about building a fire in the living room while she putters in the kitchen, putting food out for the cat. Funny how jobs divide up in coupledom. How much was in Michael's column that's now in hers? One of his last sentences was "Remember to call the chimney sweep!" She has not yet followed through.

"Where are you?" Sonny says, handing her a beer.

"I'm here." As soon as the food is opened they plate it and carry everything they need to the table by the fire in the living room. Cheri eats ravenously—this was definitely worth the trip in what's now pouring rain.

"Okay, I can't eat another bite," she says, pushing her plate away, feeling relaxed.

"There it is again."

"What?"

"Your smile. It's crooked, but it's there."

"I smile. It's not like I don't smile."

"You've got a lot of looks, but it's hard to know what you're thinking. I bet you've used that to your advantage." She purses her lips into a bit more of a smile. Sonny eyes what's left on her plate. "You going for that or can I?"

"All yours," she says. He stabs a shrimp with his chopstick. Cheri looks out the window; the sky is dark and foreboding; the rain is starting to come down harder. "It's getting apocalyptic out there. People in LA always seem to be putting sandbags out or fighting fires or dealing with earthquakes. Why do people pay all this money to live where the land is most unstable?"

"Unpredictable is more interesting," he says with his own crooked smile.

"I thought we were talking about weather."

"Are we? Then bring on the zombie apocalypse. If it's going to end, might as well go out raging against the dying of the light. Unfortunately, all my end-of-the-world provisions are in storage," he says.

"Don't tell me you're one of those guys with a homemade bomb shelter..."

"Let's say I have good survival skills, thanks to my second stepdad sending me away to wilderness training for fucked-up kids. You think cooking over a fire pit is roughing it, this was hard core. We had to eat rattlesnake and bugs, whatever we could find. Or starve. You know how hard it is to skin a rattlesnake with your bare hands when you're ten?" She wonders if that's even possible. "After the quake in '94 I got a bit extreme, I'll admit it, with the freeze-dried food and emergency generators."

"So you're saying you have sandbags."

"Correct. But if there was a tsunami or major disaster I'd be way unprepared. Bad news about being homeless means you can't carry generators and stockpiles of munitions around with you."

"You don't need stockpiles."

"Depends on how many zombies we're going to be fighting.

That's why you have this?" He puts his hand on the top of her gun tattoo.

"That's kind of personal," she says.

"I think we veered into the realm of personal when my tongue was on your pussy," he says. "But I don't mean to pry."

"I got it in a former life."

"Former life, former boyfriend. You got fucked up and got matching tattoos. I know the drill."

"We were cops." She cracks open the Macallan she's glad she remembered to bring.

"Unexpected."

"That's what a lot of people said at the time," she says, pouring them each a whiskey.

"So back up. You said you taught religion. Was that before or after being a cop? Was this in Chicago or New York?"

"The eighties, New York. In the housing projects. On the Lower East Side."

"You are definitely an interesting woman. I don't trust anything linear. Why did you become a cop?"

She considers what to say. "Probably because I knew it would piss off my parents. I wanted to get as far away from them and their world as possible."

"And did you?"

"Mission accomplished," she says, taking a drink.

"I worked with guys straight out of Compton; I can imagine it must have been pretty hard core in the projects in the eighties. And as a woman? Was pissing off your parents worth it?"

"Okay, maybe that wasn't the only reason," Cheri says. "I did have some ideas about making a difference."

"So tell me about the guy out there with the same tat. You were in love with him?" She'd been married for ten years and yet when she thinks of being in love, she goes back to Eddie Norris.

Whether it was the rain or the hangover or being properly fucked for the first time in ages, Cheri found herself telling him things that, in all the years of marriage to Michael, she had never revealed. She started with her first months on the job. Told him about the harassment; opening her locker to find bloody Tampax or, once, some rotting fish. Cops calling her Kike Dyke and Bagel Bitch. How she had the highest scores in her police academy class but wasn't put in rotation; couldn't get in a car or foot patrol because females were girls first, cops second. Until Eddie Norris. "He came from a SEU narcotics division up on One Hundred and Twelfth Street; he made twenty collars a month. A hundred hours of overtime—he barely slept he worked so much. He was a solution looking for a problem; everyone wanted to be his friend. Most guys in that position were walking egos. But not him. He got along with everyone. And he wasn't afraid he'd look like less of a man because he was letting a rookie female actually do the job. A lot of cops wanted to be in Alphabet City then; dope deals took place on nearly every corner, out of cinderblock holes in the walls of abandoned buildings. The projects were an urban blight, drug dens built into broken-down tenements. It was a hotbed, you always felt like something was about to explode, and usually it did. I know, you think adrenaline rush, power trip . . ."

"I think you said you lived there. The good-cop part," Sonny says. Cheri thinks of Yure's grandson in the wheelchair. She and Eddie had found the gangbanger who did that and put him away.

"There was that. I wouldn't have gotten on that beat if it wasn't for Eddie. He was comfortable in his skin at a time when I wanted to jump out of mine. He didn't give a shit what people thought. People were always busting his balls about his car—this piss-yellow Mazda—but he didn't care. He loved it."

"And he loved you. Not that I'm equating you with a piss-yellow Mazda."

"Yeah, we had something...a real connection."

"So what was it? I'm not going to go for the easy, cop-on-cop sex. You said fuck you to your parents and joined the police force and here was a guy who I'm assuming was the total opposite of anyone you'd grown up with..."

"No. Well, no and yes." She might have been running away, but she was also running toward something. "I guess you could say Eddie Norris caught me. He stopped me, allowed me to let down and just be myself. He accepted me." She looks around in search of what is just now sinking in as being the heart of what went so right and then so terribly wrong in their relationship. "I felt safe," she admits. Sonny gives her a knowing nod.

"So why did it end?"

"The truth?"

"No," he says, "I want a lie. Your choice, given there's no way I'm going to know the difference."

Should she tell about that night? What sent her running back to Eighty-first Street to barricade herself in her room in a tailspin of shock and heartbreak? She had never spoken about it to anyone. Eddie Norris banging on her apartment door. Insistent. The last time he'd done that, he'd taken her and fucked her from behind over the bathtub. The clear plastic shower curtain pressing against her face, like Saran Wrap, like silk. That was a fantasy. They'd done some role-playing but part of their cop-on-cop sex was they'd seen enough darkness to never let it go too far. She'd thought maybe he was going for a repeat.

"He was dressed all in black like he was going to a bridge-and-tunnel club. He said, 'Get dressed,' and I knew it was something serious. He followed me into the bathroom. I was wearing a white tank top, stretched out to the tips of my knees, brushing my teeth. My mouth was full of toothpaste and I didn't even have time to spit," she says.

"It's always the little things that stick in your memory," Sonny says. The little things, the cards Eddie laid on the table: coiled wire, a yard of heavy chain link, a switchblade, twelve-inch hunting knife, assault rifle, nightstick, stun gun.

"He pulled them out of his boot, from underneath his coat. There were no questions asked or answered. We'd all heard that a cop was killed during a buy-and-bust; the perp shot him in the head. The cop was an old friend of Eddie's, guy named Tobin. We'd hung out with him and his girlfriend, a nurse, a few times. It was a different world back then, before Rodney King, before Louima and the plunger. Crack was new to the city and hit the projects like a Mack truck. We were in the middle of a war zone. The mentality was good guys versus bad guys. We were the good guys and were going to win. There was always collateral damage," she says and looks at Sonny. "Sounds like you've seen some of that."

"Indeed I have," he says.

"Someone's kid, an innocent person in the wrong place at the wrong time. But if a cop was killed? One of us? That was personal. We handled that on our own. The sergeant let us off in shifts, fixed things so the people who needed to be out looking could do it quietly."

Sonny listened. He smoked three, maybe four cigarettes all the way down to the filter, each time waiting until she paused before he lit up the next one.

Eddie Norris invited her to cross the threshold that night, to

become part of the pack, the tribe of men. The others were waiting for them in the street below her apartment.

"It was two or three a.m. The four of them had been at it for
twenty-four hours without sleep; they were hopped up on caf-
feine, maybe a little blow off the back of a hand. Johnson was
the youngest, not too far out of high school. He was shifting
from foot to foot trying not to let on that he was nervous.
McTieg and Rayner were veterans; they weren't expecting me
and weren't happy about it, but they couldn't say anything because of Eddie. They all had a mantra: Someone's going to pay
for this, that scumbag who did it is going to pay." Stalking Alphabet City like hungry wolves, going to crack houses, drug corners,
whores and jacked-up cars and a boom box thumping. It was
an indigo night, that quality of darkness that's more blue than
black lit occasionally by the street lamps in the projects blinking on and off; broken glass, bullet holes in the windows. They'd
done walkabouts like this a thousand times, moving from outside
refuse to inside refuse. The reek of piss in the hallways, vomit
and spilled malt liquor, needles and vials crunching underfoot.
"We went to a couple of places, looking for our usual informants,
following a lead Eddie had. The shooter was a twenty-one-year-
old Puerto Rican male, spider tattoo on his neck, wearing a red
hoodie—we were going off a witness ID. Nothing was turning
up." Frustration spread through their systems; they strode through
the derelict tent city of Tompkins Square Park with tight mouths
and loud fists. McTieg slammed his foot into a cardboard tent,
causing it to collapse and sending cockroaches that could use a
leash skittling out. "What you doing, man," and then deep moans
from underneath the debris while he kept kicking. "Fuck, fuck
you, motherfucker."

"The tension ratcheted to a point where nobody said anything. Underneath the anger there was a deep sense of helplessness; if we couldn't get a cop killer, what was the point of the job? Any one of us could have been Tobin. We got a tip that Red Hood's girlfriend was in a crack den by the river. Crack spots weren't hard to find—people lined up outside of them like they were handing out welfare cheese. Anyway, she turned up in the first one. Rayner grabs her by the throat, saying, 'I'm going to choke the life out of you if you don't tell me where he is.' She didn't have to because he was stupid enough to show up there. Someone spotted him as he was pushing his way through junkies. But he started running in the other direction as soon as he saw us.

"We chase after him. He ducks into the vacant lots by Tenth Street. It was this maze of junkyards with half-demolished buildings, rotting-out appliances—it looked like a bomb had gone off; streetlights had been shot or burned out. It was dark, lots of places to hide, so we split into pairs. I'm with Rayner, Eddie's with Johnson, McTieg's on his own. We've got our flashlights out and guns drawn when Eddie's voice comes over the walkie-talkie; they've sighted him and are close behind.

"When Rayner and I get there, Red Hood's climbing a chain-link fence. Eddie grabs his leg hard, pulls his shoe off. They get him down. He's saying he didn't do nothing, 'I don't know about shooting no cop, man.'" Was it then that McTieg smashed him in the face with his bully stick so hard he split him open like a Marlboro box, or had it taken a few minutes? She can't remember time, only images: the topography of hate on Rayner's face, his mouth as he shouted, "Fucking spic, eat shit, you PR motherfucker." Saying it for all the times people had called him nigger, paying it forward to the next minority in line.

"The perp was bleeding from his mouth and nose, but his eyes were blank. He was spitting blood but kept saying, 'You got it all wrong, it wasn't me.' They all say that. You can catch them red-handed and like children they say, 'It wasn't me.' Eddie Norris was taunting him. 'You feel like a big man, killing a cop,' he screamed, spit flying out of his mouth, 'you feel like a big man *now?*' McTieg put his gun to Red Hood's head and said no more bullshit. Eddie told me to cuff him, which I did, and then search him. He wasn't armed and just as I found a joint, a dipper—meaning it was laced with PCP—Red Hood surged to his feet with the kind of crazy adrenaline you get from PCP and charged like a linebacker right at McTieg. He was cuffed. I don't know where he thought he was going to go. He was like a bull. And that was it." They were on him; fists and chains, grunts and curses.

"It was primal, like animals in a pack smelling blood. They fed off one another's anger and righteousness. I felt the adrenaline, that rush of being on high alert and in fight mode. I was right there with them as they jostled and pushed to get at him, have their turn to kick the shit out of him. But then McTieg moved over and blocked me out. And in that moment I thought: *What are we doing?* The collective rage had everyone blind. They were in a circle. I was outside, watching, realizing just how fucked up it was." Even now, she can smell the sweat of men in violent release, hear them wheezing and groaning in anger. She remembers McTieg putting his cigarette out on Red Hood's arm, saying, "That's for Tobin."

Cheri glances at the fire in the fireplace; it's burned down. The rain drums on the roof. Sonny hasn't looked away from her the whole time. His elbows are on the table; he leans toward her and asks what she knew was coming.

"So what did you do?"

"Nothing," she says heavily. "I did nothing." She can see Red Hood's fingers twitching. Then falling open, motionless.

"And he—" Sonny starts, but she cuts him off.

"Yes. He did."

Sonny is still staring at her. His expression is unreadable.

"Afterward, everyone was shaking from the high. Johnson was high-fiving, but Eddie Norris took charge. We had to tell the same story and everyone had to calm down. He laid the whole thing out. The perp was high on PCP and resisted arrest, attacked officers with deadly intent. As long as you could explain it on paper, you could pretty much do anything you wanted.

"I had to do the report because I had the lowest rank. And something was bothering me. Eddie was all, Just get this done, quick and easy. But I went back and checked Red Hood's mug shot. His tattoo was on the right side of his neck. The witnesses all said the shooter had a tattoo on the left side. The closer I looked, the more I could tell we'd got the wrong guy. Red Hood was a criminal and a scumbag, but he wasn't the guy who killed Tobin."

"And you told Eddie."

"I showed him. It was really clear. And he said, 'Forget you saw this. We got the shooter, end of story.' He took the file. I'm sure he destroyed it. And for him, that was the end of that. He went on like nothing had happened, started talking about where we'd go for a beer after work."

"He rationalized it and you didn't . . ."

"It was more than that. The thing is, I saw something in Eddie that night. I knew, deep down, that it was over then. I just didn't want to admit it." She hasn't been able to admit what she saw that night, she realizes, until right now. "He was exactly like the rest of them, but in a way, he was worse. They were in the fog of rage, like what happens in war—all you care about is getting the enemy and you forget the enemy is a living, breathing person. You don't know what someone is capable of in an extreme situation. We were trained to understand that. I couldn't know how I'd react until I was there. But I saw something in his eyes that night. After I left the circle, Eddie looked back at me. And for a split second, I saw a glint of recognition. Like he saw what I saw. I'd like to think he was going to stop it. But when he looked at me again, his eyes were empty. The man I knew wasn't in there. And then he turned around and hit Red Hood in the ribs with his nightstick." Her throat constricts for a moment; she looks down. Sonny waits for her to continue. "I'd grown up convincing myself that I could be one of the guys. If I just proved myself, worked hard enough. Being a cop, I thought I'd found my people, my tribe. But that night showed me that I could never be one of them. And it made me question if I even wanted to be. I wasn't built like that. I loved that job. But my ideas of justice—all of the right reasons I became a cop—were capsized. So I quit."

"Without saying anything? Didn't you give a reason why? Did you explain it to Eddie?"

"I just turned in my gun and badge and that was it. I wasn't one for explaining myself."

"He didn't come looking for you?"

"I went to a place I thought he'd never find me: my parents' apartment on the Upper East Side. Eddie Norris didn't know who my parents were; nobody at the NYPD did. I probably hoped he *would* find me and say he couldn't live without me. I guess I was still in love with him. I was also on a small speed binge and not thinking at all rationally."

It's dark outside. The rain picks up again, and the house rattles a bit from the wind. The last time she saw Eddie Norris was in a downpour.

"I saw him one last time. I met him at this coffee shop we used to go to, and he slid into the booth next to me, ordered coffee, and when the waiter was gone he said: 'You fucking disappear and don't say a word to me, it looks bad, very fucking bad.' He said people were worried. People who didn't know me like he knew me. 'Do I still know you?' he asked.

"I knew what he was intimating. I told him he wasted his favors finding me. If I was going to talk, why would I have quit? I wouldn't do that to him. Frankly, I didn't think about the repercussions of quitting. I just ran. But if Eddie Norris needed to hear the words, I'd give him the words. I told him I wouldn't say anything about that night or what I'd found out to anyone. And I kept my promise. Until now. But my word wasn't enough at that point. He needed to go back with insurance. He said, 'This is what you're going to do: you're going to write a statement that you quit because you have drug problems, you've been struggling with addiction.' He knew about my fondness for uppers. Nobody else did, and I never used on the job. Not once.

"He also said that if I didn't make this bogus statement, they'd do it for me. Plant drugs in my old locker and discredit me so if I ever *did* come forward, I'd never be able to get a job as a police officer anywhere again. Needless to say, I didn't write it. I wasn't going to add a lie about myself to all the other ones." Cheri flashes on the other statement, the one she didn't sign for Richards. She shakes her head at the irony, the pattern in the disparate mesh of her life, where she is the common thread.

"That's quite a story." Sonny's voice is a shared exhale. When she looks up she sees the damaged priest, the wounded healer. The rain *tip-tip-tips*. She goes to stack the plates and Sonny reaches over and touches her fingers with his. "You know the intimacy-of-strangers code? Your secret's safe with me. Thank you."

"For what?" she asks.

"For being real. It may be easier with someone you don't know, but it's not easy." Was she too real? She named names. She hadn't even known how heavy this burden was until she dropped it.

"Talking to you is pretty easy," she says. "I wish everything could be that way."

"It can be."

She believes him. For that moment, for an hour, maybe for the rest of the night. They wake up and have morning sex. He falls back asleep with his hand on her belly. She feels his breath come and go like the tide. They sleep like teenagers as the rain stops and the room lights up momentarily, then fades to gray. When they're up and in need of nicotine, they huddle beneath the deck awning, passing a cigarette back and forth. He says, "It's fucking cold and wet out here."

"Californians are pussies. Try Chicago in the winter."

"Actually, I'm going to try Seattle. Warmer but rainier."

It takes her a moment to ask: "What's in Seattle?"

"Guess I'll find that out," he says. "I'm moving there, which is why I've got all the boxes in my trunk. A friend of mine has a recording studio there, and a guesthouse. And we'll see. I'm leaving day after tomorrow." Cheri nods and looks out at the ocean. It's hard to tell the demarcation between water and air, it's tone-on-tone of gray, still, blending upward into near white. When she turns back, the acoustics have changed and they both know it. Sonny goes to take a shower.

"So . . ." Sonny says when they're at the door.

"Let's just leave it at this. If we're being honest, let's stay honest."

She hands him the cat carrier and does the obligatory embrace. "You take care," he says and kisses her forehead. She's quick to close the door behind him and listens as he starts up his truck. She feels very small and younger than she can remember; something is surging and she's taken by its tide. The outside world has come alive again in hyper-sound; the traffic on the PCH hurts her ears—it's so loud, it bleeds through the door. *I'm bleeding,* she thinks. That's what it feels like; fuck, fuck, fuck. The sobs come in soundless shudder steps. She sinks to the floor. There's no container that can hold the sadness anymore. It leaks out of her eyes, her nose, an onslaught.

Like drought-dry land after rainfall, she is unable to absorb, cannot understand why she tears up when she sees an elderly man at Ralphs struggling to get his wallet out of his pants, then forgetting why he's at the register. All music lyrics, happy or sad, remind her of Michael. Just the whiff from the fish joint at PCH brings up the Rockaways, the Eddie Norris traffic accident of her heart. A good cry is a pretty thing, and Cheri hasn't been able to cry for so long. Tear-streaked and luminous in low light, something she might be able to do in public instead of the red-eyed meltdowns she's been having. But if she is the sum of her secrets, then Sonny's releasing her to talk about Red Hood changed the equation. She'd already quit something she loved because of a man, and she'd been running from that cowardice for a long, long time. Her current career might be in shambles, but she doesn't have to rinse and repeat. She hears Michael's voice: *No conflict, no suffering.* There are pieces to pick up. She has no idea how she will assemble them or what they will form. But one thing is for certain: she will do it differently.

Meanwhile the rain has stopped, and almost instantly, Malibu is back to being 78 degrees and sunny. She has a longing for sweater weather and an escape from joggers. She sits on the deck beneath an umbrella, sunglasses, layers. A girl in cutoffs and a T-shirt runs toward her. She's pale, with short, dark hair. The girl jogs by and tilts her head, giving her a snaggletoothed smirk. She could be a younger, California version of herself. *Go home,* she seems to say. *Go home and finish it.*

YOUR OWN BACKYARD

"Don't get me wrong, it's got great bones. We just have to get rid of all this...stuff," the real estate agent says to Cheri, pointing to the jumbled assortment of books, CDs, Michael's African masks, and other eclectic totems burdening the living room of her house. The agent hands her a thick folder of comps and a list of repairs that need to be made before they put the house on the market. It's long. "You might consider staging it. Really helps get the price up. Leave it to me, I can fluff like nobody else." Cheri says thanks, shows her to the door, and promptly trashes the folder. She's grown to love this old house. The angles were quirky, the floors sloped; it was freezing in the winter and hot in the summer. Even new plumbing sighed and gurgled. She and Michael would complain, but over time, the house's eccentricities had become part of them. She thinks about Sonny, his truck full of the few belongings he had left, driving to whatever awaits him. Michael saying that the ultimate freedom lies in letting go. Although it never came up, she thinks he would have wanted her to sell the house.

She had started packing her office. Taya was right; she could write without being university-sanctioned. Yet she feels her chest clutch when she thinks about not having the title Professor before her name, that stamp of approval. She'd always been part of a big institution, and had equated work not only with a paycheck, but with the feeling of shared mission and purpose. She may never fully understand Sol's reasons for leaving her his patents, but money, she realizes, is only what you project onto it. As a teenager, she had refused Sol's money as a way to show her disdain for him. She'd never stopped running for long enough or admitted to any uncertainty. Money gave her freedom to say, "I don't know yet." But whatever she does next isn't going to be done out of fear. The rest, she tells herself, will follow. She called her publisher and said that she was ready to start working on a book, was going to investigate some new subjects and get back to them with ideas. It might not be in these files and boxes, but she'll find her subject. Or, and this was a novel concept, she'll allow the subject to find her.

⁓⁓⁓

Standing in her bedroom, she's amazed at what two self-professed nonmaterialistic people could amass. The tenor of this purge is markedly different from the one Cici helped her with; discarding her own worn-down soles and torn sheets elicits far less emotion. She feels a surprising rush of tenderness thinking of her mother folding Michael's clothes. What would people find out about her if they went through her things after she died? Not much would shock. If anyone else had to get her house ready for sale, it would simply be a testament to her bad housekeeping.

Cheri pulls a box of photographs from the top shelf of her

closet. Cheri was always a terrible subject. As a child, she'd claimed that she was part American Indian and fearful of having her spirit stolen to try to get out of school-picture day with the faux backgrounds and gap-toothed smiles.

She spills the photographs on her bed. It's a dystopian trip to random periods of her life: the pallid Girl Scout standing at the top of her driveway in Montclair; flat-chested prepubescent sandwiched between her well-endowed cousins in Varese; a Polaroid of her spiked blue hair and long-gone partying friends; grad-school-era shots of her looking tired, mouth tight, don't get too close. She can also see her under-chin developing; "Beware the under-chin," Michael would say, "you'll turn into your mother." Shots of Michael. Younger Michael, handsome and robust, his eyes crinkling as he smiled. Black-and-white snaps from their trip to city hall where they were married. In the picture, she sits on a faded wooden bench waiting to go in to say their vows. Expectant. Nervous. Michael had said, "Look at me like you do when I know you're seeing me. When we're alone." Her eyes broadcast the message *I love you. More than I can say.* Michael had a copy of this photograph in a frame in his office, but it's been years since she's really looked at it or let herself remember the day it was taken. In other photographs, their poses reveal their decline. Leaning slightly away from him at Taya's wedding; arms folded tightly against her chest at a film festival—it is clear how she'd been so afraid of human connection, of trust. And yet she was able to lay it all down with a stranger over a rainy weekend. If she'd said those same things to Michael, maybe it would have changed what he'd written in his journal.

There are photos of her parents. Scallop-edged photos from another era, Cici posed with Sol like they're in an ad for scotch.

Cici with her barely legal curves holding up a cocktail; Sol with his rakish hair, cigarette in hand. There's a snap of Sol showing off his legs in tennis shorts, posing like a cancan dancer. Those young people are her parents? Or just two young people in love. How strange. This photograph was taken the night before Sol died. She remembers Cici showing it to her, moaning, "How, how?" The waiter must have taken their picture; it's a little out of focus. After years of struggle with his weight and phlebitis, Sol looks pretty fit for someone in his late sixties. He always carried himself with the bearing of a man who knows the measure of his wealth, but she detects he might have come to know something more. They do look happy.

But amid all the detritus of her life with Michael, Cheri knows there's one object in the house she's been avoiding. It sits, day after day, in the bottom left drawer of her desk, beneath a stack of condolence cards and correspondence she hasn't opened since returning from California. The envelope Michael had handed to her, saying, "Wait for the right time to open it." One pill makes you smaller; the other makes you tall; she's Alice minus the hallucinogens. But there was never a "right time" for anything. You just made a decision, and lived with the fallout. Cheri opens the drawer, shuffles through the piles of paper until she sees the manila envelope. She tears it open and pulls out a file with a handwritten note on Michael's stationery clipped to the front.

Cheri,

Forgive me for doing this without your knowledge. If I'd asked, I think you and I both know you wouldn't have agreed. I wanted to leave you with something meaningful, and I'm glad I could accomplish it. The closet is open, kiddo. Now make the skeleton dance.

Love,
M.

She knows what the file contains before she even opens it and sees the business card for Ellen Jameson, PI. Michael had been on Cheri for years to find her birth parents, and she'd staunchly refused. The investigator's card is attached to the report and records with a paper clip. But Ellen Jameson has been thorough. She's with an agency that specializes in finding the biological parents of adopted children, and Cheri sees the record of a live birth and her birth certificate, documents from the New Jersey child welfare services, paperwork from the family who fostered her. Jameson reports her findings in a matter-of-fact style Cheri is familiar with from her years in the NYPD. It's hard to compute that the child in this file is her. The report states that her biological mother left the Trenton Family Clinic shortly after giving birth. Cheri had witnessed a crack whore leave her baby in a trash can so she could go get high, had found a homeless kid hiding in a rusted discarded refrigerator in the rubble near East First Street. Child abusers weren't only male; she'd seen firsthand how neglect killed more kids in the projects than crime did.

Miriam. That's not a crack-whore name. That's it—a first name and nothing more. The PI was unable to find any leads on Cheri's birth mother. But Ellen Jameson did find her birth father. The state apparently had his name misspelled. There's a DNA test that shows a 99.99 percent probability that she is one Gerald Dempsey's biological child. Back in 1962, the state had briefly looked for a Jerry Dempsey. Misspelled names are the first thing a detective checks for, but leave it to government workers to let that slide. She looks again at the documents. His background check shows nothing, not even an outstanding parking ticket. The photocopy of his driver's license is bad; it's hard to make out his features, as blotches of black ink further blur the typical DMV mug shot. He's looking a little sideways, like he wasn't quite ready for the photo. It's hard to believe this is real. It took the PI a year to locate this man and verify her findings, so Michael had started this long before his diagnosis.

Gerald Dempsey, age sixty-nine, living in Queens, New York. She's got his date of birth, background check, and former addresses—all in Queens; the guy stayed put. Gerry or Jerry. Something as simple as one letter on hospital records meant the difference between her being raised by Gerald Dempsey or Sol. All the time she was growing up in Montclair and then living in the city, her birth father was just an hour away. Practically in her own backyard. She could have passed him on the street or in the subway. Maybe she did. It's too much to take in.

While Michael was looking for answers about his impending death all across America, wending his way to letting go, he'd also been searching to give Cheri directions to find her beginnings. And he did all this without her knowledge. Did he get her DNA from a toothbrush, a comb? She'd be pissed off if she weren't so moved. Had this search for Cheri's full story been part of his longing for an intimacy she couldn't provide? She was indeed a stubborn fuck. If she wants to know more, she's going to have to find out herself. And that's exactly the bait Michael knew would lure her. She stares at the end of the report, where it says that Gerald "Gerry" Dempsey had consented to a DNA test. The last line of the report lists his phone number and address and states he's "open to contact."

She carries his phone number around with her for days. She thinks about what she would say to him, how she would introduce herself, but everything she says in her head comes off as absurd. She'd always been determined not to look backward; investigating her birth parents was a return to the original wound. As a child, after she found out she was adopted, she'd idealized her birth parents as the opposite of Sol and Cici: open, accepting, unpretentious. But in the end, even her fantasies led back to the harsh truth—they had given her up. The fault was in her. And them. Nobody abandons their child because of "good" circumstances, and even before she'd seen the worst in humanity, it wasn't hard to paint that picture. Michael might have been prescient or maybe he'd given her more credit than she gave herself, but she can't help laughing. *Make the skeleton dance.* Face your past. He would have appreciated the irony of her doing this now, as she's divesting herself of what was their life in Chicago to plunge forward into the total unknown.

Cheri stands at the top of the stairs to Michael's office holding the box with his ashes. It's a cold Chicago winter day; the sky is gray-streaked and if she squints she can just see a peek of sun far in the distance. She looks out on the frost-covered yard, thinking of all the times she saw Michael standing in the middle of it, of the day she'd watched him do yoga and glimpsed how we are all infinitely interconnected. She'd been looking for the perfect place, a place that said, This is what Michael would have wanted. He had loved living and creating his art here. It was where he chose to die. But it isn't about the place. Michael knew that. This, she realizes, was about her good-bye. "Okay," she says, holding up the box and tipping the plastic bag. What comes out is dense and dark and blows back in her direction, making little plinking sounds against the railing. Crap. She waits for the breeze to die down and tries again, scattering one handful at a time. She watches Michael's ashes cascade through her fingers, making a white-gray cloud that slowly dissolves into mist.

TRUTH IS

Gerry Dempsey's neighborhood in Howard Beach is lower middle class but tidy, with rows of multifamily red-brick houses decorated with blinking Christmas lights. Cheri watches two kids in braids hand-clap while singing "Miss Mary Mack" on the little patch of asphalt they call a backyard. "You're sure you're going to be okay getting here?" he asked at the end of their stilted conversation yesterday, after she'd worked up the nerve to dial his number. "I can come to you if you want." He told her to call when she reached his address and he would come down to meet her. She doesn't have to call because he's outside waiting, waving a gloved hand at her just in case she doesn't know who he is. She would have known. He looks older than his driver's license picture and taller. He's got her under-chin and a boxer's stance. She extends her hand as she approaches, but he goes in for the hug. He steps back and looks at her, holding her shoulders. Then, as if he worries he's overstepped the bounds, he drops his arms. He awkwardly points to the front door of his building. "Cold out here," he says, drawing out his vowels in a classic New York accent. "Let's go upstairs, huh?

"Gerry," he says opening the door to his apartment, "call me Gerry," although Cheri hasn't called him anything yet. She hasn't even thought about what to call him—certainly not Dad. Now that she's inside, it strikes her just how weird it is to be forty-one years old and meeting the man who spawned her. "You're very pretty, like your mother that way." She doesn't even begin to know what to do with that comment; she can tell he's nervous. She tries her nicest smile.

"Where are my manners—you want a beer? Coffee?" She says she'll have a beer; now *she's* nervous. He goes to fetch it. He has flowers in a little green vase on his kitchen table, the kind you get as a mixed bunch in the supermarket. As he hands her a cold bottle of Bud, she notices he's wearing a St. Christopher's medal. His eyes were probably once clear blue, but they've grown milky with age. He must have been blond because his eyebrows are barely visible now. His hair is white and thinning. The cleft on his chin is scarred over from—what, a bar fight? And he's got the ruddy cheeks of a drinker. They go to the living room and sit.

Is she seeing this right? He takes a pull on his beer and purses his lips around the bottle then keeps them pursed for a moment afterward, just like she does. They both take another drink. He does it again. He makes a comment about how people say Bud is piss water but he likes it. She cracks wise about no limes or imports for her, which makes Gerald laugh, just a bit too loudly. Cheri tries to take in as much of the place, and him, as she can. He leans forward and starts: "I told everything to that lady you hired. Some surprise that call was, let me tell you! All I know is this: I'd have wanted to know about you back then. But what could I do, I didn't know?" Cheri nods—nothing he could have done. She's taken aback by his admission, and not entirely sure if she should believe him. He clears his throat and continues. "I thought you'd want to know about your mother." Cheri thinks about Cici, the only mother she's known.

"Let's call her Miriam," Cheri says. "Do you know her last name?"

"Never did. I met her in Trenton. Nice girl. Looked a little on the young side, though she told me she was twenty. Pretty, with dark hair and weird eyes like yours—no offense. Had a feeling she was far from home and not going back."

"Do you know anything about her family? Sisters, brother? Where she came from?"

"All she said was that her mother was foreign. Can't for the life of me remember where. Somewhere exotic, but not too exotic. Could have been from one of those crazy countries like Russia or Iraq, for all I know. Miriam didn't stick around long. Not that I would have kicked her out of bed for eating crackers. I told her she could stay with me as long as she liked. I'd help her get a job."

"And that was it? She just left and you didn't know where?"

"She took off without a word. No note even. I went out to get cigarettes and, boom, she was gone. Never heard from her again. Certainly not about being knocked up."

"I guess the clinic couldn't find you. Did the PI tell you that it was because of a spelling mistake with your name?"

"Yeah, can you believe? Avoid hospitals at all costs. Guy I know went in for his appendix, got his gallbladder taken out." She spies some *Hustlers* poking out from under a stack of old *TV Guides* on the coffee table between them. Gerry phumphers and laughs before quickly shuffling them farther under the stack. She asks a few more questions about Miriam: Did she mention going to high school, talk about a job she had or wanted to have? He doesn't know or can't remember. "Oh, but she liked chocolate, and those wafers, what do you call them?" He snaps his fingers. "Neccos." Cheri notices a few dusty photographs in frames on the rickety bookshelf next to a few paperback crime books. "Mind if I take a look?" she asks as she gets to her feet.

"Sure, kid. Look at anything you want." Her eye is drawn to a picture of cops in dress uniforms, lined up. A younger Gerry is receiving a medal.

"Is this you?" she asks, pulse quickening.

"Yeah. That was for my nephew, Medal of Valor. Died in the line of duty. He was my sister Janice's kid, I raised him after she passed." He takes the photograph from her and dusts it a bit with his sleeve. "Closest thing to a kid of my own, Mikey was." He pauses, catching his slip. "Of course, I didn't know about—" She holds up her hand. "It's okay," she says, then adds, "I'm sorry about your nephew."

"Yeah. What are you gonna do." They share a nod. Her mind is buzzing; all these men in the photographs—Christmas morning, fishing in the Rockaways, weddings—are stamped in the Eddie Norris mold. Men whose square shoulders and broad backs cry out to wear navy blue uniforms, caps at that straight-down-the-middle angle that signals a deep knowledge of the creed, membership in the tribe. She'd had the same sense of pride and duty when she was wearing that uniform. "That there's my old man with his brothers. Think I got one of his pops somewhere, never knew him," Gerry says, rummaging.

"All the men in your family were cops?"

"Yeah, typical micks, huh? Whole family of cops, except for yours truly. Those two jokers in uniform there are my younger brothers, Johnny and Odell, both retired, living the good life off their pensions." He keeps looking for the picture of the paterfamilias, going on about all the noncop jobs he'd tried to do: speed-reading teacher, handyman, carnival barker, janitor, typewriter salesman, drunkard. "What did you expect?" he says. "You probably didn't think I'd be a lawyer or have a fancy job. Guess you could say I was the odd man out." What *did* she expect? Not mick cops. Her stomach's doing loop-the-loops. She comes from a long line of cops. Maybe heeding the call to join the NYPD was less an act of rebellion and more a return to her roots. She can't help but laugh.

"I say something funny?" he asks, slightly bewildered but wanting in on the joke.

"No," she says, putting her hand over her mouth. "Not at all."

"You laugh when you're nervous? That's me, do it all the time. It's gotten me in trouble my whole life."

She nods. They drink their beers. She asks a bit more about Johnny and Odell, and they talk about Howard Beach, the way the city has changed so much in the decade she's been away.

"Sheesh," he says, slapping his hand to his forehead. "I almost forgot to ask how things turned out for you. You got a husband? You work?" Cheri pauses, thinking about how to answer.

"My husband died. I did a few different things in my life. Looking for the next one. But it all turned out all right." She considers, for a moment, telling him about her time in the NYPD. But that would invite conversation about other parts of her life, and she isn't ready for any of that.

"Sorry about your loss," he says. They sit and nod at each other. "Here's mud in your eye," he says, tipping his bottle to her, knocking back what's left. The red Budweiser clock on the wall above their heads ticks. They slip back into an awkward silence.

"Well," she says, "thanks for the beer."

"You want another one? Can I get you something else?"

"No, thank you. I should get going."

"Look, you came here all the way from Chicago," he says. "If you want to get together again . . . I mean, meet up later or whenever . . . I'd like that."

"Okay. Well, the door is open now. And I get to New York from time to time."

"Okay, then," he says. They both rise and walk to the front door. She reaches for her coat but he takes it off the coat stand and holds it out for her. As she's about to leave, he reaches in his pocket and pulls out some bills wrapped in a rubber band. "Let me give you something for a cab or . . . for yourself. I'd like to give you something." This gesture, his hand holding out the bills and the look in his eyes, makes her sad and a little ashamed. It makes her want to stop, maybe share a little more of herself.

"I'm good," she says, "but thank you. Thank you for meeting me. We can talk again sometime, okay?" At that, he smiles. A few minutes later, as she's walking down the street, she has the desire to turn around, like a little girl, to see if he's still there.

There's nothing like a dive bar to make time stand still, and it's good to know that as much as her old neighborhood has changed, she can still count on Double Down. It's a narcoleptic remnant of the Lower East Side's grittier past with a barely ambulatory clientele in bad Santa hats. The floor is sticky, the beer shitty and cheap. Someone puts Etta James on the jukebox. She hasn't told Cici she's in town; it would break her heart to know what Cheri was doing here. But before Cheri leaves New York, there's one more stop to make. The PI also tracked down the foster family who'd briefly taken her in before her adoption. The father is deceased and the mother is in a nursing home, but she's been given the address of a William Beal in Asbury Park. He must be a relative. She's been trying the phone number listed for him. No one answers and it doesn't go to voice mail. William Beal could be out of town. But there's only one way to know for sure. Tomorrow she'll take the Path to Hoboken and, from there, rent a car and meander down the shore to Asbury Park.

As Cheri is walking to her hotel, she calls Cici. There is so much she wants to say, but she can manage only a hoarse "Thank you."

"For what? Is everything okay? You are not back in the depression?"

"I'm fine," Cheri says, realizing it's actually true. "But I wasn't, when you came to Chicago. I was an asshole. And you helped me. So thank you." There is silence on the other end of the phone. Cheri presses it closer to her ear.

"Cici. Mom? Are you crying, don't cry—"

"No, no." Cici's voice is thick with emotion. "All I ever want to do is help, *cara*. Thank you for allowing this. I love you."

"I love you too," Cheri says. When she hangs up, she feels the weight of gratitude. But also an edge of guilt, as if she's betraying Cici, the mother who had actually wanted her.

The Jersey Shore has a magical loneliness in winter. As she drives, she can see the Twin Lights lighthouse behind her, Sandy Hook to the left, and the monochromatic gray ocean ahead. It's the flip side of Malibu. If she turns her head she can make out the New York City skyline winking. Her axis of origin is all here. She thinks of the circumstances of her birth, how Cici said Sol had brought her back from what she'd assumed was an orphanage. Now she knows it must have been from the Beals'. She thinks of the freakish coincidences, that, despite her being raised by Sol and Cici, she ended up becoming a cop. Was that in her genetic predisposition, like hair color or being right-handed? If there is a God, He hides knowledge where we least expect to find it: in ourselves. Is the knowledge of who we are in our DNA? The genetic code passed down through the family, with the lies and half-truths we tell each other to protect the hope that each generation might be better, make fewer mistakes than the one before? Are the lies even necessary to survive? Was this why she didn't have a child? Was her infertility a manifestation of her deepest fear—the fear that she'd be perpetuating something she herself did not know, was afraid to face? "I could have told you that," Michael would have said. But maybe she needed to find out herself.

She stops in Sea Bright. The town is mostly boarded up, but she finds a lone fish shack that's open. The chowder is some of the best she's ever had. There's a cold drizzle that starts and stops but she needs to stretch her legs and walk down the boardwalk a bit. The beach is deserted except in the distance there's a huddle of parkas. As she gets closer she sees a group of older men and women. They strip down to bathing suits and put on caps, slap their white flesh, and start running into the frigid water. She'd heard of people swimming in the Atlantic in winter, but seeing them do it is something else. "Come in, the water's fine," someone shouts. She is moved by the audacity of these old people, the brilliance of their bodies as they bravely skip into the sea and bob under. Cheri ties to picture herself skinny-dipping in the ocean at that age. Who would she be surrounded by?

She decides to try the Beal number one last time before she's forced to go pound on his door or canvass the neighbors. She's about to hang up after the fifth ring when she hears "Yeah?" He's got a deeper voice than she imagined. She's so surprised he answered it takes her a minute to say something. "Who is this?" the voice demands after a few seconds of silence.

"Is this William Beal?"

"Billy, yeah, what do you want?"

"I've been trying to reach you," Cheri says. "Ellen Jameson, the PI who contacted you about a year ago, gave me your number. About the baby your family fostered in August 1962?"

"Yeah," he says. "And what's that got to do with you?"

"I'm that baby," she says.

When he speaks again, his voice is flat so she can't get a read on him. Billy. That's what you called a kid. By now he should have become a Bill or a William. He's fifty-seven years old, divorced, works as a super for apartment buildings. He tells her he's working, but he should be home sometime "around six." If he wasn't there, she was to buzz number 225 and a Mrs. Crenshaw would let her in to wait for him. When she hangs up, she figures there's a fifty-fifty chance he'll even show. He wasn't exactly forthcoming on the phone.

The address is north of the train station, in a part of town that looks like it's halfway between gentrification and Baghdad. His apartment building looks like renovations started and then stopped. There's still scaffolding on one side and plastic over a few windows. "I got to go to work," says Mrs. Crenshaw, letting her in the front door. "But you look okay to me. He doesn't have anything worth stealing anyway. Here's the key. Super's apartment has no number, just go to the end of the first floor. It's on the right." Mrs. Crenshaw is a tall redhead wearing a cocktail-waitress outfit under a long puffy jacket. She doesn't answer Cheri when she asks, "Did Billy say he'd be back home soon?"

Cheri's not thrilled about this half-assed arrangement, but she lets herself into Billy's apartment. It's small, sparsely furnished, and smells like medicinal Chinese herbs. He's got a fake Christmas tree in the living room with a little tinsel thrown on it and a saggy, futon-type sofa. Two bar stools are snugged up to a plastic table in the kitchen.

She tries calling Billy's cell. He doesn't answer. She might as well take off her coat. Something's on her sleeve, something gray embedded in the fabric. Ashes. She'd been wearing Michael this whole time. She can't find a napkin or a paper towel anywhere. But look what she does find: a midnight special, unloaded, badly in need of cleaning. There's no ammunition, although a quick search of the kitchen reveals a bounty of interesting items. There's a stash of what smells like very old homegrown weed, an unopened box of extra-large condoms, an extensive REO Speedwagon tape collection, tons of plastic bags tossed under the sink, and rat poison. The smell of those herbs is suddenly making her nauseated.

This is taking too long. She goes to the bathroom to pee. Stuck to the mirror above the sink there's a photograph of a boy, maybe twelve years old, in a baseball uniform posed in classic pitcher's stance. It's creased and dog-eared, like he carried it around in his wallet or pocket. His kid? She peeks into his medicine cabinets and barely has time to look at the prescription labels—lithium and Depakote, which she thinks are heavy-duty mood stabilizers—when she hears footsteps and a key in the lock.

"You Cheri?" The man who must be Billy walks in and throws his keys on the kitchen table. He takes off his hat and whatever hair hasn't receded stands up a bit from the static electricity. "You got in okay. That's good. You want to sit down?"

They sit at the kitchen table. The kid in the photo has his same wide gray eyes. Billy Beal smells like Irish Spring soap, not what she'd expect from a super who was working all day. "How do we do this? You going to ask me questions?" He's been chomping on a wad of chewing tobacco; she can tell by how he talks it's stashed in his cheek. He's taking her in. Not kindly or unkindly. Just intently.

"Okay, let's start with your parents. Where are they now?" Cheri says, going into cop mode to mask the emotional investment she has in finding out about Miriam.

"Pops died of a heart attack, and Moms is in an old-age home in Trenton."

"Sorry to hear that."

"She's got her good days and days she's in total lala land. Some days she wakes up and says she's going to open the deli." He's staring at her harder now.

"Is this a bad time? You just got home from work. I can come back."

"Nah, it's fine. Hey, let me ask you something. What's your favorite baseball team?"

"I'm not really into sports," Cheri says, taken aback at his non sequitur.

"But if you had to pick a team, who would you root for?"

"In Chicago?"

"Aw, c'mon! The Cubs or White Sox? You're from Jersey. What team did you like growing up?"

"The Yankees. Yankees over Mets any day."

"Bingo," he says, rocking back on the stool, and for the first time his face shows a little expression. "I knew it! Listen, there's something I have for you. Stay right there." Maybe this guy has taken too many mood stabilizers. She's still feeling a little queasy.

"This has been through a lot with me," Billy says, coming back into the room. "I never thought I'd see this day. I'm still blown away that PI lady found me." She looks at the gift he's holding out—a simple silver hamsa pendant on a leather cord. "Take it, it's yours," he says.

"Is this supposed to mean something to me?"

"It was hers. Your mother's."

"Miriam? She gave this to you?" There were questions she'd formulated, but now, holding something concrete, makes her voracious to know everything. Every detail, nuance, the weather on the day she was born, what Miriam was wearing, what she said to Billy Beal. "Wait," she says, "don't say anything yet. I want to start at the beginning." She gets her purse and pulls out the PI's file, a pen, and a pad of paper. "Okay, go on."

"I remember everything about that day," he says. The night before, on the top sheet of her notepad, Cheri had scribbled a list of newsworthy events that happened on her birthday: Marilyn Monroe's death, Jamaica's independence, and Nelson Mandela's arrest. She had been afraid these impersonal details were all she would ever know. She looks into Billy Beal's steel-gray eyes.

"Okay," she says. "I'm ready."

August 5, 1962

Marilyn Monroe found dead, drug overdose

Jamaica celebrates independence

Nelson Mandela arrested for illegally leaving South Africa

Trenton, New Jersey: Generator blowout at St. Mercy's

Twelve-car pileup on the New Jersey Turnpike, worst in state's history

This is the story of family.

Like any story, what happens and why changes depends on who is doing the telling. Two siblings raised by the same parents in the same house often have different versions of shared events. Multiply that over generations, and you see why wars are started, religions divided, secrets held forever.

Who really knows about their parents' life before they were parents? Who wants to know about their parents' sex life? Forget about grandparents. Throw divorce and fertility science into the equation and you can have multiple parents and more stories in the mix. What if you knew the uncut version, the whole story, not just what was interpreted for you?

What if you were adopted and got a glimpse of your birth parents? Would your biological father have your flat butt, explain your love of guns; would your birth mother have two different-colored eyes? If you discovered that your adoptive father had another family living two towns away and hated him for his deception and yourself for being complicit, would it change anything if you knew the reasons why? What if you learned that your parents had a baby who died just before they adopted you? That your adoptive mother nursed you on the milk of her dead son, a mixture of her grief and hope—hope she'd put all on you because she'd never be able to carry another child? Would it change how you feel about your parents and about yourself? Would this knowledge rewrite the story enough so you could find forgiveness for a bigamist father, compassion for a mother who stalks you with her love?

If life is a river, we can see only a small patch of it. A little in front of us, some behind. We don't know when we're going to run into a tributary or hit a waterfall. If you could pull back and up to see how it all connects to the ocean, if you could see the whole story of all of your parents and their parents, would it alter your memories of them? Would it change what you translate to your kids, what they then revise and tell their kids?

If you could do that, even for a moment, you'd get God's sense of humor. You'd know your story is perfect. That your terribly imperfect parents were perfect for you, that your life could only have been written by and for you.

This is the story of the Matzner family. Its end is its beginning. August 5, 1962: Marilyn Monroe is found dead, Jamaica celebrates its independence, Nelson Mandela is arrested. In Trenton, New Jersey, a pregnant teenage girl walks into a clinic and gives birth, then walks out, leaving her baby forever. The baby is adopted, named Cheri, wears her Girl Scout uniform to school but ditches the troop for shooting practice at the local 4-H, pierces her tongue, has a love affair with speed, becomes a cop, discovers her father leads a double life, witnesses a murder, buries her father and her husband, forgives her mother, eats a T-bone steak with a stranger in the rain, meets her biological father and the person who rescued her from the clinic, without whom this story would have been very different.

Oh, and the baby ends up having a baby. The result of that T-bone steak in the rain, some excellent whiskey, and the stranger who showed her how to open herself up, to tell her story. That baby is you, Henry. I named you Henry in honor of Michael, who wanted a Hank. I wrote this book for you. So you can smell the ocean. Have a wider view. And be able to laugh at it all just a little bit sooner than I did.

—Cheri Matzner, October 7, 2015

Acknowledgments

For their courage in helping me see them outside of their roles as my parents, I thank my mother, Cynthia Barber, and father, David Birenbaum. Tireless readers, they provided not only love and support but incisive comments. Thanks also to my stepmother, Vanessa Ruiz, for her calm and counsel.

For their enormous generosity of spirit, I am indebted to these friends who were there for me, unfailingly: Philipp Keel, A. M. Homes, Angela Janklow, Maria Semple, Tamar Halpern, Rick Mordecon, Matthias and Melodie Mazur, Ingrid Katal, Susanna Brisk, Janet Yang, Amy Raine. For their early, close reading, thanks to Cathy Coleman and Judy Sternlight.

For her encouragement, guidance, and patience, I thank my wonderful agent, Susan Golomb. Thank you to my editor and publisher, Lee Boudreaux, for putting both her heart and intellect into and behind this book. To Reagan Arthur, Lisa Erikson, Carrie Neill, Carina Guiterman, Lauren Harms, Tracy Roe, and the entire team at Little Brown, a debt of gratitude for believing in me and working so hard to bring this book into the world.

To Shaun, who was here at the conclusion, thank you for a new beginning.

Lastly, thank you to my beautiful daughter, Zoë, who has grown faster than my ability to write these words. I know you will be able to laugh at it all far sooner than I did.

About the Author

Tracy Barone earned a BA and an MFA in dramatic writing at NYU and has worked as a screenwriter and a playwright. A former film executive in Hollywood, she was the executive producer on *Wild Wild West, Rosewood,* and *My Fellow Americans* and was instrumental in acquiring and developing the films *Men in Black* and *Ali.*

LEE BOUDREAUX BOOKS

Unusual stories. Unexpected voices. An immersive sense of place. Lee Boudreaux Books publishes both award-winning authors and writers making their literary debut. A carefully curated mix, these books share an underlying DNA: a mastery of language, commanding narrative momentum, and a knack for leaving us astonished, delighted, disturbed, and powerfully affected, sometimes all at once.

LEE BOUDREAUX ON *HAPPY FAMILY*

I like a novel that surprises me, and Tracy Barone's *Happy Family* did just that, in spades, from first page to last. And the whip-smart, fiercely independent, and complicated woman at the heart of the book supplies more than her fair share of those surprises. She's not always likable, but I found myself rooting for her all the more as she simultaneously hungers for meaningful connection and pushes it away with both hands. And who can blame her for her deeply suspicious nature? After all, the whole truth of her existence is shrouded in secrecy and shame until the fact that she's adopted emerges, in all sorts of puzzling detail, when she's eight years old. As an adult, she's a flawed, messy, deeply relatable modern-day woman trying desperately to sort out her career, her marriage, her past, and her future before the clock runs out, all chronicled in a voice that's as cracklingly intelligent and wryly observant as its heroine. In the end, there's no one whose long, hard road to happiness I'd rather witness.

Over the course of her career, Lee Boudreaux has published a diverse list of titles, including Ben Fountain's *Billy Lynn's Long Halftime Walk,* Smith Henderson's *Fourth of July Creek,* Madeline Miller's *The Song of Achilles,* Ron Rash's *Serena,* Jennifer Senior's *All Joy and No Fun,* Curtis Sittenfeld's *Prep,* and David Wroblewski's *The Story of Edgar Sawtelle,* among many others.

For more information about forthcoming books, please go to
leeboudreauxbooks.com.